Judith McNaught soared to stardom with her stunning bestseller *Whitney, My Love*. Since then, she has gone on to win the hearts of millions of readers around the world with such breaktaking novels as *Once and Always* and the *New York Times* bestsellers *Something Wonderful*, *A Kingdom of Dreams* and *Almost Heaven*. Judith McNaught lives in Houston, Texas, where she is currently working on her next novel.

UNTIL YOU

Judith McNaught

CORGI BOOKS

UNTIL YOU
A CORGI BOOK : 0 552 14354 5

First publication in Great Britain

PRINTING HISTORY
Corgi edition published 1995

Set in 10/11pt Monotype Plantin by
Phoenix Typesetting, Ilkley, West Yorkshire.

Corgi Books are published by Transworld Publishers Ltd,
61–63 Uxbridge Road, London W5 5SA,
in Australia by Transworld Publishers (Australia) Pty Ltd,
15–25 Helles Avenue, Moorebank, NSW 2170,
and in New Zealand by Transworld Publishers (NZ) Ltd,
3 William Pickering Drive, Albany, Auckland.

Reproduced, printed and bound in Great Britain by
Cox & Wyman Ltd, Reading, Berks.

I write novels about very special, fictional people – men and women of courage and loyalty, of humor and integrity, people who care very much about other people.

I am honored to dedicate this novel to two real-life people who are the equal to any of those fictional characters, two people who I am privileged to call my friends . . .

To Pauli Marr, with equal parts of gratitude and admiration for all the things you are, and for all the things you've shared with me – including some of the most hilarious, and difficult, moments of my life. Occasionally, at one and the same time . . .

and

To Keith Spalding. I always imagined a knight-in-shining-armor would ride to the rescue on a destrier and carry a lance. Who would have guessed he'd ride in a BMW and carry a briefcase! But regardless of the mode of transportation or the method of defense, no knight of old could surpass you for integrity, loyalty, kindness, and humor. My life is so much the better for having known you.

I couldn't end this dedication without mentioning four other wonderful people for reasons they will know and understand:

To Brooke Barhorst, Christopher Fehlig and Tracy Barhorst – with all my love . . .

and

To Megan Ferguson, who is one *very* special young lady – with all my gratitude.

1

Propped upon a mountain of satin pillows amid rumpled bed linens, Helene Devernay surveyed his bronzed, muscular torso with an appreciative smile as Stephen David Elliott Westmoreland, Earl of Langford, Baron of Ellingwood, Fifth Viscount Hargrove, Viscount Ashbourne, shrugged into the frilled shirt he'd tossed over the foot of the bed last night. 'Are we still attending the theatre next week?' she asked.

Stephen glanced at her in surprise as he picked up his neckcloth. 'Of course.' Turning to the mirror above the fireplace, he met her gaze in it while he deftly wrapped the fine white silk into intricate folds around his neck. 'Why did you need to ask?'

'Because the Season begins next week, and Monica Fitzwaring is coming to town. I heard it from my dressmaker, who is also hers.'

'And?' he said, looking steadily at her in the mirror, his expression betraying not even a flicker of reaction.

With a sigh, Helene rolled onto her side and leaned on an elbow, her tone regretful but frank. 'And gossip has it that you're finally going to make her the offer she and her father have been waiting for these three years past.'

'Is that what the gossips are saying?' he asked casually, but he lifted his brows slightly, in a gesture that silently, and very effectively, managed to convey his displeasure with Helene for introducing a topic that he clearly felt was none of her concern.

Helene noted the unspoken reprimand and the warning it carried, but she took advantage of what had been a remarkably open – and highly pleasurable – affair for both of them for several years. 'In the past, there have been dozens of rumors that you were on the verge of offering for one aspiring female or another,' she pointed out quietly, 'and, until now, I have never asked you to verify or deny any of them.'

Without answering, Stephen turned from the mirror and picked up his evening jacket from the flowered chaise longue. He shoved his arms into the sleeves, then he walked over to the side of the bed and finally directed all his attention to the woman in it. Standing there, looking down at her, he felt his annoyance diminish considerably. Propped up on her elbow, with her golden hair spilling over her naked back and breasts, Helene Devernay was a delectable sight. She was also intelligent, direct, and sophisticated, all of which made her a thoroughly delightful mistress both in and out of bed. He knew she was too practical to nurture any secret hopes of a marriage offer from him, which was absolutely out of the question for a woman in her circumstances, and she was too independent to have any real desire to tie herself to someone for life – traits that further solidified their relationship. Or so he had thought. 'But now you are asking me to confirm or deny that I intend to offer for Monica Fitzwaring?' he asked quietly.

Helene gave him a warm, seductive smile that normally made his body respond. 'I am.'

Brushing back the sides of his jacket, Stephen put his hands on his hips and regarded her coolly. 'And if I said yes?'

'Then, my lord, I would say that you are making a great mistake. You have a fondness for her, but not a great love nor even a great passion. All she has to offer you is her beauty, her bloodlines, and the prospect of an heir. She hasn't your strength of will, nor your intelligence, and although she may care for you, she will never understand you. She will bore you in bed and out of it, and you will intimidate, hurt, and anger her.'

'Thank you, Helene. I must count myself fortunate that you take such an interest in my personal life and that

8

you are so willing to share your expertise on how I ought to live it.'

The stinging setdown caused her smile to fade a little but not disappear. 'There, you see?' she asked softly. 'I am duly chastened and forewarned by that tone of yours, but Monica Fitzwaring would be either completely crushed or mortally offended.'

She watched his expression harden at the same time his voice became extremely polite, chillingly so. 'My apologies, madame,' he said, inclining his head in a mockery of a bow, 'if I have ever addressed you in a tone that is less than civil.'

Reaching up, Helene tugged on his jacket in an attempt to make him sit down on the bed beside her. When this failed, she dropped her hand, but not the issue, and widened her smile to soothe his temper. 'You never speak to anyone in an uncivil tone, Stephen. In fact, the more annoyed you are, the more "civil" you become – until you are so very civil, so very precise and correct, that the effect is actually quite alarming. One might even say . . . *terrifying*!'

She shivered to illustrate, and Stephen grinned in spite of himself.

'That is what I meant,' she said, smiling back at him. 'When you grow cold and angry, I know how—' Her breath caught as his large hand slipped down beneath the sheet and covered her breast, his fingers tantalizing her.

'I merely wish to warm you,' he said, as she reached her arms around his neck and drew him down on the bed.

'And distract me.'

'I think a fur would do a far better job of that.'

'Of warming me?'

'Of distracting you,' he said as his mouth covered hers, and then he went about the pleasurable business of warming, and distracting, both of them.

It was nearly five o'clock in the morning when he was dressed again.

'Stephen?' she whispered sleepily as he bent and pressed a farewell kiss upon her smooth brow.

'Mmmm?'

'I have a confession.'

'No confessions,' he reminded her. 'We agreed on that from the beginning. No confessions, no recriminations, no promises. That was the way we both wanted it.'

Helene didn't deny it, but this morning she couldn't make herself comply. 'My confession is that I find myself rather annoyingly jealous of Monica Fitzwaring.'

Stephen straightened with an impatient sigh, and waited, knowing she was determined to have her say, but he did not help her do it. He simply regarded her with raised brows.

'I realize you need an heir,' she began, her full lips curving into an embarrassed smile, 'but could you not wed a female whose looks pale a little in comparison with mine? Someone shrewish too. A shrew with a slightly crooked nose or small eyes would suit me very well.'

Stephen chuckled at her humor, but he wanted the subject closed permanently, and so he said, 'Monica Fitzwaring is no threat to you, Helene. I've no doubt she knows of our relationship and she would not try to interfere, even if she thought she could.'

'What makes you so certain?'

'She volunteered the information,' he said flatly, and when Helene still looked unconvinced, he added, 'In the interest of putting an end to your concern and to this entire topic, I'll add that I already have a perfectly acceptable heir in my brother's son. Furthermore, I have no intention of adhering to custom, now or in future, by shackling myself to a wife for the sole purpose of begetting a legal heir of my own body.'

As Stephen came to the end of that blunt speech, he watched her expression change from surprise to amused bafflement. Her next remark clarified the reason for her obvious quandary: 'If not to beget an heir, what other possible reason could there be for a man such as you to wed at all?'

Stephen's disinterested shrug and brief smile dismissed all the other usual reasons for marriage as trivial, absurd, or imaginary. 'For a man such as I,' he replied with a mild amusement that failed to disguise his genuine contempt for the twin farces of wedded bliss and the sanctity of marriage – two illusions that flourished even in the brittle, sophisticated social world he inhabited, 'there does not seem to be a single compelling reason to commit matrimony.'

Helene studied him intently, her face alight with curiosity, caution, and the dawning of understanding. 'I always wondered why you didn't marry Emily Lathrop. In addition to her acclaimed face and figure, she is also one of the few women in England who actually possesses the requirements of birth and breeding in enough abundance to make her worthy of marrying into the Westmoreland family and of producing your heir. Everyone knows you fought a duel with her husband because of her, yet you didn't kill him, nor did you marry her a year later, after old Lord Lathrop finally keeled over and cocked up his toes.'

His brows rose in amusement at her use of irreverent slang for Lathrop's death, but his attitude toward the duel was as casual and matter-of-fact as her own. 'Lathrop got some maggot into his head about defending Emily's honor and putting a stop to all the rumors about her, by challenging one of her alleged lovers to a duel. I will never understand why the poor old man chose me from amongst a legion of viable candidates.'

'Whatever method he used, it's obvious age had addled his mind.'

Stephen eyed her curiously. 'Why do you say that?'

'Because your skill with pistols, and your skill on the duelling field, are both rather legendary.'

'Any child of ten could have won a duel with Lathrop,' Stephen said, ignoring her praise of his abilities. 'He was so old and frail he couldn't steady his own pistol or hold it level. He had to use both hands.'

'And so you let him leave Rockham Green unscathed?'

Stephen nodded. 'I felt it would be impolite of me to kill him, under the circumstances.'

'Considering that he forced the duel on you in the first place, by calling you out in front of witnesses, it was very kind of you to pretend to miss your shot, in order to spare his pride.'

'I did not pretend to miss my shot, Helene,' he informed her, and then he pointedly added, 'I deloped.'

To delope constituted an apology and therefore implied an admission of guilt. Thinking he might have some other explanation for standing twenty paces from his opponent and deliberately firing high into the air instead of at Lord Lathrop she said slowly, 'Are you saying you really *were* Emily Lathrop's lover? You were actually *guilty*?'

'As sin,' Stephen averred flatly.

'May I ask you one more question, my lord?'

'You can *ask* it,' he specified, struggling to hide his mounting impatience with her unprecedented and unwelcome preoccupation with his private life.

In a rare show of feminine uncertainty, she glanced away as if to gather her courage, then she looked up at him with an embarrassed, seductive smile that he might have found irresistible had it not been immediately followed by a line of questioning so outrageous that it violated even his own lax standards of acceptable decorum between the sexes. 'What was it about Emily Lathrop that drew you to her bed?'

His instant aversion to that question was completely eclipsed by his negative reaction to her next. 'I mean, was there anything she did with you – or *for* you – or *to* you, that I do not do when we're in bed together?'

'As a matter of fact,' he replied in a lazy drawl, 'there was one thing Emily did that I particularly liked.'

In her eagerness to discover another woman's secret,

Helene overlooked the sarcasm edging his voice. 'What did she do that you particularly liked?'

His gaze dropped suggestively to her mouth. 'Shall I show you?' he asked, and when she nodded, he bent over her, bracing his hands on either side of her pillow so that his waist and hips were only inches above her head. 'You're absolutely certain you wish to take part in a demonstration?' he asked in a deliberately seductive whisper.

Her emphatic nod was playful and inviting enough to take the edge off his annoyance, leaving him caught somewhere between amusement and exasperation. 'Show me what she did that you particularly liked,' she whispered, sliding her hands up his forearms.

Stephen showed her by putting his right hand firmly over her mouth, startling her with a 'demonstration' that matched his smiling explanation: 'She refrained from asking me questions like yours about *you* or anyone else, and that is what I *particularly* liked.'

She gazed back at him, her blue eyes wide with frustrated chagrin, but this time she did not fail to notice the implacable warning in his deceptively mild voice.

'Do we have an understanding, my inquisitive beauty?'

She nodded, then boldly attempted to tip the balance of power into her favor by delicately running her tongue across his palm.

Stephen chuckled at her ploy and moved his hand, but he was no longer in the mood for sexual play or for conversation, and so he pressed a brief kiss on her forehead and left.

Outside, a wet gray fog blanketed the night, broken only by the faint eerie glow of lamplights along the street. Stephen took the reins from the relieved footman and spoke soothingly to the young pair of matched chestnuts who were stamping their hooves and tossing their manes. It was the first time they had been driven in the city, and as Stephen loosened the reins to let them move into a trot, he noted that the curb horse was extremely skittish in the fog. Everything unnerved the animal, from the sound of his own hooves clattering on the cobbled streets to the shadows beneath the streetlamps. When a door slammed off to the left, he shied, then tried to break into a run. Stephen automatically tightened the reins, and turned the carriage down Middleberry Street. The horses were moving at a fast trot and seemed to be settling down a bit. Suddenly an alley cat screamed and bolted off a fruit cart, sending an avalanche of apples rumbling into the street. At the same time the door of a pub was flung open, splashing light into the street. Pandemonium broke loose: dogs howled, the horses slipped and bolted frantically, and a dark figure staggered out of the pub, disappeared between two carriages drawn up at the curb . . . and then materialized directly in front of Stephen's carriage.

Stephen's warning shout came too late.

2

Leaning heavily on his cane, the ancient butler stood in the shabby drawing room and listened in respectful silence as his illustrious visitor imparted the news that the butler's employer had just met an untimely demise. Not until Lord Westmoreland had finished his tale did the servant permit himself to show any reaction, and even then, Hodgkin sought only to reassure. 'How very distressing, my lord, for poor Lord Burleton, and for you as well. But then – accidents do happen, don't they, and one cannot blame one's self. Mishaps are mishaps, and that's why we call them that.'

'I'd hardly call running a man down and killing him a "mishap",' Stephen retorted, with a bitterness that was directed at himself, not the servant. Although the early morning accident had been much the fault of the drunken young baron who'd bounded into the street in front of Stephen's carriage, the fact was that Stephen had been holding the reins, and he was alive and unharmed, while young Burleton was dead. Furthermore, it seemed that there was no-one to mourn Burleton's passing, and at the moment, that seemed a final injustice to Stephen. 'Surely, your employer must have some family somewhere – someone to whom I could explain personally about the accident?'

Hodgkin merely shook his head, distracted by the dire realization that he was suddenly unemployed again and likely to remain so for the rest of his life. He'd obtained this position only because no-one else had been willing to work as butler, valet, footman, and cook – and for the absurdly small wages Burleton was able to pay.

Embarrassed by his temporary lapse into self-pity and his lack of proper decorum, Hodgkin cleared his throat and hastily added, 'Lord Burleton had no close living relatives, as I – I said. And since I've only been in the baron's employ for three weeks, his acquaintances aren't really known to—' He broke off, a look of horror on his face. 'In my shock, I forgot about his fiancée! The nuptials were to take place this week.'

A fresh wave of guilt washed over Stephen, but he nodded, and his voice became brisk and purposeful. 'Who is she and where can I find her?'

'All I know is that she's an American heiress the baron met when he was abroad, and that she's to arrive tomorrow on a ship from the Colonies. Her father was too ill to make the voyage, so I presume she's either travelling with a relative or, perhaps, with a female companion. Last night, Lord Burleton was commemorating the end of his bachelorhood. That's all I know.'

'You must know her name! What did Burleton call her?'

Caught between nervousness at Lord Westmoreland's terse impatience and shame at his own deteriorating memory, Hodgkin said a little defensively, 'As I said, I was new to the baron's employ, and not taken into his confidence. In my presence, he . . . he called her "my fiancée," or else "my heiress."'

'Think, man! You must have heard him refer to her name at some time!'

'No . . . I . . . Wait, yes! I do recall something . . . I recall that her name made me remember how very much I used to enjoy visiting Lancashire as a boy. Lancaster!' Hodgkin exclaimed in delight. 'Her surname is Lancaster, and her given name is Sharon . . . No, that's not it. Charise! Charise Lancaster!'

Hodgkin was rewarded for his efforts with a slight nod of approval accompanied by yet another rapid-fire question: 'What about the name of her ship?'

Hodgkin was so encouraged and so proud that he actually banged his cane upon the floor with glee as the answer popped into his mind. 'The *Morning Star*!' he crowed, then flushed with embarrassment at his boisterous tone and unseemly behavior.

'Anything else? Every detail could be helpful when I deal with her.'

'I do recall some other trifles, but I shouldn't like to indulge in idle gossip.'

'Let's hear it,' Stephen said with unintended curtness.

'The lady is young and "quite a pretty little thing,"' the baron said. I also gathered that she was rather madly in love with him and wanted the union, while it was the baron's title that was of primary interest to her father.'

Stephen's last hope that this marriage was simply one of convenience had died at the news that the girl was 'madly in love' with her fiancé. 'What about Burleton?' he asked as he pulled on his gloves. 'Why did he want the marriage?'

'I can only speculate, but he seemed to share the young lady's feelings.'

'Wonderful,' Stephen murmured grimly, turning toward the door.

Not until Lord Westmoreland left did Hodgkin permit himself to give in to despair at his own predicament. He was unemployed and virtually penniless again. A moment ago, he'd almost considered asking, even begging, Lord Westmoreland to recommend him to someone, but that would have been inexcusably presumptuous, as well as futile. As Hodgkin had discovered during the two years it had taken him to finally obtain a position with Lord Burleton, no-one wanted a butler, valet, or footman whose hands were spotted with age and whose body was so old and so stooped that he could neither straighten it nor force it to a brisk walk.

His thin shoulders drooping with despair, his joints beginning to ache dreadfully, Hodgkin turned and shuffled toward his room at the back of the shabby apartment. He was halfway there when the earl's sharp, impatient knock forced him to make his slow way back to the front door. 'Yes, my lord?' he said.

'It occurred to me as I was leaving,' Lord Westmoreland said in a curt, businesslike voice, 'that Burleton's death will deprive you of whatever wages he owed you. My secretary, Mr Wheaton, will see that you're compensated.' As he turned to leave, he added, 'My households are always in need of competent staff. If you aren't longing for retirement right now, you might consider contacting Mr Wheaton about that as well. He'll handle the details.' And then he was gone.

Hodgkin closed the door and turned, staring in stunned disbelief at the dingy room while vigor and youth began to surge and rush warmly through his veins. Not only did he have a position to go to, but a position in a household belonging to one of the most admired, influential noblemen in all of Europe!

The position hadn't been offered out of pity; of that Hodgkin was almost certain, for the Earl of Langford wasn't known as the sort of man to coddle servants, or anyone else. In fact, rumor had it that the earl was a rather distant, exacting man, with the highest standards for his households and his servants.

Despite that, Hodgkin couldn't completely suppress the humiliating notion that the earl might have offered him employment out of pity, until he suddenly remembered something the earl had said, something that filled Hodgkin with pleasure and pride: Lord Westmoreland had specifically implied that he regarded Hodgkin as *competent.* He'd used that very word!

Competent!

Slowly, Hodgkin turned toward the hall mirror, and with his hand upon the handle of his black cane, he gazed at his reflection. Competent . . .

He straightened his spine, though the effort was a bit painful, then he squared his narrow shoulders. With his free hand he reached down and carefully smoothed the front of his faded black jacket. Why, he didn't look so very old, Hodgkin decided – not a day over three-and-seventy! Lord Westmoreland certainly hadn't thought him decrepit or useless. No, indeed! Stephen David Elliott Westmoreland, the Earl of Langford, thought Albert Hodgkin would be a *worthy addition* to his staff! *Lord Westmoreland* – who possessed estates all over Europe, along with noble titles inherited through his mother and two ancestors who'd named him as their heir – thought *Albert* Hodgkin would be a worthy addition to one of his magnificent households!

Hodgkin tipped his head to the side, trying to imagine how he would look wearing the elegant Langford livery of green and gold, but his vision seemed to blur and waver. He lifted his hand, his long thin fingers touching, feeling at the corner of his eye, where there was an unfamiliar wetness.

He brushed the tear away, along with the sudden, crazy impulse to wave his cane in the air and dance a little jig. Dignity, Hodgkin very strongly felt, was far more appropriate in a man who was about to join the household staff of Lord Stephen Westmoreland.

3

The sun was a fiery disc sliding into the purple horizon by the time a seaman walked down the dock to the coach that had been waiting there since morning. 'There she is – the *Morning Star*,' he told Stephen, who'd been leaning against the door of the vehicle, idly watching a drunken brawl taking place outside a nearby pub. Before raising his arm to point out the ship, the seaman cast a cautious glance at the two coachmen, who both held pistols in clear view, and who were obviously not as indifferent as their master to the dangers lurking everywhere on the wharf. 'That's her, right there,' he said to Stephen, indicating a small ship just gliding into port, its sails dim silhouettes in the deepening twilight. 'And she's only a bit late.'

Straightening, Stephen nodded to one of the coachmen, who tossed the seaman a coin for his trouble, then he walked slowly down the dock, wishing that his mother or his sister-in-law could have been here with him when Burleton's bride disembarked. The presence of concerned females might have helped soften the blow when he delivered the tragic news to the girl, news that was going to shatter her dreams.

'This is a nightmare!' Sheridan Bromleigh cried at the astonished cabin boy who'd come to tell her for the second time that 'a gentleman' was waiting for her on the pier – a gentleman she naturally assumed was Lord Burleton. 'Tell him to wait. Tell him I *died*. No, tell him we're still indisposed.' She shoved the door closed, shot the bolt, then pressed her back to the panel, her gaze darting to the frightened maid who was perched on the edge of the narrow cot in the cabin they'd shared, twisting a handkerchief in her plump hands. 'It's a nightmare, and when I wake up in the morning, it will all be over, won't it, Meg?'

Meg shook her head so vigorously that it set the ribbons on her white cap bobbing. 'It's no dream. You'll have to talk to the baron and tell him something – something that won't vex him, and something he'll believe.'

'Well, that certainly eliminates the truth,' Sheridan said bitterly. 'I mean, he's bound to be just a trifle miffed if I tell him I've managed to misplace his fiancée somewhere along the English coastline. The *truth* is I *lost* her!'

'You didn't lose her, she eloped! Miss Charise ran off with Mr Morrison when we stopped in the last port.'

'Regardless of that, what matters is that she was entrusted to my care, and I failed in my duty to her father and to the baron. There's nothing to do but go out there and tell the baron that.'

'You mustn't!' Meg cried. 'He'll have us thrown straight into a dungeon! Besides, you have to make him feel kindly toward us because we have no-one else to turn to, nowhere to go. Miss Charise took all the money with her, and there isn't a shilling to buy passage home.'

'I'll find some sort of work.' Despite her confident words, Sherry's voice trembled with strain, and she looked about the tiny cabin, unconsciously longing for somewhere to hide.

'You don't have any references,' Meg argued, her voice filling with tears. 'And we don't have anywhere to sleep tonight and no money for lodgings. We're going to land in the gutter. Or worse!'

'What could be worse?' Sheridan said, but when Meg opened her mouth to answer, Sherry held up a hand and said with a trace of her normal humor and spirit, 'No, don't, I beg you. Don't even consider "white slavery."'

Meg paled and her mouth fell open, her voice dropping to a dazed whisper. 'White . . . slavery.'

'Meg! For heaven's sake, I meant it as a . . . a joke. A tasteless joke.'

'If you go out there and tell him the truth, they'll toss both of us straight into a dungeon.'

'Why,' Sherry burst out, closer to hysterics than she'd ever been in her life, 'do you keep talking about a dungeon?'

'Because there's laws here, miss, and you – we – we've broken some. Not on purpose, of course, but they won't care. Here, they toss you into a dungeon – no questions asked, nor answers heard. Here, there's only one sort of people who matter, and they're the Quality. What if he thinks we killed her, or stole her money, or sold her, or something evil like that? It would be his word against yours, and you aren't nobody, so the law will be on his side.'

Sheridan tried to say something reassuring or humorous, but her physical and emotional stamina had both suffered from weeks of unabated tension and stress, compounded by a long bout of illness during the voyage, followed by Charise's disappearance two days ago. She should never have embarked on this mad scheme in the first place, she realized. She'd overestimated her ability to cope with a spoiled, foolish seventeen-year-old girl, convincing herself that her common sense and practical nature, combined with her experience teaching deportment at Miss Talbot's School for Young Ladies, which Charise had attended, would enable her to deal admirably with any difficulties that arose on the trip. Charise's dour father had been so deluded by Sheridan's brisk, competent manner that, when his heart ailment suddenly prevented him from travelling to England, he'd chosen Sheridan over several older, more experienced applicants to escort his daughter to England – Sheridan, who was barely three years older than she. Of course, Charise had something to do with his decision; she'd wheedled and sulked and insisted that Miss Bromleigh be the one to accompany her, until he finally conceded. Miss Bromleigh had been the one who helped her write her letters to the baron. Miss Bromleigh, she told him, wasn't like those other sour-faced companions he'd interviewed; Miss Bromleigh would be amusing company. Miss Bromleigh, she warned him slyly, wouldn't let her become so homesick that she wanted to return to America and her papa, instead of marrying the baron!

That was certainly true, Sheridan thought with disgust. Miss Bromleigh was probably responsible for her elopement with a near-stranger, an impulsive act that loosely resembled the plot of one of the romantic novels that Sheridan had shared with Charise on the voyage. Aunt Cornelia was so opposed to those novels, and to those 'foolish romantic notions' they put forth, that Sheridan normally read them only in secret, with the curtains closed around her cot. There, in solitude, she could experience the delicious excitement of being loved and courted by dashing, handsome noblemen who stole her heart with a glance. Afterward, she could lie back on the pillows, close her eyes, and pretend that she had been the heroine, dancing at a ball in a glorious gown with pale golden hair in an elaborate upsweep . . . strolling in the park with her dainty hand resting upon his sleeve and her pale golden hair peeping from beneath the brim of her fashionable bonnet. She'd read each novel so many times that she could recite her favorite scenes from memory and substitute her own name for the heroine's . . .

The baron captured Sheridan's hand and pressed it to his lips as he pledged his eternal devotion. 'You are my one and only love . . .'

The earl was so overwhelmed by Sheridan's beauty that he lost control and kissed her cheek. 'Forgive me, but I cannot help myself! I adore you!'

And then there was her particular favorite . . . the one she most often liked to imagine:

The prince took her in his strong embrace and clasped her to his heart. 'If I had a hundred kingdoms, I would trade them all for you, my dearest love. I was nothing until you.'

Lying in bed, she would alter the plots of the novels, the dialogue, and even the situations and locales to suit herself, but she never, ever changed her imaginary hero. He and he alone remained ever constant, and she knew every detail about him, because she had designed him herself: He was strong and masculine and forceful, but he was kind and wise and patient and witty, as well. He was tall and handsome too – with thick dark hair and wonderful blue eyes that could be seductive or piercing or sparkle with humor. He would love to laugh with her, and she would tell him amusing anecdotes to make him do it. He would love to read, and he would be more knowledgeable than she and perhaps a bit more worldly. But not too worldly or proud or sophisticated. She hated arrogance and stuffiness and she particularly disliked being arbitrarily ordered about. She accepted such things from the fathers of her students at school, but she knew she wouldn't be able to abide such a superior male attitude from a husband.

And, of course, her imaginary hero would become her husband. He would propose on bended knee, and say things like, 'I didn't know there was happiness, until you . . . I didn't know what love was, until you . . . I was only half a man with half a heart . . . until you.' She liked the idea of being truly needed by her imaginary hero, of being valued for more than beauty. After he proposed with such sweet compelling words, how could she do anything but accept? And so, to the envious surprise of everyone in Richmond, Virginia, they would be married. Afterward, he would whisk her, and Aunt Cornelia, off to his wonderful mansion on a hill, where he would devote himself to making them happy, and where their most pressing worry would be which gowns to wear. He would help her locate her father, too, and he would come to live with them.

Alone in the darkness, it didn't matter that she didn't have a prayer of meeting such a man or that if by some wild chance she did encounter such a paragon of perfection, he wouldn't give Miss Sheridan Bromleigh a passing glance. In the morning, she would scrape her thick red hair back off her forehead and fasten it into a practical coil at the nape, then she would leave for school, and no-one would ever know that prim Miss Bromleigh, who was already regarded as a 'spinster' by students, staff, and parents, was an incurable romantic in her heart.

She'd fooled everyone, including herself, into thinking she was the epitome of practicality and efficiency. Now, as a result of Sheridan's boundless overconfidence, Charise was going to spend her life married to an ordinary Mister, instead of a Milord, a man who could make her life utterly miserable if he chose. If Charise's father didn't die of his fury and heartbreak, he was undoubtedly going to spend the rest of *his* life thinking of effective ways to make Sheridan's and Aunt Cornelia's lives miserable. And poor, timid Meg, who'd been Charise's overworked maid for five long years, was surely going to be turned out without a reference, which would effectively destroy her future prospects for obtaining a decent position. And these were the best possibilities!

These prospects were based on the assumption that Sheridan and Meg might somehow be *able* to return home. If Meg was correct, and Sheridan was half-convinced she was, then Meg was going to spend the rest of her life in a dungeon, and Sheridan Bromleigh – 'sensible, competent' Sheridan Bromleigh – was going to be her cell mate.

Tears of fear and guilt stung Sherry's eyes as she thought of the calamities she'd caused, and all because of her naive overconfidence and her foolish desire to see the glittering city of London and the fashionable aristocracy she'd read about in her novels. She should have listened to Aunt Cornelia, who'd lectured her for years that longing to see such wondrous sights was tantamount to reaching beyond one's station in life; that pride was as sinful in the eyes of the Lord as greed and sloth; and that modesty in a female was far more attractive to gentlemen than mere beauty.

Aunt Cornelia had been right in the first two of those beliefs, Sheridan belatedly realized. Sherry had tried to heed her aunt's warnings, but there was one major dissimilarity between her aunt and herself that made those warnings about going to England terribly difficult for Sherry to accept: Aunt Cornelia *loved* predictability. She thrived on rituals, treasured the identical day-to-day routines that sometimes made Sherry feel like weeping with despair.

4

As she stared blindly across the tiny cabin at poor Meg, Sherry wished very devoutly that she were back in Richmond, sitting across from her aunt in the tiny little three-room house they shared, enjoying a nice, routine pot of tepid tea, and looking forward to an entire *lifetime* of tepid tea and tedium.

But if Meg was right about British laws . . . then Sheridan wouldn't be going home ever, wouldn't set eyes on her aunt again, and that thought was almost her undoing.

Six years ago, when she first went to live with her mother's elder sister, the prospect of never seeing Cornelia Faraday again would have made Sheridan positively gleeful, but Sheridan's father hadn't given her a choice. Until then, he had let her travel with him in a wagon loaded with all manner of goods, from fur pelts and perfume to iron pots and pitchforks, luxuries and necessaries that he sold or bartered at farmhouses and cabins along their 'route.'

Their 'route' was whichever fork in the road took their fancy when they came upon it – usually heading south, along the eastern seaboard, in winter and north in summer. Sometimes they turned west when a particularly glorious sunset beckoned, or they angled southwest because a gurgling stream angled in that direction. In winter, when the snow sometimes made travelling difficult or impossible, there was always a farmer or a storekeeper who had need of an extra pair of willing hands, and her Irish father would trade his labor for a few nights' lodging.

As a result, by the time Sheridan was twelve, she'd slept in everything from a blanket in a hayloft to a feather bed in a house populated by a bevy of laughing ladies who wore vivid satin gowns with necklines so low their bosoms seemed to be in danger of toppling right out of them. But whether the mistress of their lodgings was a robust farmer's wife or a stern-faced preacher's wife or a lady in a purple satin dress trimmed with black feathers, their hostesses nearly always ended up doting on Patrick and fussing maternally over Sheridan. Charmed by his ready smile, his unfailing courtesy, and his willingness to work hard and long for bed and board, the ladies soon began cooking extra-large portions for him, baking his favorite desserts, and volunteering to mend his clothing.

Their goodwill extended to Sheridan too. They teased her affectionately about her mop of bright red hair and laughed when her father referred to her as his 'little carrot.' They let her stand on a stool when she volunteered to help wash dishes, and when she left, they gave her scraps of cloth or precious needles so she could fashion a new blanket or dress for her doll, Amanda. Sheridan hugged them and told them that she and Amanda were both very grateful, and they smiled because they knew she meant it. They kissed her goodbye and whispered that she was going to be very beautiful someday, and Sheridan laughed because she knew they couldn't *possibly* mean it. Then they watched Sheridan and her papa drive off in the wagon while they waved goodbye and called out 'Godspeed' and 'Come back soon.'

Sometimes the people they stayed with hinted that her papa ought to remain to court one of their daughters or a neighbor's daughter, and the smile would remain on his handsome Irish face, but his eyes would darken as he said, 'I thank you, but no. 'Twould be bigamy, since Sheridan's mama is still alive in my heart.'

The mention of Sheridan's mama was the one thing that could dim the smile in his eyes, and Sheridan always grew tense until he was himself again. For months after her mama and baby brother died from an illness called the flux, her papa behaved like a silent stranger, sitting beside the fire in their tiny cabin, drinking whiskey, ignoring the crops that were dying in the field and not bothering to plant more. He didn't talk, didn't shave, hardly ate, and seemed not to care whether their mule starved or not. Sheridan, who was six at the time and accustomed to helping her mama, tried to take over her mother's chores.

Her father seemed as unaware of Sheridan's efforts as he was of her failures and her grief. Then one fateful day, she burned both her arm and the eggs she'd cooked for him. Trying not to cry from the pain in her arm or the pain in her heart, she had lugged the wash down to the stream along with what was left of the lye soap. As she knelt on the bank and gingerly lowered her father's flannel shirt into the water, scenes from the happy past at this same spot came back to haunt her. She remembered the way her mama used to hum as she did the wash here while Sheridan supervised little Jamie's bath. She remembered the way Jamie used to sit in the water, gurgling happily, his chubby hands smacking the water in playful glee. Mama had loved to sing; she'd taught Sheridan songs from England and sung them with her while they worked. Sometimes she would stop singing and simply listen to Sheridan, her head tipped to the side, a strange, proud smile on her face. Often she would wrap Sheridan in a tight hug and say something wonderful, like, 'Your voice is very sweet and very special – just like you are.'

Memories of those idyllic days made Sheridan's eyes ache as she knelt at the stream. The words of her mama's favorite song whispered in her mind, along with the memory of her mama smiling, first at Jamie as he giggled and splashed, and then at Sheridan, who was usually getting soaked too. *'Sing something for us,'* she would say. *'Sing for us, angel . . .'*

Sheridan tried to obey the remembered request, but her voice broke and her eyes flooded with tears. With the heels of her hands, she rubbed the tears away only to discover that her father's shirt was now floating downstream, already out of her reach, and then Sheridan lost the battle to be brave and grown-up. Drawing her knees against her chest, she buried her face in her mama's apron and sobbed with grief and terror. Surrounded by summer wildflowers and the scent of fresh grass, she rocked back and forth, crying until her throat ached and her words were only a croaking whispered chant. 'Mama,' she wept, 'I miss you, I miss you, I miss you. I miss Jamie. Please come back to Papa and me. Please come back, please come back. Oh, please. I can't do it alone, Mama. I can't do it. I can't, I can't—'

Her litany of grief was suddenly interrupted by her father's voice – not the dull, lifeless, terrifyingly unfamiliar voice he'd had for months, but his old voice – hoarse now with concern and love. Crouching beside her, he'd pulled her into his arms. 'I can't do it alone either,' he'd said, cradling her tightly against him. 'But I'll wager we can do it together, sweeting.'

Later, after he'd mopped her tears, he'd said, 'How would you like to leave here and go travelling, just you and me? We'll make every day an adventure. I used to

have great adventures. That's how I met your mama –
I was having an adventure in England, in Sherwyn's
Glen. Someday, we'll go back to Sherwyn's Glen, you
and me. Only not the way your mama and I left. This
time, we'll go back in grand style.'

Before Sheridan's mama died, she'd talked nostal-
gically about the picturesque village in England where
she'd been born, about its beautiful countryside, its
treelined lanes, and the dances she'd attended at the
assembly rooms there. She'd even named Sheridan after
a particular kind of rose that bloomed at the parsonage,
a special species of red rose that she said bloomed in
gay profusion along the white fence surrounding the
parsonage.

Sheridan's father's preoccupation with returning to
Sherwyn's Glen seemed to start after her mother's death.
What puzzled Sheridan for a long while, however, was
exactly *why* her papa wanted to go back there so badly,
particularly when the most important man in the village
seemed to be an evil, proud monster of a man named
Squire Faraday who lorded it over everyone and who
would not make a good neighbor at all when her papa
built his mansion right next to his home, which was his
intention.

She knew her papa had first met Squire Faraday when
he delivered a very valuable horse from Ireland that the
squire had purchased for his daughter, and she knew that
since her father had no close family alive in Ireland, he'd
decided to stay on and work for the squire as a groom
and horse trainer. But not until she was eleven years old
did she discover that the wicked, coldhearted, hateful,
arrogant Squire Faraday was actually her mama's own
father!

She'd always wondered why her father had taken her
mother away from her beloved village and then spirited
her off to America, along with her mother's elder sister,
who then settled in Richmond and refused to budge
another inch. It had always seemed a little strange that

the only thing they took with them, besides the clothing on their persons and a small sum of money, was a horse called Finish Line – a horse that her mama had loved enough to bring along and pay his passage, and yet one she had sold soon after they arrived in America.

The few times her parents had spoken of their departure from England, it had always seemed hasty somehow, and vaguely unhappy too, but she couldn't imagine why that would have been so. Unfortunately, her father was adamantly unwilling to satisfy her curiosity on that score, which left her with no choice except to rein in her curiosity and wait until they built their mansion in Sherwyn's Glen so that she could find out for herself. She planned to accomplish her goal by asking all sorts of carefully veiled questions once she got there. As far as she could tell, her father intended to accomplish his goal by gambling at cards and dice, with whatever money they could actually spare and as often as he found a good game of either underway. The fact that he simply wasn't lucky at cards and dice was apparent to both of them, but he believed all that would change someday. 'All I need, darlin',' he would say with a grin, 'is just one nice, long lucky streak at the right table. I've had a few of those in my time, and my time is comin' again. I can feel it.'

Since he never lied to her, Sherry believed it too. And so they travelled together, talking to each other about subjects as mundane as the habits of ants and as grand as the creation of the universe. To some people, their vagabond lifestyle must have seemed strange. It had seemed that way at first to Sherry too, strange and frightening, but she soon came to love it. Before they'd left the farm, she'd truly thought the whole wide world looked exactly like their own little patch of meadow and that hardly anyone existed beyond its boundaries. Now there were new sights to see around every bend in the road and the happy expectation of meeting interesting people along their route who were heading in the same direction – travellers who were bound for, or en route from, places as distant and exotic as Mississippi, or Ohio, or even Mexico!

From them, she heard wondrous stories of far-off places, amazing customs, and strange ways of life. And because she treated everyone as her papa did – with friendliness, courtesy, and interest – many of them chose to match their pace to the Bromleighs' wagon for days at a time or even weeks. Along the way, Sheridan learned even more: Ezekiel and Mary, a Negro couple with skin like smooth shiny coal, springy black hair, and hesitant smiles, told her about a place called Africa, where their names had been different. They taught her a strange, rhythmic chant that wasn't quite a song, yet it made her spirits heighten and quicken.

A year after Mary and Ezekiel went their own way, a white-haired Indian with skin as weathered and wrinkled as dried leather appeared around a bend in the road one gray winter day, mounted upon a beautiful spotted horse that was as young and energetic as his rider was old and weary. After considerable encouragement from Sheridan's father, he tied his horse to the back of the wagon, climbed aboard, and, in answer to Sheridan's inquiry, he said his name was Dog Lies Sleeping. That night, seated at their campfire, he responded to Sheridan's question about Indian songs by giving a strange demonstration of one, a demonstration that seemed to consist of guttural sounds accompanied by the beating of his palms on his knees. It sounded so odd and unmelodic that Sheridan had to bite back a smile for fear of hurting his feelings, and even then he seemed to sense her bewildered amusement. He broke off abruptly and narrowed his eyes. 'Now,' he said, in his abrupt, commanding voice, '*you* make song.'

By then, Sheridan was as used to sitting around campfires and singing with strangers as she was speaking to them, and so she sang – an Irish song that her papa had taught her about a young man who lost his love.

When she got to the part about the young man weeping in his heart for his beautiful lassie, Dog Lies Sleeping made a strangled noise in his throat that sounded like a snort and a laugh. A swift glance across the fire at his appalled expression proved her guess was correct, and this time it was Sheridan who broke off in mid-note.

'Weeping,' the Indian informed her, in a lofty, superior tone while pointing his finger at her, 'is for women.'

'Oh,' she said, chagrined. 'I-I guess Irish men are, well, different because the song says they cry, and Papa taught it to me, and he's Irish.' She looked for confirmation to her father and said hesitantly, 'Men from the old country do cry, don't they, Papa?'

He shot her a laughing look as he dumped the dregs of his coffee onto the fire and said, 'Well, now, darlin', what if I say they do, and Mr Dog Lies Sleeping leaves us thinkin' for all time that Ireland's a sad place filled with sorry lads all weepin' their hearts out and wearin' them on their sleeves? That wouldn't be a good thing, would it? And yet, if I say they don't cry, then *you* might end up thinkin' the song and I lied, and that wouldn't be good, either.' With a conspiratorial wink, he finished, 'What if I say you misremembered the song, and it's really the *Italians* who cry?'

He'd phrased all that as if it were part of their favorite game of *'What If,'* a game they'd invented and played often to pass the time during the three years they'd travelled together. Sometimes the game was about serious possibilities, such as 'What if the horse went lame.' Sometimes it was silly, like 'What if a fairy came and gave us one wish,' but regardless of the premise, the goal was always to reach the best possible solution in the minimum amount of time. Sheridan had become so good at it that her father proudly declared that she made him work hard to stay even with her.

Sheridan's brow furrowed in concentration for a brief moment, then she announced her solution with a merry giggle: 'I think you'd best pretend there's something you have to do right now, so you don't have to answer the question. If you say anything at all, it will land you in the briars for sure.'

'You're right,' he said, laughing, then he took her advice after bidding Dog Lies Sleeping a polite good night. The lighthearted exchange didn't win even a glimmer of a smile from the stoic Indian, but across the fire, he gave Sheridan a long, intense look, then rolled to his feet and vanished into the woods for the night without a word.

The following morning, Dog Lies Sleeping offered to let her ride his horse – an honor that Sheridan suspected sprang from his desire to ride in the more comfortable wagon without actually having to admit it, and thereby save face. Sheridan, who had never ridden anything but the old, sway-backed horse that pulled their wagon, eyed the beautiful, spirited animal with a little excitement and a great deal of nervous panic. She was about to refuse when she caught the challenging look in the Indian's face. Carefully injecting a regretful tone into her voice, she pointed out that they didn't have a saddle. Dog Lies Sleeping gave her another of his lofty, superior looks and informed her that *Indian* maidens rode bareback and astride.

His unblinking stare, combined with the feeling that he knew she was afraid, was more than Sheridan could endure. Prepared to risk her life and limb rather than give him a reason to have a low opinion of her, and *all* Irish children as well, she marched over to him and took the horse's rope from his hand. He didn't offer to help her mount, so she led the horse over to the wagon, climbed into it, then spent several minutes trying to maneuver the horse into a position close enough to swing her leg over its back.

Once she was mounted, she wished she weren't. From atop the horse, the ground looked very far away, and very, very hard. She fell off five times that day, and she could practically *feel* the Indian *and* his obstinate horse laughing at her. As she prepared to mount for her sixth attempt, she was so furious and so sore that she jerked on the lead rope, grabbed the horse's ear and called him a devil, using a German word for it that she'd been taught by a German couple heading for Pennsylvania, then she hoisted herself aboard and angrily took command of her mount. It took several minutes before she realized that Indian horses apparently responded better to rudeness than timidity, because the animal stopped side-stepping and bolting and settled into an exhilarating soft trot.

That night, as she sat at the campfire watching her father cooking their supper, she shifted her position to ease the pressure on her sore backside and inadvertently met the gaze of Dog Lies Sleeping, something she'd been avoiding since she'd retied the horse to the wagon earlier that day. Instead of making some embarrassingly frank observation about her lack of riding ability in comparison to that of an Indian girl's, Dog Lies Sleeping looked at her steadily in the leaping firelight and asked what seemed an entirely inconsequential question: 'What does your name mean?'

'What does my name mean?' she repeated after a moment's thought.

When he nodded, she explained that she'd been named for a flower that grew in her mother's land of England, a place across the sea. He made a disapproving grunt, and Sheridan was so startled that she said, 'Well, then, what should my name be?'

'Not flower, you,' he said, studying her freckled face and unruly hair. 'Fire, you. Flames. Burn bright.'

'What? Oh!' she said, laughing as understanding dawned. 'You mean my hair looks like it's on fire because of its color?' Despite his aloof manner, abrupt speech, and ill-behaved horse, Sheridan was, as usual, naturally friendly, incurably curious, and incapable of carrying a grudge for more than an hour. 'My papa calls me "carrot" because of my hair,' she said with a smile. 'A carrot is an orange vegetable . . . like

. . . like corn is a vegetable,' she added. 'That is why he calls me "carrot."'

'White men are not as good as Indians for giving names.'

Politely refraining from pointing out that being named for a dog wasn't exactly preferable to being referred to as a vegetable, Sheridan said, 'What sort of name would an Indian give me?'

'Hair of Flames,' he announced. 'If you were boy, name you Wise for Years.'

'What?' Sheridan asked blankly.

'You wise already,' he clarified awkwardly. 'Wise, but not old. Young.'

'Oh, I do like being called wise!' Sheridan exclaimed, instantly reversing her earlier decision and deciding she liked him very well, indeed. 'Wise for Years,' she repeated, tossing a happy look at her amused father.

'You girl,' he contradicted, dampening her glee with his attitude of male superiority. 'Girls not wise. Call you Hair of Flames.'

Sheridan decided to like him anyway and to stifle her indignant retort that her papa thought she was very smart indeed, contrary to his opinion. 'Hair of Flames is a very nice name,' she said instead.

He smiled then for the first time, a knowing smile that took decades off his face and made it clear he was aware of her restraint in the face of his provocation. 'You Wise for Years,' he said, his grin widening as he looked at her papa and nodded.

Her father nodded his agreement in return, and Sheridan decided, as she often did, that life was really quite wonderfully exhilarating, and that no matter how different people seemed on the outside, on the inside they were much the same. They liked to laugh and talk and dream . . . and pretend that they were always brave, never in pain, and that sorrow was merely a bad mood that would soon pass. And which usually did.

5

At breakfast the next morning, her father complimented the beautiful braided and beaded belt that Dog Lies Sleeping wore around his deerskin breeches and discovered that the Indian had made it himself. Within moments, a business deal was struck, and Dog Lies Sleeping agreed to fashion belts and bracelets for her father to sell along their route.

With their new 'partner's' permission, she named the horse Runs Fast, and in the days that followed, Sheridan rode him constantly. While her father and Dog Lies Sleeping made their more dignified way along the trail in the wagon, she galloped ahead, then raced back to them, crouched low over the horse's neck, her hair tossing in the wind and mingling with the horse's flying mane, her laughter ringing out beneath the bright blue sky. On the same day she conquered her fear of a racing gallop, she proudly asked Dog Lies Sleeping if she was beginning to ride as well as an Indian *boy*. He looked at her as if such a possibility were absurd, as well as impossible, then he tossed the core of the apple he'd been eating into the grass beside the road. 'Can Wise for Years pick that up from back of running horse?' he replied, pointing to the core.

'Of course not,' Sherry said, baffled.

'Indian boy do.'

In the three years that followed, Sherry learned to do that and a great many other feats – some of which evoked worried warnings from her father. Dog Lies Sleeping greeted each of her successes with an offhand grunt of approval, followed by yet another new, seemingly impossible, challenge, and sooner or later, Sherry rose to every one. Their income increased as a result of Dog

Lies Sleeping's intricate handiwork, and they ate much better as a result of his superior hunting and fishing skills. If people found them a peculiar trio – the old Indian, the young girl who wore deerskin pants and who could ride not only bareback and astride but backward at a full-out gallop, and the amiable, soft-spoken Irishman who gambled regularly but with cautious restraint – Sherry didn't notice it. In fact, she rather thought the folk who lived in busy, crowded towns such as Baltimore, Augusta, and Charlotte led very odd, stifled lives compared to theirs. In fact, she didn't mind in the least that her papa was taking so long to win enough money to build their mansion in the village of Sherwyn's Glen.

She mentioned that very thing to Rafael Benavente, a handsome, blue-eyed Spaniard in his mid-twenties, a few days after he decided to travel with them toward Savannah on his way from St Augustine.

'*Cara mía,*' he had said, laughing heartily. 'It is good you are not in a hurry, for your papa is a very bad gambler. I sat across from him last night in a little game at Madame Gertrude's establishment, and there was much cheating.'

'My papa would never cheat!' she'd protested, leaping to her feet in indignation.

'No, this I believe,' he quickly assured her, catching her wrist as she whirled around. 'But he did not realize that *others* were cheating.'

'You should have—' her eyes dropped to the gun he wore at his hip, and she grew even angrier at the idea of someone cheating her papa out of their hard-earned money – 'shot them! Yes, shot them all, that's what!'

'That I could not do, *querida,*' he stated, while amusement again lit his face. 'Because, you see, I was one of the cheaters.'

Sheridan yanked her wrist free. '*You* cheated my papa?'

'No, no,' he said, making an unsuccessful effort to sober his expression. 'I only cheat when it is entirely necessary – such as when others are cheating – and I only cheat those who would cheat me.'

As she later learned, Rafael was something of an expert at gambling, having been, by his own admission, cast out of his family's huge hacienda in Mexico as punishment for what he called his 'many bad ways.'

Sheridan, who prized her own tiny family, was dismayed to discover that some parents actually cast their children out, and she was equally dismayed at the thought that Rafael might have committed some sort of unspeakable deed to warrant that. When she cautiously broached the subject to her father, he put his arm reassuringly around her shoulders and said that Rafael had explained the real reason he'd been sent away by his family, and that it had something to do with caring too much for a lady who was unfortunately already married.

Sheridan accepted his explanation without further question, not only because her father was always very careful about the character of any man allowed to travel with them for an extended length of time, but also because she wanted to think the best of Rafael. Although she was only twelve years old, she was positive Rafael Benavente was the handsomest and most charming man on earth – with the exception of her father, of course.

He told her wonderful stories, teased her about her ruffian ways, and told her that she was going to be a very, very beautiful woman someday. He said her eyes were as cool as gray storm clouds and that God had given them to her to go with the fire in her hair. Until then, Sheridan hadn't cared in the least about her appearance, but she hoped devoutly that Rafael was correct about her future looks and that he would wait around to find out. Until then she was content to bask in his company and be treated like a child.

Unlike most of the travellers they encountered, Rafe always seemed to have plenty of money and no particular destination or goal in mind. He gambled more often than her father did and spent his winnings as he pleased. One day, after they'd set up their wagon on the fringe of Savannah, Georgia, he disappeared for four days and nights. When he reappeared on the fifth day, he reeked of perfume and whiskey. Based on the snatches of conversation she'd overheard the year before among a group of married women heading to Missouri with their husbands in a small caravan, she concluded that Rafe's state was proof he'd been in the company of 'a harlot.' Although she had an incomplete idea of what constituted a harlot, she knew from that same conversation that a harlot was a woman who was not respectable and who possessed some sort of evil power to 'lead a man away from the path of righteousness.' Although Sherry did not know exactly what a woman did to become not respectable, she knew enough to react instinctively.

When Rafe returned that day, unshaven and smelling of harlots, Sheridan had been on her knees, trying to phrase an awkward prayer for his safety and trying not to cry with fear. Within moments, she went from fear to jealous indignation, and she stayed aloof and angry for a record full day. When his cajolery didn't soften her, he shrugged and seemed not to care, but the following night, he strolled into their camp with a mischievous grin on his face and a guitar in his hands. Pretending to ignore her, he sat down across the fire from her and began to play.

Sherry had heard other guitars played before, but *not* the way Rafe played this one. Beneath his nimble fingers, the strings vibrated with a strange, pulsating rhythm that made her heart beat faster and her toes wiggle in her boots in time with the tempo. Then suddenly the tempo changed and the music became incredibly wistful and so sad that the guitar itself seemed to be crying. The third melody he played was light and gay, and he looked at her across the campfire, gave her a wink, and began to say the words that went with the song as if he were saying them to her. They told the story of a foolish man who didn't value the things he had or the woman who loved him until he lost everything. Before Sherry could react to the shock – and possibilities – of that, he began to play another melody, lovely and soft, a song she knew. 'Sing the words with me, *querida*,' he said lightly.

Singing was a favorite pastime for many people when they travelled, including the Bromleigh group, but on that night, Sherry felt unaccountably shy and awkward before she closed her eyes and made herself think only of the music and the sky and the night. She sang along with him, his deep baritone a counterpoint to her higher notes.

Several minutes later, she opened her eyes to the sound of applause and was stunned to see that a small group of campers from across the road had come over to listen to her.

It was the first of many, many nights when she sang while Rafe played and a crowd gathered to listen. Sometimes, when they were in a village or town, people expressed their appreciation with gifts of food and even money. In the months that followed, Rafe taught her to play the guitar, though she never played as well as he did, and he taught her Spanish, which she spoke almost as well as he did, then Italian, which neither of them spoke very well. At Sherry's request, he kept an eye on the people her father gambled with, and her father's winnings began to increase. He even began to talk to Patrick about becoming partners in all sorts of ventures that sounded awfully exciting, and terribly unlikely to Sheridan, but her father always listened with interest.

The only person who seemed to be less than pleased with Rafe's presence was Dog Lies Sleeping, who regarded the other man with open disapproval and refused to do more than grunt at him, and that only in answer to a pertinent, direct question. To Sherry, he became rather withdrawn, and when she unhappily sought her father's counsel on the subject, he said Dog Lies Sleeping probably felt bad because she didn't spend as much time talking with him as she had done before Rafe joined them. After that, Sherry made it a point to seek the Indian's advice and to ride beside him in the wagon more often than she rode beside Rafe.

Geniality and accord returned to their tiny cavalcade, and everything seemed perfect and permanent . . . until her papa decided to pay a visit to her mama's spinster sister in Richmond, Virginia.

6

Sheridan had been excited about meeting her only other living relative, but she'd felt out of place in Aunt Cornelia's small, stuffy house and terrified she was going to break one of the fragile knickknacks or soil the lacy handkerchief-looking things that seemed to be on every available surface. Despite all her precautions, Sherry had the awful feeling that her aunt did not like her very much at all and that she completely disapproved of everything Sherry said and did. That suspicion was confirmed by a mortifying conversation she overheard between her aunt and her father only two days after their arrival. Sherry had been sitting on the edge of a footstool, looking out at the city street, when muted voices in the next room made her turn in surprise and curiosity at the sound of her name.

She got up and wended her way around the furniture, then she pressed her ear to the door. Within moments, she realized that her suspicion was correct: Aunt Cornelia, who taught deportment at a school for young girls of wealthy families, was *not* at all pleased with Sheridan Bromleigh, and she was treating Patrick Bromleigh to a furious scold on that very subject: 'You ought to be horsewhipped for the way you've reared that child,' Aunt Cornelia ranted in a scornful, disrespectful tone that Sheridan's father would ordinarily never have tolerated from anyone, let alone endured in silence as he seemed to be doing. 'She can't read, and she can't write, and when I asked her if she knew her prayers, she informed me she didn't "hold with too much kneeling." Then she informed me – and I quote – "The Good Lord probably doesn't like to listen to Bible-banging preachers any more than he likes harlots who lead men away from the path of goodness and righteousness." '

'Now, Cornelia—' her father began, with a sound in his voice that almost sounded like stifled laughter. Cornelia Faraday obviously thought it sounded like laughter too, because she flew straight into what Rafe called a devil-rage.

'Don't you try to get around me with your false charm, you – you scoundrel. You lured my sister into marrying you and traipsing halfway round the world with your fancy talk about a new life in America, and I'll never forgive myself for not trying to stop her. Worse, I came along! But I will not stand by and keep silent this time, not when you've turned my sister's only daughter into a – a joke! That girl, who is nearly old enough to be married, doesn't act like a female; she doesn't even look like a female. I doubt she knows she is one! She's never worn anything but pants and boots, she's as tanned as a savage, and she curses like a heathen! Her manners are deplorable, she's outrageously outspoken, her hair is untamed, and she doesn't know the meaning of the word "feminine." She announced to me, as bold as brass, that she doesn't care to marry right now, but she "fancies" someone named Rafael Benavente and she'll probably ask *him* to marry her someday. That young lady – and I use the term very loosely in Sheridan's case – honestly intends to propose matrimony herself – and furthermore, the man of her choice is apparently some Spanish vagabond who, she proudly informed me, knows everything important – including how to cheat at cards! Well,' Aunt Cornelia finished in a rising tone of angry triumph, 'I defy you to defend all that!'

Sherry held her breath and waited with some glee for her father to let loose an answering tirade in her defense at the hateful, sour-faced woman who'd wheedled her way into Sherry's confidence with her questions and was using her honest answers against her.

'Sherry does not swear!' her father retorted a little lamely, but at least he sounded as if his temper was beginning to reach the danger point.

Aunt Cornelia was not as intimidated as others were when Patrick Bromleigh finally lost his temper. 'Oh, yes she does!' she flung back. 'She bumped her elbow this morning, and she swore IN TWO LANGUAGES! I heard her myself.'

'Really,' Patrick drawled nastily, 'and how would you know what she was saying?'

'I know enough Latin to be able to translate *"Dios mío!"* into a blasphemy.'

'That means "My God",' Patrick defended, but he sounded suddenly guilty and not very convincing as he added, 'She was obviously having a go at some of that praying that you're so worked up about her not doing!' Sherry bent down and put her eye to the keyhole. Her father was flushed, either with embarrassment or anger, and his fists were clenched at his sides, but Aunt Cornelia was standing right in front of him, as cold and unmoved as stone.

'That shows what little you know of praying *or* of your daughter,' Cornelia flung back contemptuously. 'I shudder to think of the sorts of persons you've let her consort with, but I have a clear enough picture to know she's been exposed to gambling and cursing, and that you've allowed liquor-drinking card cheats, like that Mr Rafael, to see her dressed indecently. God alone knows the sort of evil thoughts she's evoked in him and every other man who's seen her with that red hair of hers flying all about like a wanton. And I haven't even *mentioned* her other favorite companion – an Indian male who sleeps with dogs! A savage who—'

Sherry saw her father's jaw clench with fury a moment before Aunt Cornelia mentioned Dog Lies Sleeping, and for a split second Sherry was half afraid – and half hopeful – that he was about to poke Aunt Cornelia right in the eye for saying such vile things. Instead, he spoke in a voice laced with biting scorn: 'You've become a foul-minded, spiteful spinster, Cornelia – the sort who pretends that all men are bestial, and that they lust after every woman they see, when the truth is that you're angry because no man ever lusted after *you*! And furthermore,' he finished, his Irish brogue thickening as his control and reason momentarily deserted him, 'Sherry may be almost fourteen, but she's as plain as a pikestaff and as flat-chested as you! In fact, Nelly, girl,' he'd finished with triumph, 'poor Sherry's showin' signs of becomin' the image of you. And there ain't enough liquor on God's earth to make a man lust after you, so I figure she's safe enough.'

At the keyhole, Sheridan realized only that a fine insult had just been scored against the 'foul-minded, spiteful spinster,' and she clamped her hand over her mouth to stifle a cheer. Unfortunately, Aunt Cornelia wasn't as undone by her brother-in-law's insults as Sherry would have liked. She lifted her chin, looked him right in the eye, and retorted with icy disdain, 'I think there was a time when *you* wouldn't have needed liquor, wasn't there, Patrick?'

Sherry didn't have the slightest notion what Aunt Cornelia meant. For a second, her father seemed blank too, and then furious, and then . . . strangely calm. 'Well done, Cornelia,' he said mildly. 'Spoken just like Squire Faraday's haughty, oldest daughter. I'd almost forgotten that's who you used to be, but you haven't, have you?' The last traces of his anger drained away completely as he looked around at the drab little room, and he shook his head, smiling ruefully. 'Never mind that you live in a house that's hardly bigger than a broom closet at Faraday manor, or that you eke out a living by teaching etiquette to other people's children, you're still Squire Faraday's daughter, proud and haughty as ever.'

'Then perhaps you'll also remember,' Aunt Cornelia said in a quieter, but unyielding, tone, 'that Sheridan's mother was my only sister. And I tell you truly, Patrick, that were she alive to see the antidote . . . the laughingstock . . . that you've made of Sheridan, she would be horrified. No,' Aunt Cornelia said with absolute finality, 'she would be *ashamed* of her.'

On the other side of the door, Sheridan went rigid with bewildered alarm. *Ashamed of her?* Surely, her mama wouldn't be ashamed of her, not of Sheridan; she'd *loved* Sheridan. Visions of her mother at the farm swirled through her mind . . . her mama putting dinner on the table and wearing a clean, starched apron, her hair wound into a neat coil at her neck . . . her mama brushing Sheridan's hair with long strokes until it crackled . . . her mama leaning closer to the light as she fashioned Sheridan a 'special dress' from scraps of lace and cotton someone had traded them.

With a vision of her mother's starched apron and shiny hair still in her mind, Sheridan spread her arms wide and looked down at herself. She was wearing men's boots because she didn't like to bother with laces, and they were scuffed and dusty. Her buckskin pants were stained, not to mention worn thin at the seat; around her waist a braided belt that Dog Lies Sleeping had made for her was serving the dual purpose of holding her pants up and her jacket closed. *Ashamed* . . .

Involuntarily, she turned to the little looking glass on her aunt's washstand and moved closer to it to peer at her face and hair. The image in the mirror made her rear back in alarm; then she stopped and blinked her eyes and gave her head a shake to chase the vision away.

For a moment she stood stock-still, completely at a loss as to what to do to fix matters, then she raised her hands to her head and tried to comb her fingers through the tangled mass of long, 'wanton' red hair. Her fingers stopped, unable to penetrate more than a few inches into the snarls, so she tried to remedy things by putting her palms against the sides of her hair and pressing down hard. Then she warily approached the mirror again. Ever so cautiously she lifted her hands away. Her hair sprang back out. She didn't in the least look like her mother. She didn't actually resemble any female she'd ever seen – a fact that she'd been both aware of, and unconcerned with, until that moment.

Aunt Cornelia had said she looked like a . . . *laughingstock*, and now that Sheridan thought about it, people had been reacting to her a little oddly lately – especially men. They stared at her in a peculiar way. Lustfully? Her father obviously hadn't noticed it, but in the last year, Sheridan's chest had been swelling quite embarrassingly and sometimes it showed no matter how carefully she tried to keep her jacket closed.

Aunt Cornelia said she looked wanton. *Wanton?* Sheridan furrowed her brow, trying to recollect when and how she'd heard that word used. 'Wanton' had some sort of connection to a harlot . . . a *hussie* . . . A 'wanton' hussie! That was it! That was Sheridan?

An unfamiliar lump of tears swelled in her throat at the realization. Aunt Cornelia was probably right about that and everything else – and, worst of all, that Sheridan's mama would be ashamed of her now.

Ashamed.

Sheridan was so stricken that she simply stood there, immobilized. Minutes later she realized that her aunt was demanding that Sheridan be left with her so that Sheridan could have a decent home and upbringing, and that Sheridan's father was putting up only a feeble protest. When it finally sank in, she bolted forward, tripping over her aunt's silly footstool in her haste, and yanked the door open. 'No, Papa, don't! Don't leave me here! Please!'

He looked haunted and torn, and Sheridan took advantage of his indecision, flinging herself into his arms. 'Please, I'll wear ladies' boots and fix my wanton hair, and everything else, but don't leave me here.'

'Don't, darlin',' was all he said, and she sensed that she was losing the battle.

'I want to go with you and Rafe and Dog Lies Sleeping! That's where I belong, no matter what she says!'

Sheridan was still saying that the next morning when he left. 'I'll be back before you know it,' he said firmly. 'Rafe has some good ideas. We'll make ourselves a pile of money, and we'll all come back for you in a year – two at the most. You'll be all grown up by then. We'll go to Sherwyn's Glen, and I'll build us that grand house, just like I promised you, honey. You'll see.'

'I don't want a grand house,' Sheridan cried, looking first at Rafe, who was standing in the street, looking handsome and grim, and then at Dog Lies Sleeping, whose expression revealed nothing. 'I just want you and Rafe and Dog Lies Sleeping!'

'I'll come back before you know I'm gone,' he'd promised, ignoring her sobs and giving her his warm, Irish smile that ladies always found so appealing. In a stroke of inspired cajolery, he added, 'Think how shocked Rafe will be when we come for you and you're a lovely young lady, wearing skirts and . . . and doing the things your aunt will teach you.'

Before she could protest, he untangled her arms from around his neck, put his hat on, stepped back, and looked at Cornelia. 'I'll send what money I can to help out.'

Cornelia nodded as if accepting alms from a peasant and said nothing, but her manner didn't seem to disturb him in the least.

'Who knows,' he said with a roguish grin, 'maybe we'll even take you back to England with us. You'd like

47

that, wouldn't you, Nelly – living right under Squire Faraday's nose, holding court in a house bigger than his? I seem to remember that the drawing room was always filled with your beaux.' With a mocking smile, he added, 'None of them were good enough for you, though, were they, Nelly? But then, maybe they've improved with age.'

Sheridan, who was trying to breathe slowly so she wouldn't weep like a baby, watched him shrug his shoulders in utter indifference at her aunt's rigid silence, then he turned and gave Sheridan a quick, hard hug. 'Write to me,' she implored him.

'I will,' he promised.

When he left, Sherry turned slowly to look at the expressionless face of the woman who had caused the complete destruction of her life and who was her only living female relative. Her gray eyes brimming with tears, Sherry said very softly and very clearly, 'I . . . I wish we'd never come here. I wish I'd never set eyes on you! I hate you.'

Instead of slapping her, which Sherry knew she was entitled to do, Aunt Cornelia looked her straight in the eye and said, 'I'm sure you do, Sheridan. I daresay you'll hate me much more before this is over. I, however, do not in the least hate you. Now, shall we have a bit of tea before we begin your lessons?'

'I hate tea too,' Sheridan informed her, lifting her chin to its haughtiest angle and returning her aunt's stony stare – a stance that was not only instinctive but identical to her aunt's. Her aunt noticed the similarity, even though Sheridan was unaware of it. 'Do not try to stare me out of countenance with that expression, child. I perfected that very look long ago, and I'm quite immune to it. In England, it would have served you well, were you Squire Faraday's acknowledged granddaughter. However, this is America, and we are no longer the proud Squire's relations. Here we are shabby-genteel at best. Here, I teach deportment to the children of

48

people whom I would have once regarded as my inferiors, and I am lucky to have the work. I thank my Maker that I'm able to have this cozy house for my very own, and I do not look back at the past. A Faraday does not lament. Remember that. And I am not completely regretful of my life's choices. For one thing, I am no one's puppet anymore. I no longer awaken wondering what sort of uproar will occur today. I lead an orderly, quiet, respectable life.'

She stepped back as she finished that speech, and with something that might actually have been amusement, she surveyed her unmoving niece. 'My dear, if you wish to carry off that look of stony hauteur to its best advantage, I recommend that you look down your nose at me just the tiniest bit – yes, just so. That's how I would have done it.'

If Sheridan hadn't been so forlorn and so bitter, she would have laughed. In time, she learned to laugh again – just as she learned Latin and ladylike behavior. Her aunt was a relentless teacher, determined that Sheridan learn everything she herself knew, and yet Sheridan soon realized that beneath her aunt's formal rigidity, there was a deep concern and even affection for her wayward niece. Sheridan was a quick student, once she got over her resentment. Book learning, as she discovered, helped to relieve the tedium of a life that no longer involved wild rides on spotted horses or the humming of guitar strings or laughter under the stars. Exchanging even a nodding glance with a member of the opposite sex was evidence of easy virtue and, therefore, forbidden; striking up a conversation with a stranger verged on criminal behavior. Singing was done only in church, and never, ever, *ever* was one to accept payment in any form for it. In place of the exhilarating things she used to enjoy, there was the dubious challenge of learning to pour tea while holding the pot at just the right angle, of placing one's fork and knife in the correct place after dining – trivial things, to be sure, but as Aunt Cornelia said, 'Knowing how to behave is your most valuable asset – your only one, in our circumstances.'

Her reasoning became evident when Sheridan turned seventeen: Garbed in a simple brown gown with her hair tucked into a neat chignon, held in place by a cap she'd crocheted herself, Miss Sheridan Bromleigh was presented to Mrs Adley Raeburn, the headmistress of the school where Aunt Cornelia taught. Mrs Raeburn, who had come to the house at Aunt Cornelia's invitation, stared for a split second at Sheridan's hair and face – a peculiar reaction from city people that had become more pronounced of late. A few years ago, a younger, less well-bred and serene Sheridan Bromleigh would have self-consciously looked down at her boots or tugged her hat down over her face or else demanded to know what the stranger was gaping at.

But this was a new Sheridan, a young woman who was well aware that she had been a financial burden. Now she was determined to become a wage-earner, not only for her aunt's sake, or merely for the present, but for her own sake and for always. In the city, she had seen the face of widespread poverty and hunger – things that had seemed rare in the country. Sheridan was a city dweller now, and likely to remain so for the rest of her life. In the last two years, her father's letters, which had come frequently at first, had ceased altogether. He wouldn't simply forget her here, of that she was sure, and the possibility that he might be dead was so unbearable that she couldn't endure it. That left her no choice except to find a way to look after herself and to tell herself that it was only until he and Rafe came for her. She told herself that as Mrs Raeburn said courteously, 'I've heard some very good things about you from your aunt, Miss Bromleigh.'

And Sheridan Bromleigh, who once would have shoved her hands into the waistband of her pants and replied with blunt shyness that she couldn't think what those good things might have been, stretched out her hand instead, and replied with equal courtesy, 'And I of you, Mrs Raeburn.'

Now, as Sheridan stood below decks on the *Morning Star*, she suddenly realized there was a very good chance she would never see any of the people from her old life again: not Aunt Cornelia, or the little girls at school or the other teachers who'd become her friends and who gathered at the house every Saturday afternoon for tea and conversation. She might never again set eyes on their smiling faces. Or on Rafe . . . or her father.

Her mouth felt dry and at the same time wet tears stung her eyes as she thought of the father she might never see again. When he finally appeared at Aunt Cornelia's, anxious to see her and explain the reason for his long silence, she wasn't going to be there . . . She might never know what happened to him.

She closed her eyes and could almost see Rafe and Dog Lies Sleeping and her father standing in her aunt's parlor, waiting to see her. She'd brought all of this on herself by insisting on accompanying Charise on this voyage, and money hadn't been her only motive. No, indeed. She'd been daydreaming about England ever since she'd started reading those romantic novels. They had sparked her longing for adventure, ignited the streak of dreamy recklessness that she hadn't been able to completely conquer, despite her aunt's diligent efforts, and her own.

Well, she was certainly having an adventure! Instead of sitting in a classroom, surrounded by little faces listening with rapt attention as she read them a story or taught them to walk decorously, she'd landed herself in a strange, unfriendly country – trapped, defenseless, and completely devoid of the wit and courage on which she'd prided herself, preparing to face a nobleman who, according to Meg, would not be required by British law to govern his justifiable rage or delay his vengeance when she told him what had happened. What she, in her pride, had *allowed* to happen.

Fear, the weakness Sheridan despised above all others, spread through her, evading her efforts to subdue it, and she shivered uncontrollably at the thought of the misery she had caused everyone who trusted and loved her. After a lifetime of determined optimism and robust health, she suddenly felt weak, frantic, and alarmingly dizzy. The room began to revolve, and she clutched at the back of a chair for support; then she forced her eyes open, drew a deep breath, and smoothed her hair back into its stern chignon as she reached for her cloak and aimed a reassuring smile at the terrified maid.

Trying to sound flippant, she said, 'It's time to meet the beastly baron and face my fate,' then she sobered and ceased trying to pretend there was no need for alarm. 'You stay here, out of sight. If I don't come back for you right away, wait for a few hours and then leave as quietly as you can. Better yet, stay aboard. With luck, no-one will discover you until the ship is already under way in the morning. There's no point in both of us being arrested and hauled away, if that's what he decides to do.'

7

After the relative quiet of their tiny, dim cabin, the noise and bustle on the torchlit deck was jarring. Stevedores with trunks and crates on their shoulders were swarming up and down the gangplank, unloading cargo and taking on new provisions for the *Morning Star*'s voyage the next day. Winches creaked overhead as cargo nets were slung over the side of the vessel and lowered onto the pier. Sherry picked her way carefully down the gangplank, searching among the throng for a man who looked like her notion of a villainous English nobleman – a thin, pale, overbred, pompous male with a streak of cruelty was certain to be decked out in satin knee breeches and dripping with fobs and seals to impress his bride.

And then she saw the tall, dark man standing on the pier, impatiently slapping his gloves against his thigh, and she knew in an instant it was he. Despite the fact that he was wearing dark trousers, not knee breeches, and that when the wind blew his cloak open, there wasn't a gleaming fob or golden seal in sight, everything about him still set him apart and stamped him indelibly as 'privileged.' His square jaw was set with cool purpose, and there was a confident strength emanating from every inch of his broad-shouldered frame, right down to the tips of his shiny boots. He was already frowning as he watched her approach, and Sherry's fear promptly escalated to panic. For the past two days, she'd secretly counted on her own ability to calm and cajole the affronted bridegroom into seeing reason, but the man whose dark brows were drawn together in a scowl of grim displeasure looked about as malleable as granite. He was doubtlessly wondering where the devil his fiancée was and why Sheridan Bromleigh, not Charise Lancaster, was walking down the gangplank. And he was clearly annoyed.

Stephen wasn't annoyed, he was stunned. He'd expected Charise Lancaster to be a giddy seventeen- or eighteen-year-old with bouncing curls and rosy cheeks, decked out in ruffles and lace. What he saw in the flickering shadows of the torches was a composed, pale young woman with high cheekbones and extraordinarily large, light eyes that were set off by gracefully winged, russet brows and a luminous fringe of long lashes. Her hair was an indeterminate color, pulled back severely off her forehead and concealed with a hood. Instead of ruffles, she was wearing a sensible, but unattractive, brown cloak, and his first thought as he held out his hand to shake hers was that Burleton must have been either mad or blind to describe her as 'quite a pretty little thing.'

Despite her outward composure, she looked extremely tense, frightened, as if she already sensed that something was terribly wrong, so Stephen changed his mind and decided the best course for both of them was probably the most direct one.

'Miss Lancaster,' he said, after quickly introducing himself, 'I'm afraid there's been an accident.' Guilt tore at him as he added tightly, 'Lord Burleton was killed yesterday.'

For a moment, she simply stared at him in shocked incomprehension. 'Killed? He isn't here?'

Stephen had expected her to dissolve into tears, at the very least, or even to have hysterics. He had not expected her to withdraw her cold hand from his and say in a dazed voice, 'How very sad. Please give my condolences to his family.' She'd turned and taken several steps up the pier before he realized she was obviously in complete shock. 'Miss Lancaster—' he called, but his voice was drowned out by an alarmed shout from above as a cargo net loaded with crates swung wide from its winch: 'STEP ASIDE! LOOK OUT!'

Stephen saw the danger and lunged for her, but he wasn't in time – the cargo net swung wide, striking her in the back of the head and sending her flying onto the pier on her face. Already shouting to his coachmen, Stephen crouched down and turned her over in his arms. Her head fell back limply and blood began to run from the huge lump at the back of her scalp.

8

'How is our patient today?' Dr Whitticomb asked as the Westmoreland butler ushered him into the earl's study. Despite Dr Whitticomb's brisk tone, he felt as pessimistic about her chances of recovery as Stephen

Westmoreland, who was sitting in a chair by the fireplace, his elbows propped on his knees, his head in his hands.

'There's no change,' the earl said, wearily rubbing his hands over his face before he looked up. 'She's as still as death. The maids in her chamber are under orders to keep talking to her as you suggested. I even tried talking to her myself a few minutes ago, but she didn't respond. It's been three days,' he pointed out as frustrated impatience edged his voice, 'can't you do something?'

Dr Whitticomb pulled his gaze from the earl's haggard features, curbed the impulse to insist he get some rest, which he knew would be futile, and said instead, 'She's in God's hands, not mine. I'll go up and look in on her, however.'

'A damned lot of good that's going to do,' his lordship fired at his departing back.

Ignoring that outburst of noble temper, Hugh Whitticomb walked up the grand staircase and turned left at the top.

When he returned to the study sometime later, the earl was sitting as he had been before, but Dr Whitticomb's expression had brightened considerably. 'Evidently,' he said dryly, 'my visit did do some good, after all. Or perhaps she simply liked my voice better than the maids'.'

Stephen jerked his head up, his gaze searching the physician's face. 'She's conscious?'

'She's resting now, but she came around and was even able to speak a few words to me. Yesterday, I wouldn't have given a farthing for her chances, but she's young and strong, and I think she may pull through.'

Having said all he had to say on that subject, Dr Whitticomb looked at the deeply etched lines of fatigue and strain at Stephen's eyes and mouth and embarked on the second of his primary concerns: 'You, however, look like the very devil, my lord,' he pronounced with the blunt familiarity of a longtime family friend. 'I was going to suggest we go up to see her together after supper – providing you invite me to stay for supper, of course – but the sight of you might frighten her into a relapse if you don't have some sleep and a shave first.'

'I don't need any sleep,' Stephen said, so relieved that he felt positively energized as he stood up, walked over to a silver tray, and pulled the stopper out of a crystal decanter. 'I won't argue about the shave, however,' he said with a slight smile as he poured brandy into two glasses and held one of them out to the physician. Lifting his own glass in the gesture of a toast, he said, 'To your skill in bringing about her recovery.'

'It wasn't my skill, it was more like a miracle,' the physician said, hesitating to drink the toast.

'To miraculous recoveries, then,' Stephen said, raising his glass to his lips, then he stopped again as Whitticomb negated the second toast with another shake of his head.

'I . . . didn't say she was recovered, Stephen. I said she's conscious and she's able to speak.'

The earl caught the hesitation in his voice, and a pair of piercing blue eyes narrowed sharply on Dr Whitticomb's face, demanding an explanation.

With a reluctant sigh, the physician acceded to the demand. 'I'd hoped to delay telling you this until after you'd had some rest, but the fact is that even if she pulls through physically – and I can't promise you she will – there's still a problem. A complication. Of course, it may be very temporary. Then again, it might not.'

'What the hell is that supposed to mean?'

'She has no memory, Stephen.'

'She what?' he demanded.

'She doesn't *remember* anything that took place before she opened her eyes in the bedchamber upstairs. She doesn't know who she is or why she's in England. She couldn't even tell me her own name.'

9

With his hand on the ornate brass door handle, Dr Whitticomb paused before entering his patient's bedchambers. Turning to Stephen, he lowered his voice and issued some last-minute warnings and instructions: 'Head wounds are very unpredictable. Don't be alarmed if she doesn't remember speaking to me a few hours ago. On the other hand, she may have already regained her memory completely. Yesterday, I spoke with a colleague of mine who's had more experience with serious head injuries than I, and we both felt it would be a mistake to give her laudanum no matter how severe her headache might become. Even though it would help her pain, laudanum will put her to sleep, and we both think it's imperative to keep her conscious and talking.'

Stephen nodded, but Whitticomb wasn't finished. 'Earlier today, she grew very anxious and frightened when she couldn't remember anything, so do not, under any circumstances, say or do anything to add to her anxiety. When we go in there, try to make her feel calm and reassured, and make certain any servant who enters this bedchamber is under the same orders. As I said, head wounds are very dangerous and very unpredictable, and we wouldn't want to lose her.' Satisfied that he'd covered everything, he turned the handle.

Sheridan sensed the presence of people in the darkened room as she floated in a comforting gray mist, drifting in and out of sleep, her mind registering neither fear nor concern, only mild confusion. She clung to that blissful state, because it allowed her to escape the nameless fears and haunting questions nagging at the back of her mind.

'Miss Lancaster?'

The voice was very near her ear, kind but insistent and vaguely familiar.

'Miss Lancaster?'

He was speaking to her. She forced her eyes open and blinked, trying to focus, but her vision was strangely blurry and she saw two of everything, each object superimposed over the other.

'Miss Lancaster?'

She blinked again, and the images separated into two men, one of them middle-aged and gray-haired, with wire-rimmed spectacles and a neat mustache. He looked kindly and confident, just as he sounded. The other man was much younger. Handsome. Not so kindly. Not so confident, either. Worried.

The older man was smiling at her and speaking. 'Do you remember me, Miss Lancaster?'

Sheridan started to nod, but movement made her head hurt so horribly that spontaneous tears burned her eyes.

'Miss Lancaster, do you remember me? Do you know who I am?'

Careful not to move her head when she spoke, she answered his question: 'Doctor.' Her lips felt dry and cracked, but talking didn't seem to make her headache more intense. The moment she realized that, her own questions began to rush in on her. 'Where am I?'

'You're safe.'

'Where?' she persisted.

'You're in England. You sailed here from America.'

For some reason, that made her feel uneasy, depressed. 'Why?'

The two men exchanged a glance, then the doctor said reassuringly, 'That will all come back to you in due time. Don't concern yourself with anything right now.'

'I . . . want to know,' she insisted, her whisper hoarse with tension.

'Very well, child,' he agreed at once, patting her arm. After a slight hesitation he smiled as if he were giving

58

her happy news and said, 'You came here to join your fiancé.'

A fiancé. Evidently, she was betrothed . . . to the other man, she decided, because he was the one who'd looked the most worried about her. Worried and exhausted. She shifted her gaze to the younger man and gave him a wan, reassuring smile, but he was frowning at the physician, who was shaking his head at him in some sort of warning. That frown bothered her for some reason, and so did the physician's warning look, but she didn't know why. It was incongruous, but at that moment, when she knew not who she was or where she'd been or how she came to be here, the only thing she *did* seem to know for certain was that one must always apologize for causing unhappiness to another. She knew that rule of courtesy as if it were deeply ingrained in her – instinctive, imperative, urgent.

Sherry surrendered to the overwhelming compulsion, and in a faint, thready voice, she waited until her fiancé was looking at her and said, 'I'm sorry.'

He winced as if her words had hurt him, and then for the first time in her recollection, she heard his voice – deep, confident, and incredibly soothing. 'Don't apologize. Everything is going to be fine. All you need is a little time and some rest.'

The act of speaking was beginning to require more effort than she could make. Exhausted and bewildered, Sherry closed her eyes, then she heard the men move as if to leave. 'Wait . . .' she managed. Suddenly and irrationally terrified of being alone, of sinking back into the dark void that was tugging at her and never being able to surface again, she looked at both men, then settled her imploring gaze on her fiancé. He was the stronger of the two, younger, more vital – he would keep the demons in her brain at bay, with sheer force of will, if they came back to torment her. 'Stay,' she said in a faint whisper that was draining the last of her strength. 'Please.' When he hesitated and looked at the doctor,

Sheridan wet her cracked lips and, drawing a labored breath, she framed into one feeble word all the thoughts and emotions that were warring inside her. 'Afraid.'

Her eyelids felt like lead weights, and they closed against her will, shutting her away from the world of the living. Panic set in, pressing her down, making her fight for air. . . And then she heard the sharp scrape of chair legs on the polished wood floor as a heavy chair was pulled up beside the bed. 'There's nothing to fear,' her fiancé said.

Sheridan moved her hand an inch forward on the coverlet, a child blindly seeking reassurance from a parent she couldn't even remember. Long masculine fingers closed over her palm and held it in a reassuring grip. 'Hate . . . afraid,' she mumbled.

'I won't leave you. I promise.'

Sheridan clung to his hand, and his voice, and his promise, and she took all three with her into a deep, dreamless sleep.

Guilt and fear made Stephen's chest ache as he watched her drifting deeper and deeper into slumber. Her head was swathed in bandages and her face was ghostly pale, but what struck him forcibly was how *small* she looked in that bed, swallowed up by pillows and bedcovers.

She had apologized, when he was entirely to blame, not only for the death of her fiancé and her dreams, but for this calamity as well. He knew the dangers on a dock, and yet he'd positioned himself, and her, directly in the path of a winch. On top of that, he'd been so preoccupied with her reaction to Burleton's death that he'd failed to see the loaded cargo net swinging toward her, and then he'd failed to react in time to the stevedore's warning shout. And if she hadn't been in such a state of shock over what Stephen had told her, and the blunt, clumsy *way* he'd told her, then she might have been able to react in time to save herself.

As it was, he had put her in the path of danger, failed

to protect her, and then made it all but impossible for her to protect herself. If she died, the fault would be entirely his, and he knew he'd never be able to live with that on his conscience. He already carried enough of a burden over young Burleton's death to torment his nights and haunt his days.

Her breathing changed suddenly, and fear clawed at him. He held his own breath until her chest rose and fell in what seemed like a reasonably steady rhythm, then he exhaled and looked down at the hand resting trustingly in his palm. Her fingers were long and graceful and smooth, but her nails were trimmed very short – an aristocratic hand belonging to a prim and proper young lady with an obvious penchant for tidiness and practicality, he decided.

He lifted his gaze to her face, and if he hadn't been half crazed with fear and half dead from exhaustion, he would have smiled as he wondered how she felt about that face of hers, given her prim and practical streak. There was certainly nothing prim about those soft, generous lips, and nothing practical about those incredibly long, curly lashes that lay like lush crescents against her cheeks. He had no idea what color her hair or eyes were, but her cheekbones were delicately molded, her ivory skin almost translucent. In contrast to all her other features that seemed to exemplify fragile femininity, there was a firmness to that small chin of hers that hinted of willfulness. No, Stephen corrected himself, it more likely hinted of courage. She hadn't wept with pain or fear; she'd said she *hated* being afraid, which implied she preferred to fight that debilitating emotion, rather than succumb to it.

She undoubtedly had courage, he decided, and kindness as well – enough to try to apologize for worrying him. Courage and gentleness, a remarkable combination in any woman, but particularly in one so young.

And so *vulnerable*, he realized with a fresh surge of panic as her chest rose and fell in fitful little gasps.

Tightening his grip on her hand, he watched her seem to struggle for air while a lump of pure terror swelled in his throat. God! She was dying! 'Don't!' he whispered fiercely. 'Don't die!'

10

Bright sunlight was peeking between the green draperies at the far end of the room when Sheridan opened her eyes again. Her fiancé was seated in a chair beside the bed, still holding her hand, fast asleep. Sometime in the night, he'd removed his coat and neckcloth, opened his collar, and fallen asleep with his arms crossed on the bed and his head resting on them. His face was toward her, and Sheridan cautiously turned her head on the pillow, breathing a sigh of relief when the slight movement didn't unleash the hammers in her brain.

In the peaceful daze that comes after a deep sleep, she idly studied the man to whom she was betrothed. He was tanned, she realized, as if he spent time outdoors, and his thick hair was a rich dark brown, beautifully trimmed to lie flat at the sides and to barely touch the collar of his shirt. At the moment, his hair was rumpled from sleep and there was something endearingly boyish about that and the way his spiky black lashes lay against his face. There was nothing boyish about the rest of him, however, and she felt a mixture of fascination and an inexplicable uneasiness at the discovery. The shadowy beginnings of a dark beard had appeared on a square jaw that was hard and resolute even in slumber. His straight, dark brows were drawn together into a scowl that boded ill for someone in his dreams. The fine white fabric of his shirt was stretched taut over powerful shoulders and muscular arms. Crisp, dark hair peeked from the deep vee of his open collar and lightly covered his forearms. He was all rugged angles and sharp planes, from his finely carved nose to his chiselled jaw and long fingers. He looked stern and uncompromising, she decided.

And handsome.

Dear God, he was so handsome!

Reluctantly, she lifted her gaze from his face and, for the first time, she looked at her surroundings. Her eyes widened in shocked awe at the glittering opulence of the green and gold room. Pale, apple green silk covered the walls and the windows and floated gracefully from the bed's canopy, held in place by shimmering golden cords and tassels. Even the cavernous fireplace at the far end of the room was of a wondrous green marble, adorned with golden birds mounted at the corners and ornate brass fittings. Two curved sofas upholstered in pale green watered silk faced each other in front of the fireplace, separated by a low oval table.

Her attention drifted back to the dark head resting near her hip, and she felt her spirits lift a little. She was obviously very fortunate, because her betrothed was not only startlingly handsome, but he was obviously extremely wealthy too. Moreover, he'd stayed with her all night, sleeping in that dreadfully uncomfortable position and never letting go of her hand; therefore, he must be very much in love with her.

He had obviously courted her and asked her to marry him. She closed her eyes tightly, searching for any recollection of him or of her past, but there was nothing except a black void. No woman could possibly forget being courted and loved by a man like this; it just wasn't possible. She'd remember it all in a minute, she told herself fiercely, fighting back a surge of panic so strong it made her feel nauseated. In her mind, she said things to herself that he must have said to her: *'Will you do me the honor of becoming my wife, Miss . . . ?'* Miss who? Miss WHO?

'*Stay calm!*' Sheridan warned herself desperately. '*Concentrate on other things . . . sweet things he must have said.*' Unaware that she was breathing faster and clutching his hand so hard that her nails were digging into it, she tried to think, to remember some of their times together. He would have treated her in a courtly manner as befitted a proper suitor. He'd have brought her flowers and told her that she was clever and charming and beautiful. She'd have to be all those things in order to have captured the heart of such a supremely eligible suitor. . .

She tried to think of something clever, but her mind went blank.

She tried to think of a charming phrase, and her mind remained blank. Trying to stay calm, she settled for thinking of her face. Her face . . .

She had no face.

SHE HAD NO FACE!

Some instinct or latent character trait was struggling to keep her calm, but terror was beginning to quake through her. She couldn't remember her name. She couldn't remember his name. SHE COULDN'T REMEMBER HER OWN FACE.

Stephen felt as if his hand had suddenly been clamped in a vise that was biting into his fingers, cutting off their blood supply. He tried to pull free of its painful grasp, but it held onto him. After three days without sleep, it took a supreme effort just to force his eyes open enough to peek between the heavy lids at whatever was causing his hand to go numb. Instead of finding a pitchfork buried in his fingers, he saw a woman lying in the bed beside him. Since that situation certainly wasn't unusual enough to startle him from his dazed stupor, he simply twisted his hand to free it a little so that he could go back to sleep. But because courtesy to the opposite sex had been drummed into his head since childhood, and because the woman had looked truly frantic, he managed to form a polite inquiry about her problem just as his eyes closed and he began sinking into a deep sleep. 'What's wrong?'

Her voice shook with alarm. 'I don't know what I look like!'

Stephen had known other women who were obsessed with their appearance, but this female's concern – in a dimly lit boudoir in the middle of the night – verged on the ridiculous. Given that, he didn't feel obliged to even open his eyes when she tightened her grip and frantically implored, 'What do I look like?'

'Ravishing,' he stated tonelessly. His entire body ached, which, he belatedly realized, was because she was in the bed and he wasn't. He was trying to muster the strength to ask her to move over, when he heard the unmistakable sound of stifled crying. Turning his head away from the sound, he wondered irritably what he had done to make her cry and resolved to have Wheaton send her a pretty trinket to atone for whatever it was – a ruby brooch, or something. The desire for an expensive piece of jewelry was, more often than not, the underlying cause of most feminine bouts of delicate tears. Even in his sleep, Stephen knew that.

Her crying promptly escalated to serious, anguished weeping, punctuated with gulped breaths and shuddering. Whatever he'd done to cause *this* outburst, it was far more than merely forgetting to compliment her gown or breaking an engagement for the theatre. This outburst was going to cost him a diamond necklace!

A convulsive sob shook her entire body along with the bedcovers.

And a matching bracelet.

Exhausted in body and spirit, he drifted deeper into slumber, reaching for the bliss of it, but something she'd said was holding him back, tugging at him. *'I don't know how I look . . . don't know . . . don't KNOW.'*

Stephen's eyes snapped open, and he jerked his head toward her. She'd turned her face away and covered her mouth with her left hand in an attempt to silence her cries, but shudders were still racking her body. Her eyes were closed, but tears were trickling steadily from beneath her long wet lashes and streaking down her pale cheeks. She was weeping her heart out, but she was fully conscious and lucid and his relief at that outweighed his guilt over her tears.

'I wasn't awake enough to understand your question before,' he said quickly. 'I apologize.'

Her body stiffened at the sound of his voice, and he saw the gallant struggle she made to bring herself under control before she turned her head on the pillow and looked at him.

'What's wrong?' he said carefully, gentling his voice to what he hoped was a soothing tone.

Sheridan swallowed, taken aback by how tired he still looked and how relieved. He must have been worried to death about her for days, she realized, feeling foolish and ungrateful for weeping like an infant over what in reality was little more than a temporary inconvenience. A bizarre, frightening inconvenience, to be sure, but it wasn't as if she'd been crippled or maimed or diagnosed with some deadly ailment. Guided by an instinctive desire to make the best of a difficult situation, she drew a shaky breath and gave him an apologetic smile. 'I – It sounds absurd, but I don't know what I look like, and it—' She broke off, unwilling to distress him by telling him how frightening that was. 'It's a trifling thing, really, but since you're already awake, could you just describe me a little?'

Stephen recognized her attempt to control her fear as well as reassure him – which struck him as remarkably and touchingly brave. 'Describe you . . .' he said, stalling for time. He didn't know the color of her hair, and he was afraid of how she might react if she saw herself in a mirror, so he tried to pass the entire issue off as a joke. 'At the moment, your eyes are puffy and red,' he said with a smile as he flicked a quick glance at her eyes to gather additional information, 'but they're

. . . very large and . . . gray,' he concluded with some surprise.

In fact, she had startling eyes, Stephen realized – light silvery gray at the center with a thin outline of black at the edges and set off with that luxurious fringe of long sable lashes.

'Gray?' Sheridan said, disappointed. 'I don't think I like that.'

'Right now, when they're wet, they look like liquid silver.'

'Perhaps they aren't so very bad. What about the rest of me?'

'Well, your face is pale and streaked with tears, but it's a rather nice face, despite that.'

She looked torn between horror, tears, and laughter. To his relief and surprise, she decided to smile. 'What color is my hair?'

'At the moment,' he prevaricated quickly, 'your hair is concealed by a large white . . . er . . . turban. Wearing a turban to bed has become all the rage, as you know.' The night of the accident, the light had been poor and her hair had been covered, first with a hood and then with her blood. Still, her lashes were brown, so it stood to reason her hair would be. 'Your hair is brown,' he said decisively. 'Dark brown.'

'It took you rather a long time to decide.'

She was watching him closely, puzzled but not suspicious.

'I'm not very observant – about some things,' he countered, inanely he thought.

'May I see a mirror?'

Stephen wasn't certain how she'd react if she didn't recognize her face even when she saw it in a mirror, and he wasn't certain if she'd panic when she saw her head swathed in bandages and the dark bruise near her temple. He was, however, certain that when the time came for her to look in a mirror, he wanted Whitticomb here in case she needed medication. 'Another day,' he said. 'Perhaps tomorrow. Or when the bandages are removed.'

Sheridan sensed why he didn't want her to look at a mirror, and since she wasn't up to another bout of terror and had no desire to make things any more trying for him than she already had, she reverted to their earlier remarks about turbans. 'Turbans are very practical, I suppose. They save one the bother of using brushes and combs, and all that.'

'Exactly,' Stephen said, marvelling at the grace and courage she displayed under such extreme duress. He was so grateful she was able to talk and so touched by her attitude that it seemed perfectly natural, perfectly right, to cover her hand with his, smile into those amazing silvery eyes, and tenderly inquire, 'Are you in much pain? How do you feel?'

'I have a bit of a headache, that's all,' she admitted, returning his smile as if that, too, were natural and right. 'You needn't worry that I feel as badly as I look.'

Her voice was soft and sweet, and yet her expression was open and direct. She'd indicated a feminine concern about her appearance earlier, then calmly accepted that she did not look her best, and now she was actually joking about it. All those things gave Stephen the distinct impression that pretense and pretension were completely foreign to her, and that she was refreshingly unique in those ways and probably many other delightful ways, as well.

Unfortunately, that realization led instantly to another – one that banished his pleasure and made him quickly withdraw his hand from hers. There was nothing natural, nothing right, about what he was doing or the way he was thinking about her. He was not her fiancé, as she believed; he was the man who was responsible for her fiancé's *death*. Common decency, respect for the young man he had killed, and just plain ordinary good taste all dictated that he keep his distance mentally and physically. He was the last man on earth who had the right to touch her or think about her in any personal sort of way.

Hoping to end his visit on a light note, he stood up, rotating his sore shoulders, trying to work the kinks out of them. Reverting to her last comment about her looks, he said, 'All in all, if I had to describe you at this moment, I'd say you look like a fashionable mummy.'

She giggled weakly at that, but she was tiring, and he saw it. 'I'll send a maid in with breakfast. Promise me you'll eat something.' She nodded, and he turned to leave.

'Thank you,' she said quietly behind him, and he turned back, puzzled.

'For what?'

Those candid eyes lifted to his, searching, delving, and Stephen had the fleeting impression that, with time, she might see straight into his blackened soul. She obviously hadn't gotten his true measure, however, because a warm smile touched those soft lips of hers. 'For staying with me all night.'

Her gratitude only made him feel more guilty about everything, more of a disgusting fraud, for letting her think of him as some gallant white knight, instead of the black villain he actually was. Inclining his head in the mockery of a bow, Stephen gave her a bold grin and a deliberate insight into his true character: 'That is the *first* time I've ever been thanked by a beautiful woman for spending the night with her.'

She looked confused, not appalled, but that didn't diminish Stephen's own sense of relief. He hadn't made that subtle 'confession' about his true nature because he needed or desired absolution, or wished to do penance. What mattered most to him at the moment was that he had at least been honest with her for a change, and that redeemed him a little in his own eyes.

As he headed down the long hall to his own chamber, Stephen felt completely elated about something for the first time in weeks, no, months: Charise Lancaster was on the way to a full recovery. He was completely certain of it. She was going to pull through, which meant he could now notify her father of her accident and at the same time give the man some needed reassurance about her eventual recovery. First he had to locate him, but that task and the delivery of the letter could both be handed over to Matthew Bennett and his people.

11

Stephen glanced up from the letter he was reading and nodded a greeting at the light-haired man in his early thirties who was walking toward him. 'I apologize for interrupting your holiday in Paris,' he told Matthew Bennett, 'but the matter is urgent, and delicate enough to require your personal attention.'

'I'm happy to be of assistance in any way I can, my lord,' the solicitor replied without hesitation. The earl gestured toward a leather chair in front of his desk, and Matthew sat down, feeling no affront – and no surprise – that the man who had summoned him from a badly needed holiday was now making him wait while he finished reading his mail. For generations, Matthew's family had been privileged to act as the Westmoreland family's solicitors, and as Matthew well knew, that honor and its enormous financial rewards carried with it the obligation to make oneself available whenever and wherever the Earl of Langford desired.

Although Matthew was a junior member of the family firm, he was well versed in the Westmorelands' business affairs, and he'd even been called upon several years ago to handle an extremely unusual personal assignment from the earl's brother, the Duke of Claymore. On that occasion, Matthew had felt a little intimidated and off-balance when he answered the duke's summons, and he'd suffered an embarrassing lack of composure when he heard the nature of his assignment. However, he was older now and wiser, and quite happily confident that he could handle whatever 'delicate' matter of the earl's that required his attention – and without so much as a blink of surprise.

And so he waited with perfect equanimity to discover what 'urgent' detail needed his particular attention, ready to give his advice on the terms of a contract, or perhaps a change in a will. Given the use of the word 'delicate,' Matthew was inclined to think the matter probably involved something more personal – perhaps the settlement of a sum of money and property on the earl's current mistress, or a confidential, charitable gift.

Rather than keep Bennett waiting any longer, Stephen put the letter from his steward on his Northumberland estate aside. Leaning his head against the back of his chair, he gazed absently at the intricate plasterwork on the frescoed ceiling twenty-five feet above, his mind switching from the steward's letter to the other, more complicated problem of Charise Lancaster. He was about to speak when the under-butler, an elderly man whom Stephen belatedly recognized as Burleton's former manservant, interrupted with a polite cough and said a little desperately, 'Miss Lancaster is insisting upon getting out of bed, milord. What shall we tell her?'

Stephen transferred his gaze to the butler without lifting his head, smiling a little because she was obviously feeling much better. 'Tell her I do not intend to let her out of bed for a full week. Tell her I'll join her after supper.' Oblivious to the mixture of shock, admiration, and dismay that flickered across Matthew Bennett's normally bland features, or the erroneous conclusions the other man might draw from his smiling remark, Stephen decided to tackle his problem head-on. 'I seem to have acquired a "fiancée,"' he began.

'My heartiest felicitations!' Matthew said.

'She isn't *my* fiancée, she's Arthur Burleton's.'

After a distinct pause, during which Matthew struggled to think of some appropriate response to that revelation, he said, 'In that case, please convey my . . . er . . . felicitations to that gentleman.'

'I can't. Burleton is dead.'

'That's a pity.'

'I killed him.'

'That's much worse,' Matthew said before he could stop himself. There were laws against duelling, and the courts were taking a stern posture of late. Furthermore, the blatant presence of the dead man's fiancée in the earl's bed wasn't going to do his case any good either. The solicitor's mind already searching for the best possible line of defense, Matthew said, 'Was it swords or pistols?'

'No, it was a carriage.'

'I beg your pardon?'

'I ran over him.'

'That's not as straightforward as swords or pistols,' Matthew said absently, 'but it *is* much easier to defend.' Too worried to notice the odd look the earl was aiming at him, he continued thoughtfully, 'The courts might be persuaded to take the point of view that if you'd truly meant to kill him, you'd have chosen a duel. After all, your skill with pistols is widely known. We can call dozens of witnesses to attest to that fact. Theodore Kittering would make an excellent witness in that regard – he was a crack shot before you wounded him in the shoulder. No, we'd better leave him out of it, because he isn't fond of you, and the duel would be bound to come out during the trial. Even without Kittering's testimony, we should be able to convince the court that Burleton's death wasn't what you actually intended – that it was incidental to the event and, therefore, loosely speaking, an accident!' Very pleased with his logic, Matthew withdrew his thoughtful gaze from across the room and finally looked at the earl, who said very clearly, and very slowly, 'At the risk of

72

appearing hopelessly obtuse, may I inquire what in the living hell you are talking about?'

'I beg pardon?'

'Am I to understand you think I ran him down deliberately?'

'I was under that impression, yes.'

'May I ask,' his lordship drawled, 'what possible reason I could have for such a deed?'

'I assume your reason had something to do . . . er, was directly related to . . . er . . . the presence of a certain young lady who is not permitted to leave your . . . ah . . . bedchambers.'

The earl gave a sharp crack of laughter that had a rusty sound to it, as if laughter were foreign to him.

'Of course,' Stephen said, 'how foolish of me. What other conclusion could you have reached?' Straightening in his chair, he spoke in a brisk, businesslike tone. 'Last week, the young woman upstairs – Charise Lancaster – arrived in England from America. She was betrothed to Burleton, and their marriage was to take place the following day by special license. Since I was responsible for his death, and since there was no-one else to tell her what had happened, I naturally met her ship and gave her the sad news. I was talking to her on the dock when some idiot lost control of a loaded cargo net and it struck her in the head. Since her only travelling companion was a ladies' maid, and since Miss Lancaster is too ill to leave England for a while, I'll have to depend upon you to notify her family of all this and to escort any family member who wishes to come back here to England. In addition, I want to settle Burleton's affairs. Put together as complete a dossier on him as you can so I can see where to begin. The least I can do is make sure his name is cleared of debts that he didn't have time to settle before he died.'

'Oh, I see!' Matthew said with a smile of relief that he was happy to see the earl return.

'Good.'

Reaching for a quill and paper on the desk, Matthew said with pen poised, 'Where does her family reside and what are her relatives' names?'

'I don't know.'

'You don't . . . know?'

'No.'

'Perhaps,' Matthew suggested, very cautiously, and very respectfully, 'we might make inquiries of the young lady?'

'We might,' Stephen said dryly, 'but she will have precious little to tell you.' Taking pity on the solicitor, he added, 'Her injury was to the head and severe enough to cause a loss of memory, which Dr Whitticomb believes is a temporary condition. Unfortunately, although her health is mostly restored, her memory isn't.'

'I'm sorry to hear that,' Matthew said sincerely. Thinking that concern for the young woman had somewhat diminished the earl's usual perspicacity, he suggested diplomatically, 'Perhaps her maid could be of help?'

'I'm certain she could. If I knew where she was.' With veiled amusement, Stephen watched the solicitor struggle to keep his face from showing any emotion whatsoever. 'I sent someone to her cabin within minutes after the accident, but the maid was nowhere to be found. One of the crew members thought she might have been English, so perhaps she went home to her family.'

'I see,' Matthew replied, but he still wasn't overly concerned. 'In that case, we'll begin our inquiry on the ship.'

'It sailed the following morning.'

'Oh. Well, what about her trunks? Was there anything in them to give us a clue as to her family's direction?'

'There might have been. Unfortunately, her trunks sailed with the ship.'

'You're certain?'

'Quite. In the immediate aftermath of the accident, my only concern was to get her medical attention at once. The following morning, I sent for her trunks, but the *Morning Star* had already sailed.'

'Then we'll begin our search at the ship's office. There's bound to be a passenger manifest and a cargo manifest, and they'll be able to tell us what her ports of call were in America.'

'Start with the shipping office,' Stephen agreed. He stood up, concluding the interview, and Matthew promptly arose, his mind already on the search he was about to instigate.

'I've only been to the Colonies once,' he said. 'I shan't mind another visit.'

'I'm sorry to have cut your holiday short,' Stephen repeated. 'However, there's another reason for urgency, beyond the obvious one. Whitticomb is becoming concerned that her memory hasn't shown the slightest sign of returning. I'm hoping that seeing people from her past may help.'

12

As he'd promised, Stephen went upstairs to see her later that evening. He'd made it a practice to visit her twice each day, and although he kept them very brief and impersonal, he found himself nevertheless looking forward to them. He knocked on her door, and when there was no response, he hesitated then knocked again. Still no reply. Evidently his instructions that a maid was to be with her at all times had not been followed. Either that or the servant had fallen asleep on duty. Both possibilities angered him, but his primary emotion was alarm for his houseguest. She'd wanted to leave her bed. If she'd decided to try it, despite his instructions, and then collapsed with no-one there to help her or sound an alarm . . .

Or if she'd lapsed back into unconsciousness . . .

He shoved the door open and strode into the chambers. The *empty* chambers. Baffled and annoyed, he looked at the bed, which had been neatly made up. Evidently the little idiot had not seen fit to follow his orders, and neither had the maid!

A soft sound made him swing around. And stop cold.

'I didn't hear you come in,' his houseguest said, walking out of the dressing room. Clad in a white dressing gown that was too large for her, with a hairbrush in one hand and a blue towel loosely draped over her head, she stood before him barefoot, unselfconscious, and completely unrepentant for ignoring his instructions.

Having just been needlessly subjected to several awful moments of fear, Stephen reacted with a flash of annoyance, followed by relief, and then helpless amusement. She'd borrowed a gold cord from the draperies and tied it around her waist to hold the white dressing robe closed, and with her bare toes peeping out from beneath the long robe and that light blue towel over her head like a veil, she reminded him of the barefoot Madonna. Instead of the real Madonna's serenely sweet smile, however, this madonna was wearing an expression that looked bewildered, accusing, and distinctly unhappy, all at once. She did not make him wait to find out the cause.

'Either you're extremely unobservant, my lord, or else your eyesight is afflicted.'

Caught completely off-guard, Stephen said cautiously, 'I'm not certain what you mean.'

'I mean my hair,' she said miserably, pointing an accusing finger to whatever was concealed beneath the towel.

He remembered that her hair had been matted with blood, and assumed the wound to her scalp had bled even after Whitticomb had stitched it. 'It will wash right out,' he assured her.

'Oh, I don't think so,' she said ominously. 'I already tried that.'

'I don't understand . . .' he began.

'My hair is *not* brown—' she clarified as she swept the towel away and picked up a fistful of the offending tresses to illustrate the problem. 'Look at it. It's *red*!'

She sounded revolted, but Stephen was speechless, completely transfixed by a heavy mass of shiny, flaming strands that tumbled in waves and curls over her shoulders and the bodice of her robe and down her back. She released the handful she was holding, and it ran through her fingers like liquid fire. '*Jesus* . . .' he breathed.

'It's so . . . so brazen!' she said unhappily.

Belatedly realizing that her real fiancé wouldn't be standing there, staring at something he would have already seen, Stephen reluctantly withdrew his gaze from the most magnificent, and unusual, head of hair he had ever seen. 'Brazen?' he repeated, wanting to laugh.

She nodded and then impatiently shoved aside a glossy panel of coppery locks that slid away from her center part and draped itself over her forehead and left eye.

'You don't like it,' he summarized.

'Of course not. Is that why you didn't want to tell me its real color?'

Stephen seized the excuse she'd inadvertently handed him and nodded, his gaze shifting back to that exotic hair. It was a perfect frame to set off her delicate features and porcelain skin.

It began to register on Sheridan that the expression on his face wasn't revulsion at all. In fact, he looked almost . . . admiring? 'Do *you* like it?'

Stephen liked it. He liked every damn thing about her. 'I like it,' he said casually. 'I gather that red hair isn't quite the thing in America?'

Sheridan opened her mouth to answer, and realized she didn't know the answer. 'I . . . don't see how it could be. And I don't think it is in England.'

'What makes you say that?'

'Because the maid who helped me admitted after I

pressed her that she had never seen a head of hair this color in her *entire* life. She looked perfectly appalled.'

'Whose opinion matters most?' he countered smoothly.

'Well, when you put it that way . . .' Sheridan said, feeling shy and overheated beneath the warmth of his smile. He was so beautiful – in a dark, manly way – that it was difficult not to stare at him and even more difficult to believe he'd actually chosen her above all the women in his own country. She loved his company, his humor, and the gentle way he treated her. She counted the hours between his visits, looking forward eagerly to each one, but the visits had all been very brief and completely uninformative. As a result, she still knew nothing about herself, or about him, or about their past relationship. She was no longer willing to exist in limbo, waiting for her capricious memory to return at any moment and provide the answers.

She'd understood Lord Westmoreland's point of view, which was that she shouldn't jeopardize her health by over-taxing her mind, but her body was healed now. She'd gotten out of bed, bathed, and washed her hair, and then put on the dressing robe, in order to prove to him that she was well enough now to ask questions and hear answers. Her legs felt wobbly, but that might be due to a lingering weakness from her ordeal or, more likely, it was another symptom of the flustered nervousness she sometimes felt in his presence.

She nodded toward a pair of inviting green-silk-covered sofas positioned near the fireplace. 'Would you mind if we sat down? I'm afraid I've been in bed so long that my legs have grown weak from disuse.'

'Why didn't you say something before?' Stephen said, already stepping aside so that she could precede him.

'I wasn't certain it was allowed.'

She curled up on the sofa, tucked her bare feet beneath her, and arranged the dressing robe neatly around her. One of the things she'd obviously forgotten, Stephen noted, was that well-bred young ladies did not entertain gentlemen who were not their husbands in their boudoir. Stephen, on the other hand, was as aware of this as he was his own transgression in being there. He chose to ignore both issues in favor of his own desires. 'Why did you say you weren't certain you were allowed to sit down?'

Her embarrassed gaze slid to the fireplace, and Stephen felt absurdly deprived of the delight of her face, and absurdly pleased when she looked back at him. 'I understand from Constance – the maid – that you're an earl.'

She looked at him as if she almost hoped he'd deny it, which made her the most unusual woman he'd ever met.

'And?' he said when she didn't continue.

'And that I ought properly to address you as "my lord."' When he merely lifted his brows, waiting, she admitted, 'Among the things I do seem to know is that in the presence of a king, one does not sit unless invited to do so.'

Stephen suppressed the urge to shout with laughter. 'I am not a king, however, merely an earl.'

'Yes, well, I wasn't certain if the same protocol applied.'

'It doesn't, and speaking of the maid, where the devil is she? I specifically said you were not to be left alone at any time.'

'I sent her away.'

'Because of her reaction to your hair,' he assumed aloud. 'I'll see that—'

'No, because she'd been with me since dawn, and she looked exhausted. She'd already tidied the room, and I certainly didn't want to be bathed as if I were a child.'

Stephen heard that with surprise, but then she was full of surprises, including her next announcement, which was stated with a great deal of resolve and only a tremor of uncertainty. 'I've been making some decisions today.'

'Have you now,' he said, smiling at her fierce

expression. She was not in any position to make decisions, but he saw no reason to point that out to her.

'Yes. I've decided that the best way to cope with the loss of my memory is to believe that it's merely a passing inconvenience, and for us to treat it that way.'

'I think that's an excellent idea.'

'There are a few things I'd like to ask you, however.'

'What would you like to know?'

'Oh, the usual things,' she said, choking on a laugh. 'How old am I? Do I have a middle name?'

Stephen's defenses collapsed, leaving him torn between the wild urge to laugh at her wonderful, courageous sense of humor and the wilder urge to pull her off the sofa, shove his hands into that mass of gleaming hair and bury his lips in hers. She was as enticing as she was sweet, and more sexually provocative in that robe and curtain cord than any gorgeously dressed – or undressed – courtesan he'd ever known.

Burleton must have been in an agony to take her to bed, he thought. No wonder he intended to marry her the day after she arrived . . .

Guilt abruptly doused Stephen's pleasurable contemplation of her appealing assets, and shame ate at him like acid. Burleton, not he, should have been sitting across from her. It was Burleton who should have been the one to enjoy this cozy moment with her, to see her curled up on the sofa, barefoot; it was Burleton who had the right to be mentally undressing her and thinking of taking her to bed. No doubt he'd been thinking of little else while he waited for her ship to arrive.

Instead of all that, her ardent young lover was lying in a coffin, and his *killer* was enjoying the evening with his bride. No, Stephen corrected himself with savage self-disgust, he wasn't merely enjoying a pleasant evening with her, he was *lusting* after her.

His attraction to her was obscene! It was insane! If he wanted diversion of any kind, he could choose from among the most beautiful women in Europe.

Sophisticated or naive, witty or serious, outgoing or shy, blondes, brunettes, *and redheads* – they were his for the asking. There was no reason on earth to feel a wild attraction to this woman, no reason to react to her like some randy adolescent or aging lecher.

Her quiet voice jerked him from his furious self-reproach, but his feelings of revulsion lingered. 'Whatever it is,' she said half-seriously, 'I don't think it has very long to live.'

Stephen's gaze snapped back to her face. 'I beg your pardon?'

'Whatever it is that you've been glowering at over my left shoulder for the last minute – I hope it has legs and can run very quickly.'

He gave her a brief, humorless smile. 'My thoughts drifted. I apologize.'

'Oh, please do not apologize!' she said with a nervous laugh. 'I am vastly *relieved* to know you were thinking of something other than my questions with that black scowl on your face.'

'I'm afraid I've forgotten the questions entirely.'

'My age?' she provided helpfully, her delicate brows lifting. 'Do I have a middle name?' Despite her lighthearted tone, Stephen realized she was watching him very, very closely. He was disconcerted by the way her eyes were searching his, and he hesitated for a second, still struggling to switch his attention to the topic at hand. She broke the silence before he could, by heaving a great, comical sigh of dismay and warning him in an exaggerated, dire voice, 'Dr Whitticomb told me this malady I have is called am-ne-si-a, and it is *not* contagious. Therefore, I shall be very much aggrieved if you mean to pretend you have it too, and thus make me look quite ordinary. Now, shall we start with something a little easier? Would you care to tell me *your* full name? *Your* age? Take your time, think about the answers.'

Stephen would have laughed if he hadn't hated himself so much for wanting to. 'I am three and thirty,' he said. 'My name is Stephen David Elliott Westmoreland.'

'Well, that explains it!' she joked. 'With so many names, it's little wonder it took you awhile to recall them all!'

A grin tugged at his lips, and Stephen tried to negate it by chiding as sternly as he could, 'You impertinent baggage, I'll thank you to show me a little more respect.'

Unchastened and unrepentant, she tipped her head to the side and inquired curiously, 'Because you're an earl?'

'No, because I'm *bigger* than you are.'

Her peal of laughter was as musical as bells and so infectious that Stephen's face hurt from the effort to keep his expression blank.

'Now that we've established that I am impertinent and you are larger than I,' she said, giving him a laughing, innocent look from beneath her lashes, 'would it be equally correct to assume that you are also older than I?'

Stephen nodded because he couldn't trust his voice.

She pounced instantly. 'By how many years?'

'Persistent little chit, aren't you?' he said, caught between amusement and admiration at how neatly she'd twisted the subject back around to her questions.

She sobered, her gray eyes infinitely appealing. 'Please tell me how old I am. Tell me if I have a middle name. Or don't you know?'

He didn't know. On the other hand, he didn't know the ages or middle names of many of the women who'd occupied his bed. Since she'd spent very little time with her fiancé, the truth seemed safe and even reasonable. 'Actually, neither of those issues ever came up.'

'And my family – what are they like?'

'Your father is a widower,' Stephen said, recalling what he'd learned from Burleton's butler, and feeling quite capable of handling the discussion, after all. 'You are his only child.'

She nodded, absorbing that, then she smiled at him. 'How did we meet?'

'I imagine your mother introduced you to him shortly after you were born.'

She laughed because she thought he was joking. He frowned because he hadn't anticipated questions like that, he didn't feel capable of either answering or evading them, and no matter what he did or said, he was still going to be a fraud.

'I mean, how did you and I meet?'

'The usual way,' he said curtly.

'Which is?'

'We were introduced.' He got up to avoid the puzzlement and scrutiny in those wide gray eyes of hers, and walked over to a sideboard, where he'd seen a crystal decanter earlier.

'My lord?'

He glanced over his shoulder as he pulled the stopper out of the decanter and raised it to the glass. 'Yes?'

'Are we very much in love?'

Half the brandy sloshed over his thumb and ran down the side of the glass onto the gold tray. Swearing silently, he realized that no matter what he told her now, she was going to feel duped when she recovered her memory. Between that and the fact that he was also responsible for the death of the man she did care for, she was going to hate him thoroughly when this was over. But not as much as he hated himself for everything, including what he was about to do. Raising the glass, he tossed down what little brandy he'd actually managed to get into it, then he turned around and faced her. Left with no choice, he answered in a way that he knew would destroy any good opinion she had of him. 'This is England, not America—' he began.

'Yes, I know. Dr Whitticomb told me that.'

Inwardly Stephen winced at the reminder that she'd had to be told what country she was in, which was also his fault. 'This is England,' he repeated curtly. 'In England, in the upper classes, couples marry for a variety of reasons, nearly all of which are purely practical.

Unlike some Americans, we do not expect or desire to wear our hearts on our sleeves, nor do we prose on and on about that tenuous emotion called "love." We leave that to the peasants and the poets.'

She looked as if he'd slapped her, and Stephen put the glass down with more force than he'd intended. 'I hope I haven't upset you with my bluntness,' he said, feeling like a complete bastard. 'It's getting late, and you need your rest.'

He gave her a slight bow to indicate the conversation was over, and then waited for her to stand up, carefully looking away when the dressing robe parted to reveal a glimpse of shapely calf. He already had his hand on the door handle, when she finally spoke.

'My lord?'

'Yes?' he said without turning.

'You do have one, though, do you not?'

'One what?'

'A heart.'

'Miss Lancaster,' he began, furious with himself and with fate because he was in this untenable situation. He turned around and saw that she was standing at the foot of the bed, her hand resting on the poster in a pretty pose.

'My name is—' she hesitated, and he felt another stab of unbearable guilt as she had to think to remember her own name, 'Charise. I wish you would call me that.'

'Certainly,' he said, intending to do nothing of the sort. 'And now, if you'll excuse me, I have some work to do.'

Sheridan waited until the door closed behind him, then she grabbed the poster with the other hand as dizziness and nausea overwhelmed her. Carefully, she eased herself into a sitting position on the satin coverlet, her heart hammering from weakness and fear.

What sort of person was she, she wondered, to have wanted to wed a man who thought as he did? What sort of person was he? Her stomach churned when she

84

remembered the cold way he'd looked at her and the callous way he'd spoken about love.

What could she have been thinking of to have pledged herself to such as he? Why would she have done that, Sheridan wondered bitterly.

But she already suspected the answer to that: it lay in the wondrous way she felt when he smiled at her.

Only he hadn't been smiling when he left. She'd given him a disgust of her with all her talk about love. When he came to see her in the morning, she'd apologize. Or leave the matter entirely alone and simply try to be lighthearted and amusing company.

Reaching for the edge of the coverlet, she climbed into bed and pulled it up to her chin. Wide awake, her throat aching with tears, she stared at the canopy above her. She would *not* cry, she told herself. Surely no irreparable damage had been done to their relationship tonight. They were betrothed, after all. He would surely overlook her small error in viewpoint. Then she remembered that she'd asked him if he had a heart, and the lump of tears in her throat felt the size of a fist.

Tomorrow, everything would look brighter, she told herself. She was still weak and tired right now from the exertion of bathing and dressing and washing her hair.

Tomorrow, he would come to see her and everything would be all right again.

13

Stephen was in the middle of dictating to his secretary when Whitticomb arrived three days later. He was smiling, Stephen noticed, as the butler showed him past the double doors that opened into the study. A half hour later, when he came downstairs after visiting his patient, he did not look nearly as pleased. 'I'd like to talk to you privately, if you can spare me a few minutes,' he said, waving off the appalled butler who was standing in the doorway, trying to announce him.

Stephen had an uneasy premonition of what he was going to hear, and with an irritated sigh, he dismissed his secretary, shoved his correspondence aside, and leaned back in his chair.

'I distinctly remember telling you,' Hugh Whitticomb began, as soon as the doors closed behind the secretary, 'that it is imperative to keep Miss Lancaster from becoming upset. The specialist I consulted on memory loss stressed that to me, and I stressed it to you. Do you remember that conversation?'

Stephen reined in a sharp retort at the physician's tone, but his voice turned curt. 'I do.'

'Then will you please explain to me,' Dr Whitticomb said, noting his adversary's warning tone and tempering his own accordingly, 'why you have not gone up to see her in three days. I told you it was important that she have diversions to distract her thoughts from her troubles.'

'You told me, and I made certain she has every conceivable sort of feminine diversion I could think of, from books and fashion plates to embroidery frames and watercolors.'

'There's one "feminine diversion" you have not offered, and one she has a right to expect.'

'And that is?' Stephen said, but he already knew.

'You have not offered her even a modicum of conversation with her fiancé.'

'I am *not* her fiancé!'

'No, but you *are* inadvertently responsible for the fact that she doesn't have one. I'm amazed you've forgotten that.'

'I'll overlook that insult,' Stephen warned icily, 'as having been spoken by an aging, overwrought family friend.'

Dr Whitticomb realized that he had not only chosen

the wrong tactic with his opponent, but also pushed him too far. He had forgotten that the cool, uncompromising nobleman seated behind the desk was no longer the mischievous little boy who'd sneaked to the stables in the middle of the night to ride a new stallion, then bravely refused to cry while Hugh set his broken arm and lectured him on the folly of inviting danger.

'You're quite right,' he said mildly. 'I am upset. May I sit down?'

His opponent accepted his apology with a tentative nod. 'Certainly.'

'We "overwrought, aging" fellows tend to tire rather easily,' he added with a grin, and was relieved to see a trace of amusement soften Stephen's features. Stalling for time, Hugh gestured toward the brass cigar box on the leather inlaid table beside his chair. 'Every now and then I develop a sudden urge for an excellent cigar. May I?'

'Of course.'

By the time Hugh had the cigar lit, he had decided on a better way to convince Stephen of the gravity of Charise Lancaster's situation, and he was satisfied that enough time had elapsed to dissipate any lingering hostility Stephen might have felt about Hugh's last ill-advised attempt. 'When I went upstairs just now,' he began, studying the thin trail of white smoke curling off the cigar in his hand, 'I found our patient thrashing about in bed, moaning.'

Alarm sent Stephen partway to his feet before the physician held up his hand and added, 'She was sleeping, Stephen. Dreaming. But she felt a little feverish,' he added, dishonestly, to help attain his goal. 'I was also informed that she's not eating well, and that she's so lonely, and so desperate for answers, that she talks to the chambermaids, the footmen – anyone at all who might be able to tell her about this house, about herself, or about you, her own fiancé.'

Stephen's guilt tripled at this vividly drawn picture

of Charise Lancaster's suffering, but that only made him more adamant. 'I am *not* her fiancé. I am the man who is responsible for his death! First I murder him, and then I take his place,' he gritted caustically. 'The whole notion is obscene!'

'You did not murder him,' Hugh said, astonished by the true depth of Stephen's guilt. 'He was foxed and he ran out in front of you. It was an accident. These things happen.'

'You wouldn't be able to shrug it off as easily as that if you'd been there,' he shot back savagely. 'You weren't the one who pulled him out from under the horses. His neck was broken, and his eyes were open, and he was trying to whisper and trying to breathe. Christ, he was so young, he didn't look like he ought to be shaving yet! He kept trying to tell me to "Get Mary." I thought he was asking me to find someone named Mary. It didn't occur to me until the next day that, with his dying breath, he was talking about getting married. Had you been there and seen and heard all that, you wouldn't find it so goddamned easy to excuse me for running him down and *then* lusting after his fiancée!'

Hugh had been waiting for Stephen to end his guilty tirade so he could point out that Burleton reportedly had a penchant for recklessness, drunkenness, and gambling, none of which would have made him a decent husband for Miss Lancaster had he lived, but Stephen's last revealing sentence banished everything else from his mind. It explained Stephen's uncharacteristic cruelty in leaving her alone upstairs.

The forgotten cigar clamped between his teeth, Hugh leaned back in his chair and regarded the angry earl with amused fascination. 'So, she appeals to you in *that* way, does she?'

'In exactly "that way",' Stephen bit out.

'Now I understand why you've been avoiding her.' Narrowing his eyes against the smoke, Hugh considered the situation thoughtfully for a moment, then continued.

'Actually, it's little wonder you find her irresistible, Stephen. I myself find her utterly refreshing and completely delightful.'

'Excellent!' Stephen said caustically. 'Then you tell her *you're* really Burleton, and then *you* wed her. That would set everything to rights.'

That last sentence was so subtly revealing, and so interesting, that Hugh carefully withdrew his gaze from Stephen's face. He removed his cigar from his mouth, held it in his fingertips, and studied it with apparent absorption. 'That is a very interesting line of thought, especially for you,' he remarked. 'I might even say a *revealing* line of thought.'

'What are you talking about?'

'I am talking about your statement that if someone were to marry her, "that would set everything to rights." ' Without waiting for a reply, he continued, 'You feel responsible for Burleton's death and her memory loss, and you're physically attracted to her. Despite that – or because of all that – you're adamantly opposed to doing something as simple and therapeutic as pretending to be her fiancé, is that right?'

'If you want to put it that way, yes.'

'That's it then,' Hugh said, slapping his knee and smiling with satisfaction. 'That's the whole puzzle, all nicely put together.' Without waiting for his annoyed adversary to demand an explanation, Hugh provided it: 'Miss Lancaster has no fiancé because of an accident for which you were unavoidably responsible, but responsible nonetheless. Now, if you were to pretend to be her affianced husband, and if she were to develop a deep affection for you while you were pretending to be that, then under those circumstances, she might expect – might even have a *right* to expect – that you turn the deception into a reality.

'Based on your prior attitude toward the female set, which by the way has your mama in complete despair of ever seeing you married, there would be no chance

89

of Miss Lancaster bringing you up to scratch. But Miss Lancaster is not as easy for you to dismiss as the others have been. You find her physically desirable, but you also fear that you might find her *irresistible* on longer acquaintance, otherwise you wouldn't be letting her presence drive you into hiding in your own home. Nor would you be callously avoiding someone who clearly needs your company and attention.

'If you had nothing to fear, you wouldn't be avoiding her. It's as simple as that. But you *do* have something to fear: For the first time in your life, you have reason to fear the loss of your cherished bachelorhood.'

'Are you finished?' Stephen inquired blandly.

'Quite. What do you think of my summation of the situation?'

'I think it is the most impressive combination of unlikely possibilities and faulty logic I have ever heard in my life.'

'If so, my lord,' Dr Whitticomb said with a congenial smile, peering at him over the tops of his spectacles, 'then why are you denying her the comfort of your presence?'

'I can't answer that at the moment. Unlike you, I haven't stopped to analyze all my misgivings.'

'Then let me provide you with an added motivation to overcome any misgivings you may have or invent,' Hugh said, his tone turning brisk and firm. 'I've been reading articles on the subject of memory loss, and consulting with those few colleagues who have some experience in it. It appears that it can be brought on, not only by an injury to the head, but by hysteria, or in the worst cases – a combination of both. According to what I've learned, the more desperate Miss Lancaster becomes to recover her memory, the more upset and depressed and *hysterical* she will become when she cannot. As her agitation increases, the harder she'll find it to recall anything.' With satisfaction, he watched the younger man frown with concern. 'Conversely, *if* she is made to feel safe and happy, it stands to reason her memory will return much sooner. If it *ever* returns, that is.'

Dark brows had drawn together over alarmed blue eyes. 'What do you mean "if it ever returns"?'

'Precisely what I said. There are cases of permanent memory loss. There was one in which the poor devil had to be taught to speak and read and feed himself all over again.'

'My God.'

Dr Whitticomb nodded to reinforce his point, then he added, 'If you have any lingering doubts about doing what I've suggested, consider this as an added incentive: The young lady is aware that she had not spent a great deal of time with her fiancé before coming here, because I've told her that. And she's also aware that she's never been in this house, or even this country before, because I've assured her of that too. Because she knows she's among unfamiliar people in unfamiliar surroundings, she hasn't already made herself sick with anxiety over not recognizing everyone and everything. *But*, that's not going to be true if she hasn't recovered her memory before her family arrives. If she can't remember her own people when she sees them, she's going to start falling apart mentally and physically. Now, what are you willing to risk in order to save her from that fate?'

'Anything,' Stephen said tightly.

'I knew you would feel just that way when you understood the true gravity of the situation. By the by, I told Miss Lancaster that she need not remain in bed any longer, provided she doesn't attempt anything strenuous for another week.' Taking out his watch, Hugh Whitticomb flicked the cover open and stood up. 'I must be off. I had a note from your lovely mother. She said she's planning to come up for the Season with your brother and sister-in-law in a sennight. I'm looking forward to seeing all of them.'

'So am I,' Stephen said absently. Whitticomb was on his way out when it occurred to Stephen that in addition to everything else, he was going to have to involve his family in the deception he was about to put into full force. And even that wouldn't suffice, he realized as he shoved papers into his desk drawer. In a week, when his family arrived in London for the Season, so would the rest of the *ton*, and invitations to balls and all the other entertainments would begin arriving at his house by the hundreds along with a daily stream of callers.

He put the key into the drawer's lock and turned it, then he leaned back in his chair, frowning as he considered his alternatives: If he turned down all the invitations, which he was certainly willing to do, that wouldn't solve the problem. His friends and acquaintances would begin calling until they saw him and had an opportunity to try to discover why he had come to London for the Season only to behave like a recluse.

Frowning, Stephen realized his only choice was to spirit Miss Lancaster out of the city and take her to one of his estates – the remotest of his estates. That meant he'd have to make his excuses to his sister-in-law and his mother, at whose pleading insistence he'd come to London for the Season in the first place. They'd both argued very prettily and very persuasively that they hadn't seen enough of him in the last two years and that they enjoyed his company immensely, both of which Stephen knew they truly meant. They had not mentioned their third reason, which Stephen knew was to get him married off, preferably to Monica Fitzwaring, which was a campaign they'd undertaken with amusing – and increasing – perseverance of late. Once his mother and Whitney understood his reason for leaving London, they would immediately forgive him for foiling their plans, but they were going to be disappointed.

14

Now that he fully understood the importance of Whitti-comb's reasons for wanting Stephen to play the part of her devoted fiancé, Stephen was determined to set matters to rights at once. He paused outside her door, braced himself for the inevitable bout of tears and recriminations that were bound to pour forth from her the moment she saw him, then he knocked and asked to see her.

Sheridan started at the sound of his voice, but when the maid hurried forward to admit him, she returned her gaze to information she was copying out of the London newspaper, and said very firmly, 'Please tell his lordship that I am indisposed.'

When the maid relayed the information that Miss Lancaster was indisposed, Stephen frowned worriedly, wondering just *how* sick she had made herself because of his neglect. 'Tell her that I came to see her and that I'll return in an hour.'

Sheridan refused to feel even a trace of pleasure or relief that he intended to return. She knew better now than to depend on him for anything. Dr Whitticomb had been so distressed over the state he'd found her in that morning, that his alarm had communicated itself to her, shaking her out of her dazed misery. If she was going to fully recover, he'd warned her, it was absolutely imperative that she take care of herself physically and that she keep her mind active.

He'd rushed through a disjointed – and, Sherry suspected, dishonest – explanation about her fiancé's neglect that included statements such as 'absorbed by pressing business matters,' and 'obligations of his rank,' and 'problems with the stewardship on one of his estates.' He'd even implied that the earl hadn't been feeling quite himself lately. Unfortunately for the kindly physician, the more he tried to explain away Lord Westmoreland's inexcusable disinterest in his fiancée, the more obvious it became to Sheridan that her presence, and her illness, were apparently less important to the earl than the tiniest details of his business and social life! Furthermore, she had every reason to believe that he was actually punishing her, or teaching her a cruel lesson, for having had the nerve to bring up the topic of love.

She had spent days tormenting herself for doing that and blaming herself for asking him if he had a heart. But as she'd listened to Dr Whitticomb's lecture about her health and watched the somber look on his face, her guilt and hurt had finally turned to justifiable indignation. She wasn't engaged to the physician, but *he'd* been worried about her. *He'd* gone to the trouble to travel a distance to see her. If love was a laughable, forbidden emotion to sophisticated English noblemen, then the earl could at least have made allowances for her lost memory!

As to marrying the earl, Sheridan couldn't imagine what madness could have caused her to make such a decision. Thus far, the only positive attribute he seemed to possess was that he was remarkably handsome, which was certainly not reason enough to wed him. Furthermore, when her memory returned, if she didn't recall things that completely altered her opinion of him, she fully intended to tell him to take his marriage proposal and make it to some other female, one who was as cold and impersonal about marriage as he was! She found it almost impossible to believe that, in her right senses, she would have felt differently about the matter of marriage. Perhaps her father had been deceived into believing the earl would make her a good husband and had insisted she wed the man. If so, she would go to her father and explain why she'd decided not to do so. In the last few days, whenever she tried to think of her father, she couldn't conjure a face, but she could feel faint stirrings of emotion – a gentle warmth, a loving closeness, a sense of loss as if she missed him terribly. Surely, a father who evoked feelings like that wouldn't be the sort to force his daughter to marry a man she didn't admire in the least!

Exactly an hour later, Stephen knocked at the door again.

Sheridan looked at the clock on the mantel, angrily noting that he was at least punctual, but that didn't influence her decision. Continuing to study the newspapers that she'd spread out on the writing desk by the windows, she spoke to the maid: 'Please tell his lordship that I am resting.' As she said the words, she felt a spurt of pride in herself. Although she didn't know anything factual about Charise Lancaster, at least she didn't lack spirit or resolve!

On the other side of the portal, Stephen's guilt was replaced by the beginning of alarm. 'Is she ill?' he demanded of the maid.

The chambermaid looked pleadingly at Sheridan, who shook her head, and the maid answered him in the negative.

An hour after that, when Stephen again knocked upon the door, he was informed she was 'having a bath.'

An hour after that, he was no longer worried, he was annoyed. He knocked sharply, and this time he was advised that 'Miss is sleeping.'

'Tell "Miss,"' he ordered in a dire, warning tone, 'that I will return in exactly one hour, and I expect to see her, very clean and very rested and ready to go downstairs for supper. We dine at nine.'

An hour later, when the earl knocked on the door, Sheridan experienced a degree of amused satisfaction. Smiling to herself, she sank deeper into the warm bubbles that threatened to spill over the marble bath.

'Tell his lordship that I prefer to eat in my room this evening,' she instructed, feeling sorry for the poor maid, who looked as if she'd rather be flogged – or else was afraid of being flogged.

Stephen flung open the door before the maid had finished the sentence and stalked inside the bedchamber, nearly knocking the servant over. 'Where is she?' he snapped.

'In – in the bath, my lord.'

He started toward the doorway that led into the special marble bath suite he'd had installed off this bedchamber several years ago, then he caught the maid's appalled expression and changed direction. Walking over to the table by the window, he glanced at the open newspaper and saw a piece of writing paper lying beside it. 'Miss Lancaster!' he said, raising his voice and using a tone that made the poor chambermaid blanch. 'If you are not downstairs in exactly ten minutes, I will come up here and haul you down there myself in whatever state of dress, or undress, I happen to find you! Is that clear?'

To his disbelief, the chit didn't dignify his ultimatum with a reply! Wondering who she could possibly be writing to, Stephen picked up the writing paper. He was thinking sardonically that poor Burleton was probably better off dead, because Charise Lancaster would have made his life a hell with her outrageous obstinacy and temper, when he picked up the paper and realized what she'd been doing. In a precise, elegant hand, she'd recorded facts she'd gathered from the morning *Post*, facts that she must have known before, but which she was having to relearn, because of him:

King of England – George IV. Born 1762.
George IV's father was George III. Died two years ago.
Called 'Farmer George' by English people.
The King is fond of ladies and fine clothing and excellent wines.

After every few recorded facts, she'd tried to list similar facts about herself, but there were only blank spaces where easy answers should have been.

I was born in 18_____?
My father's name is_____?
I am fond of_____?

Guilt and sorrow raged through Stephen, and he closed his eyes. She didn't know her own name, or her father's, or the year of her birth. Worse, when her memory did return, she was in for the biggest blow of all – the tragedy of her fiancé's death. All of that . . . and all because of him.

The words on the paper felt as if they were searing his hand, and he dropped it onto the desk, drew an unsteady breath and turned to leave. He would not lose patience with her again, no matter what she said or did, he vowed. He had no right to feel anger or frustration; he had no right to feel anything except guilt and responsibility.

Determined to do everything in his power to atone for the hurt he had inflicted on her with his neglect – and was going to inflict on her when she ultimately learned her real fiancé was dead – Stephen headed for the door. However, since he couldn't begin his program of atonement until she left the bathing room, he warned, in a more courteous, but very firm, voice, 'You have eight minutes left.'

He heard the bath water slosh, nodded with satisfaction, and left. As he walked down the upper hall toward the staircase, he realized he was going to have to do more than apologize for neglecting her; he was going to have to come up with an explanation she would accept. Before she lost her memory, Charise Lancaster had obviously harbored youthful, idealistic notions about love and marriage, since she'd plainly asked him if they were 'very much in love.' Inwardly, Stephen recoiled from the mere mention of the word.

As he'd discovered, with age and experience, very few women were actually capable of feelings or behavior that even approximated that tender emotion, though nearly all women talked as if it were as natural to their sex as breathing. For his part, he instinctively mistrusted the word and any woman who mentioned it.

Helene shared his feelings in that regard, which was one more reason he enjoyed her company. Moreover, she was faithful to him, which was more than could be said of most of the wives of his acquaintances. For those reasons, he kept her in a style that would have befitted the legitimate wife of a nobleman, complete with a beautiful London townhouse, a large staff of servants, closets full of gowns and furs, and a splendid silver-lacquered coach with pale lavender velvet squabs – a color combination that was Helene Devernay's 'signature.' Few but she could wear it, and others who tried never managed to carry it off or look as lovely in it. She was sophisticated and sensual; she understood the rules and did not confuse lovemaking with love.

Now that he thought about it, not one female, including those he'd spent enough time with to start betrothal rumors circulating, had ever presumed to try to engage him in a discussion about love, let alone expect him to actually profess it.

Charise Lancaster, however, was obviously not so practical or so sensible. She clearly expected her fiancé to discuss it – at length, no doubt – and that was something Stephen intended to avoid for his sake and her own. Once her memory returned, she was going to hate him for all his deceptions, but she would hate him far more for humiliating her with false protestations of undying affection that he didn't feel.

Two footmen stepped forward as he reached the drawing room and swept open the doors. His forehead furrowed in thought, Stephen walked past them and then over to the sideboard, where he poured sherry into a glass. Behind him, the doors closed silently, and he turned his attention to the most pressing problem at hand. Within the next minute or two, he had to invent some truly plausible explanation to give her for his blatantly unloverlike behavior the last night they'd talked, and for avoiding her since then. When he'd first gone upstairs to see her, he'd intended to apologize and soothe her with a few vague platitudes. Now that he had a better idea of her temperament, he had the uneasy conviction that she wouldn't settle for that.

15

Seething and hurrying, Sheridan clasped the front of the long lavender gown closed as she rushed down the hall from her bedchamber, past startled footmen, whose heads turned in unison as she passed, their mouths agape. Just when she thought she must surely be coming to the living areas of the house, she emerged onto a balcony with a white marble banister that continued downward in a wide, graceful spiral for two full stories before it ended in a vast entrance hall below.

Snatching up the hem of her gown, she ran down the staircase, past framed portraits of what must have been sixteen generations of the arrogant earl's ancestors. She didn't have the slightest idea where he was or how he expected her to find him. The only thing she knew for certain was that in addition to all his other unpleasant traits, he'd spoken to her as if she were a piece of his chattel, and that he was undoubtedly relishing the prospect of hauling her downstairs like a sack of flour in front of his servants if she didn't meet his deadline.

To deprive him of that pleasure, she was willing to go to almost any lengths. She could not imagine how she could have been in her right mind and still have agreed to bind herself for life to a man like him! As soon as her father arrived, she would break her engagement and ask him to take her home at once!

She didn't like the earl, and she was quite certain she wouldn't have anything in common with his mama either. According to the chambermaid, this gown belonged to the earl's mother. It was appalling to imagine an elderly dowager such as his mother, or any other respectable female for that matter, prancing around at balls or entertaining visitors in a flimsy, frivolous lavender gown with nothing but silver ribbons to hold the bodice together or keep the entire front from coming open. She was so angry and so absorbed in her own woes that she didn't give even a passing notice to the splendor of the great hall with its four immense chandeliers, glittering like giant tiers of brilliant diamonds, or to the exquisite frescoes on the walls and intricate plasterwork on the ceiling.

As she neared the bottom step, she saw an elderly man in a black suit and white shirt hurry into a room that opened off the main hall on the left. 'You rang, my lord?' she heard him say in the doorway. A moment later, he backed out, bowing reverently, and closed the doors. 'Excuse me—' Sherry began awkwardly, tripping on the hem of her gown and reaching for the wall to steady herself.

He turned, saw her, and his body froze. At the same time all his facial features seemed to twist and quiver in some sort of palsied shock.

'I'm perfectly all right,' Sheridan hastily reassured him as she righted herself and jerked the hem from beneath her left foot. Noting that he still looked a little queer, Sheridan held out her hand to him and said, 'Dr Whitticomb said I'm well enough to come downstairs. We haven't met, but I am Charise . . . um . . . Lancaster,' she remembered after an awkward pause. He raised his hand toward hers, and since he seemed uncertain about what to do next, she took his hand in hers, and prompted with a gentle smile, 'And you are—?'

'Hodgkin,' he said, sounding as if he had a blockage in his throat. Then he cleared it and said again, 'Hodgkin.'

'I am happy to meet you, Mr Hodgkin.'

'No, miss, just "Hodgkin."'

'I couldn't possibly address you by your surname alone. It's disrespectful,' Sheridan said patiently.

'It's required here,' he said, looking harassed.

Indignation made Sheridan's left hand clench on the front of her gown. 'How very like that arrogant beast to deny an older man the dignity of being addressed as "mister"!'

His features contorted again, and he seemed to stretch his neck as if gasping for air. 'I'm sure I don't know whom you might be referring to, miss.'

'I am referring to . . .' She had to think to remember the maid's answer when Sheridan had asked her the earl's name. It had seemed the woman had recited an entire litany of names, but his family name had been . . . Westmoreland! That was it. 'I am referring to Westmoreland!' she said, refusing to dignify his name with his own title. 'Someone should have taken a stick to his backside and taught him common courtesy.'

On the balcony above, a footman who'd been flirting with a passing chambermaid twisted around and gaped at the entrance hall, while the maid banged against his side in her eagerness to lean over the banister for a better view. A few yards from Sheridan, four footmen who had been filing decorously into the dining room carrying platters suddenly crashed into each other because the lead footman had stopped dead in his tracks. Another white-haired man, younger than Hodgkin but dressed exactly like him, materialized from the dining room, scowling ferociously as the lid of a silver chafing dish hit the marble floor with a crash and rolled into his leg. 'Who is responsible for—' he demanded, then he, too, looked at Sheridan and seemed to momentarily lose control of his expression as his gaze ran over her hair, her gown, and her bare toes.

Ignoring the commotion around her, Sheridan smiled at Hodgkin and said gently, 'It's never too late, you know, for most of us to see the error of our ways if they're pointed out to us. I shall mention to the earl at an appropriate moment that he ought properly to address a man of your age as "Mr Hodgkin." I could suggest that he put himself in your position and imagine himself at your age . . .'

She stopped in puzzlement as the elderly man's white brows shot up into his hairline and his faded eyes seemed to pop out of their sockets. Anger with the earl had overruled her sense for those moments, but Sheridan finally realized that the poor man was obviously afraid of losing his position if she interfered. 'That was foolish of me, Mr Hodgkin,' she said meekly. 'I won't say anything about this, I promise.'

On the balcony above and in the hall below, servants exhaled a collective sigh of relief that was abruptly cut off as Hodgkin opened the doors to the drawing room and they heard the American girl say to the master in a haughty, unservile tone, 'You rang, my lord?'

Stephen whirled around in surprise at her choice of words and then stopped dead. Choking back a laugh that was part appalled and part admiring, he stared at her as she stood before him, with her pert nose in the air and her gray eyes sparking like large twin flints. In sharp contrast to the stony hauteur of her stance and expression, she was clad in a soft, billowing peignoir made of voluminous lavender silk panels that draped off both her shoulders, leaving them beguilingly bare. She was clutching the front closed, which lifted the hem just high enough off the floor to expose her bare toes, and her titian hair, still damp at the ends, was spilling over her back and breasts as if she were a Botticelli nude.

The pale lavender color should have clashed with her hair, and it did, but her creamy skin was so fair that the overall effect was somehow more dramatic than actually displeasing. It was, in fact, so startlingly effective that it took him a moment to realize that she'd not deliberately selected Helene's peignoir out of some defiant desire to flaunt custom or annoy him, but because she didn't have anything else to wear. He had forgotten that her trunks had sailed with her ship, but if that ugly brown cloak she'd been wearing was indicative of her preference in clothing, he preferred to see her in Helene's peignoir. The servants wouldn't share his liberal view, of course, and he made a mental note to remedy her apparel problem first thing in the morning. For now, there was nothing he could do except be grateful that the peignoir actually covered enough of her to verge on decency.

Biting back an admiring smile, he watched her struggle to maintain her frosty facade in the face of his silent scrutiny, and he marvelled that she could convey so many things without moving or speaking. She was innocence on the brink of womanhood, outrageous daring untempered by wisdom or hampered by caution. A vision of that gleaming hair of hers spilling over his chest flashed through his mind, and Stephen abruptly shook it off just as she broke the silence: 'Have you finished staring at me?'

'I was admiring you, actually.'

Sheridan had come downstairs fully prepared for a confrontation, longing for it, in fact, and she'd already suffered one setback when he looked at her with that peculiarly flattering expression in his bold blue eyes; his smiling compliment was the second. Reminding herself that he was a coldhearted, dictatorial beast whom she was *not* going to marry, no matter how he looked at her or how sweetly he spoke, she said, 'I presume you had some reason for summoning me into your august presence, your worship?'

To her surprise he didn't rise to her barbs. In fact, he looked rather amused as he said with a slight bow, 'As a matter of fact, I had several reasons.'

'And they are?' she inquired stonily.

'First of all,' Stephen said, 'I wanted to apologize.'

'Really?' she said with a shrug. 'For what?'

Stephen lost the battle to suppress his smile. She had spirit, you had to give her that. A great deal of spirit . . . and a great deal of pride. He couldn't think of a man, let alone a woman, who'd dare to face him down and verbally bait him as she was doing. 'For the abrupt way I ended our conversation the other night, and for not coming up to see you since then.'

'I accept your apology. Now, may I go upstairs?'

'No,' Stephen said, suddenly wishing she had a little less courage. 'I need . . . no, want . . . to explain why I did that.'

She gave him a scornful look. 'I'd like to see you try.'

Courage was an admirable trait in a man. In a woman, he decided, it was a pain in the ass. 'I *am* trying,' he warned.

Now that he'd lost a little of his composure, Sheridan felt much better. 'Go ahead,' she invited. 'I'm listening.'

'Will you sit down?'

'I might. It all depends upon what you have to say.'

His brows snapped together and his eyes narrowed, she noticed, but his voice was carefully controlled as he began his explanation. 'The other night, you seemed to be aware that I . . . that things between us weren't . . . all that you'd expect from a fiancé.'

Sheridan acknowledged the truth of that with a slight, regal inclination of her head that indicated nothing more than mild interest.

'There's an explanation for that,' Stephen said, disconcerted by her demeanor. He gave her the only reason he'd been able to invent that seemed logical and acceptable. 'The last time we were together, we quarrelled. I didn't think about our quarrel while you were ill, but when you began to recover the other night, I found it was still on my mind. That is why I may have seemed . . .'

'Cold and uncaring?' she provided, but with more puzzlement and hurt than real anger in her voice.

'Exactly,' Stephen agreed. She sat down then, and he breathed an inner sigh of relief that the skirmish and lies were over, but his relief was short-lived.

'What did we quarrel about?'

He should have known that a defiant American redhead with an unpredictable disposition and no regard for noble titles or respect for dress codes would insist on prolonging a disagreement, instead of accepting his apology and politely letting the matter drop. 'We quarrelled about your disposition,' Stephen countered smoothly.

Puzzled gray eyes gazed straight into his. 'My disposition? What was wrong with it?'

'I found it . . . quarrelsome.'

'I see.'

Stephen could almost hear her wondering if he was so small-minded that he'd continue to harbor a grudge over a quarrel when she'd been so sick. She looked down at her hands folded neatly in her lap, as if she suddenly couldn't face him, and asked in a disappointed, hesitant tone, 'Am I a shrew, then?'

Stephen gazed at her bowed head and drooping shoulders, and he felt a resurgence of the peculiar tenderness she seemed to evoke in him at unexpected times. 'I wouldn't say that exactly,' he replied with a reluctant smile in his voice.

'I have noticed,' she admitted meekly, 'that my disposition has been a little – uncertain – these past few days.'

Whitticomb had said he found her utterly delightful, and Stephen had the feeling that was a vast understatement. 'That's completely understandable in these circumstances.'

She lifted her head, her eyes searching his, as if she, too, were trying to reassess him. 'Would you tell me exactly what we quarrelled about the last time we were together?'

Trapped, Stephen turned toward the drinks tray and

reached for the crystal decanter of sherry, thinking quickly for an answer that would soothe and placate her. 'I thought you paid too much notice to another man,' he said on a stroke of inspiration. 'I was jealous.' Jealousy was an emotion that he'd never experienced in his life, but women were inevitably pleased when they could evoke it in a man. He glanced over his shoulder and was relieved to discover that in that one respect, Charise Lancaster was like all her sisters, because she looked amused and flattered. Hiding his smile, he poured sherry into a small crystal goblet. When he turned to hand it to her she was still looking at her hands. 'Sherry?' he asked.

Sheridan's head snapped up, an inexplicable surge of delight in her heart. 'Yes?'

He held the goblet toward her and she looked at him expectantly but not at the glass. 'Would you like some wine?' Stephen clarified.

'No, thank you.'

He put the glass on the table. 'I thought you said yes.'

She shook her head. 'I thought you were talking to me and – *Sherry!*—' she exclaimed, surging to her feet, her face positively radiant. 'I thought it was me. I mean, it is me. I mean, it must be what I was called, what—'

'I understand,' Stephen said gently, experiencing a sense of relief that was nearly as strong as hers. They stood within arm's reach, smiling at each other, sharing a moment of triumph that seemed to bind them together and send their thoughts in similar directions. Stephen suddenly understood how Burleton could have been 'madly in love' with her, as Hodgkin had claimed. As Sherry looked into his smiling blue eyes, she saw a warmth and charm that made her understand why she might have pledged herself to him. Odd phrases began to flit through the blankness of her memory, suggesting what ought to happen next . . .

The baron captured her hand and pressed it to his lips as

he pledged his eternal devotion. 'You are my one and only love . . .'

The prince took her in his strong embrace and clasped her to his heart. 'If I had a hundred kingdoms, I would trade them all for you, my dearest love. I was nothing, until you . . .'

The earl was so overwhelmed by her beauty that he lost control and kissed her cheek. 'Forgive me, but I cannot help myself! I adore you!'

Stephen saw the soft invitation in her eyes, and in that unguarded moment of complete accord, it seemed right, somehow, to respond. Tipping her chin up, he touched his lips to hers and felt the gasp of her indrawn breath at the same time her body seemed to tense. Puzzled by her rather extreme reaction, he lifted his head and waited for what seemed a long time for her to open her eyes. When her long lashes finally fluttered up, she looked confused and expectant and, yes, even a little disappointed. 'Is something amiss?' he asked cautiously.

'No, not at all,' she said politely, but it seemed as if the opposite were true.

Stephen looked at her in waiting silence, a tactic that normally prompted others to continue speaking, and which was predictably successful on his 'fiancée.'

'It is only that I seemed to expect something different,' she explained.

Telling himself that he was merely trying to help her jog her memory, he said, 'What was it that you expected?'

She shook her head, her smooth brow furrowed, her eyes never leaving his. 'I don't know.'

Her hesitant words and steady gaze only confirmed what he already suspected, which was that her real fiancé had evidently given freer rein to his passion. As Stephen gazed into those inviting silvery eyes, he abruptly decided that he was practically *obligated* to live up to her memory of Burleton. His conscience shouted that he had another, selfish reason for what he was about to do, but Stephen ignored it. He had, after all, promised Whitticomb that he would make her feel safe and cherished. 'Perhaps you were expecting—' he said softly as he slid his arm around her waist and touched his lips to her ear, 'something more like this.'

His warm breath in her ear sent shivers up Sheridan's spine, and she turned her face away from the cause, which brought her lips into instant contact with his. Stephen had intended to kiss her as Burleton might have done, but when her soft lips parted on a shaky breath, his intentions slipped from his mind.

Sheridan knew the moment his arm tightened on her waist and his lips began to move insistently against hers that she couldn't have been expecting this . . . not the stormy rush of sensation that made her gasp and cling tighter to him, nor the compulsion to yield her mouth to his searching tongue, nor the frantic beating of her heart when his fingers shoved into the hair at her nape, holding her mouth tighter to his while her body seemed to want to meet and forge into his.

Stephen felt her lean into him and fell helpless victim to it. When he finally managed to drag his mouth from hers, he lifted his head and stared down at her flushed face, stunned by his unprecedented reaction to a few virginal kisses from an inexperienced girl who hadn't seemed to have the slightest idea how to kiss him back. He watched her lids open and gazed into her slumbrous eyes, a little annoyed with his loss of control and distinctly amused by the fact that an untutored slip of a girl was responsible for it.

At three and thirty, his preferences ran toward passionate, experienced, sophisticated women who knew how to give and receive pleasure. The notion that he could have been so violently aroused by a child-woman who was currently draped in an ill-fitting peignoir belonging to his current mistress was almost comical. On the other hand, she had shown herself to be an eager and willing student during those minutes in his arms, and there hadn't been a sign of maidenly shyness, not even now, as she stood in his arms, steadily returning his gaze.

All things considered, he decided, Charise Lancaster was probably not inexperienced, but rather improperly tutored by Burleton and his predecessors. The realization that he himself had been the naive one made Stephen grin as he lifted his brows and inquired dryly, 'Was that more what you expected?'

'No,' she said, giving her head a firm shake that sent her shining hair spilling over her right shoulder. Her voice shook, but her eyes never left his as she confessed softly, 'I know I could never have forgotten anything that feels like that.'

Stephen's amusement vanished, and he felt an unfamiliar ache in his chest. Without realizing what he was doing, he laid his hand against her cheek, his fingers splaying over the incredible softness of it. 'I wonder,' he mused aloud, 'if you can possibly be as sweet as you seem.'

He hadn't intended to voice the thought, and he didn't expect any reply, let alone the amazing one she gave him. In the voice of one confessing a terrible secret, she said, 'I don't think I am sweet at all, my lord. You may not have noticed it, but I believe I have a rebellious nature.'

Stephen squelched his shout of laughter and fought to keep his face straight, but she mistook his silence for dissent. 'It would seem,' she said in a shaky whisper, as her eyes dropped guiltily to the front of his shirt, 'that I must have been quite good at hiding it from you when I had all my wits about me?'

When he didn't reply, Sheridan stared at the tiny ruby studs winking in his snowy shirtfront, savoring the sensation of a strong masculine arm around her waist. And yet she had the hazy feeling that there was something wrong in what she was doing. She concentrated on the feeling, trying to force it to take shape and reveal itself, but nothing happened. It was as unreliable as her own reactions to her betrothed; to everything, in fact. One minute she hated her gown, her fiancé, and her loss of memory, and she wanted to be rid of all of them. And then he could change all that with a warm smile or an admiring glance . . . or a kiss. With a single smile, he could make her feel as if her gown were fit for a princess and that she was beautiful and that her memory was best lost. She couldn't understand any of that, particularly why there were fleeting moments when she felt she didn't *want* to remember. And, dear God, the way he kissed her! Her whole body seemed to melt and burn, and she loved the feeling at the same time that it made her uneasy and guilty and uncertain. In an effort to explain all that to him and even perhaps ask his counsel, Sheridan drew an unsteady breath and confessed to his shirtfront, 'I don't know what sort of person you think I am, but I seem to have a . . . a *formidable* temper. One might even say I have a . . . a completely unpredictable disposition.'

Helplessly enchanted by her candor, Stephen put his fingers beneath her chin and tipped it up, forcing her to meet his gaze. 'I've noticed,' he said huskily.

Her expressive eyes searched his. 'That doesn't bother you?'

There were several things that 'bothered' Stephen at that moment, and they were not related to her disposition. Her full breasts were pressed against his chest, her molten hair was gliding over his hand at her back, and she had a soft, full mouth that positively invited a man's kiss. The name 'Sherry' suited her perfectly. She was dangerously and subtly intoxicating. She was *not* his fiancée, she was *not* his mistress; she deserved his respect and his protection, not his lust. Intellectually, he knew that, but his brain seemed to be hypnotized by her smile and her voice, and his body was being ruled by an arousal that was becoming almost painful. Either she didn't understand why he was rigid, or she hadn't noticed, or she didn't mind, but whatever the reason, he was content with the result. 'You "bother" me very much,' he said.

'In what way—' Sherry asked, watching his gaze drop to her lips and feeling her heartbeat triple.

'I'll show you,' he murmured huskily, and his lips seized hers with violent tenderness.

He kissed her slowly, urging her to participate this time, not merely to yield, and Sheridan sensed the subtle invitation. His hand curved round her nape, stroking it softly, while his other hand drifted up and down her spine in an endless caress. His parted lips moved back and forth on hers, urging them to open for him, and Sheridan responded with tentative uncertainty. She matched the stroking movements of his mouth, and felt his lips part more; she touched her tongue to them, exploring the warm male contours, and she felt his hand clamp tighter against the base of her spine.

She leaned up on her toes, sliding her hands up the hard muscles of his chest, over his shoulders, arching her body as she brought him closer to her. . . and suddenly his arms went around her like iron bands, and the kiss became fiercely hard and urgent. His tongue caressed hers and then drove into her mouth, sending shivers of primitive sensations through Sheridan's quaking body, and she clung tighter to him, kissing him back. His hands shifted, sliding up the sides of her breasts, starting to caress them. . .

Warned by an instinct she didn't understand and didn't challenge, Sheridan tore free of his mouth and shook her head at him in a near-panic, even though a part of her desperately wanted him to kiss her again.

Stephen reluctantly loosened his grip on her and dropped his arms to his sides. With a mixture of disbelief and amusement he gazed down at the exquisite young beauty who had just managed to drug not only his senses, but his mind. Her face was flushed, her chest was heaving gently with each apprehensive breath she drew, and her dark-lashed eyes were wide with confusion and desire. She looked as if she wasn't certain what she wanted to do.

'I think it's time we did something else,' he said, making the decision for both of them.

'What do you have in mind?' she asked shakily.

'What I have in mind,' Stephen replied wryly, 'and what we are *going* to do are very far apart.' He decided, after dinner, to teach her the rudiments of chess.

It was a mistake. She beat him twice in a row because he couldn't seem to keep his mind on the game.

16

Stephen scrupulously avoided all thoughts of her the following day, but as his valet laid out his clothes for the evening, he found himself looking forward to supper with Sherry more than he could remember anticipating a meal in a very long time. He'd ordered some decent clothing for her from Helene's dressmaker and insisted that at least one gown be delivered to her later that day with the remainder to be delivered as they were readied. When the modiste had reminded him hysterically that the Season was about to begin and her seamstresses were all working night and day, Stephen had politely asked her to do the best she could. Since Helene's purchases at the exclusive shop resulted in astronomical charges, he had every faith the dressmaker would manage to put a decent wardrobe together and that she would charge him exorbitantly for the added haste.

Within hours, three seamstresses had arrived at the house, and although he wasn't naive enough to suppose that, on such short notice, his dinner partner would be garbed in the highest fashion, he was rather eager to see how she looked in a proper gown. As he tipped his head back so his valet could brush lather under his chin, Stephen decided that no matter what Charise Lancaster wore, she would do it with her own special flair, whether it was a golden drapery cord or a ball gown.

He was not disappointed in that, or in their evening. She walked into the dining room, her titian hair tumbling over her shoulders and framing her vivid face, looking like an exotic ingenue in a soft aqua wool gown with a low, square neckline and fitted bodice that managed to call attention to the tops of her full breasts and accent her narrow waist before it fell in simple folds to the floor. Shyly avoiding Stephen's frankly admiring gaze, she nodded graciously at the footmen standing at attention near the sideboard, complimented the silver bowls of white roses and banks of ornate silver candelabra on the table, then she slid gracefully into the chair across from him. Only then did she lift her face to his, and the smile she gave him was so warm, so filled with generosity and unconscious promise, that it took a moment for Stephen to realize she was merely thanking him for the gown. ' . . . you were much too extravagant, though,' she finished with quiet poise.

'The gown is far from extravagant and not nearly as lovely as the woman wearing it,' Stephen replied, and when she looked away as if she were truly embarrassed by his remark, he reminded himself very firmly that she didn't *intend* to seduce him with that melting smile of hers, or the graceful sway of her hips, or the swell of her soft breasts, and that this was a very inappropriate time, place, and woman to evoke thoughts of satin pillows beneath glossy titian hair and full breasts swelling to fit his seeking hands. In view of that, he turned his thoughts to safer topics and asked what she had done with her day.

'I read the newspapers,' she replied, and with candlelight shimmering on her hair and glowing in her laughing eyes, she began to regale him with a hilarious commentary about the gushing reports she'd been reading in the back issues of the newspapers about the doings of the *ton* during the London Season. Her original intent, she explained, had been to learn all she could from the newspapers about his acquaintances and all the other members of the *haut ton* before she was introduced to them. Stephen's conscience rebelled at letting her do that when she wasn't going to meet anyone at all, but, he reasoned, the endeavor seemed to have cheered and occupied her, and so he asked her what she had learned thus far.

Her answers, and her facial expressions, kept him amused, diverted, and challenged throughout the entire ten-course meal. When she talked about some of the outrageous frivolities and excesses she'd read about, she had a way of wrinkling her pert nose in prim disapproval or rolling her eyes in amused disbelief that invariably made him feel like laughing. And while he was still struggling to hide his amusement, she could turn thoughtful and phrase a quiet question that took him completely aback. Her damaged memory seemed to have random blanks when it came to understanding how and why people in his social stratum – or her own in America, for that matter – did things in a particular way, and so she asked pointed questions that made him reevaluate customs he'd taken for granted.

'According to the *Gazette*,' she laughingly informed him as the footmen placed a serving of succulent duck on their plates, 'the Countess of Evandale's court gown was embellished with three thousand pearls. Do you suppose that was an accurate tally?'

'I have every faith in the journalistic integrity of the *Gazette's* society reporter,' Stephen joked.

'If that is correct,' she said with an infectious smile, 'then I can only assume they were either very *small* pearls or she is a very *large* lady.'

'Why is that?'

'Because if the pearls were large and she was not, she'd have surely required a winch to haul her upright after she curtsied to the king.'

Stephen was still grinning at the image of the coldly dignified and very rotund countess being hoisted aloft and swung out of the way of the throne when Sherry made a lightning shift from the frivolous to the serious. Propping her chin on her linked fingers, she'd regarded him down the length of the dining table and asked, 'In April, when everyone of importance gathers in London for the Season and remains until June, what do people do with their children?'

'They stay in the country with their nannies, governesses, and tutors.'

'And the same is true in the autumn during the Little Season?'

When Stephen nodded, she tipped her head to the side and said gravely, 'How lonely English children must be during those long months.'

'They aren't alone,' Stephen emphasized patiently.

'Loneliness has nothing to do with being alone. Not for children or adults.'

Stephen was so desperate to avert a topic that he feared would lead directly into an impossible discussion of *their* children, that he didn't realize his tone had chilled or that in her vulnerable state, his remarks might hit her like daggers. 'Are you speaking from experience?'

'I . . . don't know,' she said.

'I'm afraid that tomorrow evening, you're going to be.'

'Alone?'

When he nodded, she looked quickly at the delicate pastry shell filled with pâté that was on the plate in front of her, then she drew a deep breath, as if gathering her courage, and looked at him directly. 'Are you going out because of what I just said?'

He felt like a beast for making her ask that, and very emphatically he said, 'I have a prior engagement that cannot be cancelled.' And then, as if his need to exonerate himself in her eyes weren't already reaching the absurd, he announced, 'It may also set your mind at ease to know that my parents had my brother and me brought to London at least once every fortnight during the London Season. My brother and his wife, and a few of their friends, bring their children and an entourage of governesses here during the Season.'

'Oh, that's lovely!' she exclaimed, her smile dawning like the sun. 'I am vastly relieved to know there are such devoted parents amongst the *ton*.'

'Most of the *ton*,' he informed her dryly, 'is vastly *amused* by that same parental devotion.'

'I don't think one ought to let the opinions of others influence what one does, do you?' she asked, frowning a little.

Three things hit Stephen at once, and he was torn between laughter, pity, and chagrin: Whether she realized it or not, Charise Lancaster was 'interviewing' him, weighing his merits, not only as a prospective husband, but as the prospective father of her children – neither of which were roles he was going to fulfill. And that was a very good thing, because in the first place, he didn't seem to be rating very high in her estimation, and in the second, her disinterest in the opinions of others would surely get her banished from polite society within a week, were she ever to set foot in it. Stephen had never cared for anyone's opinion, but then he was a man, not a woman, and his wealth and illustrious name gave him the right to do as he damn well pleased and to do it with impunity. Unfortunately, the same upright society matrons who were eager to lure him into marrying their daughters, and who were perfectly willing to overlook any of his vices and excesses, would pillory Charise Lancaster for the most minor social infraction – let alone a major one such as dining alone with him, as she was doing now.

'Do you think one ought to let the opinions of others influence one's actions?' she repeated.

'No, definitely not,' he solemnly averred.

'I'm happy to hear that.'

'I was afraid you would be,' Stephen said, biting back a grin.

His good humor continued unabated during their meal and afterward in the drawing room, but when it was time to bid her good night, he realized he couldn't trust himself to do more than press a brotherly kiss on her cheek.

17

'Whatever you did, it certainly has turned the trick,' Hugh Whitticomb announced early the following evening, as he poked his head into the drawing room, where Stephen was waiting for Sherry to join him for dinner.

'She's feeling well, then?' Stephen replied, pleased and relieved that his passionate and willing 'fiancée' had not decided to indulge in a fit of virginal guilt over the few liberties he'd taken the night before and confessed it all to Whitticomb. Stephen had been closeted all day, first with one of his stewards, and then with the architect who was laboring over the plans for renovating one of his estates, and so he hadn't caught a glimpse of her, though the servants had kept him informed of her whereabouts in the large townhouse and reported that she appeared to be in good spirits. He was looking forward to a thoroughly enjoyable evening, first with Sherry and later with Helene. As to which part of the evening he was most looking forward to, that was something he did not care to consider.

'She's feeling more than well,' the physician remarked. 'I'd say she's glowing. She said to tell you she'd be down in a moment.'

Stephen's pleasurable contemplation of his evening was substantially diminished by the fact that the physician was now strolling into the room, uninvited

– and unwanted – and he was studying Stephen with an open, intense interest that was distinctly disturbing from someone as astute as he. 'What did you do to accomplish such a miraculous transformation?'

'I did as you suggested,' Stephen said mildly, turning and walking over to the fireplace mantel where he'd left his glass of sherry. 'I made her feel . . . er . . . safe and secure.'

'Could you be more specific? My colleagues – the ones I've consulted about Miss Lancaster's amnesia – would surely be interested in your method of treatment. It's amazingly effective.'

In answer, Stephen propped an elbow on the mantelpiece and quirked a mocking brow at the inquisitive physician. 'Don't let me keep you from another appointment,' he countered dryly.

The broad hint that he should leave led Hugh Whitticomb to conclude that Stephen wished to enjoy the evening alone with her. Either that or he simply didn't want a witness to the charade he was being forced to play as her devoted fiancé. Hoping to discover it was the former, he said sociably, 'As it happens, I'm free for the evening. Perhaps I could join you at supper and witness firsthand your methods with Miss Lancaster?'

Stephen gave the physician a look as bland as his own, but his voice carried a wealth of meaning. 'Not a chance.'

'I rather thought you were going to say something like that,' Dr Whitticomb said with a grin.

'A glass of Madeira instead?' the earl suggested, his expression as inscrutable as his tone.

'Yes, thank you. I believe I will,' Dr Whitticomb said, no longer quite so certain what Stephen's motives were for wanting him to depart. The earl nodded a silent instruction at a footman standing near a cabinet filled with decanters and glasses, and in moments a glass of wine was handed to him.

Dr Whitticomb was asking Stephen what he intended to do about his houseguest when the *ton* descended en masse on London for the Season next week, when the earl's gaze suddenly snapped to the doorway and he straightened from his lounging position against the fireplace. Turning in the direction of his gaze, Dr Whitticomb saw Miss Lancaster walk into the room wearing a fetching yellow gown that matched the wide ribbon that twined in and around the heavy curls at her crown. She saw him too, and she came directly to him as good manners and his age dictated she should. 'Dr Whitticomb,' she exclaimed with a delighted smile, 'you didn't tell me you would be here when I came down!'

She held out both hands to him in a gesture that, for a well-bred English girl, would have been much too cordial for such a brief acquaintance. Hugh took her hands in his own and decided he liked her unaffected warmth and spontaneity very well, and the devil with custom. He liked her very well indeed. 'You look lovely,' he said feelingly, standing back a little to survey her gown. 'Like a buttercup, in fact,' he added, though the compliment sounded unflattering somehow.

Sheridan was so nervous about facing her fiancé that she prolonged the moment before she had to look at him. 'But I look exactly as I did when you saw me a few moments ago. Of course, I didn't have clothes on then,' she added, and then felt like dropping through the floor when the earl made a choked, laughing sound.

'What I meant was,' she amended swiftly, looking up at Lord Westmoreland's handsome, smiling face, 'I didn't have *these* clothes on.'

'I know what you meant,' Stephen said, admiring the rosy blush that tinted her cheeks and the porcelain skin above the gown's square neckline.

'I cannot thank you enough for the lovely gowns,' she told him, feeling as if she could drown in the depths of his blue eyes. 'I confess that I was very much relieved by their arrival.'

'Were you?' Stephen said, grinning for no reason at all except that she gave him an odd kind of pleasure when she walked into a room . . . or looked at him with such unconcealed delight over a trifling thing like a few hastily fashioned, simple gowns. 'Why were you relieved?' he asked, noticing that she did not offer her hands to him to clasp as she had to Whitticomb.

'I wondered the same thing,' Dr Whitticomb said, and Sheridan pulled loose from Lord Westmoreland's mesmerizing gaze with a mixture of embarrassment and reluctance. 'I was very much afraid they might all be like the one I wore two nights ago,' she explained to the physician. 'I mean, it was truly lovely, but . . . well . . . *drafty.*'

'Drafty?' Dr Whitticomb repeated blankly.

'Yes, you know – it rather floated about and I felt like I was wearing a lavender *veil,* instead of a sturdy gown. I was in constant fear that one of those silver ribbons would come undone and I would find myself . . .' She trailed off, as all the physician's attention shifted and narrowed on the earl. 'So it was *lavender,* was it?' he asked her without taking his gaze from her fiancé. 'And flimsy?'

'Yes, but it was perfectly proper to wear it in England,' she put in quickly, sensing increasing censure in the look the older man was giving the earl.

'Who told you that, my dear?'

'The maid – Constance.' Determined that he not misjudge her fiancé, who looked mildly amused despite the doctor's continued, narrowed scrutiny, she added very firmly, 'Dr Whitticomb, the maid assured me it was meant to be worn "for one dinner bell." Those were her very words – "For One Dinner Bell"!'

For some reason, that emphatic announcement caused both men to finally break off their visual duel and aim their twin gazes at her. 'What?' they said in unison.

Wishing she'd never brought the matter up, Sheridan drew a long breath and patiently explained to both baffled male faces, 'She said that the lavender gown was suitable for only *one dinner bell*. *I* didn't know you rang a bell, and I realized I was coming down to supper, not dinner, but since I didn't have anything else to wear, and I hadn't worn it for any other dinner bell, I didn't—' She broke off as understanding dawned on the earl's face, and she saw him struggling to keep his expression straight. 'Have I said something amusing?'

Dr Whitticomb looked at Stephen and demanded a little testily, 'What does she mean?'

'She means *"En déshabillé."* The chambermaid was butchering the French pronunciation.'

Dr Whitticomb nodded his instant understanding, but he did not find the explanation at all humorous. 'I should have guessed. I certainly suspected it from the description of that *lavender* gown. I trust you'll find a qualified ladies' maid for Miss Lancaster at once and that you'll completely remedy the clothing problem, so that sort of misunderstanding won't happen again?'

Dr Whitticomb had drained his glass and passed it to the footman who materialized at his elbow with a silver tray before he realized that his host hadn't replied. Intending to insist on an answer, he turned and realized that Stephen had evidently forgotten not only the question but Hugh's presence. Instead of attending the discussion, he was grinning at Charise Lancaster, and saying in a lightly chastising tone, 'You have not yet bade me good evening, mademoiselle. I'm beginning to feel quite devastated.'

'Oh, yes, I can see that you are,' Sheridan said, laughing at the outrageous – but flattering – exaggeration. Leaning casually against the mantel, with his blue eyes smiling into hers and that lazy white smile upon his handsome face, Stephen Westmoreland epitomized male confidence and potency. Nevertheless, his teasing gallantry and the warmth in his eyes had a strangely exhilarating effect on her; and her own smile warmed as she admitted wryly, 'I did intend to greet you at once, but I've forgotten how it should be done, and I've been meaning to ask you about it.'

'What do you mean?'

'I mean, am I to curtsy?' she explained with a desperate little laugh that Stephen found utterly endearing. Somehow, she managed to confront her enormous problem and all its obstacles with a smiling honesty that he found astonishing and incredibly courageous. As to how he wished her to greet him, he would have preferred that she offer both her hands to him as she'd done to Hugh Whitticomb, or better yet that she offer her mouth for the kiss he suddenly wanted to put there, but since neither was feasible right now, he nodded in answer to her question and said casually, 'It's customary.'

'I rather thought it was,' she said and sank into a graceful, effortless curtsy. 'Was that acceptable?' she asked, putting her hand into Stephen's outstretched palm as she arose.

'More than acceptable,' he said with a grin. 'How did you spend your day?'

From the corner of his eye, Hugh Whitticomb carefully noted the warmth of the earl's smile, the absorbed way he watched her as she answered his question, and the fact that he was standing far closer to her than was necessary or even seemly. If he was merely acting a part, then he was certainly enjoying it. And if he wasn't merely acting . . .

Dr Whitticomb decided to test the latter possibility, and in a casual joking tone, he addressed their profiles, 'I could still be coerced into staying for supper, were I invited—'

Charise Lancaster looked around at him, but Stephen didn't so much as glance in his direction. 'Not a chance,' he said dryly. 'Go away.'

'Never let it be said I don't know a hint when I hear one,' Dr Whitticomb said, so encouraged, so utterly delighted by everything, including Stephen's unprecedented lack of hospitality, that he almost clasped the butler's outstretched hand at the front door when the butler gave him his hat and cane.

'Keep an eye on the young lady for me,' he said instead, with a conspiratorial wink. 'It will be our little secret.' He was halfway down the front stairs before he realized that the butler hadn't been Colfax, but another, much older man.

It didn't matter. Nothing could have dampened his spirits right then.

His carriage was waiting at the curb, but the night was so fine and his hopes so high that he decided to walk and motioned to his coachman to follow him. For years, he and the Westmoreland family had watched in helpless consternation as women threw themselves at Stephen, all of them so damned eager to trade themselves for his title, his wealth, and an alliance with the Westmoreland family that Stephen, who had once been the personification of elegant charm and relaxed warmth, had become a hardened cynic.

He was sought after by every hostess and matchmaking mama in England, treated with the deferential respect that his immense wealth and powerful family commanded amongst the *ton*, and desperately desired – not for what he was, but for *who* he was and *what* he had.

The longer he remained unattached, the more of a challenge he had become, to married and unmarried women alike, until it reached the point that he could not walk into a ballroom without creating a veritable frenzy amongst the female population. He saw it happening, he understood the reasons, and his opinion of women continued to degenerate in direct proportion to his increase in popularity. As a result, his attitude toward the entire female sex was now so jaded and so low that he publicly preferred the company of his mistress to that of any respectable female of his own class. Even when he came to London for the Season, which he hadn't done in two years, he disdained to put in an appearance at any of the major social functions, preferring to spend his evenings either at the gaming tables with male friends or else at the theatre and opera with Helene Devernay. So openly did he flaunt her in front of the offended *ton* that it was causing a scandalbroth that was deeply distressing to his mother and his sister-in-law.

Until a year or two ago, he had at least tolerated the women who made cakes of themselves over him. Until then, he had treated them with nothing worse than amused condescension, but lately his patience had seemed to come to an end. These days, he was fully capable of delivering a crushing setdown or a biting incivility that was guaranteed to reduce a lady to mortified tears and to outrage her relatives when they heard of it.

And yet . . . tonight, he had been smiling into Charise Lancaster's eyes with some of his old warmth. No doubt part of his attitude owed itself to the fact that Stephen felt responsible for her plight – and he was. She needed him desperately right now, but in Dr Whitticomb's opinion, he needed her just as badly. He needed gentleness in his life and sweetness. Most of all, he needed hard proof that there were unmarried females in the world who wanted and needed more from him than just the use of his title, his money, and his estates.

Even in her vulnerable state of mind, Charise Lancaster seemed to place no importance in his title or the size and elegance of his home. She wasn't intimidated by him, or his possessions, nor was she awed by his attention. Tonight she had greeted Hugh with a natural warmth that was irresistible, then she had laughed out loud at Stephen's gallantry. She was refreshingly frank and unselfconscious, yet she was sweet and soft too – enough to have been crushed by Stephen's neglect. She was the sort of rare young woman who thought of others' needs before her own and who obviously forgave offenses with grace and generosity. During the first few days of her recovery, when she was still confined to her bed, she'd invariably asked Hugh to reassure 'the earl' that she was going to recover her health and her memory so that he wouldn't worry needlessly. Moreover, she'd been thoughtful enough – and astute enough – to realize that he would blame himself for her accident. In addition to that, Hugh was completely enchanted by her friendly, unaffected cordiality toward everyone, from the servants to himself, and even her betrothed.

Monica Fitzwaring was a fine young woman of excellent character and breeding, and Hugh liked her very well, but not as a wife for Stephen. She was lovely, gracious, and serene – as she'd been taught to be – but because of that same upbringing, she had neither the desire nor the ability to evoke deep emotions in any husband, and particularly not in Stephen. Not once, in all the times Hugh had seen Stephen with her, had he ever looked at her with the sort of gentle warmth he'd shown to Charise Lancaster in the last hour. Monica Fitzwaring would make Stephen an excellent hostess and charming dinner companion, but she would never be able to touch his heart.

Not long ago, Stephen had alarmed his entire family by announcing that he had no intention of ever marrying Monica or anyone else merely to beget an heir. Hugh found that more reassuring than alarming. He didn't approve one bit of these modern marriages of convenience that were so *de rigueur* amongst the *ton* – not for anyone he cared about, and he cared very much about the Westmorelands. For Stephen, he wanted nothing less than the sort of marriage Clayton Westmoreland had, the sort of marriage Hugh himself had when his Margaret was alive.

His Margaret . . .

Even now, as he strolled past the stately mansions that marched along Upper Brook Street, the thought of her made him smile. Charise Lancaster rather reminded him of his Margaret, he realized. Not in looks, of course, but in her kindness and her pluck!

All things considered, Hugh was quite convinced that fate had finally given Stephen Westmoreland the sort of blessing he deserved. Of course, Stephen didn't want that sort of blessing, and Charise Lancaster wasn't likely to feel very 'blessed' when she discovered she'd been duped by her 'fiancé' and her own physician. Nevertheless, fate had Hugh Whitticomb as an ally, and Dr Whitticomb fancied himself as something of a potent force when the need arose.

'Maggie girl,' he said aloud, because even though his wife had died ten years before, he still felt she was very close and he liked to talk to her to keep her close, 'I think we're going to pull off the best match in years! What do you think?'

Swinging his cane, he tipped his head and listened, and then he started to chuckle because he could almost hear her familiar response: *I think you should call me Margaret, Hugh Whitticomb, not Maggie!*

'Ah, Maggie girl,' Hugh whispered, grinning, because he *always* replied the same way, 'you've been my Maggie since the day you slid backwards off that horse and dropped right into my arms.'

'I did not slide off, I dismounted. A little awkwardly.'

'Maggie,' Hugh whispered, 'I wish you were here.'

'I am, darling.'

18

Stephen had intended to spend the night with Helene, at the theatre and then in her bed, but three hours after he'd left, he found himself back at his own front door, frowning because his knock hadn't been answered. Inside the entrance hall, he looked around for a butler or a footman, but the place seemed deserted, despite the relatively early hour. Dropping his gloves on a hall table, he strolled into the main salon. No butler materialized to divest him of his coat, so he shrugged out of it and tossed it over the arm of a chair. Then he took out his watch, wondering if it had stopped.

His watch indicated the hour was half past ten, and when he turned to study the ormolu clock on the mantel, both timepieces agreed. Normally, he never returned from an evening with Helene, or any of his clubs, until dawn, and even then a sleepy-eyed footman was always in the hall to greet him.

His thoughts turned to the evening he'd just spent with Helene, and Stephen reached up, idly rubbing his hand over the back of his neck, as if he could somehow rub away the discontent and ennui that had plagued him all night. Seated beside her in his box at the theatre he'd paid scant attention to the performance on stage, and then it was only to find fault with the actors, the musicians, the stage setting, and the perfume worn by the elderly dowager in the next box. In his state of restlessness, everything seemed to either bore or grate on him.

The unusually pleasant mood he'd enjoyed earlier, as Sherry partook of an early dinner and regaled him with her amusing – and often astute – observations about her latest discoveries in the newspapers, had begun to dissipate as soon as he left the house.

By the end of the play's first act, Helene had sensed his discontent, and smiling invitingly behind her fan, she had whispered, 'Would you prefer to leave now, and create our own "second act" in more congenial surroundings?'

Stephen had readily acceded to her suggestion that he take her to bed, but his performance there was as unsatisfying as the performance he'd witnessed at the theatre. Once he'd gotten his clothes off, he discovered he didn't want to indulge in the sort of leisurely sexual preliminaries he normally enjoyed; he simply wanted to spend himself in her. He'd wanted physical relief, not sensual pleasure; he'd gotten the former and given none of the latter.

Helene had noticed, of course, and as he shoved off the bedcovers to get up, she raised up on an elbow and watched him dressing. 'What occupies your thoughts tonight?'

Guilty and frustrated, Stephen had bent down to press an apologetic kiss on her furrowed forehead, as he replied, 'A situation that is entirely too complicated and too vexing to trouble you with.' The explanation was an evasion, and they both knew it, just as they both knew a mistress was not ordinarily entitled to explanations or recriminations, but then Helene Devernay was far from ordinary. She was as sought-after and admired in her own right as any of the *ton*'s acclaimed beauties. She chose her lovers to suit herself, and she had a wide field to choose from, all of them wealthy noblemen who were only waiting for the chance to offer her their 'protection,' as Stephen had done, in exchange for the exclusive right to her bed and her company.

She'd smiled at his evasion and traced her fingertip down the deep vee of his open shirt as she inquired with sham innocence, 'I understand from a seamstress at Madame LaSalle's that you had urgent need of several gowns that you desired to be delivered to your home with utmost haste for a visitor there. How is that . . . situation?' she finished delicately.

Stephen straightened and regarded her with a mixture of amusement, irritation, and admiration for her perception. 'The situation,' he admitted bluntly, 'is "vexing" and "complicated."'

'I rather thought it might be,' she said with a knowing smile, but Stephen heard the underlying note of sorrow in her voice. She was obviously concerned about the presence of an unknown woman in his home, and that puzzled him. In his elite social circle, not even the presence of a wife had any bearing on a man's decision to have a mistress. Amongst the *ton*, marriages generally took place between two congenial strangers who expected to remain exactly that, once the requisite heir was produced. Neither party was expected to alter their lifestyle to suit the other, and affairs were as rampant among women as men. Discretion, not morality, was what mattered to both parties in a *ton* marriage. Since both Helene and he understood all that, and since he was *not* married, Stephen was amazed that she would give even a passing thought to his female houseguest. Leaning down, he kissed her on the mouth as he ran his hand familiarly over her bare thigh. 'You are making entirely too much of the matter. She is a homeless waif who is merely recovering from an injury at my home, while we await the arrival of her family.'

But as Stephen left the house he provided for Helene, he reluctantly faced the fact that Charise Lancaster was a far cry from a pitiable homeless waif. In reality, she was courageous, intelligent, spontaneous, amusing, naturally sensual, and thoroughly entertaining. And the surprising, irritating truth was that he'd enjoyed her company tonight far more than he'd enjoyed taking Helene to the theatre or to bed. Sherry enjoyed his company too. She liked talking to him, and she liked being in his arms . . .

Those thoughts gave birth to an impractical possibility that he actually let himself consider as his carriage neared his home on Upper Brook Street: Burleton hadn't had anything to offer her except a minor noble title and the respectability of marriage, but she and her father had been willing to settle for only that. Within hours of Burleton's death, Stephen had made plans for a funeral and had begun making inquiries into the young man's affairs to see if any other final arrangements were needed. What he learned was that the young baron had a predilection for gaming. Not until this morning, when Matthew Bennett's firm provided him with a full dossier, did Stephen learn that Burleton had completely depleted what little fortune he'd inherited. Beyond a small mountain of gambling debts, which Stephen intended to settle, Burleton had nothing to leave behind – not an estate or the family jewels or even a coach. His excessive gambling had already depleted whatever money he'd gained by agreeing to marry Charise Lancaster.

Within a year or two, Sherry would have been living in genteel poverty, just as Burleton had been doing at the time of his death, with no benefit from her marriage beyond a noble title that wasn't equal to the least of the titles Stephen held. Stephen had no intention of marrying her, but he was able – and perhaps even willing – to offer her the world, provided they continued to enjoy each other in the weeks to come, and so long as she actually understood the arrangement and its terms . . .

So long as she actually understood the arrangement . . .

The ugliness of what he was actually considering hit him, and it sickened him. Charise Lancaster was a naive virgin, not a courtesan. Even if she had had the background and experience to understand what such a relationship would entail, which she did not, she was still much too young for him, and he was entirely too jaded for her.

Fortunately, he was not quite jaded enough, or debauched enough, or *bored* enough to actually offer her an arrangement that would have robbed her of her virtue and all chances of respectability. He could not believe he was so utterly lacking in morality, so vile, that he was capable of killing a young, would-be bridegroom and then, in less than a fortnight, actually considering making a mistress of the young man's affianced bride. It wasn't merely revolting, it was madness. He accepted that he obviously had lost all his ideals over the years, but until that moment, he'd never felt he'd lost his mind as well.

Feeling like a complete degenerate, Stephen resolved to fulfill his role as Sherry's temporary guardian from that moment forward and to think of her only in the most impersonal terms. In keeping with this, he would henceforth see that she was not only amused and made to feel secure but also spared any future physical advances from him!

She might think they were betrothed, but he damned well knew better, and in the future, he would remember it! One person with a faulty memory was enough!

He wished, very devoutly, that she would recover quickly, but he was beginning to feel less guilty for depriving her of her real fiancé. She deserved someone better than young Burleton. He would never have been man enough for her; he was too callow for her, too irresponsible, and too poor. She needed, she deserved, to be garbed in furs and kept in the lap of sumptuous luxury.

In the back of his mind, he was aware that the responsibility for finding her someone like that was very probably his, but he didn't want to contemplate that now. It dimmed his pleasure, and he wanted to salvage the rest of the evening and make it enjoyable for both of them.

Wondering when he had developed such a weakness for damsels in distress – and such a bizarre partiality for distressed damsels with flame-colored hair – Stephen stood in the empty salon, prepared to do his duty as guardian by entertaining his houseguest.

Except the house was as silent and deserted as an empty tomb.

Shoving his hands into his pockets, he turned slowly, still half-expecting Sherry, or a servant, to materialize from the corners of the empty room. When no-one did, he started forward, undecided whether to go to bed or rouse his normally efficient servants – who'd suddenly become inexcusably lax in their duties. He was reaching for the bell pull when he heard the faint sound of raised voices speaking in unison from somewhere at the back of the house, and then the sound died away.

Puzzled, Stephen headed in the direction of the sound, his booted footsteps echoing on the floor of the colonnaded entry hall as he crossed it and turned down a long corridor that ran toward the back of the house. At the end of the corridor he stopped again, his head tipped to the side, listening to the silence. Sherry had undoubtedly retired hours ago, he decided, growing thoroughly annoyed with himself for rushing home from his mistress's inviting arms to devote himself to her like some overardent nursemaid.

He started to turn in disgust then stopped dead as Sherry's merry voice wafted down the hallway from the direction of the kitchen. 'All right, everyone, let's try it again – only Mr Hodgkin, you must stand right near me and sing louder, so I don't get the words wrong again. Ready?' she said.

A chorus of servants' voices suddenly burst into a jaunty Yuletide song that every English child since the Middle Ages had learned to sing. Stephen strode toward the kitchen, his annoyance increased by the thought of Sherry being in the kitchen with his dawdling servants instead of his being waited upon by them. In the doorway of the large, tiled room, Stephen stopped short, staring in amused disbelief at the sight that greeted him.

Fifty servants in their various household uniforms were standing in five perfect rows, with Sherry and old Hodgkin positioned in front of them. Normally the household staff conformed to a rigid, centuries-old hierarchy, with the head butler and the housekeeper at the pinnacle of it, but it was obvious to Stephen that Sherry had organized them without regard to either rank or decorum and probably according to singing ability instead. Poor Colfax, Stephen's lofty head butler, was relegated to the back row, between a chambermaid and a laundress, while his archrival for household supremacy – Stephen's valet, Damson – had managed to obtain a more important placing in the front row. Damson, a rigidly superior gentleman's gentleman, who rarely deigned to speak to anyone but Stephen, had actually slung his arm around a footman's shoulders, and the two of them were harmonizing with shared gusto, their rapturous gazes cast toward the ceiling, their heads nearly touching.

The vignette was so unprecedented, so beyond Stephen's wildest imaginings, that for several minutes he remained where he stood, watching and listening as grooms, ushers, and footmen in full livery sang in democratic harmony with chambermaids, laundresses, and plump scullery maids in soiled white aprons, all of whom were taking direction from a stooped, ancient under-butler who was waving his hands as if he were conducting a symphonic chorus.

Stephen was so riveted by the scene before him that it was several moments before he realized that Damson and the footman, and several of the others, had very pleasant voices, and several minutes more before it occurred to him that he was enjoying the amateur performance in his kitchen far more than the professional one at the theatre.

He was wondering why they were singing a Christmas song in the middle of spring, when Sherry suddenly joined the chorus, and the sound of her voice soaring gently above the would-be tenors and aspiring baritones nearly stopped Stephen's breath. When the notes were low, she sang them with a jaunty earthiness that made her makeshift chorus break into grins as they sang with her, and when the melody climbed higher, she matched it with effortless ease until every corner of the vast room seemed to reverberate with the soaring beauty of her voice.

When the song came to its rousing end, a footboy of about seven years of age stepped forward, holding out his bandaged forearm to Sherry. Smiling bashfully at her, he said, 'Me hand would feel much better, ma'am, if I was to hear one more happy song.'

In the doorway, Stephen straightened and opened his mouth to order the boy not to plague her, but Damson leapt in with what Stephen thought would be a similar order. Instead, the valet said, 'I'm sure I speak for all of us, miss, when I say that you've made this evening into an extraordinarily fine one by sharing your company and your – may I be so bold as to say – your *exquisite* voice with us!'

That long, flowery speech won a hesitant, confused smile from Sherry, who had crouched down to adjust the bulky bandage on the little boy's arm. 'What Mr Damson means,' Colfax, the butler, translated with a disgusted look at the valet, 'is that we all enjoyed this evening very much, miss, and that we would be deeply appreciative if you might extend it just a little.'

The little boy rolled his eyes at the butler and the valet, then beamed at Sherry, who was at his eye level, frowning at whatever she saw beneath the bandage. 'They mean, may we sing another song, please, miss?'

'Oh.' Sheridan laughed, and Stephen saw her wink conspiratorially at the butler and valet as she straightened and said, 'Is *that* what you meant?'

'Indeed,' said the valet, glowering huffily at the butler.

'I know it is what *I* meant,' the butler retorted.

'Well, can we?' the little boy said.

'Yes,' she said, sitting down at the kitchen table and drawing him onto her lap, 'but I'll listen to you this time, so that I can learn another of your songs.' She looked at Hodgkin, who was beaming at her and waiting for further suggestion. 'I think that first song, Mr Hodgkin – the one you all sang for me about "a snowy Christmas night with a Yule log burning bright."'

Hodgkin nodded, held up his thin hands for silence, waved his arms dramatically, and the servants instantly burst into exuberant song. Stephen scarcely noticed. He was watching Sherry smile at the little boy in her lap and whisper something to him, then she lifted her hand to his cheek, gently cradling his smudged face to the bodice of her gown. The picture they made together was one of such eloquent maternal tenderness that it snapped Stephen out of his distraction, and he stepped forward, inexplicably anxious to banish the image from his mind. 'Is it Christmas already?' he said, strolling into the midst of the cozy scenario.

If he'd been holding loaded guns in both hands, his presence couldn't have had a more dampening, galvanizing effect on the merry occupants of the room. Fifty servants stopped singing and began backing out of the room, bumping into each other in their haste to scatter. Even the child in Sherry's lap wriggled away before she could catch him. Only Colfax, Damson, and Hodgkin made a more dignified – but very cautious – retreat and bowed their way out of the room.

'They are quite terrified of you, aren't they?' Sherry asked, so happy that he'd returned early that she was beaming at him.

'Not enough to stay at their posts, evidently,' Stephen retorted, then he smiled in spite of himself because she looked so guilty.

'That was my doing.'

'I assumed it was.'

'How did you know?'

'My magnificent powers of deduction,' he said with an exaggerated bow. 'I have never heard them sing, or ever come home to an empty house until tonight.'

'I felt at loose ends and decided to explore a little. When I wandered in here, Ernest – the little boy – had just put his arm against one of those kettles and burned it.'

'And so you decided to cheer him by organizing all the servants into a choir?'

'No, I did that because everyone seemed to be as much in need of a little cheering as I was.'

'Were you feeling ill?' Stephen asked worriedly, scanning her face. She looked fine. Very fine. Lovely and vibrant – and embarrassed.

'No. I was . . .'

'Yes?' he prompted when she hesitated.

'I was sorry you were gone.'

135

Her candid answer made his heart lurch in surprise . . . and something else, some other feeling he couldn't identify. And didn't want to try. On the other hand, for the moment she was his fiancée, and so it seemed both appropriate, and pleasurable, to lean down and press a kiss to her flushed cheek, despite the fact that he had vowed in that same hour to maintain a completely platonic relationship from that moment on. And if the kiss drifted to her lips, and his hands caught her shoulders, drawing her closer for a moment, then that, too, seemed harmless enough. What was not appropriate or harmless was the instantaneous response of his sated body when she pressed lightly against him and put her hand against his chest or the tender thought that suddenly sprang to his mind . . . *I missed you tonight.*

Stephen released her as if his hands were burned and stepped back, but he kept his expression bland so that his confused annoyance wouldn't show. He was so preoccupied that he automatically complied when she suggested he wait while she fixed them something to drink.

When she had the cups and pot arranged on a tray, Sheridan returned to the table and sat down across from him.

She propped her chin in her hands and studied him with a slight smile while Stephen watched the way the firelight glinted on her hair and made her cheeks glow. 'It must be exhausting work being an earl,' she remarked. 'How did you become one?'

'An earl?'

She nodded, glanced at the pot and got up quickly. 'The other night, after supper, you mentioned that you have an older brother who is a duke, and then you said you inherited your titles by default.'

'I was being glib,' Stephen answered idly, his attention pulled inevitably to her quick, graceful movements as she readied whatever she was preparing. 'My brother inherited the ducal title and several others through our father. Mine came to me from an uncle. Under the terms of a Letters Patent and a special remainder granted to one of my ancestors generations ago, the earls of Langford were allowed to designate the heir to their titles if they were childless.'

She gave him a distracted smile and nodded, and Stephen realized with a jolt that she wasn't particularly interested in a topic that was normally a matter of avid fascination to every unwed female of his acquaintance.

'The chocolate is ready,' she said, picking up a heavy tray laden with a pot, cups, spoons, and several delicate pastries she'd evidently discovered in a cupboard.

'I hope you like it. I seem to know exactly how to make it,' she said, putting the tray into his hands as if it were perfectly natural for him to march about bearing it. 'Only I don't know whether I make it well or not.' She looked thoroughly pleased that she remembered how to make the drink, but it struck Stephen as a little odd that she would know how to perform a task that was always relegated to the servants. On the other hand, she was American, and perhaps American women were more familiar with kitchens than their English counterparts.

'I hope you like it,' she repeated dubiously as they headed toward the front of the house.

'I'm sure I will,' Stephen replied dishonestly. The last time he'd drunk hot chocolate, he'd been in leading strings. These days, his preferences ran toward a glass of aged brandy at this hour. Afraid she'd somehow read his thoughts, he added for emphasis, 'It smells delicious. All that singing about snow and Yule logs must have whetted my appetite for it.'

19

Stephen carried the ornate silver tray down the hall, past three gaping footmen, to the drawing room. Colfax was at his regular station near the front door, and he rushed forward with the obvious intent of prying the tray loose from him, but Stephen stopped him with a mocking remark to the effect that they had already fended for themselves without any help and he saw no reason to change that, now that most of the work was already done.

They were halfway into the drawing room when the door knocker was raised and lowered with emphatic regularity. Stephen had given instructions that all callers were to be informed he was not in, and he paid the sound no heed, but an instant later, he heard a chorus of cheerful voices that made him groan inwardly.

'He most certainly *is* at home, Colfax,' Stephen's mother was telling the butler. 'When we arrived in London two hours ago, there was a note from him announcing his intention to remove to the country. If we had not arrived several days early, he would have been gone. Now, where is he hiding himself?'

Swearing under his breath, Stephen turned just as his brother, his brother's wife, and a friend of hers accompanied his mother into the drawing room – a fleet of ships sailing determinedly into battle against what they perceived as his antisocial behavior.

'I won't have it, darling!' his mother announced, marching forward to press a kiss on his cheek. 'You are too much . . .' Her eyes riveted on Sherry, and her voice trailed off lamely, '. . . alone.'

'Entirely too much!' Whitney Westmoreland announced, her back to the room as she allowed Colfax to divest her of her cape. 'Clayton and I intend to see that you attend every important ball and rout for the next six weeks,' she continued as she linked her arm through her husband's and started forward. Two steps into the drawing room, they stopped.

Stephen glanced apologetically at Sherry, who looked completely disoriented and panicky, and whispered, 'Don't worry. They will like you once they recover from their surprise.' In the space of a few tense seconds, Stephen rapidly considered every plausible, and implausible, way of handling what looked to be impending disaster; but without ordering Sherry to leave so that he could explain – which would only humiliate and distress her – he had no choice but to improvise and to play out the farce in his family's presence and then explain the truth to them after Sherry went up to bed.

In keeping with that plan, Stephen sent a warning look to his older brother that insisted on his unquestioning cooperation, but Clayton's amused attention was on Sherry and the forgotten tea tray in Stephen's hands. 'Very domestic, Stephen,' Clayton remarked dryly.

Impatiently putting the tray down, Stephen looked at the doorway, where Colfax was waiting for instructions about refreshments, and nodded emphatically to produce them at once. Then he turned to the waiting group and began the introductions. 'Mother, may I present Miss Charise Lancaster.'

Sherry looked at her future mother-in-law, realized she was being introduced to a dowager duchess and promptly panicked because she couldn't think what to say. She threw an agonized look at Stephen and said in a whisper that seemed to shriek through the silent, waiting room, 'Will an ordinary curtsy suffice?'

Stephen put his hand beneath her elbow, partly for support and partly to urge her forward, and gave her a reassuring smile. 'Yes.'

Sherry sank into a curtsy and felt her knees wobble, then she drew on courage she didn't know she possessed and straightened. Meeting the older woman's piercing gaze, she said courteously, 'I am very happy to make your acquaintance, ma'am, I mean, *your grace.*' Turning, she waited as Stephen introduced her to his sister-in-law, a stunning brunette he referred to as Whitney, whose green eyes were regarding Charise with veiled puzzlement. Another duchess! Sherry thought frantically, older than she, but not a great deal. To curtsy or not to curtsy? As if the other woman sensed her uncertainty, she held out her hand and said with a hesitant smile, 'How do you do, Miss Lancaster?'

Sherry was grateful for the hint, and after shaking the young woman's hand she turned to be introduced to the duke, a very tall, dark-haired man who bore a distinct resemblance to her fiancé in his facial features, height, and broad-shouldered physique. 'Your grace,' she murmured, curtsying again.

The fourth member of the group, a handsome man in his mid-thirties whose name was Nicholas DuVille, pressed a gallant kiss to the back of her hand and told her that he was 'enchanted' to meet her, then he smiled into her eyes in a way that made her feel as if she'd just received a very great compliment.

Finished with the introductions, she waited for one of Stephen's relatives to welcome her to the family or to at least wish her happiness, but no-one seemed able to speak. 'Miss Lancaster has been ill,' her fiancé said, and three pairs of eyes turned to her, as if concerned that she might swoon which she felt very much as if she might actually do.

'Not ill, actually,' Sherry amended. 'It was an injury – a blow to the head.'

'Why don't we all sit down,' Stephen suggested; cursing perverse fate for making what had already been a difficult situation into one that was bound to worsen. Sherry obviously didn't understand what his family was thinking, but Stephen did. They had walked in on him while he was entertaining an unchaperoned female in his home, which meant that her morality was in serious question, not to mention his own judgment for bringing such a woman into his home, particularly at an hour when callers might arrive. Furthermore, if she were some doxy with whom he was dallying, then he'd committed an unforgivable breach of decency by introducing her to his female relatives. Rather than believe he would descend to that, they were now waiting patiently for some sort of explanation as to who she was . . . or where her chaperone was . . . or where his mind was. Stalling for time, Stephen stood up as the butler came forward bearing a tray of decanters and glasses. 'Ah, here is Colfax right now!' he said with grim desperation. 'Mother, what will you have to drink?'

His tone won a startled glance from his mother, but she sensed his desire for her unquestioning cooperation and complied at once. With a polite smile, she shook her head at the tray the butler was placing on the table in front of the sofa and looked instead at the one Stephen had already put there. 'Is that hot chocolate I smell?' she asked brightly, and without waiting for a reply, she said to the butler, 'I believe I prefer the chocolate, Colfax.'

'I'd have the sherry if I were you,' Stephen advised with feeling.

'No, I think I'd prefer the chocolate,' his mother said firmly, then she demonstrated her legendary grace under pressure by turning to Sherry. 'I noticed you have an American accent, Miss Lancaster,' she said politely. 'How long have you been in England?'

'A little over a sennight,' Sherry said, her voice tense with confusion and uncertainty. No-one in that room seemed to know anything at all about her, even though she was betrothed to a member of their own family. Something was odd – dreadfully odd.

'Is this your first visit?'

'Yes,' Sherry managed, looking desperately at Stephen, her chest tightening with anxiety and irrational foreboding.

'And what brings you here?'

'Miss Lancaster came to England because she is betrothed to an Englishman,' Stephen said, coming to Sherry's rescue and praying that his mother's heart was strong.

The dowager duchess's entire body seemed to relax and her expression to warm. 'How delightful,' she said, pausing to frown at the butler, who had poured sherry into a glass and was holding it toward her, despite her stated preference for the chocolate. 'Colfax, do stop waving that wine under my nose. I'd prefer hot chocolate.' She smiled at Sherry as Colfax distributed glasses of wine to the remaining guests. 'To whom are you betrothed, Miss Lancaster?' she inquired brightly, reaching forward and helping herself to a cup of the chocolate.

'She is betrothed to me,' Stephen said flatly.

Silence exploded in the room. If the situation hadn't been so grave, Stephen would have laughed at the myriad reactions to his announcement. 'To . . . you?' his mother said dazedly. Without another word, she put the cup of chocolate down and plucked a glass of wine from Colfax's tray on the table. Off to Stephen's right, his brother was regarding him with fascinated disbelief, and his sister-in-law had gone perfectly still, a forgotten glass of sherry uplifted in her outstretched hand, as if she'd been about to offer someone a toast. Colfax was dividing his anguished sympathy between Stephen's mother and Sherry, while Nicholas DuVille was studying the edge of his coat sleeve, undoubtedly wishing he were somewhere else.

Ignoring their plight for the moment, Stephen looked at Sherry, who was staring at her lap, her head bent with mortification at what surely struck her as an insulting lack of enthusiasm from her future in-laws. Reaching for her hand, Stephen clasped it reassuringly and gave her the first feasible explanation that sprang to mind: 'You wanted to wait until my family met you before we told them we are betrothed,' he lied, with what he hoped was a convincing smile. 'And that is why they seem so surprised.'

'We seem surprised because we *are* surprised,' his mother said sternly, looking at him as if he'd taken leave of his senses. 'When did you meet? *Where* did you meet? You haven't been to—'

'I'll answer all your questions in a few minutes,' Stephen interrupted in a terse voice that silenced his mother before she could blurt out that he hadn't been to America in years. Turning to Sherry, he said gently, 'You look very pale. Would you like to go upstairs and lie down?'

Sherry wanted very much to flee from that room with all its tension and undercurrents, but there was something so very strange about everything that she was half afraid to be absent. 'No, I – I think I'd prefer to stay.'

Stephen gazed into her wounded, silvery eyes and thought how this moment would have been for her if he had not killed her real fiancé. True, Burleton wasn't much of a matrimonial prize, but they had cared for each other, and she certainly wouldn't have been subjected to such a degrading lack of enthusiasm from Burleton's family, if he'd had one. 'If you would rather stay,' he teased, 'then *I'll* go upstairs and lie down and *you* stay here to explain to my family that I was such a . . . a sentimental idiot . . . that I let you twist me around your finger and convince me that they ought not to be told of our betrothal until *after* they'd met you and had an opportunity to know you.'

Sherry felt as if an enormous weight had just fallen off her shoulders. 'Oh,' she said with an embarrassed laugh, as she looked around at the occupants of the room. 'Is *that* what happened?'

'Don't *you* know?' the dowager burst out in what was, to Stephen's recollection, her first total loss of composure in her entire life.

'No – you see, I've lost my memory,' Sherry replied

with such sweetness and courage that Stephen's chest ached with admiration. 'It is a dreadful inconvenience right now, but at least I can assure you it isn't a hereditary madness. It's merely the result of a silly accident that occurred on the dock beside the ship . . .'

Her voice trailed off, and Stephen forestalled another embarrassing barrage of questions by taking matters into his own hands and standing up, forcing her to follow suit. 'You're tiring, and Hugh Whitticomb will have my head if you aren't rosy and healthy when he arrives tomorrow morning,' he told her gently. 'Let me walk you to your bedchamber. Say good night to everyone. I insist.'

'Good night, everyone,' Sherry echoed with a disconcerted smile. 'As I'm certain you know, Lord Westmoreland is terribly protective.' As she turned away, she noticed that while everyone else seemed to find her very odd, Nicholas DuVille was watching her with a faint smile, as if he found her more interesting than hopelessly peculiar. Sherry clung to the memory of his encouraging glance as she closed the door to her bedchamber and sat down on her bed, her mind whirling with frightening doubts and hopeless questions.

20

When Stephen walked back into the drawing room a few moments later, four pairs of eyes tracked his progress across the room, but his family waited until he was seated before they launched their questions. The instant he touched the chair, however, the two women spoke simultaneously.

His mother said, 'What accident?'

His sister-in-law said, 'What ship?'

Stephen looked to his brother for his first question,

but Clayton merely regarded him with raised brows and said dryly, 'I can't seem to get past the staggering discovery that you are not only a "sentimental idiot" but "terribly protective" as well.'

Nicholas DuVille politely refrained from saying anything at all, though Stephen had the distinct feeling the Frenchman was rather amused by his predicament. He considered rudely volunteering to provide DuVille with a coach so that he could leave, but the man was a longtime friend of Whitney's, and, besides, his presence would deter Stephen's dignified mother from indulging in what would have been her first bout of hysterics.

Satisfied that the group was as ready as they were ever likely to be to hear the truth, Stephen leaned his head against the back of his chair and addressed the ceiling in a terse, composed voice. 'The scene you just witnessed between Charise Lancaster and myself is actually a giant farce. The entire debacle began with a carriage accident over a week ago, an accident for which I was responsible and which has resulted in a chain of events that I am about to describe to you. The young woman whom you have just met is as much a victim of those events as her deceased fiancé, a young baron by the name of Arthur Burleton.'

From the other side of the room, Whitney said in an appalled voice, 'Arthur Burleton is – was a complete scapegrace.'

'Be that as it may,' Stephen replied with a ragged sigh, 'they cared for each other and were going to be wed. As you're about to discover from my tale, Charise Lancaster, whom you all suspect of being either a complete birdwit or else a scheming fortune-hunter who has somehow enticed me into offering her marriage, is actually a completely innocent, and very pitiable, victim of my own negligence and dishonesty . . .'

When Stephen had completed his tale and answered everyone's questions, a long silence fell over the room's occupants as everyone tried to gather their thoughts. Lifting his wineglass, Stephen took a long drink, as if the wine could somehow wash away the bitterness and regret he felt.

His brother spoke first. 'If Burleton was inebriated enough to run in front of a team of horses on a public street in the fog, then surely he is responsible for his own death.'

'The responsibility is mine,' Stephen replied curtly, dismissing Clayton's well-meaning attempt to absolve him. 'I was driving a raw team. I should have been able to keep my horses under control.'

'And following that logic, I gather you feel equally responsible for the loaded cargo net that injured Charise Lancaster?'

'Of course I do,' Stephen bit out. 'She would not have been standing in harm's way, nor would I have let her, if we hadn't both been preoccupied with Burleton's death. If it had not been for my carelessness on two occasions, Charise Lancaster would be a healthy, married woman tonight with an English baron for a husband and the life she wanted stretching before her.'

'Now that you've convicted yourself,' Clayton countered, momentarily forgetting DuVille's presence, 'have you decided on your penalty yet?'

Everyone in the room knew Clayton was merely frustrated and alarmed by the bitter self-recrimination that had permeated Stephen's voice, but it was Nicholas DuVille who defused the charged atmosphere by interrupting in a humorous drawl, 'In the interest of avoiding a nasty duel between the two of you at dawn, which would force me to arise at a very inconvenient and uncivilized hour in order to act as your joint second, may I respectfully suggest you turn your excellent minds to possible solutions to the problems, rather than dwelling on the cause?'

'Nicholas is quite right,' the dowager duchess murmured to her empty glass, her expression somber and preoccupied. Lifting her gaze to his, she added, 'Though it's unfair to embroil you in our family problems, it is obvious that you are better able to think clearly because you are not so deeply involved.'

'Thank you, your grace. In that case, may I offer you my thoughts on the matter?' When both women nodded emphatically and neither man voiced an objection, Nicki said, 'If I understood everything correctly, it appears that Miss Lancaster was betrothed to a penniless ne'er-do-well, for whom she harbored tender feelings, but who had nothing to offer her other than a noble title. Do I have it right so far?'

Stephen nodded, his expression carefully neutral.

'And,' Nicki continued, 'because of two accidents for which Stephen feels responsible, Miss Lancaster now has no fiancé and no memory. Correct?'

'Correct,' Stephen said.

'As I understood it, her physician believes her memory will return in its own good time, is that also correct?'

When Stephen nodded, Nicki said, 'Therefore, the only permanent loss she has suffered – for which you can possibly feel responsible – is the loss of a fiancé who possessed a meaningless title and several very unsavory habits. In which case' – he lifted his glass in a mocking toast to his own powers of reason – 'it appears to me that you could discharge your debt to her by simply finding her another fiancé to take Burleton's place. And if the fiancé you select also happens to be a decent fellow, capable of supporting her in a respectable style, then you could not only soothe your guilt, but you might rightly feel as if you've saved her from a life of torment and degradation.' He glanced at Whitney and then at Stephen. 'How am I doing so far?'

'I'd say you're doing rather well,' Stephen replied with a slight smile. 'I'd given some thought to a similar idea. But,' he added, 'the idea is far easier to contemplate than to execute.'

'Oh, but I know we could pull it off if we put our

147

heads to it!' Whitney exclaimed, anxious to pursue any solution at all that would derail his guilt and give them all a direction. 'All we need do is see that she's introduced to a few of the hundreds of eligible men who will be here for the Season.' She looked at her mother-in-law for support and received an overbright smile that belied unspoken worries.

'Actually, there are one or two minor problems associated with that plan,' Stephen said dryly, but he couldn't bring himself to dampen her enthusiasm. Besides, the plan seemed far more feasible now, with the women in his family ready to lend their enthusiasm and assistance, than it had in the past days. 'Why don't you give the entire project some careful thought, and we'll discuss the various aspects of it on the morrow – at one o'clock here?' he suggested. When everyone agreed, he cautioned, 'For Sherry's sake, it is important that we foresee problems and avert them in advance. Remember that, when you are thinking about all this. I'll send a note to Hugh Whitticomb and ask him to come round and join the discussion, so that we are certain we aren't imperiling her recovery in any way.'

As the group arose, he looked at his mother and Whitney and said, 'Unless I miss my guess, Sherry is wide awake and torturing herself with questions she can't possibly answer about everyone's reaction to her tonight.' He didn't have to complete the request. Both women were already heading for the door, anxious to atone for any unhappiness they'd caused his temporary fiancée.

21

Standing at the windows, gazing out into a night as dark and blank as her memory, Sherry whirled around at the soft knock on the door of her bedchamber and called for her visitors to enter.

'We've come to beg your forgiveness,' Stephen's mother said as she walked over to the windows. 'We didn't understand – about your betrothal, or your accident, or all the rest – until Stephen explained to us.'

'I'm so glad you're still awake,' Stephen's beautiful sister-in-law said, her green eyes filled with an odd kind of regret as they searched Sherry's. 'I don't think I could have slept, after the way we behaved to you downstairs.'

Momentarily mired down in the social technicalities of how she ought properly to respond to an apology from two regal duchesses, Sherry gave up worrying about protocol and did what she could to soothe their obvious unease. 'Please don't trouble yourselves about it,' she said with soft sincerity. 'I don't know what could have possessed me to want to keep the betrothal a secret, but I wonder sometimes if, when I am quite myself, I am perhaps a little . . . eccentric.'

'I think,' Whitney Westmoreland said, looking as if she were trying to smile when she felt rather sad, 'that you are very brave, Miss Lancaster.' And then as if she'd belatedly thought of it, she held out her hands and exclaimed with a bright smile, 'Oh – and, welcome to the family. I – I've always wanted a sister!'

Something about that forced, desperate cheer in her voice set off the alarm bells in Sherry's brain, and she felt her hands tremble as she held them out to her future sister-in-law. 'Thank you.' That sounded so inadequate that an awkward pause followed, and Sherry stifled a hysterical laugh as she explained, 'I haven't the *slightest* idea if I've always wanted a sister . . . but I'm perfectly certain that I must have and that I would have wished for her to be as lovely as you are.'

'What an utterly charming thing for you to say,' the dowager duchess said with a catch in her voice as she enfolded Sherry in a brief, almost protective hug and then ordered her to 'go straight to sleep,' as if Sherry were a child.

They left, promising to come to see her tomorrow, and Sherry gazed in stupefaction at the door when it closed behind them. Her future husband's relatives were as unpredictable as he was – one minute cool and distant and unreachable, and then warm and affectionate and kind. Sherry sank down onto the bed, her brow furrowed in puzzlement as she searched for some explanation for their range of behavior.

Based on various statements she'd read in the *Post* and the *Times* in the past week, Americans were often regarded by the British in a variety of unflattering ways – from amusingly ill-bred Colonists to uncouth barbarians. No doubt, both duchesses had wondered what could have possessed Lord Westmoreland to want to marry one of them – that would explain their negative reaction to her when they first arrived. Evidently, Lord Westmoreland had told them something to reassure them, but what . . . Weary of the endless questions that revolved in her mind during every waking moment, Sherry raked her hair off her forehead and flopped down on her back, staring at the canopy above the bed.

The Duchess of Claymore rolled onto her side, studying her husband's rugged features in the light of a single candle beside their bed, but her troubled thoughts were on Stephen's 'fiancée.'

'Clayton?' she whispered, absently trailing her fingertip down his arm. 'Are you awake?'

His eyes remained closed, but his lips quirked in a lazy half smile as her finger traced a return path to his shoulder. 'Do you want me to be?'

'I think so.'

'Let me know when you are certain,' he murmured.

'Did you notice anything odd about Stephen's behavior tonight – I mean about the way he treated Miss Lancaster and their betrothal, and all that?'

His eyes opened just enough to slant her a wry glance. 'What could possibly be considered "odd" behavior in a man who is temporarily betrothed to a woman whom he does not know, does not love, and does not wish to wed . . . and who thinks he is someone else?'

Whitney gave a sighing laugh at his summation of the predicament, then lapsed into thought again. 'What I meant is that I glimpsed a softening in him that I haven't seen in years.' When he didn't immediately reply, she continued to pursue her hazy line of thought. 'Would you say that Miss Lancaster is extremely attractive?'

'I would say almost anything if it will entice you to either let me make love to you, or else go back to sleep.'

She leaned over and kissed him gently on the mouth, but when he started to turn toward her, she put her hand against his chest and said with a laugh, 'Could you say that Miss Lancaster is extremely attractive – in an unconventional sort of way?'

'If I say yes, will you let me kiss you?' he teased, already tipping her chin up for his kiss.

When he finished, Whitney drew a steadying breath, determined to voice her thoughts before she inevitably sank into the sensual spell he could weave so easily around her. 'Do you think Stephen could be developing a special fondness for her?' she whispered.

'I think,' he teased, his hand drifting down her collarbone to her breast, 'that you are indulging in wishful thinking. DuVille is more likely to want her than Stephen – which would please me almost as much.'

'Why would that please you?'

'Because,' he said as he raised up on an elbow and forced her back onto the pillows, 'if DuVille had a wife of his own, he'd stop longing for *mine.*'

'Nicki doesn't "long" for me in the least! He—'

Whitney forgot the rest of her protest as his mouth smothered her words and then her thoughts.

22

Standing on tiptoe, Sherry removed a book on America from one of the bookcases in the library, then she carried it to one of the polished mahogany tables scattered about the room and sat down. Looking for something to jog her memory, she flipped through the pages, searching for information that she might recognize. There were several intricate drawings of harbors teaming with ships and spacious city streets bustling with carriages, but nothing at all that seemed even remotely familiar. Since the heavy tome was arranged in alphabetical order, and since it seemed logical that pictures would jog her memory better than the written word, she went to the beginning of the book and began slowly turning the pages until she came to a drawing. Under 'A' she found information on agriculture along with an illustration of verdant wheat fields against a backdrop of gentle hills. She'd started to turn the page when another picture flashed through her mind. Only the fleeting vision of fields that she saw had crops with fat white tufts on the top. The image faded instantly, but it made her hand begin to tremble as she reached for the next page and the next. The illustration of a coal mine triggered nothing, nor did anything else she saw, until she came to a picture of a man with a craggy face, prominent nose, and long, flowing dark hair. 'American Indian,' the caption above the illustration read, and Sherry felt the blood begin to pound in her temples as she stared hard at that face. A familiar face . . . or was it? She clenched her eyes closed, trying to focus on the images dancing and fading in her mind. Fields . . . and wagons . . . and an old man with a missing tooth. An ugly man who was grinning at her.

'Sherry?'

Sherry stifled a startled yelp as she whirled around in her chair and stared at the handsome man whose voice normally soothed and excited her.

'What's wrong?' Stephen demanded, his voice sharp with alarm as he noted her stricken, white face, and started forward.

'Nothing, my lord—' she lied with a nervous laugh, standing up. 'You startled me.'

Frowning, Stephen put his hands on her shoulders and scrutinized every feature on her pale face. 'Is that all? What were you reading over there?'

'A book on America,' she said, revelling in the sensation of his strong hands gripping her shoulders and steadying her. Sometimes, she almost felt as if he truly cared for her.

Another vision drifted through her mind, hazier by far than the others . . . but soothing and, oh, so sweet: Kneeling before her with flowers in his hand, a handsome, dark-haired man who may have been the earl proclaimed, *I was nothing until you came into my life . . . nothing until you gave me your love . . . nothing until you . . . until you . . .*

'Should I summon Whitticomb?' Stephen demanded, raising his voice and giving her a slight shake.

His tone snapped her out of her reverie, and she laughed, shaking her head. 'No, of course not. I was only remembering something, or perhaps only imagining it happened.'

'What was it?' Stephen said, releasing his grip on her shoulders, but holding her pinned with his gaze.

'I'd rather not say,' she stated, flushing.

'What was it?' he repeated.

'You would only laugh.'

'Try me,' he said, his words clipped.

Rolling her eyes in helpless dismay, Sherry stepped back and perched her hip on the library table beside the open book. 'I wish you would not insist on this.'

'But I do insist,' Stephen persisted, refusing to be swayed by the infectious smile trembling on her soft lips. 'Perhaps it was a real memory, and not just your imagination.'

'You would be the only one to know that,' she admitted, becoming very preoccupied with the study of the cuticle on her thumb. Looking sideways at him from beneath her long lashes, she asked, 'By any chance, when you asked me to marry you, did you happen to mention that you were nothing at all, until me?'

'I beg your pardon?'

'Inasmuch as you look revolted by the thought,' Sherry said without rancor, 'I don't suppose you would have gone down on one knee when you did propose?'

'Hardly,' Stephen said dryly, so offended by the image of himself assuming such a foolish position that he'd forgotten he'd never proposed to her at all.

Sherry's disappointment in his answers was offset by his increasing discomfiture at the questions. 'What about flowers? Did you happen to offer me a bouquet when you said, "I was nothing until you gave me your love, Sherry. Nothing at all until you came into my miserable life"?'

Stephen realized she was actually relishing his discomfort, and he chucked her under the chin. 'Brat,' he said lightly, noting that she seemed never to be intimidated by him. 'I merely came to invite you to join me in my study. My family will be gathering there any moment for a "conference."'

'What sort of conference?' Sheridan asked, pausing to close the book and return it to the shelf.

'A conference about you, actually – about the best way to "launch" you into Society,' Stephen replied distractedly, watching her lean up on tiptoe, and trying not to concentrate on how utterly fetching she looked in a deceptively simple peach gown with a high mandarin collar and tightly fitted bodice that cleverly called attention to every inviting curve she had without displaying so much as a glimpse of skin.

After a full night's sleep, he'd awakened feeling more optimistic about Sherry's plight than he had since she collapsed at his feet on the dock. With the aid of his family, who'd volunteered their cooperation and assistance, the idea of finding a suitable husband for her during the Season seemed not only an ideal solution, but an achievable one. In fact, he was so enthusiastic about it that he'd sent notes to them early this morning, asking each of them to bring two lists: one of eligible men, and another itemizing those things that would also have to be handled in order to launch her properly.

Now that he had a specific goal, Stephen saw no reason not to pursue it with the same single-minded efficiency and determination that he used to achieve his other business successes. Like his brother and a very few other noblemen, he preferred to handle most of his own business and financial affairs, and he had a well-deserved reputation for doing so with brilliance and daring. In contrast to many of his peers who were sinking further and further into debt because they regarded any business dealings as the province of the 'merchant class,' and therefore beneath them, Stephen was steadily increasing his already vast holdings. He did it because it was sensible, but mostly, he did it because he thoroughly enjoyed the challenge of testing his judgment and timing; he liked the exhilaration that came with successfully acquiring and disposing of assets.

He intended to handle Sherry Lancaster as if she were any other very desirable 'asset' he possessed and of which he intended to dispose. The fact that Sherry was a woman, not a rare artifact or a warehouse full of precious spices, had no bearing on his thinking or his strategy, except that he intended to ensure that her purchaser was worthy and responsible. The only remaining difficulty was to enlist her cooperation in being 'disposed of.'

He'd considered that delicate problem earlier, while he bathed. By the time Damson removed a jacket of biscuit superfine from one of the wardrobes and held it up for Stephen's approval, he'd arrived at the best, and only, solution. Rather than add yet another lie to the ones Sherry had already been told, Stephen was going to tell her a partial truth. But not until after he'd met with his family.

Sherry put away the remaining books she'd intended to look through, as well as the quill and paper she'd removed from a desk drawer. Then she turned and he offered his arm to her. The gesture was so gallant and the smile in his eyes so warm that she felt a helpless burst of joy and pride. Clad in a light tan coat, his long legs encased in coffee brown trousers and shiny brown top boots, Stephen Westmoreland was the stuff that dreams were made of . . . tall, broad-shouldered, and breathtakingly handsome.

As they started down the staircase, she stole another glance at his chiselled profile, marvelling at the strength and pride carved into every feature on that starkly beautiful, tanned face. With that lazy, intimate smile of his and those deep blue, penetrating eyes – why, he must have been making female hearts flutter all over Europe for years! No doubt he'd kissed a great many of those females too, for he certainly knew how to do it, and he didn't seem the least hesitant about it when he chose to kiss her. Thousands of women all over Europe had probably found him as completely irresistible as she did, and yet, for some incomprehensible reason, he'd chosen her above them. That seemed so unlikely, so inconceivable, that it made her uneasy. Rather than surrender to doubt and uncertainty, Sherry returned to the lighthearted conversation they'd had in the library.

As they neared the open doors of his study, she gave him a jaunty, teasing smile. 'Since I can't remember your proposal, you might at least have *pretended* that you made me a proper one – on bended knee. Considering my weakened condition, that would have been the more chivalrous thing to do.'

'I am a very unchivalrous man,' Stephen replied with an impenitent grin.

'Then I hope I at least had the good sense to make you wait a very long time before I accepted your ungallant offer,' she retorted severely, stopping in the doorway. She hesitated and then with a helpless laugh at her inability to remember, she said, '*Did* I make you wait, my lord?'

Helplessly enthralled by this new, teasingly flirtatious side of her, Stephen automatically matched her mood. 'Certainly not, Miss Lancaster. In fact, you flung yourself at my feet and wept with gratitude at the offer of my splendid self.'

'Of all the arrogant, dishonest—' she said on a choked, horrified laugh. 'I did no such thing!' Looking for some sort of confirmation, Sherry glanced at Colfax who was standing at attention holding one of the study doors open, while trying to look as if he weren't hearing – and enjoying – their banter. Her fiancé looked so supremely self-satisfied, his expression so bland and complacent, that Sherry had the awful feeling he was telling the truth. 'I didn't actually do that—' she said weakly, 'did I?'

Stephen's shoulders lurched with suppressed mirth at the appalled expression on her upturned face, then he shook his head and put her out of her misery. 'No,' he said, unaware that he was flirting with her in an open doorway and looking happier than he had in years, in view of his mesmerized servants and his fascinated family and friends, who'd arrived while he was with Sherry in the library. 'After you greet everyone, I'm sending you for a ride in the park, so that you can take in the sights and get some fresh air while we discuss arrangements—' He broke off as some slight movement from inside the study attracted his attention, and he turned fully around, somewhat surprised to find Sherry and himself the focus of a roomful of people who oddly hadn't made a single sound to alert him they were present.

Blaming their lack of conversation on awkwardness about their forthcoming topic, Stephen led her into the study and waited while Sherry greeted everyone with the same warm, unaffected cordiality that she seemed to feel for everyone from the servants to her physician. Anxious to get down to the purpose for the meeting, he interrupted Hugh Whitticomb, who was embarking on an enthusiastic recounting of Sherry's recuperative powers and bravery, and said, 'Since you're all present, why don't you begin discussing the various ways to ease Sherry's way into Society while I walk her out to the carriage.' To Sherry, he added, 'I'll wait while you find a light wrap, then we'll go to the carriage and discuss your itinerary with my coachman.'

Sherry felt his hand under her elbow, firmly drawing her away from people she would very much have liked to spend more time with, but she did as he asked and bade them good bye.

Behind them, Dr Whitticomb signalled Colfax to close the doors, then he looked round at Stephen's family, noting their distracted, thoughtful expressions. The scene he had witnessed a few moments ago as Stephen and Charise Lancaster stood just outside the doors had only confirmed what he already believed, and he was almost certain that the others in the room had noted the same delightful alteration in Stephen that he had.

He hesitated, vacillated, then made his decision, and cautiously endeavored to see if their thoughts truly marched with his. Keeping his voice casual, he glanced at the dowager duchess. 'Lovely girl, isn't she?'

'Lovely,' Stephen's mother agreed unhesitatingly. 'Stephen seems very protective of her, I noticed. I haven't seen him treat any female quite that way before.' Her smile turned wistful. 'She seems to like him very well too. I cannot help wishing he weren't so set on finding a husband for her. Perhaps with time, he might have—'

'My thoughts, exactly,' Hugh said, and so emphatically that she gave him an odd, startled look. Satisfied that he had her unwitting support, Hugh turned to Stephen's sister-in-law. 'What do you think, your grace?' Whitney Westmoreland smiled at him – a slow, knowing smile that warmed his heart and promised her full cooperation. 'I find her completely delightful, and I think Stephen does too, though I doubt he'd want to admit it.'

Restraining the absurd urge to wink at her, Hugh looked to Nicholas DuVille. Until that moment, Hugh had been the only outsider whom the Westmoreland family had regarded as a confidant. DuVille was not a family member or even a close family friend. He had in fact been Clayton's rival for Whitney's hand, and although Whitney regarded him as a dear and close friend, Hugh doubted that Clayton harbored quite the same fondness for him. Hugh wasn't certain why DuVille had been invited to attend what was an intensely private family discussion.

'Charming,' the Frenchman said with a tranquil smile. 'And unique, I suspect. Based on what I have witnessed, I cannot believe Stephen is immune to her attractions.'

Satisfied that he'd gathered all the support he could have hoped, Hugh looked at Clayton Westmoreland, the one member of the group who he knew could, and would, put a stop to any sort of intervention if he didn't agree. 'Your grace?' he invited.

The duke gave him a steady look, and said one word, very clearly and very distinctly: 'No.'

'No?'

'Whatever you're thinking, forget it. Stephen will not welcome our interference in his personal life.' Oblivious to his wife's swift intake of breath as she started to argue, he said, 'Furthermore, the entire situation he is in with Miss Lancaster is already impossibly complicated and fraught with deceit.'

'But you *do* like her, don't you?' Whitney put in a little desperately.

'Based on what little I know of her,' Clayton emphasized, 'I like her very well. However, I am also thinking of her best interests. It would be wise if we all remember that when she recovers her memory and realizes that Stephen was responsible for her fiancé's death, and that he has been lying to her about everything since then, she is not going to like him nearly so well. In fact, she is unlikely to think very well of any of us, when that day arises.'

'It's likely she will be embarrassed and angry when she first realizes she'd never set eyes on Stephen until last week,' Dr Whitticomb conceded. 'However, even before she was out of danger, she showed great concern for Stephen. Kept asking me not to let him worry, and so forth. I think that shows a remarkable understanding – the sort that could enable her to see very quickly why we all had to lie to her.'

'As I said before,' Clayton said firmly, 'Stephen will not welcome our interference in his personal life. If anyone in the family feels the need to try to dissuade him from finding her a husband or to influence him in her favor in any way, then it should be done openly. Today. After that, the matter should be left to Stephen and Miss Lancaster and fate.'

Surprised when there was no objection from his wife, Clayton turned to tease her about her uncharacteristic acquiescence, but she was frowning at DuVille, who, in turn, seemed to be vastly amused about something. He was wondering about that silent exchange when Stephen strode swiftly into the study.

23

'Sherry is safely out of hearing and out of the house,' Stephen announced as he carefully closed the study doors behind him. 'I'm sorry to have kept you waiting, but you were all more prompt than I anticipated.' Walking over to his desk, he sat down behind it, passed a cursory glance over his accomplices, who were seated in a semicircle in front of the desk, and went directly to the point.

'Rather than getting mired down in the minor complications and details of sending Sherry out into Society,' he said in a cordial, but businesslike tone, 'let's go directly to the subject of prospective husbands. Did you bring your lists of acquaintances who might serve the purpose?'

A rustling followed as the women searched their reticules and Whitticomb reached into his pocket to extract the lists they had prepared that morning at his instruction. Stephen's mother leaned forward and handed her folded sheet of writing paper to him, but she pointed out a major encumbrance. 'Without a dowry, Miss Lancaster is at a terrible disadvantage, no matter how desirable she might be. If her father isn't the man of means that you suspect—'

'I'll provide a generous dowry,' Stephen said as he unfolded the notepaper. He glanced at the first few names on the list, and his reaction veered from horror to hilarity. 'Lord Gilbert Reeves?' he repeated, looking at her. 'Sir Frances Barker? Sir John Teasdale? Mother, Reeves and Barker must be fifty years older than Sherry. And Teasdale's grandson was at university with me. These men are ancient.'

'Well, *I'm* ancient!' she protested defensively.

'You said we were to list any unmarried acquaintances for whom we could personally vouch, and that's what I did.'

'I see your point,' Stephen said, struggling to keep his face straight. 'While I look over the other lists, perhaps you could concentrate on some younger men of good reputation with whom you are not *quite* so personally acquainted?' When she nodded agreeably, Stephen turned to his sister-in-law and smiled as he reached for her list.

His smile faded, however, as he looked down the long list of names.

'John Marchmann?' he said with a frown. 'Marchmann is a compulsive sportsman. If Sherry was ever going to see him, she'd have to slog down every stream in Scotland and England and spend the rest of her life in the hunting field.'

Whitney managed a look of innocent confusion. 'He is exceedingly handsome, however, and he is also very amusing.'

'Marchmann?' Stephen repeated incredulously. 'He's terrified of women! The man still blushes in the company of a pretty girl, and he's nearly forty!'

'Nevertheless, he is very kind and very nice.'

Stephen nodded absently, looked at the next name, and then at her. 'The Marquis deSalle won't do at all. He's a habitual womanizer, not to mention a complete hedonist.'

'Perhaps,' Whitney graciously conceded, 'but he does have charm, wealth, and an excellent address.'

'Crowley and Wiltshire are both too immature and hot tempered for her,' he said, studying the two names. 'Crowley isn't too bright, but his friend Wiltshire is a complete bacon-brain. They duelled a few years ago and Crowley shot himself in the foot.' Oblivious to her startled giggle, he added disgustedly, 'A year later they decided to settle another argument on the field of honor, and Wiltshire shot a tree.' Bending a reproving look on his laughing sister-in-law, he added, 'It wasn't funny. The ball from Crowley's pistol ricocheted off the tree and hit Jason Fielding, who'd raced out there to try to stop them. If it hadn't wounded Jason in the right arm, Crowley probably wouldn't have walked away in one piece. If Sherry married either one of them, they'd manage to make her a widow by their own hand, mark my word.'

He looked at the next two names and then scowled at her. 'Warren is a mincing fop! Serangley is a dead bore. I can't believe you think these men are eligible suitors for anyone, let alone an intelligent, sensible young woman.'

For the next ten minutes, Stephen dismissed every name on the list for a variety of reasons that seemed very sound to him, but he began to have the annoying feeling that the group gathered around the desk was finding his rejection of suitor after suitor amusing.

The last name on Whitney's list made his brows snap together and his smile vanish. 'Roddy Carstairs!' he exclaimed in disgust. 'I wouldn't let Sherry near that overdressed, egotistical, razor-tongued little gossip for anything. He's never married because he's never found a woman who he thinks is worthy of him.'

'Roddy is not little,' Whitney pointed out firmly, 'though I'll grant he's not precisely tall, but he is a particular friend of mine.' Biting her lip to hide her smile, she added, 'You are being excessively particular, Stephen.'

'I'm being practical!'

Discarding that list, he reached for Hugh Whitticomb's, glanced at it, frowned, and tossed it aside. 'Apparently you and my mother have a great many friends in common.' With an irritated sigh he got up and walked restlessly around to the front of his desk. He perched his hip on the edge of it, crossed his arms over his chest, and regarded his brother with frustration and hope. 'I see you haven't brought a list, but you must know someone who'd be right for her.'

'As a matter of fact,' his brother replied in a voice tinged with ironic amusement, 'I've been thinking that over as I listened to you eliminate the other candidates.'

'And?'

'And I realized I do know someone. He doesn't meet *all* of your lofty criteria, but I'm no longer in any doubt he's the right man for her.'

'Thank God! Who is he?'

'You.'

The word hung on the air while Stephen bit back a strange and irrational bitterness. 'I am *not* a candidate!' he said frigidly.

'Excellent—' Nicholas DuVille's amused exclamation drew everyone's instant attention as he removed a sheet of writing paper bearing his family crest from his pocket. 'In that case I did not waste my time in making out my own list. I assumed,' he added as Stephen slowly unfolded his arms and reached for the paper, 'that since I was invited here today, I was also to bring a list?'

'It's good of you to have gone to the trouble,' Stephen said, wondering why he'd let his brother's absurd jealousy of DuVille color his own impression of the man. Nicholas DuVille was not only a handsome, educated, well-bred man, he was witty and he was damned nice. Stephen opened the list and looked at the single name scrawled across it, then he lifted his head and regarded DuVille with narrowed eyes. 'Is this your idea of a joke?'

'I hadn't expected you to find the notion laughable,' he countered smoothly.

Unable to believe he was serious, Stephen studied him in cool silence, noticing for the first time that there was an infuriating arrogance about the man, his smile, and even the way he was sitting in the chair, his driving gloves dangling idly from one hand. Realizing that no-one else understood what he was talking about, Stephen managed to clarify the matter and still challenge DuVille's integrity. 'You seriously want to be considered as a suitor for Charise Lancaster?'

'Why not?' Nicki countered, visibly enjoying the other man's discomfiture. 'I am not too old, too short, nor have I ever shot myself in the foot. I dislike fishing, I haven't an excessive attachment to the hunt, and though I do have some vices, no-one has ever accused me of being overdressed, razor-tongued, or a gossip.'

. . . *But egotistical, they have!* Stephen thought with another flash of hostility. *And jaded.* In his mind, he saw the suave Frenchman locked in a passionate embrace with Sherry, her hair spilling over his arm like satin fire, and his hostility escalated to outrage. All her warmth and innocence, that rebellious, jaunty spirit of hers, her courage and thoughtfulness would belong to DuVille, who would . . .

Marry her.

Stephen's inexplicable wrath abruptly gave way to common sense and the realization that fate had just delivered the ideal solution to his problems. DuVille was perfect. He was, in fact, regarded as a tremendous matrimonial prize amongst the *ton*.

'Am I to take your silence for assent?' DuVille inquired, looking as if he knew perfectly well that Stephen couldn't have any objection to his suit. Recovering his manners, if not his cordial attitude toward the other man, Stephen nodded and said with scrupulous civility, 'Certainly. You have my blessings as her . . .' He had started to say guardian and broke off because he was not her legal guardian.

'As her unwilling fiancé?' Nicki suggested. 'Who wishes to be relieved of the obligation to marry her himself so that he can continue as a bachelor without the tiresome burden of a guilty conscience over her unmarried state?'

Whitney saw Stephen's jaw tighten, and she recognized the ominous glitter in those narrowed blue eyes. In a mood like this one, she knew Stephen could and would flay Nicki alive, regardless of the fact that he was her friend or a guest in his home. Her fear was confirmed as Stephen recrossed his arms and subjected Nicki to a contemptuous, raking stare that slid slowly down his entire length. She opened her mouth, waiting to see if Stephen might somehow rise to Nicki's bait by saying he would marry Sherry himself. Instead, Stephen announced in an insulting drawl, 'I think we ought to discuss your qualifications or lack thereof a little further, DuVille. In rejecting one of the other contenders, I believe the word "lecher" was mentioned—'

'No, it was not!' Whitney burst out so desperately that Stephen looked at her, and while he'd momentarily lost some of his momentum, she said fiercely, 'Stephen, *please* do not take your frustration out on Nicki. He wants to help.' She glanced swiftly at Nicki, who had gone perfectly still from the moment Stephen launched his tirade and who looked more like he was contemplating murder than marriage. Her exasperating husband was sitting there looking as if he was *enjoying* both men's predicament, but he responded to her silent appeal and intervened. 'Really, Stephen, this is no way to treat your prospective son-in-law,' he said dryly, using humor to dispel the tension.

'My what?' Stephen demanded with disgust.

Clayton replied with a mocking grin, 'Since you not only promised to provide a dowry, but a "generous" one, I'd say that puts you in the role of father. Now, since DuVille has merely offered himself as a possible suitor, not a husband, my advice is to wait to antagonize him until *after* the nuptials.'

The absurdity of that scenario was not lost on either of the combatants, who visibly relaxed, but Whitney scarcely breathed until Stephen finally held out his hand to Nicki in a gesture of conciliation. 'Welcome to the family,' he said ironically.

'Thank you,' Nicki said, leaning forward and accepting the handshake. 'How large a dowry should I expect?' he joked.

'Now that we've overcome that hurdle,' Stephen said,

walking back around his desk and sitting down, 'let's get down to the problems we're likely to face when we introduce Sherry to Society.'

Whitney surprised him with an instant objection. 'There's no need to do that. Nicki has already offered himself as a prospective suitor.'

Stephen flicked a quelling glance at her as he withdrew a sheet of writing paper from his desk. 'I would like Sherry to have more than one suitor from which to choose, which means she will have to be out in Society. I'd also like her to have her affections set on someone by the time her memory returns, if at all possible. That will help diminish whatever grief she may feel when she learns of Burleton's death.'

DuVille's objection was next. 'That is hoping for too much in too short a time.'

Stephen overruled that with a shake of his head. 'Not in this case. She scarcely knew Burleton. He could not have become the entire center of her universe during the short time he was with her in America.'

No-one could argue the logic of that, but from there on, everything concerning Sherry's actual introduction to Society went up for endless debate. Stephen listened in growing frustration as everyone suggested various pitfalls and problems, from the possible to the absurd, that might be encountered if Sherry were introduced to the *ton* during the Season.

24

At the end of an hour, when impatience finally drove Stephen to begin brushing aside everyone's objections to his plan, Hugh Whitticomb suddenly decided to give his professional medical opinion of it as Sherry's physician. 'I'm sorry, I cannot allow it,' he said flatly.

'Would you care to enlighten me as to your reason?' Stephen said caustically when the physician acted as if the matter was settled and there was nothing more to be said.

'Certainly. Your contention that Society will overlook Miss Lancaster's lack of knowledge about our ways because she is American may be partially correct. However, Miss Lancaster is sensitive enough to notice immediately that she's lacking in certain social skills, and *she* is likely to become her harshest critic. That will add to the extreme stress she is already under, which I cannot permit to happen. The Season begins in a few days, and that's an impossibly short time for her to learn everything she'd need to know to make a full-fledged debut, as intelligent as she is.'

'Even if that weren't an obstacle,' Whitney added, 'we still wouldn't be able to outfit her for the full Season on such short notice. It will take a great deal of pressure to influence Madame LaSalle, or any other acceptable modiste, to set to work on a wardrobe for Miss Lancaster when they're already impossibly busy working for their regular clients.'

Ignoring that problem for the moment, Stephen directed his remarks to Whitticomb. 'We can't keep her locked away from everyone. That won't help her meet potential suitors, and furthermore, people will begin to talk and wonder why we feel the need to hide her. More important, Sherry herself will begin to wonder about that, and I suspect the conclusion she'll draw is that we're ashamed of her.'

'I hadn't considered that,' Whitticomb admitted, looking deeply troubled by the possibility.

'I suggest we compromise,' Stephen said, wondering why everyone else seemed bent on finding problems, instead of solutions. 'We'll keep her social appearances to a minimum. So long as one of us stays at her side whenever she attends a function, we can shield her from too many questions.'

'You can't shield her completely,' Whitticomb argued. 'What will you tell people about who she is and how she lost her memory?'

'We'll tell them the truth, but without going into too much detail. We will say that she suffered an injury, and though we can all vouch for her identity, as well as for her being of unexceptional birth and character, she simply cannot answer questions for a while.'

'You know how cruel people can be! Why, her lack of knowledge could be mistaken for stupidity.'

'Stupidity?' Stephen scoffed with a harsh laugh. 'How long has it been since you went to a debutante ball and tried to carry on a sensible conversation with any of the chits making their annual debut?' Without waiting for a reply, he said, 'I can still remember the last time I did – half of them were incapable of discourse on any topic beyond the latest fashion and the weather. The rest of them couldn't do anything but blush and simper. Sherry is extremely intelligent, and that will be evident to anyone with enough wit to recognize intelligence when it is right in front of them.'

'I don't think she'll seem stupid to anyone,' Whitney put in slowly. 'They're more likely to think her wonderfully mysterious, particularly the younger beaux.'

'It's settled then,' Stephen said with an implacable finality that warned further argument would be futile. 'Whitney, you and Mother make the arrangements to see her appropriately attired. We'll introduce her to Society under our own aegis, and then make certain that at least one of us is always with her. Let's begin by taking her to the opera, where she can be seen but not easily approached. After that, a musicale, a few teas. Her looks are so extraordinary that she's bound to attract considerable attention, and when she doesn't immediately appear at all the balls, the mystery surrounding her will grow, and as Whitney pointed out, that's actually to our advantage.' Feeling satisfied that all the important considerations had been resolved, Stephen looked around and said, 'Does anyone have anything else that needs to be discussed?'

'One thing,' his mother said very emphatically. 'She cannot possibly stay under your roof with you another night. If it were known she'd been in this house alone and unchaperoned, nothing we could do or say would salvage her reputation or enable her to make a suitable match. It will be a miracle if servants' gossip hasn't already spread.'

'The servants adore her. They wouldn't utter a word to hurt her.'

'Be that as it may, they are bound to talk with other people's servants without intending to harm her. By the time the *on-dits* have circulated through the city, she'll have become your paramour, and we cannot risk that sort of gossip.'

'I suppose Clayton and I could invite her to stay with us,' Whitney said reluctantly when Stephen seemed to be waiting for her to make the offer, but she wasn't at all pleased with the solution. She didn't want to remove Sherry from Stephen's immediate sphere. Once the round of social activities began with the crushes of people at all of them, Stephen might not encounter her for days at a stretch, or only for a few minutes at a time.

'Fine,' Stephen agreed with annoying satisfaction. 'She'll stay with you.'

Hugh Whitticomb removed his wire-rimmed spectacles and began to polish the lenses with his handkerchief. 'I'm afraid that plan isn't fine with me.'

Stephen made a Herculean effort to keep his impatience with the balky physician under control. 'What do you mean?'

'I mean I cannot allow her to be removed into unfamiliar surroundings among people she does not know.' When Stephen's brows snapped together and he opened his mouth to argue, Hugh Whitticomb looked around at the gathering, his tone dire with warning.

'Miss Lancaster believes she is betrothed to Stephen and that he cares deeply for her. He is the one who stayed by her bedside when she was hovering near death, and he is the one she relies upon.'

'I'll explain to her about the social stigma she risks by remaining here,' Stephen said briskly. 'She will understand that it simply isn't appropriate.'

'She does not have the slightest concept of the importance of appropriate behavior, Stephen,' Whitticomb contradicted smoothly. 'If she had, she wouldn't have been standing down here in a lavender peignoir the night I came by to visit her.'

'Stephen!' his mother exclaimed.

'She was fully covered,' he said with a dismissive shrug. 'And it was all she had to wear.'

Nicki DuVille joined the debate. 'She cannot stay here unchaperoned. *I* won't permit it.'

'*You* have nothing to say about it,' Stephen countered.

'I think I do. I will not have the character of my future wife besmirched. I, too, have a family who must accept her.' Leaning back in his chair, Stephen steepled his hands and regarded him with unconcealed dislike for several moments before he remarked in a voice as cold as his gaze, 'I do not recall hearing you actually offer for her, DuVille.'

Nicki lifted a challenging brow. 'Would you like to hear me do so now?'

'I told you that I want her to have a choice of suitors,' he said in an ominous voice. Stephen wondered how his brother could countenance such an arrogant bastard within a mile of his wife. 'At this time, you are nothing but a possible contender for her hand. If you wish to retain that status for another sixty seconds, I suggest—'

'I could stay here with Miss Lancaster,' the dowager interjected desperately.

The two men reluctantly ended their visual duel and looked to Hugh Whitticomb for a decision. Instead of immediately replying, Hugh began polishing his other lens while he considered the dampening effect the dowager's presence was likely to have on a budding romance. A regal, imposing woman even late in her fifth decade, she was much too keen to permit the sort of cozy atmosphere Hugh wanted to see preserved between Stephen and Sherry Lancaster. Moreover, she would be bound to intimidate Sherry, no matter how she tried to do the opposite. Rapidly considering the most persuasive argument against her solution, he said, 'In the interest of your own health, your grace, I do not think you ought to tax yourself with the responsibilities of a constant chaperone. I would not want to see a recurrence of last year's problem.'

'But you said it wasn't serious, Hugh,' she protested.

'I'd like to keep it that way.'

'He's right, Mother.' Feeling that he'd already over-burdened his family with his own problems, Stephen seconded the motion and added, 'We need to find someone who can stay with her at all times, a chaperone of unimpeachable character and reputation who could also serve as a ladies' companion.'

'There's Lucinda Throckmorton-Jones,' the dowager duchess said after a moment's thought. 'No-one would dare to question the acceptability and character of any young lady in her charge.'

'Good God, no!' Hugh exclaimed, so forcefully that everyone gaped at him. 'That hatchet-faced dragon may be the duenna of choice among some of our best families, but she'd drive Miss Lancaster back to her sickbed! The woman actually refused to budge from my elbow when I put salve on a burned thumb belonging to one of her charges. Acted like she suspected I might want to seduce the silly chit.'

'Well, then who do *you* suggest?' Stephen snapped, losing all patience with the balky, unhelpful physician.

'Leave that matter to me,' Hugh amazed him by saying. 'I may know just the lady, if her health is adequate to the task. She's quite lonely, and feeling rather useless these days.'

The dowager duchess regarded him with interest. 'Whom do you mean?'

Rather than risk having the astute lady immediately veto his choice, Hugh decided to take matters into his own hands and then present them with a *fait accompli*. 'Let me give it further thought, before I narrow the choice down to one. I may bring her by tomorrow. Another night under Stephen's roof cannot do Sherry any more harm than has already been done.'

They broke off as Colfax knocked on the door and said that Miss Lancaster was just returning in the carriage.

'I think that covers everything.' Stephen stood up, concluding the meeting.

'Everything, but two small details,' Clayton pointed out. 'How do you intend to gain your fiancée's co-operation in your scheme to find her another husband without crushing her or humiliating her? And what do you intend to do when she tells someone she is betrothed to you? They'll laugh her out of London.'

Stephen opened his mouth to point out yet again that he was *not* her fiancé, and then gave up. 'I'll handle that tonight or tomorrow,' he said instead.

'Be tactful,' Hugh warned. 'Do not upset her.'

Whitney stood up, pulling on her gloves. 'I think I'd better pay a personal call on Madame LaSalle at once. Persuading her to drop everything and go to work on a complete wardrobe now, when the Season is about to go into full swing, will require a miracle.'

'It will require a great deal of Stephen's gold, not a miracle,' her husband said with a chuckle. 'I'll drop you at LaSalle's shop on my way to White's.'

'White's is in the opposite direction, Claymore,' Nicki pointed out. 'If you would allow me to escort your wife to the modiste, perhaps along the way she could suggest the best way for me to gain Miss Lancaster's confidence.'

With no feasible reason to object, Clayton nodded curtly, and DuVille offered his arm to Whitney, who paused to press a kiss on Clayton's cheek. As the foursome departed, both brothers watched DuVille's retreating back with matching scowls.

'How often,' Stephen asked cynically, 'have you wanted to knock DuVille's teeth down his throat?'

'Not as often as I suspect you are going to,' Clayton said dryly.

'What do you think, Nicki?' Whitney asked after glancing behind her to make certain Stephen's butler was closing the door and not eavesdropping in the doorway.

He shot her a sideways smile as he signalled for his carriage. 'I think that, at this moment, your husband and your brother-in-law are longing for any excuse to draw my blood.'

Whitney smothered a laugh as a footman rushed forward to let down the steps, and she climbed into the carriage. 'I think Stephen is the more eager.'

'An alarming thought,' he said, chuckling, 'since he has the hotter temper and the reputation as a crack shot.'

She sobered. 'Nicki, my husband was very specific in there about our not interfering. I thought you understood the warning I was trying to give you to forget all about volunteering yourself as Miss Lancaster's suitor. You will have to excuse yourself from the contest at the first opportunity. Clayton rarely forbids me anything, and I will not defy him when he does.'

'You are not defying him, *chérie*. I am. Furthermore, he said only that the "family" could not interfere. I am not part of your family, to my everlasting regret.'

He grinned to take the solemnity out of it, and Whitney knew he was merely flirting. 'Nicki—'

'Yes, my love?'

'Do not call me that.'

'Yes, Your Grace?' he teased.

'Do you remember how painfully naive and gauche I was when you decided to help "launch" me into Society by attending my debut and paying me particular attention?'

'You were never gauche, *chérie*. You were refreshingly innocent and unconventional.'

'Charise Lancaster,' she persisted, 'is as inexperienced as I was. More so. Do not let her mistake your attention for real devotion. I mean, do not let her care for you too much. I couldn't bear it if we were responsible for hurting her more than she has been.'

Nicki stretched his long legs out in front of him, looked at them in thought for a moment, then he slanted her a smile. 'When I attended your debut, I remember warning you that you must not confuse a harmless flirtation for something more meaningful. I did that so you would not be hurt. Do you recall the occasion?'

'Yes.'

'And in the end, you were the one who rejected me.'

'After which you soothed your "broken heart" with an endless string of willing ladies.'

He didn't deny it, but said instead, 'Charise Lancaster reminded me of you from the moment I saw her. I cannot say why I think she is very out of the ordinary, or how deep the resemblance to you goes, but I am looking forward to the discovery.'

'I want her for Stephen, Nicki. She is right for him. I know Dr Whitticomb thinks as I do. All you were supposed to do is pay her enough attention to make Stephen a little jealous—'

'I think I can handle that without trying,' he chuckled.

'—so that Stephen will have to see how desirable she is and that he's at risk of losing her to another.'

'If you mean to adhere to your husband's dictate about not becoming involved, I am afraid you are going to have to leave the methods to me. Agreed?'

'Agreed.'

25

Summoned to the earl's study by a footman, Sherry bade a cheerful good morning to the servants she passed in the upper hall, paused in front of a gilt-framed mirror to ensure her hair was tidy, then she smoothed the skirt of her new lime dress and presented herself to Hodgkin, who was stationed at the open doors to the study, watching as footmen applied beeswax to graceful tables and polish to silver candelabra. 'Good morning, Hodgkin. You're looking especially fine today. Is that a new suit?'

'Yes, miss. Thank you, miss,' Hodgkin said, fighting unsuccessfully to conceal his pleasure at the discovery that she, too, noticed how well he looked in the new suit of clothes that he was entitled to twice each year as part of his employment. Straightening his shoulders to their most rigid angle, he confided, 'It arrived yesterday, directly from the tailors.'

'I have a new gown,' she confided in return. Stephen had looked up at the sound of her voice and now watched her pick up her skirts and do a slow pirouette for the under-butler's benefit. 'Isn't it lovely?' he heard her ask.

The scene was so unaffectedly charming that Stephen smiled and answered before the under-butler could. 'Very lovely,' he replied, which caused Hodgkin to jump nervously and Sherry to drop her skirts, but she smiled that winsome smile of hers as she came toward his desk, her hips swaying gently. Most of the women Stephen knew had been taught exactly how to walk and how to carry themselves, so they moved with the practiced precision of a drill team. Sherry had an effortless grace about her, as if walking was what it should be – a distinctive, naturally feminine act.

'Good morning,' she said. Gesturing toward the sheaf of documents and correspondence on his desk, she added, 'I hope I'm not interrupting you. I thought you wished to see me at once—'

'You aren't interrupting,' Stephen assured her. 'In fact, I sent my secretary away so that we could be private. Sit down, please.' Glancing at Hodgkin, he nodded toward the doors in a silent order that they were to be closed. As the tall oaken panels swung silently into place, Sherry settled her skirts around her. She took painstaking care with her new gown, Stephen noticed, smoothing her hand over a wrinkle and looking down at her feet to make certain the hem didn't lie beneath the toe of her slipper. Satisfied that everything was arranged in becoming order, she looked at him expectantly, her lovely eyes inquisitive. And trusting.

She trusted him implicitly, Stephen realized, and in return he was about to abuse that trust by manipulating her. As the silence lengthened to the point of awkwardness, he realized that he had been dreading this moment more than he'd realized – enough to have put it off last night so that they could enjoy supper together. However, there was no point in delaying it another minute. And yet, that's exactly what he found himself doing.

He searched quickly for a topic, failed to come up with one, and filled the expectant silence with the first remark that came to mind, 'Have you had a pleasant morning?'

'It's a little too soon to tell,' she solemnly replied, but her eyes lit with laughter. 'We finished breakfasting only an hour ago.'

'Has it only been an hour? It seems longer,' Stephen said inanely, feeling as awkward and ill-at-ease as an untried youth alone with a woman for the first time. 'Well, what have you done since then?' he persevered.

'I was in the library looking for something to read when you sent for me.'

'You can't mean you've finished all those magazines I had sent over for you! There was a stack as high as my waist.'

She bit her lip and gave him a laughing look. 'Did you actually *look* at any of them?'

'No, why?'

'I don't think you'd find them very edifying.'

Stephen knew nothing of women's magazines, except that women read them faithfully, but in an effort to keep the conversation going, he politely inquired about the names of the magazines she'd received.

'Well, there was one with a very long name. If I remember correctly, it was called, *The Ladies Monthly Museum, or Polite Repository of Amusement and Instruction: being an Assemblage of what can Tend to please the Fancy, Instruct the Mind or Exalt the Character of the British Fair.*'

'All of that in one magazine?' Stephen teased. 'That's quite an ambitious undertaking.'

'That's what I thought, until I looked at the articles. Do you know what one of them was about?'

'Based on that look on your face, I'd be afraid to hazard a guess,' he said, chuckling.

'It was about rouge,' she provided.

'What?'

'The article was about how to rouge one's cheeks. It was absolutely *riveting*. Do you suppose that falls under the heading of "Instructing the Mind" or of "Exalting the Character"?' she inquired with sham gravity as Stephen's shoulders shook with helpless laughter at her wit.

'Some of the other magazines did have articles of far more import, however. For example, in the one called *La Belle Assemblée, or Bell's Court and Fashionable Magazine addressed particularly to the Ladies*, there was an informative treatise on the correct way for a lady to hold her skirts when she curtsies. I was spellbound! I had never realized it was preferable to use only the thumb and forefinger of each hand to spread one's skirts, instead of all the fingers God gave us. Dainty perfection is the ideal to which every woman must aspire, you know.'

'Is that your theory, or the magazine's?' Stephen asked with a grin.

She gave him a sidewise, laughing look that was a miracle of jaunty irreverence. 'What do you think?'

Stephen thought he'd take her jaunty irreverence over dainty perfection every day of his life. 'I think we should have that rubbish removed from your bedchamber.'

'Oh, no, you mustn't. Truly you mustn't. I read the articles every night in bed.'

'You do?' Stephen asked because she looked perfectly serious.

'Oh, yes! I read one page and nod right off. It's ever so much more effective than a sleeping draught.'

Stephen pulled his gaze from her entrancing face and watched her shove her hair back off her forehead and give it an impatient shake that sent a veil of coppery locks sliding off her shoulder. He'd liked it where it had been, draped artlessly over her right breast. Annoyed with the impossible direction of his thoughts, Stephen said abruptly, 'Since we've ruled out rouge and curtsying, what are you interested in?'

You, Sherry thought. *I am interested in you. I am interested in why you seem uneasy right now. I am interested in why there are times when you smile at me as if you see only me and I am all that matters. I am interested in why there are times when I sense that you don't want to see me at all, even when I'm in front of you. I am interested in anything that matters to you because I want so much to matter to you. I am interested in history. Your history. My history.* 'History! I like history,' she provided brightly after a pause.

'What else do you like?'

Since she couldn't speak from memory, she gave him the only answer that came to mind. 'I think I like horses very well.'

'Why do you say that?'

'Yesterday, as your coachman drove me through a park, I saw ladies riding, and I felt . . . happy. Excited. I think I must know how to ride.'

'In that case, we'll have to find you a suitable mount and find out. I'll send word to Tattersall's and have someone over there choose a nice, gentle little mare for you.'

'Tattersall's?'

'It's an auction house.'

'May I go along and watch?'

'Not without causing an uproar.' She gave him a startled look, and he smiled. 'Females are not allowed at Tatt's.'

'Oh, I see. Actually, I'd rather you didn't spend money on a horse. It may turn out that I don't know how to ride at all. Could I not use one of your horses first, to find out? I could ask your coachman—'

'Don't even consider it,' Stephen warned sharply. 'I do not own a horse suitable for you or any other woman to ride, no matter how accomplished you may be. My animals are not the sort for a demure jog through the park.'

'I don't think that's what I imagined yesterday. I felt like I wanted to gallop and feel the wind in my face.'

'No gallops,' he decreed. No matter how much riding she'd done, she was no rawboned country girl; she was slender and delicate, without the strength to handle a spirited gallop. When she looked bewildered and mutinous, he explained gruffly, 'I don't want to carry you home unconscious for a second time.'

He suppressed a shudder at the memory of her limp body in his arms, and that reminded him of another accident . . . another limp body belonging to a young baron with a life ahead of him and a beautiful girl who wanted to marry him. The recollection banished all desire to delay coming to the real point of their visit.

Leaning back in his chair, Stephen gave her what he hoped was a warm, enthusiastic smile and put his plan for her future into action. 'I'm delighted to tell you that my sister-in-law has persuaded the most fashionable modiste in London to abandon her shop in its busiest time and to come here, with seamstresses in tow, in order to design a wardrobe for you to wear during the Season's activities.' Instead of being thrilled, she furrowed her brow a little at the news. 'Surely, that doesn't displease you?'

'No, of course not. But you see I don't need any more gowns. I still have two that I haven't yet worn.'

She had a total of five ordinary day dresses, and she actually believed that was a wardrobe. Stephen decided her father must have been a selfish miser. 'You will need a great many other things, besides those few items.'

'Why?'

'Because the London Season calls for an extensive wardrobe,' he said vaguely. 'I also wanted to tell you that Dr Whitticomb will be arriving this afternoon with an acquaintance of his, an elderly lady who, I understand from the doctor's note, is eager and competent to be an acceptable duenna for you.'

That startled an instantaneous chuckle from her. 'I don't need a ladies' companion,' she laughed. 'I *am* a—' Sherry's stomach churned and the words simply stopped coming. The thought that prompted them vanished into the ether.

'You are what?' Stephen prompted, watching her closely and noting her agitation.

'I—' She reached for the words, the explanation, but they evaded her, retreating further from her mind's grasp. 'I – don't know.'

Eager to get the distasteful part of the discussion over with, Stephen brushed that aside. 'Don't worry about it. Everything will come back to you in good time. Now, there is something else I want to discuss with you . . .'

When he hesitated, she lifted those large silvery eyes to his and smiled a little to reassure him that she felt quite well enough to go on. 'You were about to say?'

'I was about to say that I have arrived at a decision with which my family agrees.' Having closed off her only possible avenue of appeal by warning her that his family concurred with him, Stephen presented her with a carefully worded ultimatum: 'I want you to have an opportunity to enjoy the Season, and the attention of other men, before we announce our betrothal.'

Sherry felt as if he had slapped her. She didn't want attention from strange men, and she couldn't imagine why he would like that. Steadying her voice, she said, 'May I ask why?'

'Yes, of course. Marriage is a very great step, which should not be undertaken lightly—' Stephen broke off, mentally cursing himself for idiotically paraphrasing the actual ceremony, and switched to what he felt was a convincing explanation she wouldn't see through. 'Since we did not know each other well before you came to England, I've decided that you ought to have the opportunity to look over the other eligible suitors in London, before you settle on me as a husband. For that reason, I'd like our betrothal to remain a secret between us for a while.'

Sherry felt as if something were shattering inside. He *wanted* her to find someone else. He was trying to rid himself of her, she could *feel* it, and why not? She couldn't even remember her own name without a reminder and she was nothing like the gay, beautiful women she'd seen in the park yesterday. She couldn't even begin to compare to his sister-in-law or his mother, with their self-assured manner and regal ways. Apparently, they didn't want her in the family either, which meant their cordiality to her had all been a pretense.

Tears of humiliation burned the backs of her eyes, and she hastily got to her feet, trying to recover her control, fighting desperately to hold on to her shattered pride. She couldn't face him, and she couldn't run from the room without giving her feelings away, so she carefully kept her back to him and strolled over to the windows that looked out upon the London street. 'I think that is an excellent idea, my lord,' she said, staring blindly out the window, struggling to keep her voice steady. Behind her, she heard him get up and come toward her, and she swallowed and drew a deep breath before she could go on. 'Like you, I have had . . . some reservations about our suitability . . . ever since I arrived here.'

Stephen thought he heard her voice break, and his conscience tore at him. 'Sherry,' he began and put his hands on her shoulders.

'Kindly take your hands . . .' she paused for another shattered breath, 'off me.'

'Turn around and listen to me.'

Sherry felt her control collapsing, and though she closed her eyes tightly shut, hot tears began to race down her cheeks. If she turned now he'd see that she was crying, and she would rather die than suffer that humiliation. Left with no recourse, she bent her head and pretended to be absorbed in tracing her finger over the etchings on the leaded glass pane.

'I am trying to do what is best,' Stephen said, fighting the desire to wrap her in his arms and beg her forgiveness.

'Of course. Your family could not possibly think I am suitable for you,' she managed in a relatively normal voice after a moment. 'And I'm not at all certain how my father could have thought you were suited to me.'

She sounded composed enough that Stephen was about to let go of her, when he saw the tears dropping onto the sleeve of her gown, and his restraint broke. Grabbing her shoulders he turned her around and pulled her into his arms. 'Please don't cry,' he whispered into her fragrant hair. 'Please don't. I'm only trying to do what is best.'

'Then let go of me!' she said fiercely, but she was crying so hard, her shoulders were quaking.

'I can't,' he said, cradling the back of her head and holding her hot cheek pressed to his shirt, feeling the

183

wetness seeping through it. 'I'm sorry,' he whispered, kissing her temple. 'I'm sorry.' She felt so soft against him. She was too proud to struggle and too shattered to stop crying, so she stood rigidly in his embrace, her body racked with silent sobs. 'Please,' he whispered hoarsely, 'I don't want to hurt you.' He stroked his hand over her back and nape in a helpless attempt to soothe her. 'Don't let me hurt you.' Without realizing what he was doing, he forced her chin up with his hand and touched his mouth to her cheek, trailing a light kiss over the smooth skin, feeling the wetness of her tears. With the single exception of the night she regained consciousness, she had not shed a single tear over the absence of her memory, or the blinding pain from her injury, but she was crying in silent earnest now, and suddenly Stephen lost his mind and his control. He rubbed his mouth over her trembling lips, tasting their salty softness, and crushed her closer to him, delicately teasing her lips with his tongue, urging them to part. Instead of sweetly offering him her mouth, as she had done before, she tried to turn her face away. He felt her rejection like a physical blow, and he doubled his efforts to make her succumb, kissing her with demanding hunger, while in his mind he saw her smiling up at him a few minutes ago, and leading a chorus of servants in the kitchen, and flirting with him yesterday: *I hope I had the good sense to make you wait a very long time before I accepted your ungallant proposal,* she'd teased. She was rejecting him now, permanently, and something deep within Stephen gave out a keening cry, mourning the loss of her tenderness and passion and warmth. Shoving his hands into her hair, he turned her face up to his and gazed into wounded, hostile silver eyes. 'Sherry,' he whispered thickly as he purposefully lowered his mouth to her, 'kiss me back.'

She couldn't free her mouth from his, so she fought him with rigid, unmoving indifference, and Stephen fought back. Using all of the sexual expertise he'd acquired during two decades of dalliance with the opposite sex, he ruthlessly laid siege to the defenses of an inexperienced, virginal twenty-year-old. Slanting his arm across her back, holding her pressed fiercely close to him, he teased and seduced her with his hands and mouth, and then his voice. 'Since you're going to be comparing me with your other suitors,' he whispered without realizing that he was undoing everything he thought he'd wanted to accomplish, 'don't you think you ought to know how I compare?'

It was his words, not the seduction of his hands and mouth that crumbled Sherry's resistance. Some protective feminine instinct warned her that she must never again let herself trust him, never again let him touch or kiss her, but just this once . . . just one more time, to yield to that insistent mouth that was possessing hers . . . Her lips softened imperceptibly, and Stephen claimed his victory with the swiftness of the hunter, except gentleness was his weapon now.

Reality set in finally, and Stephen lifted his mouth from hers and dropped his arms. She stepped back, breathing hard; her entrancing smile was overbright. 'Thank you for the demonstration, my lord. I shall endeavor to grade you fairly when the time for comparison arrives.'

Stephen scarcely heard her, nor did he try to stop her when she whirled on her heel and left him standing there. Reaching out, he braced his hand against the window frame, staring blindly at the ordinary scene in front of his house. 'Son of a *bitch!*' he whispered savagely.

Careful to smile at each servant she passed so that they wouldn't know how she felt, Sherry walked up the stairs, her lips feeling swollen and bruised from the plundering kisses that had destroyed her and meant nothing to him.

She wanted to go home.

The phrase became a chant with every carefully paced step she took, until she finally gained the privacy of her own chamber. She curled into a protective ball on the bed, her knees drawn to her chest, her arms wrapped tightly around them, feeling as if she could splinter into a thousand pieces if she let go. Turning her face into the pillow to stifle her sobs, Sheridan wept for a future she couldn't have and a past she couldn't remember. '*I want to go home,*' she cried in a broken chant. 'I want to go home. Papa,' she wept, 'why are you taking so long to come for me?'

26

A beautiful spotted horse was grazing nearby, and in a fit of exuberance, Sherry got up and jumped onto its back, and they rode off in the moonlight, her laughter echoing on the wind. The horse and she were flying . . . flying. . . 'You'll break your neck, *cara!*' the younger man called, and he was in hot pursuit, his horse's hooves pounding closer and closer, and they were both laughing and flying across the meadow . . .

'*Miss Lancaster!*' Another voice, a female voice was calling from a further distance. 'Miss Lancaster!' A hand touched her shoulder, shaking her lightly, and Sherry jolted back to harsh reality. 'I'm sorry to wake you, ma'am,' the maid said, 'but Her Grace is in the sewing room with the seamstresses, and she asked if you would join them there.'

Sherry wanted to wrap herself in the bedcovers like a cocoon and seek out her dream again, but how did one tell a duchess and her seamstresses to go away so one could dream, particularly when one was an unwanted fiancée of the duchess's son. Reluctantly, Sherry got up, washed her face, and followed the maid upstairs to a huge, sunny room.

The duchess who was waiting turned out to be the earl's sister-in-law, not his mother.

Refusing to disgrace herself further by revealing any of her emotions, Sherry gave her a scrupulously polite greeting that was neither cool nor warm.

If Whitney Westmoreland noticed anything different in Sherry's demeanor, she didn't show it, but then she was carried away with enthusiasm about seeing Sherry outfitted 'in all the latest fashion.'

With Whitney Westmoreland smiling and chatting about balls and routs and Venetian breakfasts, and seamstresses buzzing around her like gnats, Sherry stood for what seemed an eternity on a raised platform in a huge sunny room, being measured, pinned, pushed, tugged, and turned. This time, she was not gullible enough to believe Whitney's warm smile and encouraging comments were sincere. She simply wanted Sherry off their hands, engaged to someone else, and obviously a wardrobe was the first step toward that goal. Sherry understood that, but she had plans of her own. She was going back home, wherever home was, and she couldn't possibly get there fast enough to suit herself. She intended to reassure the duchess of that as soon as this absurd fuss over clothing was over, but when the seamstresses finally let her step off the platform and pull on a dressing robe, they didn't leave. Instead, they began opening trunks and swirling bolts of fabrics over furniture, window seats, and carpet, until the entire room was a riot of colors in every imaginable shade, from emerald green to sapphire blue and sunny yellows, down to the palest pinks and shades of cream.

'What do you think?' Whitney asked her.

Sherry looked around at the dizzying array of sumptuous silks and soft batistes, of gossamer chiffon and delicate lawn. Jaunty striped fabrics were scattered among silks that were richly embellished with gold and silver and bolts of batiste heavily embroidered with flowers of every color and type. Whitney Westmoreland was smiling, waiting for Sherry to express her pleasure or her preferences. What did she think? Sherry wondered a little hysterically. Putting up her chin, she looked at the woman named Madame LaSalle who spoke with a French accent and behaved like a general, and she stated her preference, though she didn't know where it came from. 'Do you have anything in red?'

'Red!' the woman gasped, her eyes popping. 'Red! No, no, no, mademoiselle. Not with your hair.'

'I like red,' Sheridan persisted stubbornly.

'Then you must have it,' she said, recovering her diplomatic self, but not yielding a bit artistically. 'You must use it to upholster furniture or hang at the windows, but it is not a color that can be worn on your lovely self, mademoiselle. Heaven has already blessed you with hair of the rarest red, and so it would be wrong, sinful, to wear anything that would not flatter your special gift.'

That flowery speech was so absurd that Sherry bit back a wan smile and saw the duchess struggling to keep her own countenance straight. Momentarily forgetting that Whitney Westmoreland might pretend to be her friend, but was nothing of the sort, she said, 'I think that means it would look dreadful on me.'

'*Oui*,' said Madame with great feeling.

'And that there is nothing on earth that would compel her to make me a red gown, no matter how much I insisted,' Sherry added.

The duchess returned Sherry's laughing look and said, 'Madame would sooner throw herself into the Thames.'

'*Oui!*' all of the seamstresses chorused, and for a few moments the room was filled with the convivial laughter of eight women with a common goal.

For the next several hours, Sherry stood mostly aside while the duchess and Madame talked endlessly about the correct styles and fabrics to be used. Just when she thought it was all settled, they began to discuss embellishments, and there was more talk about bows and laces and satin edging. When she finally realized the seamstresses were actually going to remain at the house, working day and night in this room, Sherry firmly interceded. 'I have five gowns already – one for every day for nearly a week.'

Conversations dropped off and gazes swivelled to her. 'I'm very much afraid,' the duchess said with a smile, 'that you will be changing gowns five times a day.'

Sherry frowned at the amount of time that must take, but she held her silence until they left the sewing room. Planning to retreat back into the solitude of her room after she told the duchess she had no intention of marrying into the family, she headed in that direction with the duchess by her side. 'I really cannot change gowns five times a day,' Sherry began. 'They will all be wasted—'

'No they will not,' Whitney said with a confident smile that was not returned. Wondering worriedly why Sherry Lancaster seemed reserved and distant today, she said, 'During the Season, a well-dressed lady needs carriage dresses, walking dresses, riding habits, dinner dresses, evening gowns, and morning dresses. And those are only the barest necessities. Stephen Westmoreland's fiancée will be expected to have opera dresses, theatre dresses—'

'I am not his fiancée, nor have I any desire to be,' Sherry interrupted implacably, as she stood with her hand on the handle of the door to her bedchamber. 'I've tried to make it clear all day and in every way possible that I do not need or want all that clothing. Unless you will let my father repay you for it, I ask you to cancel everything. And now, if you will excuse me—'

'What do you mean you aren't his fiancée?' Whitney said, and in her alarm, she laid her hand on the other woman's arm. 'What has happened?' A laundress padded down the hall with an armload of linen, and

Whitney said, 'Could we talk in your bedchamber?'

'I do not wish to be rude, your grace, but there is nothing to talk about,' Sherry said very firmly, proud that her voice didn't waver in the least, and that there was nothing plaintive in the way she was speaking to the other woman.

To her surprise, the duchess did not stiffen in affront. 'I disagree,' she said with a stubborn smile and reached forward to nudge the door open. 'I think there is a great deal to talk about.'

Fully expecting some sort of deserved reprimand for her discourtesy or ingratitude, Sherry walked into the bedchamber, followed by the duchess. Refusing to cower or apologize, she turned around and waited in silence for whatever was to come.

In the space of seconds, Whitney considered Sherry's denial of her betrothal, noted the total absence of her normal, unaffected warmth, and correctly assumed her current attitude of proud indifference was a facade to conceal some sort of deep hurt. Since Stephen was the only one who had the power to truly hurt her, that meant he was the likely cause of the problem.

Prepared to go to great lengths to undo whatever damage her idiot brother-in-law had done to the one woman who was surely meant for him, Whitney said cautiously, 'What has happened to make you say you aren't betrothed to Stephen and don't wish to be?'

'Please!' Sherry said with more emotion than she wanted to show. 'I do not know who I am or where I was born, but I do know that there is something inside of me that cries out against the deceit and pretense I've been told. I'll surely begin to scream if I have to endure more of it right now. There's no need, no purpose, in your pretending to want me as a sister-in-law, so please do not!'

'Very well,' the duchess said without rancor, 'we shall put an end to pretense.'

'Thank you.'

'You have no idea just how badly I hope to have you as a sister-in-law.'

' And I suppose you are now going to try to convince me that Lord Westmoreland is as eager a bridegroom as there ever was.'

'I couldn't even say that with a straight face,' the duchess admitted cheerfully, 'let alone be convincing.'

'What?' Sherry uttered in blank astonishment.

'Stephen Westmoreland has the liveliest reservations about marrying anyone, *especially* you. And for some very good reasons.'

Sherry's shoulders shook with helpless laughter. 'I think you are all quite mad.'

'I cannot blame you for thinking that,' Whitney said with a gusty sigh. 'Now, if you would like to sit down, I shall tell you what I can about the Earl of Langford. But first, I have to ask you what he told you this morning that has made you think he does not desire to marry you.'

The offer of information about a man who was a total mystery to her was nearly irresistible, but Sherry wasn't certain why the offer was being made or if she should accept it. 'Why do you wish to become involved in all this?'

'I wish to become involved because I like you *very* much. And because I'd like you to like me also. But most of all, because I truly believe you are perfect for Stephen and I'm desperately afraid this set of circumstances may keep you both from finding that out until it is too late to undo the damage. Now, please tell me what happened, and then I'll tell you what I can.' For the second time, Whitney carefully avoided saying she would tell her everything. The phrase she'd used was misleading, but at least it was not another lie.

Sherry hesitated, searching Whitney's face for some sign of malice and saw only earnestness and concern. 'I suppose it can't do any harm – except to my pride,' she said with a weak attempt at a smile. In a relatively unemotional voice, she managed to recount what had happened that morning in the earl's study.

Whitney was impressed by the simplicity and cleverness of Stephen's chosen method to enlist Sherry's cooperation, and she was equally impressed that a naive girl, who was in a strange land, surrounded by strangers, and with not even a memory of her past, could have seen right through his smoothly worded ploy. Moreover Sherry had evidently been wise enough and proud enough not to voice a single objection to it. Which, Whitney decided with an inner smile, probably accounted for Stephen's black scowl earlier, when she bade him good day before coming upstairs. 'Is that everything?'

'Not exactly,' Sherry said angrily, looking away in embarrassment.

'What else happened?'

'After he gave me all that fustian about wanting me to have choices, I was so angry and confused that I – I felt a little overemotional.'

'Had I been in your place, I'd have felt for a heavy, blunt object to hit him with!'

'Unfortunately,' Sherry said with a shaky laugh, 'I didn't see anything suitable to use, and I felt this – this stupid urge to cry, so I walked over to a window to try to compose myself.'

'And then?' Whitney prodded.

'And then he had the audacity, the arrogance, the – the gall to try to kiss me!'

'Did you allow it?'

'No. Not willingly.' That wasn't entirely true, and she looked away again in helpless misery. 'I wasn't willing, *at first,*' she amended. 'But you see, he's very good at it, and—' She broke off as a realization hit her, and she said it aloud, her expression turning ferocious: 'He's very good at it, and he *knows* it! That is why he insisted on kissing me, as if that would make everything all right again. And in a way he won, because in the end

I gave in. Oh, he must be very *proud* of himself,' she finished with withering scorn.

Whitney burst out laughing. 'I very much doubt that. In fact, he was in the foulest mood imaginable when I arrived. For a man who wishes to break a betrothal, and has every reason to believe he's well on the way to accomplishing it, he is *not* in an exultant frame of mind.'

Somewhat cheered by that, Sherry smiled; then her smile faded and she shook her head. 'I do not understand any of this. Perhaps, even when I am in full possession of all my faculties, I am somewhat lacking in understanding.'

'I think you are amazingly perceptive!' Whitney said with feeling, 'and brave. And very, very warmhearted too.' She watched uncertainty flicker in expressive gray eyes, and Whitney wanted desperately to trust Charise Lancaster with the entire truth, every bit of it, beginning with Burleton's death and Stephen's part in it. As Stephen had pointed out, Sherry had scarcely known Burleton. Moreover, it was very clear that she had strong feelings for Stephen.

On the other hand, Dr Whitticomb had emphasized the real danger of upsetting her too much, and Whitney was terribly afraid the news of Burleton's death and Stephen's part in it might do just that.

She settled for telling her everything but that, and, returning the other girl's level gaze, she said with a sad smile, 'I am going to tell you a story about a very special man, whom you may not at first recognize. When I met him, four years ago, he was vastly admired for his tremendous charm and delightful manners. Men respected his skill at gaming and sports, and he was so handsome that women actually stared at him. His mother and I used to go into whoops over the effect he had on them, and not merely innocent young girls in their first Season, but sophisticated flirts, as well. I know he thought their reaction to his face was excessively silly, but he was unfailingly gallant to all of them. And then three things happened that changed him drastically – and the odd part is that two of them were good things: First, Stephen decided to take more of a personal interest in his business affairs and investments, which my husband had been handling along with ours. Stephen immediately began taking daring chances on large, risky ventures that my husband would never have considered – not with someone else's money. Time after time Stephen took enormous risks, and time after time, they paid off in enormous profits. And while all that was happening, so did something else that eventually contributed to his change from friendly gallantry to cold cynicism: Stephen inherited three titles from an elderly cousin of his father's, one of them the Earl of Langford. Normally, titles pass to the eldest son, except in certain instances, and this was one of them. Some of the titles held by the Westmoreland family date back over three hundred years, to King Henry VII. Among them are three titles granted by him that, at the request of the first Duke of Claymore, contain recorded exceptions to the normal line of descent. The exceptions allowed the holder of the title, if childless, to designate his own heir, so long as the heir was a direct descendant of one of the dukes of Claymore.

'The titles Stephen inherited were old and prestigious, but the land and income that went with them were insignificant. However – and here is where everything began to go "wrong," as it were – Stephen was already doubling and redoubling his own wealth. He loves architecture and studied it at university, so he bought fifty thousand of the most beautiful rolling acres imaginable and began working on a design for a house that would serve as his primary seat. While that house was under construction, he bought three lovely old estates in different parts of England, and began restoration on them as well. So there you have the whole picture – a man who was already wealthy, handsome, and from one of the most important families in England, and who, quite suddenly, acquired three titles, amassed a very large fortune, and bought four splendid estates. Can't you guess what happened next?'

'I presume he moved into one of his new homes.'

Whitney gaped at her in laughing delight, pleased at her straightforward outlook and lack of guile. 'He did do that,' she said after a moment, 'but that's not to the point.'

'I don't understand.'

'What happened was that a thousand families who would settle for nothing less than a titled husband for their daughters – and daughters who expected nothing less than that for themselves – suddenly added Stephen Westmoreland to their lists of desirable husbands. To the very *top* of their lists, in fact. Stephen's desirability and popularity exploded so quickly and so – so *noticeably* – that it was rather appalling to see. Because he was nearly thirty at the time, it was believed he would have to wed very soon, and that added a degree of desperation and urgency to the chase. Entire families descended on him if he walked into a room, daughters were thrust in his way – subtly of course – no matter where he went.

'Most men with titles and fortunes are born to them, as my husband was, and they learn to accept and ignore all that, though my husband admitted to me there were many times he felt like a hunted hare. In Stephen's case, it all seemed to happen overnight. If it had been otherwise, if the change hadn't been so sudden and drastic, Stephen might have adjusted to it with more patience, or at least more tolerance. And I think he still would have done so if he hadn't also become involved with Emily Kendall.'

Sherry felt her stomach clench at the mention of a woman he'd been 'involved' with, and at the same time she was helpless to control her curiosity. 'What happened?' she asked when Whitney hesitated.

'Before I tell you, you will have to give me your pledge never to breathe a word of this to anyone.'

Sheridan nodded.

Whitney got up and restlessly wandered over to the windows, then she turned and leaned back against the pane, her hands behind her back, her face somber. 'Stephen met Emily two years before he inherited his titles. She was the most beautiful woman I've ever seen, and one of the wittiest and most amusing . . . and haughty. I thought her haughty. In any case, half the bachelors in England were mad about her, and Stephen was one of them, though he was clever enough not to let her see it. She had the most amazing way of bringing men to their knees, but Stephen wouldn't bend to her, and I suppose that was part of his appeal – the challenge. In what I can only think of as a moment of madness, Stephen asked her to marry him. She was stunned.'

'Because he loved her?' Sherry asked.

'Because he was so dreadful as to *ask* her.'

'What?'

'According to my husband, who had the story directly from Stephen, Emily's primary reaction was shock and then anguish that he'd put her in such an untenable position. She was – is – the daughter of a duke, and it seemed that her family would not countenance a marriage to a mere mister. She was to be married in a fortnight to William Lathrop, the Marquess of Glengarmon, an old man whose father's estate marched beside Emily's father's. No-one knew about the betrothal as yet because it had just been finalized. Emily burst into tears and told Stephen that, before he'd asked her to marry him, she had at least been able to resign herself to marrying Lord Lathrop, but that now, her life was going to be unbearable. Stephen was furious that she was to be "wasted" on a pathetic old man, but she convinced him there was no point in trying to reason with her father – which he actually wanted to do, even though he knew perfectly well that it is a daughter's duty to marry wherever her family wills.'

She paused and gave Sherry an abashed smile and added, 'I did not necessarily agree with that when *my* father claimed the right to choose a husband for me.' Returning to the story, she continued, 'In any case, when Stephen still insisted on talking to her father, Emily told him he would beat her if he knew she'd complained to Stephen about her fate or her feelings about Lord Lathrop.'

'And so they parted?' Sherry ventured when Whitney seemed to hesitate.

'I only wish they had! Instead, Emily convinced him that the only way she could endure her fate, now that she knew he loved her, was if they continued their . . . friendship . . . after she was married.' Sherry frowned because it was difficult to hear about how much he had loved another. Whitney mistook her frown for disapproval and hastened to defend the indefensible, partly out of loyalty to Stephen and partly so that Sherry wouldn't condemn him out of hand. Unfortunately, within moments she found herself on shaky ground as she tried to impart information while obscuring its full meaning. 'It's not that unusual or even scandalous. Amongst the *ton*, there are many females who desire the . . . *attention* . . . and the . . . *companionship* of an attractive man whom they know . . . ah . . . *think* . . . would be very . . . *entertaining* in . . . er . . . a-variety-of-ways,' Whitney finished breathlessly. 'It's all very discreet, of course.'

'You mean they must be sly about their friendship?'

'I suppose you could say that,' Whitney said, as it dawned on her that Sherry was blissfully unaware that Stephen had been much more than Emily's 'friend' during her marriage, and that they were not discussing friendships at all. In retrospect, Whitney realized she should have expected that. Well-bred English girls often had no clear idea of what couples did in the bedchamber, but they usually had overheard the gossip of older sisters and other married females. By the time they were Sherry's age, they at least suspected that something more than friendly handshakes occurred.

'What happens if the truth is discovered?'

Having gotten by this far by telling truth with impunity, Whitney stuck to the same practice with the rest of her questions. 'Then the husband is usually displeased, particularly if there has been cause for gossip.'

'And if he is displeased, does he insist that his wife restrict herself to female companions?'

'Yes, but he occasionally has a discussion with the gentleman as well.'

'What sort of discussion?'

'The sort that takes place at dawn at twenty paces.'

'A duel?' Sherry exclaimed, thinking that seemed like a severe overreaction to what had merely been, at worst, too close a friendship between opposite sexes to be seemly.

'A duel,' Whitney confirmed.

'And did Lord Westmoreland agree to continue being Emily Kendall's—' She paused, discarding the word 'suitor' because it sounded ridiculous if the lady was already married, '—her close friend,' she improvised, since that was correct, 'even after she was married?'

'Yes, for over a year, until her husband found out about it.'

Sherry drew in a long breath, half afraid to ask. 'Was there a duel?'

'Yes.'

Since Lord Westmoreland was still very much alive, Sherry assumed Lord Lathrop was very much dead. 'He killed him,' she said flatly.

'No, he didn't, though it might well have come to that. I think Stephen may have intended that it should. He was desperately in love with Emily, and loyal to her to the point of blindness. He despised Lord Lathrop. He hated him for ever offering for Emily in the first place, for being a disgusting old roué who'd stolen her youth and life, and for being too old to give her children. The morning of the duel, Stephen mentioned some of those opinions to him, though I'm certain he expressed himself more eloquently.'

'And then what happened?'

'The old marquess nearly died, but of shock, not from a pistol shot. It seems that Emily and her father, not he, had sought the marriage. Our Emily wanted to be a duchess, which she would have become when Lathrop's ancient father died and Lathrop inherited his father's title. On the morning of the duel, Stephen believed Lord Lathrop. He said no man alive could have feigned such a stunned reaction to Stephen's accusations. Besides, Lathrop had no reason to lie.'

'Did they still duel?'

'Yes and no. Stephen deloped, which amounts to an apology. In doing that he gave the elderly man the satisfaction he was entitled to have from him. Emily's father sent her to Spain within the week, and she stayed there for over a year, until after Lord Lathrop died. She came home a "new woman" – more beautiful than before, but also more serene and less haughty.' Whitney had intended to end the story there and explain the point she'd been trying to make with it, but Sherry's question obliged her to finish. 'Did they ever see each other again?'

'Yes, and by that time Stephen had inherited his title. Oddly enough – or perhaps not oddly at all, considering the timing – it was Emily's father who went to see Stephen first. He told Stephen that Emily was in love with him, and always had been, which, in her own selfish way, I believe she was. He asked Stephen to at least talk to her.

'Stephen agreed, and I'm quite sure her father left in happy expectation that everything would be all right and that his daughter was going to be the Countess of Langford. Emily came to see Stephen the following week, and she confessed to everything, from her selfishness to her deceit. She begged his forgiveness and pleaded with him to give her a chance to prove that she truly loved him, to show him that she'd changed.

'Stephen told her he would think about it. The very next day, her father paid a "casual social call" on Stephen and brought up the subject of a betrothal contract. Stephen volunteered to have something drawn up, and her father left believing Stephen was the most forgiving and generous of men.'

'He was going to marry her after what she'd done?' Sherry burst out in disbelief. 'I cannot believe he would! He must have been quite out of his head.' The words were out before Sherry realized that the emotion she felt was as much jealousy as righteous indignation. 'Then what happened?' she asked more calmly.

'Emily and her father came to see him, as they'd arranged to do, but the paper that Stephen handed them was not a betrothal contract.'

'What was it?'

'It was a list of suggested second husbands for her. Every man on it had a title, and every man was between the ages of sixty and ninety-two. It was not merely an intentional insult to both of them; it was doubly cutting because he'd deliberately let Emily believe she was going to be given a betrothal contract.'

Sherry digested all that for a moment. 'He isn't very forgiving, is he? Particularly when you said earlier that it is not at all unusual for married ladies to do what she did.'

'Stephen could not forgive her for wanting to marry Lathrop in the first place, not when she did it for his title. He could not forgive her for lying to him. But most of all, he could not forgive her for letting him nearly kill her husband in a duel.

'If you consider all I've told you, I think you will begin to understand why he mistrusts his own judgment of women and why he mistrusts their motives. Perhaps you'll even find that his desire to have you meet other gentlemen, before you decide permanently on him, isn't so very wrong or even cruel. I am not saying he was right,' Whitney added when her conscience issued another irate protest. 'I don't know that he is, and what I think doesn't matter in any case. I am only asking – suggesting – that you listen to your heart and decide for yourself, based on the new information I've given you. And there is one more thing I can tell you that may help you to decide.'

'What is it?'

'Neither my husband nor I have ever seen Stephen look at any woman quite the way he looks at you, not with the same degree of gentleness and warmth and humor.' Having done and said everything she could think of to help matters, Whitney walked over to the sofa to collect her things, and Sherry stood up.

'You've been very kind, Your Grace,' Sherry said with soft sincerity.

'Please call me Whitney,' the duchess said as she picked up her reticule, and with a sidewise smile, she added, 'and do *not* call me "kind," for then I will have to confess the truth, which is that I also have a selfish reason for wanting you in the family.'

'What selfish reason is that?'

Turning fully toward her, the duchess said with soft candor, 'I think you are my best chance of ever having a sister, and probably my only chance of having one with whom I could be completely delighted.'

In a world where everything and everyone seemed unfamiliar and suspicious, the words she'd said and the soft smile that accompanied them had a profound effect on Sherry. As they smiled at each other, Sherry reached out to shake the duchess's hand and the duchess reached forward to meet it, and somehow the polite handshake became a tight squeeze of encouragement that lasted an extra moment longer than it needed to. And then it became a hug. Sherry had no idea who made the first move, but she did not think it was she, and it didn't matter. They both stepped back from it, smiling a little sheepishly at such an unseemly display between two virtual strangers who should have been calling each other 'Miss Lancaster' and 'your grace' for at least another year of acquaintance. None of that mattered because it was too late to go back. The bond had already been felt and acknowledged and accepted. The duchess stood quietly for a moment, a tiny, amused smile at the corner of her lips, and she shook her head as if pleased and puzzled. 'I like you so much,' she said simply, and then she was gone in a swirl of fashionable cherry skirts.

A moment after the door closed, it opened again and she put her head inside, still smiling. 'By the by,' she whispered, 'Stephen's mother likes you too. And we'll see you at supper.'

'Oh, that's lovely.'

Whitney nodded and said with another irrepressible smile, 'I'm on my way downstairs to convince Stephen it's his idea.'

And then she was gone.

Sherry wandered over to the windows that overlooked Upper Brook Street. Crossing her arms, she gazed absently at the fashionably dressed men and women alighting from carriages and strolling down the street, enjoying the balmy afternoon.

She thought about everything she'd heard, turned it over and over in her mind, and the earl took on new dimensions. She could imagine how it would feel to be wanted for what he had and not for what he was. The fact that he didn't appreciate that sort of attention, that sort of fawning and pretense, proved that he was not a boastful or prideful man.

The fact that he had not abandoned his friendship with the woman he'd loved, even after she was lost to him, was irrefutable proof that he was steadfast and loyal. And the fact that he'd been prepared to risk his life in a duel . . . that was downright noble.

In return Emily Lathrop had deceived and used and betrayed him. In view of that it was little wonder he wanted to be very, very certain he did not make a second mistake when he chose a wife.

Idly rubbing her hands over her elbows, Sherry watched a carriage with a high perch tear down the street, scattering pedestrians, while she contemplated the vengence he had enacted on the woman he had once obviously loved.

He was not boastful or prideful . . .

He was not forgiving either.

She turned away from the window and wandered over to her desk, idly turning the pages of the morning newspaper trying to distract herself from another truth: she had not learned one thing today, or any other day, that would indicate he had any feelings for her at all.

He liked to kiss her, but somewhere in her darkened memory, Sherry had the feeling that that did not necessarily signify love. He liked her company, sometimes. And he liked to laugh with her, always. She could sense that.

She so much wished her memory would return, because all the answers she needed would be there.

Restlessly, she bent down and picked a scrap of paper from the carpet, trying to decide how to behave to him from this point on. Pride demanded that she seem unaffected by his crushing announcement downstairs. Her instincts demanded that she not give him a second opportunity to hurt her again.

She would act as naturally as she could, she decided, but she would be just reserved enough to warn him to keep his distance.

And she would find some way to stop remembering how his hands slid up and down her spine and across her shoulders when he kissed her . . . or how his fingers sank into her hair, holding her mouth pressed so tightly to his that it was as if he couldn't get enough of it. She would not think about the insistent hunger of those kisses, or the way his arms felt around her. And under no circumstances would she let herself dwell again on the way he smiled. . . that lazy, dazzling smile that swept slowly across his tanned face and made her heart stop . . . or the way his dark blue eyes crinkled at the corners when he smiled . . .

Thoroughly disgusted with herself for doing precisely what she was telling herself she would not do, Sherry sat down at her desk and concentrated all her attention on the newspaper.

HE HAD LOVED EMILY LATHROP.

Frustrated, Sherry closed her eyes tightly as if she could shut him out of her mind. But she couldn't. He had loved Emily Lathrop to distraction and though she knew it was foolish, the knowledge hurt terribly, because she loved him.

27

Sheridan was still reeling from her realization when she was summoned to join Dr Whitticomb and her future 'duenna.'

Longing for more time to think about all she'd learned that day and depressed at the prospect of living under the icy eye of some vigilant Englishwoman, Sherry reported to the drawing room, where Dr Whitticomb was hovering near an elderly lady seated upon the sofa. Instead of the grim-faced English Amazon Sherry had imagined, her chaperone looked more like a tiny, plump china doll with pink cheeks and silver hair tucked neatly under a frilled white cap.

She was dozing at the moment, her chin resting against her chest.

'This is Miss Charity Thornton,' Dr Whitticomb whispered to Sherry when she was standing beside him, '—the Duke of Stanhope's maiden sister.'

Swallowing an astonished chuckle at the absurdity of

this diminutive, sleeping person being in charge of her, Sherry lowered her own voice to a whisper, and politely replied, 'It is very good of her to come here to look after me.'

'Oh, she was thrilled to be asked.'

'Yes,' Sherry joked helplessly, watching the gentle rise and fall of the elderly lady's bosom, 'I can see that she is *very* excited.'

Off to the left, out of Sherry's line of vision, Stephen leaned against a carved satinwood table, observing the meeting, and he smiled at her quip.

'Her younger sister, Hortense, wanted to accompany her,' Dr Whitticomb confided in his hushed voice, 'but they bicker incessantly about everything, including their ages, and I didn't want to see your peace cut up.'

'How old is her sister?'

'Eight and sixty.'

'I see.' Biting her trembling lower lip in an effort to hide her mirth, Sherry whispered, 'Do you think we should awaken her?'

From his corner of the room, Stephen joined the conversation in a normal tone of voice. 'Either that,' he joked, 'or we can bury her where she sits.'

Sherry stiffened in shock at the discovery of his presence, but Miss Charity jolted awake as if someone had fired off a cannon in her ear. 'Goodness, Hugh!' she exclaimed severely. 'Why didn't you awaken me?' She looked at Sherry and held out her hand, smiling. 'I am so very pleased to come to your assistance, my dear. Dr Whitticomb told me you're recovering from an injury, and that you're in need of a chaperone of unimpeachable reputation while you stay here with Langford.' Her smooth brow furrowed in bewilderment. 'I can't quite remember what sort of injury it was, however.'

'A head injury,' Sherry provided helpfully.

'Yes, that was it.' Her bright blue gaze darted to Sherry's head for a moment. 'It looks as if it has healed.'

Dr Whitticomb intervened. 'The injury has healed,'

he reminded her. 'But there is still a troublesome aftereffect. Miss Lancaster has not yet recovered her memory.'

Miss Charity's face fell. 'My poor child. Do you know who you are?'

'Yes.'

'Do you know who I am?'

'Yes, ma'am.'

'Who am I?'

Perilously close to a fit of giggles, Sherry looked aside, struggling for composure, and inadvertently encountered the earl's grin and sympathetic wink. Deciding it was best to ignore his friendly overture until she had more time to sort out her own feelings, she jerked her gaze back to her chaperone, and dutifully answered the question she assumed had been put to her as a test. 'You are Miss Charity Thornton, the Duke of Stanhope's sister.'

'That is what I thought!' the elderly lady exclaimed with relief.

'I t-think I'll ring for t-tea!' Sherry said, already fleeing from the room, her hand clamped over her mouth, her shoulders rocking with helpless laughter.

Behind her, Miss Charity said sadly, 'Such a beautiful child, but if that was a stammer I just heard, we're going to have a time of it, trying to make a good match for her.'

Hugh gave her shoulder a reassuring squeeze. 'You're just the one to do it, though, Charity.'

'I shall show her just how to go about in Society,' Charity was saying when Sherry returned. Now that the elderly lady was fully awake, she seemed remarkably more alert and lucid, and she beamed brightly at Sherry as she patted the seat beside her on the sofa, in a clear invitation to sit down. 'We are going to have a lovely time,' she promised as Sherry complied with the invitation. 'We will attend soirées, levees, and balls, and we'll shop in Bond Street and drive in Hyde Park and along Pall Mall. Oh, and you *must* attend a ball at Almack's Assembly Rooms at once. Do you know about Almack's?'

'No, ma'am. I'm afraid not,' Sherry replied, wondering how her chaperone could possibly keep up such a pace.

'You will love it,' said Charity, clasping her hands in prayerful ecstasy. 'It is "The Seventh Heaven of the Fashionable World," and more important than a presentation at court. The balls take place on Wednesday evenings, and they are so exclusive that once the patronesses have given you a voucher of entry, you are virtually assured of acceptance at all the *ton* functions. The earl will escort you the first time, which will make you the envy of all the females and an object of special interest to all the males who are present. Almack's is just the place for you to make your first appearance in Society—' She broke off and looked worriedly at the earl. 'Langford, does she have vouchers for Almack's?'

'I'm afraid I never gave Almack's a thought,' Stephen replied, turning away in order to hide the revulsion that he felt for the place.

'I shall speak to your mama about the vouchers. It will take all of her influence to pull it off, but she will be able to prevail on the patronesses.' Her blue eyes riveted disapprovingly on the earl's finely tailored claret jacket and trousers, and she warned in alarmed tones, 'You will not be admitted to Almack's if you are not properly attired, Langford.'

'I will warn my valet of the dire social consequences should he fail to turn me out appropriately,' Stephen promised, straightfaced.

'Tell him you must wear a formal black coat with long tails,' she emphasized, still doubting the competence of the excellent Damson.

'I'll relay that information verbatim.'

'And a formal white waistcoat, of course.'

'Of course.'

'And a white neckcloth.'

'Naturally,' he replied in a tone of perfect gravity, inclining his head in a little bow.

Satisfied that he was duly forewarned, Miss Charity turned to Sherry and confided, 'The patronesses once turned back the Duke of Wellington himself when *he* appeared at Almack's in those dreadful trousers men wear nowadays, instead of formal knee breeches.' In a lightning switch of topic, she said, 'You do know how to dance, do you not?'

'I—' Sherry hesitated and shook her head. 'I'm not certain.'

'We must find you a dancing instructor then at once. You will need to learn the minuet, country dances, cotillions, and the waltz. But you must not dance the waltz anywhere until after the patronesses at Almack's have approved you for it.' In a dire voice, she warned, 'Were you to do it, it would be worse than if Langford weren't appropriately attired, for he would not be admitted, so no-one would know, while you would be thought "fast" and therefore disgraced. Langford will lead you onto the floor for the first dance, then he may dance one more dance with you, but no more. Even two dances could be construed as singling you out for *particular* attention, which is the last thing we would wish to happen. Langford,' she said, startling Stephen out of his study of Sherry's flawless profile, 'are you attending all this?'

'I am hanging on every word,' Stephen replied. 'However, I believe Nicholas DuVille will wish the honor of escorting Miss Lancaster to the assembly and onto the floor for her first dance.' Leaning imperceptibly to the side to get a better look at Sherry's reaction to his last announcement and his next one, he added, 'I have another engagement next Wednesday and will have to content myself with a later place on her dance card for that evening.' Her expression didn't change. She was looking at her hands in her lap, and he had the impression she was mortified by all this discussion of attracting suitors.

'The doors close at eleven sharp, and the Lord himself wouldn't be admitted after that,' Miss Charity warned, and while Stephen was marvelling at her ability to remember some things and forget others, she said, 'DuVille? Is that the same young man who once had a tendre for your sister-in-law?'

'I believe,' Stephen evaded cautiously, 'that he is now quite taken with Miss Lancaster.'

'Excellent! Next to you, he is the best catch in England.'

'He will be ecstatic to know that,' Stephen replied, mentally applauding his sudden and inspired decision to force DuVille to escort Sherry to Almack's hours before Stephen had to arrive. It was delightful vengeance just to envision the suave Frenchman surrounded like a trapped hare by a roomful of eager debutantes and their avaricious mothers who would look DuVille over like a choice meal, calculating his financial worth and wishing he had a title to go with it. Stephen hadn't set foot in 'The Marriage Mart' in over a decade, but he remembered it well: The gambling available in the anteroom was for stakes so low it was absurd, and the food was as boring as the gaming – weak tea, warm lemonade, tasteless cakes, orgeat, and bread and butter. Once DuVille had his two dances with Sherry, the rest of the evening would be sheer, undiluted purgatory for him.

Stephen, however, intended to escort Sherry to the opera himself the next night. She liked music – he knew that from the night he found her singing with the servants' chorus – so she would surely enjoy *Don Giovanni*.

Arms folded over his chest, he watched Charity Thornton lecturing Sherry. When he first walked in to meet the new duenna, he'd taken one look at Charity Thornton and wondered if Whitticomb had lost his mind. But as he listened to her happy chatter, he decided the physician had actually made an excellent choice that would suit everyone, including Stephen, perfectly. When she wasn't dozing, or pausing to remember something that suddenly evaded her, she was cheerful company. If anything, she amused Sherry, rather than intimidating or flustering her. He was thinking about all that when he realized the woman was talking about Sherry's hair.

'Red is not at all the thing, you know, but once my excellent maid has cut it off and styled it, you won't *see* so very much of it.'

'Leave it!' Stephen rapped the order out before he could stop himself or temper his tone, and the other three occupants all gaped at him.

'But Langford,' Miss Charity protested, 'girls are wearing their hair short these days.'

Stephen knew he ought to stay out of it, knew it was not his place to interfere in an entirely feminine judgment about coiffeur, but the thought of Sherry's heavy mass of shiny hair lying in a molten heap on the floor was unthinkable. 'Do not cut her hair,' he said in a tone of icy command that sent most people scurrying for cover.

Inexplicably, his tone made Whitticomb smile.

It made Charity look chastened.

It made Sherry momentarily consider cutting her hair off at the nape.

28

Whitney smiled as she watched Sherry's new maid put the finishing touches on her coiffeur. Downstairs Nicki was waiting to accompany Sherry and Charity Thornton to Almack's for Sherry's first official London appearance. Stephen was to join them there later, and the foursome would then proceed to the Rutherfords' ball, where Whitney, Clayton, and the dowager duchess would lend their protection and influence to ensure that nothing went wrong during the Season's most important opening ball. 'Stephen was absolutely right when he implored you not to cut your hair.'

'He did not exactly implore me,' Sherry pointed out. 'He *forbade* it.'

'I have to agree with him,' Stephen's mother said. 'It would have been a crime to cut such extraordinary hair.'

Sherry gave her a helpless smile, unable to argue the point, partly out of courtesy, but mostly because in the three days since Lord Westmoreland had told her she was to consider other suitors, Sherry had become very fond of Whitney Westmoreland and the dowager. They'd been with her almost constantly, accompanying her on her sightseeing and shopping excursions, watching as she had her dancing instructions, and telling her amusing stories about people she was going to meet. In the evenings they dined as a group with the earl and his brother.

Yesterday, Whitney had brought her three-year-old son, Noel, to the earl's house, where Sheridan was having a dancing lesson in the ballroom given by a humorless dancing master who should have been a military general. With little Noel in her lap, Whitney and the dowager duchess, who was seated beside her, had watched as Sheridan tried to master the steps of dances she seemed never to have done. When the dancing master's clipped orders began to embarrass her, Whitney had stood up and volunteered to dance with the dancing instructor so that Sherry could see how the steps were done. Sherry had happily switched places with her and held Noel in her lap. In no time at all, the dowager duchess decided to show both Whitney and Sherry some of the dances that were done in *her* day, and by the end of that session all three women were convulsed with laughter over the dancing master's indignation when they began dancing with each other.

At supper that night, they regaled both men with hilarious descriptions of the lesson and the teacher. Sherry had dreaded that first supper with her reluctant fiancé, but the presence of the dowager, Whitney, and the duke served as a buffer and a distraction. Sherry was inclined to think that that was exactly their purpose in coming to supper. If that was their plan, it was certainly effective, because by the end of that first evening, Sherry was able to be in the earl's presence and to treat him with courtesy, but nothing more and nothing less. There were times when she had the gratifying feeling that it irritated him to have her treat him thus, times when she was laughing with his brother, that she caught the earl frowning, as if he were piqued about something. There were also times when Sherry felt as if Clayton Westmoreland was perfectly aware of his brother's unreliable disposition, and that for some reason the duke found it amusing. For her part, Sherry thought the Duke of Claymore was the kindest, most amiable, charming man she had ever met. She said as much to the earl the following morning when he surprised her by coming down early for breakfast. In hopes of avoiding him, she'd begun eating earlier and in the morning room, and so she'd been surprised when he wandered in as if he'd always dined there instead of in the grandeur of his dining room. She was equally surprised when her praise of his brother's disposition and character caused the earl's mood to take a sudden turn for the sarcastic as he said, 'I'm happy to know you have met your ideal of the perfect man.' He then had gotten up from the table, with his breakfast not finished, and with an excuse about having work to do, he had left Sherry sitting alone at the table staring after him in stupefaction. Last night after supper he'd gone to the theatre with a friend and the night before to another late function, and Hodgkin said he'd returned each night just before dawn.

Whitney and his mother had arrived shortly afterward and found her sitting at the table, wondering if lack of adequate sleep was making him cross. When she explained to both women about his ill humor and what had preceded it, Whitney and the duchess looked at each other and exclaimed in unison, 'He's jealous!' That possibility, though seemingly unlikely, had been intriguing enough that when Nicholas DuVille called for her in the afternoon to take her for a brief ride in the park, Sherry had made it a point to comment on *his* attributes as a cheerful and amiable companion in the drawing room before supper that night. The earl's reaction had been similar to his reaction that morning, though his words were different. 'You're certainly easy to please,' he said scornfully.

Since Whitney and the dowager had asked to be kept apprised of everything Stephen said and did, Sherry shared his comment with them the next morning, and they again chorused, 'He's jealous!'

Sherry wasn't certain if she was pleased or not. She only knew that she was afraid to believe he really cared for her, but a part of her was completely unable to stop hoping that he did.

She knew he was coming to Almack's tonight to single her out for attention because Charity Thornton thought that would assure Sherry's instant popularity. Sherry wasn't interested in popularity; she was only interested in not shaming herself or his family or him. She'd been nervous all afternoon about the evening to come, but Whitney had arrived unexpectedly to keep her company while she dressed for the evening, an activity that had taken so much time she was actually beginning to long to be on her way.

A seamstress stood off to the side, holding a spectacular gown that had been completed only minutes ago, and Sherry again glanced at the clock. 'I am keeping Monsieur DuVille waiting,' she said nervously.

'I am perfectly certain Nicholas expects to be kept

waiting,' Whitney said dryly, but it wasn't Nicholas DuVille Sherry was concerned about. Lord Westmoreland was downstairs, and she hoped to see if the final effect of all this preparation had any noticeable effect on the way he looked at her.

'All ready – no, don't look yet,' Whitney said, when Sherry started to turn to the mirror to see her new coiffeur. 'Wait until you have your gown on, so that you can see the full effect.' Smiling whimsically, she added, 'I was staying with my aunt and uncle in Paris when I was of an age to make my first appearance in Society. I had never seen myself done up in a real gown until the moment my aunt let me turn around and look in the mirror.'

'Really?' Sherry said, wondering how that could be true when from all she'd seen and read, wealthy English girls were turned out like princesses from the time they were quite little.

Whitney saw the question she was too polite to ask, and laughed. 'I was a "late bloomer."'

Sheridan found it impossible to imagine that the gorgeous brunette seated on the edge of the bed had ever known an awkward moment in her life, and she said so.

'Until shortly before that night in Paris, my two greatest ambitions were to master the use of a slingshot, and to force a local boy to fall madly in love with me. Which is why,' she finished with a confiding smile, 'I was sent off to France in the first place. No-one could think what else to do with me in order to stop me from disgracing myself.'

Sherry's joking reply was muffled as the maid and seamstress gently lowered the gown over her head. Behind her, the dowager duchess walked into the bedchamber. 'I was too eager to see how you looked to wait until we saw you at the Rutherfords,' she confided, standing back and watching the robing procedure.

'Is Monsieur DuVille annoyed because this is taking

so long?' Sherry asked, lowering her arms and obediently turning around so that her helpers could begin to fasten the tiny hooks at the back of her gown.

'Not in the least. He is having a glass of sherry with Stephen, and— Oh!' she breathed as Sherry turned around.

'Please do not tell me anything is wrong,' Sherry said. 'I refuse to endure one second more of primping.'

When Stephen's mother didn't seem able to speak, Sherry turned to Whitney, who was slowly standing up, a smile dawning across her face.

'I wish someone would say something,' Sherry said anxiously.

'Show Miss Lancaster how she looks,' Whitney said to the maid, already longing to see Stephen's reaction when he witnessed the transformation. 'No, wait – gloves first, and the fan.' To Sherry, she added, 'You must have the full effect when you see yourself, don't you agree?'

Sherry had no idea if she agreed. With an inexplicable combination of anticipation and grave foreboding, she drew on the long, ivory, elbow-length gloves, took the ivory and gold fan the maid held out to her, then she turned and slowly lifted her gaze to the full-length looking glass that the maids were holding.

Her lips parted in pleasure and disbelief at the gorgeously gowned woman looking back at her.

'I look . . . very nice!' she exclaimed.

Stephen's mother shook her head incredulously. 'That is an understatement.'

'A masterpiece of understatement,' Whitney agreed, so eager to see Stephen's reaction that she had to suppress the temptation to grab Sherry's hand and drag the younger woman downstairs to the salon, where she knew he would be waiting with Nicki and Miss Charity.

29

Originally, Stephen had been amused at the thought of forcing Nicholas DuVille to spend a large part of his evening at Almack's – and under the watchful eye of Charity Thornton, no less – but now that the moment for their departure was near, he was far less pleased with his joke. As he sat in the drawing room, listening to Miss Thornton and DuVille chatting while they waited for Sherry to come downstairs, Stephen noticed that the elderly peagoose seemed to hang on to DuVille's every word and to beam approvingly at him as he uttered each syllable – an attitude that struck Stephen not only as highly inappropriate in a chaperone but damned incomprehensible, considering that DuVille's reputation as a womanizer was legendary.

'Here they are now!' Charity Thornton said excitedly, tipping her head toward the hall and bolting to her feet with more enthusiasm and energy than she'd displayed all week. 'We shall have such a wonderful evening! Come along, Monsieur DuVille,' she said, gathering up her shawl and reticule.

Stephen followed them into the entry hall, where DuVille stopped to gaze at the staircase as if transfixed, an appreciative smile working its way across his face. Stephen followed the direction of his gaze, and what he saw filled him with bursting pride. Coming down the staircase, wrapped in a gold-spangled gown of ivory satin, was the same woman who'd dined with him in an overlarge peignoir and bare feet. Considering how delectable she'd looked that way, he should have expected her to be a sensation in a formal gown, but somehow he wasn't prepared for what he saw. Her hair was pulled back off her forehead and entwined with slender ropes of pearls at the crown, then it spilled over her shoulders in a tumble of molten waves and curls. She took his breath away.

She suspected it too, Stephen realized, because although she'd looked through him as if he were invisible for most of the last four days, she was finally looking at him . . . not for long of course. Only a fleeting glance to see his reaction, but he let her see it.

'Madam,' he said, 'I shall have to hire an army of chaperones after tonight.'

Until that moment, Sherry had almost managed to forget that his whole purpose for this expensive charade was to lure suitors so that he could hand her off to someone else, but his unhidden pleasure in the thought that she might attract considerable notice came as an agonizing reminder. It cut so deeply – coming in the precise moment when she had thought she actually looked nice, and hoped he might also – that she went numb inside. Extending her hand for his kiss, she said with quiet, but unmistakable, determination, 'I will endeavor to make *certain* you need to do *exactly* that.'

Inexplicably, that rejoinder made his dark brows snap together into a frown of displeasure. 'Don't "endeavor" too much; that is how reputations are made.'

30

'What was that all about, Damson?' Stephen glanced at his valet in the mirror as he deftly tied the last of a series of elaborate knots into his white neckcloth, then leaned forward and ran a hand over his jaw to check the closeness of his shave.

'Mr Hodgkin thought you ought to be given this letter before you left, in case it was important,' Damson said as he laid the tattered missive on the bed and went about the more pressing business of seeing that his lordship was properly turned out for an evening at Almack's. Removing a formal black coat with long tails from one of the wardrobes, he padded across the suite, shaking out nonexistent wrinkles from it. Holding up the coat, he waited while Stephen plunged his arms into the sleeves, then he smoothed his hands over the shoulders, adjusted the front, and stepped back to survey the excellent results of his care and attention.

'Did Hodgkin say who the letter was from?' Stephen asked, tugging his shirt cuffs into position and adjusting the sapphire studs at the cuff.

'Lord Burleton's former landlord had it sent round to you. It was directed to the baron at his old lodgings.'

Stephen nodded without much interest. He had settled Burleton's bill with his landlord and directed that gentleman to forward all of Burleton's mail to him. So far all the mail had been from establishments where Burleton had made purchases for which he had not paid. Having deprived Burleton of his life and the opportunity to clear his debts himself, Stephen felt honor-bound to do so in his behalf.

'Give it to my secretary,' Stephen said, in a hurry to be off. He'd promised to join his brother for a few leisurely hands of cards or rounds of faro at The Strathmore, and he was running late. After an hour or two of high-stakes gambling, he planned to put in his appearance at Almack's, and at the earliest possible opportunity, whisk her out of the 'Marriage Mart,' and then to Lord Rutherford's ball, which would be far more enjoyable for both of them. DuVille, he decided with amused satisfaction, could content himself with escorting Charity Thornton to the Rutherfords'.

'I suggested Mr Hodgkin give it to your secretary, my lord,' Damson replied, vigorously brushing away any invisible but offensive bits that might have decided to implant themselves somewhere on his lordship's immaculate person. 'But he was very insistent that you see it, lest it turn out to be news of import. It was posted from America.'

Thinking it was probably a charge for something Burleton had purchased while he was visiting there, Stephen reached for the letter and headed downstairs, opening it as he walked.

'McReedy is out front with the coach,' Colfax advised him, holding out his gloves, but Stephen neither heard nor saw him.

All his attention was riveted on the contents of the letter sent to Burleton by Charise Lancaster's father's solicitor.

Colfax noted his employer's deep preoccupation with the letter and his darkening expression and immediately worried that the letter's contents might somehow cause the earl to alter his plans for the evening. 'Miss Lancaster was certainly in her best looks when she left for Almack's – and very much anticipating her evening, if I may say so,' he pointedly remarked. It was the truth, but it was also Colfax's cautiously worded reminder, spoken out of fondness for the American girl, that the earl's appearance at Almack's in her behalf was vitally important.

Stephen slowly refolded the letter and stared past the butler, his thoughts clearly on something, something far removed from Almack's – and very dire. He left without a word, his strides long and purposeful, as he headed toward his waiting coach.

'I fear it was disagreeable news, Hodgkin,' Colfax said to the under-butler who was hovering worriedly at the edge of the hall. 'Very disagreeable indeed.' He hesitated, feeling it was beneath his dignity to conjecture, but his concern for the lovely American girl overrode even his abiding concern for his dignity. 'The missive was addressed to Lord Burleton . . . perhaps it pertained only to him, and had naught to do with Miss Lancaster.'

31

Situated in St James's Square behind a dark green canopy that stretched from the front door to the street, The Strathmore catered to a relatively small, highly select group of the nobility who preferred to gamble in more luxurious surroundings than the glaringly lit, noisy game rooms at White's, and to partake of better fare than the tasteless boiled fowl, beef steaks, and apple tarts served at Brooks's and White's.

In contrast to Brooks's, White's, and Watier's, The Strathmore had been founded by, and was owned by, its one hundred and fifty illustrious members, rather than by an outside proprietor. Membership was handed down from generation to generation and was rigidly limited to the descendants of its original founders. The club existed, not to make a profit, but to provide an unbreachable, comfortable fortress where members could bet staggering fortunes on a hand of cards, talk in desultory tones without having to shout to be heard, and dine on superb fare prepared by its French and Italian chefs. Discretion was expected from – and granted to – each member. Gossip about members' giant losses and gains at the gaming tables spread from White's and Brooks's and then all over London like wildfire. At The Strathmore, where the stakes were astronomical by comparison, not a word about such things ever passed beyond The Strathmore's green canopy. Within the club's confines, however, gossip was passed from member to member and room to room with astonishing alacrity and considerable masculine enjoyment.

Guests were not allowed beyond the marble pillars that flanked the front door, even if accompanied by members, a discovery that had enraged Beau Brummell when he attempted to gain entry during the days he reigned supreme at every other fashionable gentlemen's club in London.

Prinny himself had been denied membership on the grounds that he was not a descendant of the founders, which caused the then-Prince Regent to react with as much ire as Brummell but with uncharacteristic common sense and foresight: He founded his own club, installed two of the royal chefs in prominent positions, and named it Watier's, after one of his chefs. The Prince Regent could not, however, replicate the aura of hushed dignity – of utter exclusivity and understated elegance – that pervaded the spacious rooms.

Nodding absently to the manager, who greeted him with a bow at the door, Stephen wended his way through the large, oak-panelled rooms, paying scarcely more attention to the members conversing in comfortable, high-backed dark green leather chairs or seated at the gambling tables, than he had to the club's employee. The third room he came to was virtually deserted, which suited him perfectly, and he sat down at a table with three vacant chairs. Staring fixedly into the empty fireplace, he considered the grave contents of the letter and contemplated the most momentous decision of his life.

The more he thought about the problem the letter created, the more obvious the solution became . . . and the better he felt about it. In the space of half an hour, Stephen's mood veered from grim to thoughtful to philosophical – and finally to gladness. Even without the letter, Stephen knew that he probably would have ended up doing exactly what he was about to do. The difference was that the contents of the letter virtually obliged him to do it, which meant he could act on his desire without surrendering all claim to honor and decency. From the moment he'd told Sherry that he wanted her to consider other suitors, he'd regretted it. He could hardly contain his jealousy if she praised DuVille, and he had no idea to what irrational lengths he might have gone when other suitors started appearing at his door. No doubt the day would have soon come when some besotted suitor screwed up the courage to ask Stephen for her hand, and found himself sprawled in the street instead.

Whenever she was in a room with him, Stephen had trouble keeping his eyes off her, and if they were alone, it took all of his control to keep his hands off her. If she was gone, he couldn't seem to keep his mind off her. Sherry wanted him too. He'd known that from the very first, and she hadn't changed, no matter how much she tried to behave as if he were merely a distant acquaintance with whom she had little in common. She'd melt in his arms again if he kept her there for longer than a few moments, he was certain of it.

His brother's joking remark made Stephen look up in surprise. 'At the risk of intruding on what appears to be a complicated discussion you're having with yourself,' Clayton drawled, 'would you care to include me in it, or would you rather play cards?' A half-finished drink was on the table in front of him, and as Stephen glanced around the room, he noticed it had filled up considerably since he had arrived.

While Clayton waited with lifted brows for his decision, Stephen leaned back in his chair and contemplated for the last time the decision he'd made and the desirability of acting on it at once. Since that was exactly what he wanted to do, he considered only the advantages of haste and ignored any disadvantages. 'I'd prefer to talk,' he said. 'I'm not in the mood for cards.'

'I noticed that. So did Wakefield and Hawthorne who invited us to join them while you were lost in thought.'

'I didn't realize they were here,' Stephen admitted, looking over his shoulder for the two friends he'd inadvertently offended. 'Where are they now?'

'Nursing their affronted sensibilities at the faro table.' Despite his offhand manner, Clayton was very aware that something important was on Stephen's mind. Hoping for an explanation, he waited patiently for a few moments, and finally said, 'Did you have any particular topic of conversation in mind, or should I choose one?'

In answer, Stephen reached into his pocket and withdrew the letter that had arrived from Charise's father's solicitor. 'This is the topic on my mind at the moment,' he said, handing it to his brother along with the modest bank draft that accompanied it.

Clayton unfolded the letter and began to read.

Dear Miss Lancaster,

I have directed this letter to your new husband so that he may first prepare you for the news it contains.

It is with deep personal regret that I must inform you of the death of my friend, your father. I was with him at the end, and it is for your own sake, that I tell you he expressed regret for what he felt were his many failures in your upbringing, including having spoiled you by giving you everything and too much of it.

He wanted you to attend the best schools, and to make a brilliant marriage. He accomplished all those goals, but in doing so and in providing your large dowry, he spent virtually all that he had, and mortgaged the rest. The bank draft I have enclosed represents the full value of his assets as they are known to me.

I know you and your father disagreed on many things, Miss Lancaster, but it is my fond hope – as it was his – that you will someday appreciate his efforts on your behalf and make the best of your opportunities. Like you, Cyrus was strong-willed and hot-tempered. Perhaps it is those very similarities that you shared with him which prevented the two of you from seeking a better understanding.

Perhaps that lack of closeness will now enable you to cope better with the news of his death than might otherwise have been. More likely, you will feel a deep regret someday when you realize that it is too late to say and do those things which might have mended the rifts between the two of you.

In his desire to spare you such painful thoughts, your father instructed me to tell you that, though he may not have shown it, he loved you, and though you did not show it, he died believing you also loved him.

Finished, Clayton handed the letter back, his somber expression reflecting the same regret and concern that Stephen felt for Sherry. . . and the same puzzlement over some of what he read. 'A pity about her father,' he said. 'She has had a staggering run of ill luck. Although it is probably fortunate that they weren't close.' After a moment's hesitation, he frowned and added, 'What do you make of the solicitor's tone? The young woman he referred to in that letter is nothing like the one I've met.'

'Nor I,' Stephen confirmed. 'Except for her willfulness and temper,' he amended with a wry grin. 'Other than that, I can only assume her father – and his solicitor – must have been of like minds when it came to raising females, and both regarded any sort of spirit as intolerable defiance.'

'That is the same conclusion I reached, based on my knowledge of my father-in-law.'

'Lancaster must have been quite a pinchpenny if he regarded that ugly serviceable brown gown she was wearing on the ship as giving her "everything",' Stephen remarked as he stretched his long legs out in front of him, crossed them at the ankles, and settled more comfortably into the chair. Shoving his hands into his pockets, he glanced over his shoulder to signal a servant. 'Champagne,' he requested in answer to the servant's inquiry.

In the immediate aftermath of such grim news and its dire ramifications for Sherry, Clayton thought Stephen's indolent posture, and his request for champagne, were both a little odd. He waited for some indication as to how and when he intended to break the news to her, but Stephen seemed perfectly content to watch the servant pour champagne into two glasses and place them on the table.

'What do you intend to do next?' Clayton finally demanded.

'Propose a toast,' Stephen said.

'To be more specific,' Clayton said, growing extremely impatient with his brother's deliberate obtuseness, 'when do you intend to tell her about the letter?'

'After we're married.'

'I beg your pardon?'

Instead of repeating his answer, Stephen quirked an amused brow at his brother, picked up his champagne, and lifted the glass in a mock toast. 'To our happiness,' he said dryly.

In the moment it took Stephen to drain the glass, Clayton recovered his composure, carefully disguised his delight with that turn of events, and stretched out in his own chair. He picked up his glass of champagne, but instead of drinking it, he turned it absently in his fingers while he eyed his brother with unhidden amusement.

'Are you wondering if I'm making a mistake?' Stephen asked finally.

'Not at all. I am merely wondering whether you're aware that she seems to have developed a certain, shall we say, "mild aversion" to you?'

'She wouldn't throw water on me if I were on fire,' Stephen agreed. 'At least not if she had to come close to me to do it.'

'And do you see that as an obstacle to her accepting your generous offer of marriage?'

'Possibly,' Stephen said with a chuckle.

'In that case, how do you intend to persuade her to agree?'

'Actually,' Stephen lied straight-faced, 'I thought I would point out how wrong it was of her to mistrust my intentions and integrity, and then I'll prove it to her by proposing. Afterward, I'll tell her that if she cares to ask my forgiveness, I'll grant it to her.'

He was so convincing that his brother gave him a look of sarcastic disgust. 'And then what do you suppose will happen?'

'And then I will spend the next few days and nights in the pleasant confines of my home.'

'With her, I presume?' Clayton mocked.

'No, with compresses on both my eyes.'

Clayton's laughing rejoinder was interrupted by the return of Jordan Townsende, the Duke of Hawthorne, and Jason Fielding, Marquess of Wakefield. Since Stephen had nothing more to discuss with his brother, he invited them to stay and the four friends got down to the serious business of highstakes gaming.

Concentrating proved to be difficult, however, because Stephen's thoughts kept drifting to Sherry and their immediate future. Despite his joking banter about how he intended to propose to her, he had no notion of what he would actually say. It didn't even seem important. All that mattered was that they were going to be together. She was actually going to be his, and without the taint, the lifelong guilt, that had made Stephen recoil from marrying young Burleton's fiancée. Her father's death made it imperative that she have someone to care for her – and for whom she cared – when she learned about it.

Their marriage would have happened anyway. Stephen accepted the truth of that now. Somewhere in the back of his mind, he'd known it from the moment she had confronted him in a robe tied with a gold curtain cord and her hair covered with a blue towel, reminding him of a barefoot Madonna – a Madonna with a horrifying problem. *'My hair – it's red!'*

No, Stephen thought, he'd felt something for her even before that . . . from that very first morning when he awoke beside her bed and she'd asked him to describe her face. He'd looked into those mesmerizing gray eyes of hers and seen such courage, such softness. It had started then and was strengthened by everything she did and said. He loved her irreverent wit, her intelligence, and her unaffected warmth toward everyone she encountered. He loved the way she felt in his arms, and the way her mouth tasted. He loved her spirit and her fire and her sweetness. And especially her honesty.

After an adulthood surrounded by women who hid avarice behind inviting smiles and ambition behind lingering glances, and who pretended passion for a man when the only passion they were capable of feeling was for possessions, Stephen Westmoreland had finally found a woman who wanted only him.

And he was so damned happy, that he couldn't decide what to buy her first. Jewels, he decided, as he paused to bet on his hand of cards. Carriages, horses, gowns, furs, but first the jewels . . . Fabulous jewels to set off her exquisite face and more to twine in her lustrous hair. Gowns adorned with . . .

Pearls! Stephen decided with an inner laugh as he recalled her mirthful commentary on the Countess of Evandale's gown. A gown adorned with three thousand and *one* pearls. Sherry didn't seem to have any interest in gowns, but that particular gown would appeal to her sense of humor, and she would like it because it was a gift from him.

Because it was from him . . .

He knew she would feel that way as surely as he knew Sherry wanted him. From the moment he brushed his mouth over her lips and felt them tremble, felt her body strain instinctively closer to his, he'd known she wanted him. She was too inexperienced to hide her feelings, too candid to want to try.

She wanted him, and he wanted her. In a very few days, he would take her to bed for the first time, and there he would teach her the delights of 'having.'

Jason Fielding spoke his name, and Stephen glanced up, realized they were all waiting for his bet, and tossed more chips onto the stacks in the middle of the table.

'You've already won that one,' Jason pointed out in an amused drawl. 'Wouldn't you like to clear it away, so you can win a nice fresh pile of our money?'

'Whatever is on your mind, Stephen,' Jordan Townsende remarked, eyeing him curiously, 'it must be damned engrossing.'

'You looked right through us earlier,' Jason Fielding added as he began to deal the cards. 'The most crushing setdown I've had in years.'

'Stephen has something *very* engrossing on his mind,' Clayton joked.

As he finished that sentence, William Baskerville, a middle-aged bachelor, strolled over to the table, a folded newspaper in his hand, and idly watched the play.

Since Stephen's courtship of Sherry would be common gossip by morning, and his betrothal a fact by the end of the week, Stephen saw no reason to conceal what had been on his mind. 'As a matter of fact—' he began, when he suddenly thought to glance at a clock. Three hours had passed already. 'I'm late!' he said, startling the others as he shoved his cards back into the center, and abruptly stood up. 'If I'm not inside Almack's before eleven, they'll have locked the damned doors.'

Three astounded males watched his retreating shoulders as Stephen stalked swiftly out of the club – evidently in a hurry to reach a destination that no man of sophistication or maturity ever set foot in willingly, let alone anxiously. The thought of Stephen Westmoreland willingly setting foot in that place with its ballroom filled with blushing misses fresh from the schoolroom and eager to snag an eligible husband was utterly ludicrous. Baskerville spoke first. 'Egad!' he breathed, looking around at the others in stunned horror, 'did Langford say he was bound for *Almack's*?'

The Marquess of Wakefield tore his amused gaze from the doorway and looked at the others. 'That's what I heard.'

The Duke of Hawthorne nodded, his voice dry. 'Not only did I hear him say Almack's, but I noticed he seems to be in rather a hurry to get there.'

'He'll be lucky if he gets out of there alive,' Jason Fielding joked.

'And still a bachelor,' Jordan Townsende agreed, grinning.

'Poor devil!' said Baskerville in a dire voice. Shaking his head, he departed to join some acquaintances at the hazard table – and to share the highly diverting information that the Earl of Langford had rushed off in order to make it into the 'Marriage Mart' before the doors were closed.

The consensus of opinion among the hazard players, who were throwing dice on long tables with high wooden sides, was that Stephen had yielded to the deathbed wish of a dying relative to appear at Almack's on behalf of some young chit to whom the dying person was related.

At the green felt-covered faro tables, where gentlemen were placing bets on what card a dealer was going to draw, face up, from a box, the general opinion was that the unfortunate Earl of Langford had lost a wager that required him to spend a night at Almack's as his noxious forfeit.

Gentlemen who were playing even-odd, wagering on the numbers most likely to appear when the rotating even-odd wheel came to a stop, were of the opinion that Baskerville had lost his hearing.

Whist players, concentrating on the cards they held, were of the opinion that Baskerville had lost his mind.

But whatever opinion the particular individual held, his reaction was always the same as everyone else's: hilarity. In every one of The Strathmore's rooms, the refined atmosphere was repeatedly disrupted by loud guffaws, hearty chuckles, and snorts of laughter as word circulated from member to member, and table to table, that Stephen Westmoreland, Earl of Langford, had gone to Almack's for the evening.

32

It was five minutes past eleven of the clock when Stephen strode swiftly past the two chagrined young bucks who were retreating to their carriages after having been turned away by Lady Letitia Vickery for failing to arrive before eleven. The patroness was in the act of closing the door when Stephen called out to her in a low, warning voice, 'Letty, don't you dare close that damned door in my face!'

Bristling with affront, she peered into the darkness beyond the lighted entry, as she swung it closed. 'Whoever you are, you are too late to enter.'

Stephen put his toe against the panel to stop her. 'I think you should consider making an exception.'

Her disdainful face appeared in the wedge of light between the jamb and the edge of the door. 'We do not make exceptions, sirrah!' She saw who he was, and a look of comical disbelief momentarily shattered her expression of stony hauteur. 'Langford, is that *you*?'

'Of course it is, now open the door,' Stephen commanded quietly.

'You cannot come in.'

'Letty,' he said with strained patience, 'do not make me resort to unpleasant reminders of times when you've invited me in to less appropriate places than this one – and with your poor husband practically within earshot.'

She opened the door, but placed herself in the opening. Stephen contemplated the efficacy of lifting her by the shoulders and moving her out of his way while she implored in a fierce whisper, 'Stephen, for God's sake, be reasonable! I cannot let you in. The other patronesses will have my head if I do.'

'They will kiss you on both cheeks for making an

exception in my case,' he said flatly. 'Only think of the boost in attendance you'll have tomorrow, when it's learned that *I* was actually lured to this boring assembly of virtuous innocents for the first time in fifteen years.'

She hesitated, weighing the obvious truth of that against the peal that was likely to be rung over her head by the other patronesses before she could explain her motivations. 'Every eligible male in London will want vouchers to get in, so that he can see for himself what female could possibly have been exquisite enough to lure you here.'

'Exactly,' Stephen said sardonically. 'You'll have so many eligible men inside that you'll have to lay in an extra supply of warm lemonade and bread and butter.'

She was so delighted with the possibility of receiving credit for all the splendid matches made during her season as patroness, that she overlooked his disdainful slurs on the hallowed halls of Almack's, its refreshments, and its occupants. 'Very well. You may come in.'

The evening had not been the disaster Sherry had feared it would be. She had danced and been made to feel quite welcome. In fact, with a few uncomfortable exceptions, the evening had been very pleasant, but she had remained tense and expectant until a few minutes ago, when the clock finally indicated the hour of eleven. Now that the possibility of the Earl of Langford's appearance was eliminated, she felt incredibly disappointed, but she refused to succumb to anger or rejection. She'd sensed he wasn't enthusiastic about coming here, and it was foolish to expect him to inconvenience himself for her. That would have implied some sort of concern or caring for her that she now accepted he simply did not have. Whitney and his mother had been wrong. Determined not to let thoughts of him occupy one more moment of her evening, she concentrated on the conversation of the young ladies and their mamas who were standing in a circle with her, talking among themselves, but politely including her.

231

Most of the girls were younger than she, and very amiable, if not particularly given to intelligent discourse. They were however amazingly well-informed on the income, prospects, and lineage of every bachelor in the room, and she had only to look twice at a male to have them – or their mamas and chaperones – lean aside and obligingly share all their knowledge. The deluge of data confused Miss Charity and alternately embarrassed and amused Sherry.

The Duchess of Clermont, a stern elderly lady who was introducing her granddaughter, another American named Dorothy Seaton, tipped her head toward a handsome young man who'd asked Sherry for the honor of a second dance, and warned, 'I would not show young Makepeace more than the briefest civility, were I you. He is only a baronet, and his income is a mere five thousand.'

Nicholas DuVille, who'd spent most of the evening in the card room, heard that as he returned to Sherry's side. Leaning down, he said in a low amused voice, 'You look quite terribly embarrassed, *chérie*. Amazing, is it not, that a country that prides itself on its refined manners has no compunction at all in discussing such things.'

The musicians who'd paused briefly for refreshments were returning to their instruments, and music began to fill the ballroom. 'Miss Charity looks exhausted,' Sherry said, raising her voice to be heard above the increasing volume of music and conversation.

Miss Charity heard her name and looked up sharply. 'I am not weary, my dear child. I am exceedingly vexed with Langford for not making his appearance as he promised, and I intend to scold him soundly for treating you so shabbily!'

All around them heads were beginning to turn and conversations were dropping off, then escalating to frantic whispers, but Sherry was blissfully unaware of the cause. 'It doesn't signify, ma'am. I've done perfectly well without him.'

Miss Charity was not soothed. 'I do not remember being this annoyed in the last thirty years! And if I *could* remember all of the last thirty years, I'm *still* certain I wouldn't remember being this annoyed!'

Beside them the Duchess of Clermont stopped eavesdropping on Charity Thornton's irate monologue, and she glanced up, her gaze riveting on something across the room. 'I cannot believe my own eyes!' she burst out. Hectic conversations were erupting all around them, and she leaned sideways, raising her voice to be heard above it all as she commanded her granddaughter, 'Dorothy, attend to your hair and gown. This is a chance you may *never* have again.' That gruff order drew Sherry's attention to Dorothy, who had obediently reached up to pat her coiffure into place as were half the debutantes in Sherry's range of view. Those who weren't checking their hair were smoothing their skirts. Debutantes who weren't already lining up with their partners on the dance floor were making a mass exodus toward the retiring room, and *they* were also patting and smoothing on the way. 'What is happening?' she asked, lifting quizzical eyes to Nicki, who was blocking her view.

His gaze shifted over the blondes and brunettes, registering heightened color of cheeks and eager gazes, and without bothering to look over his shoulder, he said, 'Either a fire has broken out in the middle of the dance floor, or else Langford has just arrived.'

'It can't be him! It's after eleven and the doors are locked.'

'Nevertheless, I would wager a small fortune that Langford's the cause. The hunting instincts of the female of the species are at a fever pitch, which means prime prey is in sight. Shall I look round and see?'

'Try not to be obvious about it.'

He complied, turned back around, and confirmed it. 'He's stopped to greet the patronesses.'

Sherry did the last thing she'd planned to do if he came: she ducked around Nicki and beat a hasty retreat

233

to the retiring room – not to primp, though, or check her appearance. No indeed. Merely to compose herself. And then primp just a little.

As she waited to get into the retiring room, she discovered her fiancé was the talk of the crowd, and the talk she was hearing was as illuminating as it was embarrassing to her: 'My older sister will swoon when she hears Langford was here tonight and she was not!' one of the girls was telling her friends. 'Last autumn, he singled her out for particular attention at Lady Millicent's ball and then dropped her completely. She has carried a tendre for him ever since.'

Her friends looked shocked. 'But last autumn,' one of them corrected, 'Langford was on the verge of offering for Monica Fitzwaring.'

'Oh, I do not think that's possible. I heard my sisters talking and they were positive he was having—' she cupped her hand over her lips, and Sherry strained helplessly to eavesdrop, 'a *torrid* affair with a certain married lady last autumn.'

'Have you ever seen his *chère amie*?' another asked, and the girls in front of that group turned around. 'My aunt saw him at the theatre with her two nights ago.'

'*Chère amie*?' The question flew out before Sherry could stop it, prompted by the discovery that he had escorted a female to the theatre, immediately after dining with Sherry and his family.

The girls, whom she'd been introduced to earlier, were happy to oblige Sherry with all the information a newcomer to their circle, and an American, might need in order to fully appreciate the finer subtleties of the gossip.

'*Chère amie* is a courtesan, a woman who shares a man's baser passions. Helene Devernay is the most beautiful courtesan of them all.'

'I heard my brothers talking one evening, and they said Helene Devernay is the most heavenly creature on earth. She loves lavender, you know . . . and Langford had a special silver coach built for her with lavender velvet squabs.'

Lavender. That flimsy lavender gown that Dr Whitticomb had objected to, the meaningful way he'd said, '*Lavender, was it*' to the earl. It had belonged to the woman who shared his 'baser passions.' Sherry knew kissing qualified as passion. She didn't know what constituted baser, but she could sense the fact that they were intense and somehow scandalous and personal. And he shared all that with another woman only *hours* after dining with his unwanted fiancée.

Even though Miss Charity now knew Lord Westmoreland was somewhere in the ballroom, she was almost as angry with him when Sherry returned as she'd been when Sherry left. 'I intend to report Langford's conduct to his mama, first thing in the morning! She will ring a peal over his head for this night's work.'

Stephen's bland, amused voice made Sherry stiffen in angry shock as he strolled up behind them and spoke to Miss Charity first. 'For what am I to be called to task by my mother, ma'am?' he asked, a lazy, white smile sweeping across his features.

'For being late, you naughty boy!' she said, but all traces of animosity were vanishing from her voice as he aimed that lethally attractive smile directly at her and kept it there. 'For stopping too long to speak to the patronesses! And for being entirely too handsome for your own good! Now,' she finished, forgiving him entirely, 'kiss my hand properly and lead Sherry onto the dance floor.'

Nicki had been shielding her by keeping his back to the room, but he had no choice except to step aside. Sherry's anger escalated when she heard Miss Charity cave in so easily, and it doubled when she reluctantly turned and found *herself* the object of amused blue eyes and a smile so warm it could have baked bread. Aware that every head in the ballroom seemed to be turned their way, Sherry reluctantly extended her hand, because that was what she was required to do. 'Miss Lancaster,' he said, pressing a brief kiss to the back of it, continuing to hold it despite her effort to jerk it free, 'may I have the pleasure of the next dance?'

'Let go of my hand,' Sherry said, her voice shaking with anger. 'Everyone is looking at us!'

Stephen studied her hectic color and flashing eyes, and he marvelled that he'd been able to ignore how magnificent she looked when she was angry. If he'd realized during the last few days that a slight lack of punctuality could rouse her from her indifference to ire, he'd have come down late for every meal.

'Let go of my hand!'

Grinning helplessly because he was happy and she was evidently this *un*happy over his near-absence, Stephen teased, 'Are you going to make me drag you onto that dance floor?'

Some of his satisfaction with that faded as she yanked her hand free and said, 'Yes!'

Momentarily thwarted, Stephen stepped aside as some young dandy squeezed past him and bowed before her. 'I believe the next dance is mine, if you don't mind, my lord.' Left with no choice, he backed off a step and watched her curtsy prettily to him and stroll onto the dance floor. Beside him, DuVille observed him with amusement. 'I believe you have just been the recipient of a crushing setdown, Langford.'

'You're right,' he replied affably, leaning his shoulders against a pillar behind him. He was so happy he even felt charitably toward DuVille for a change. 'I suppose there's nothing alcoholic to drink?' he said, watching Sherry dancing with her partner.

'Not a thing.'

To the vast disappointment of everyone in the room, neither Lord Westmoreland nor Nicholas DuVille seemed inclined to ask anyone to dance except the American girl. When Sherry remained on the dance floor for a second dance with the same young man, Stephen frowned. 'Didn't anyone warn her that it's a mistake to show partiality by dancing twice with the same partner?'

'You are beginning to sound like a jealous beau,' Nicki remarked, slanting him an amused look from the corner of his eye.

Stephen ignored him, glancing around at the hungry, eager, expectant, hopeful female faces watching him and feeling like a human banquet being served up to an audience of refined, elegantly dressed cannibals. As the music wound to its end, Stephen said, 'Do you happen to know if her next dance is taken?'

'All of her dances are taken.'

Stephen saw Sherry's partner politely return her to Charity Thornton, and he observed the crowd of men crossing the dance floor to claim their partners for the waltz that was just beginning so that he could see in advance who he was about to preempt. Beside him, DuVille shoved away from the pillar they'd been sharing. 'I believe this dance is mine,' he said.

'Unfortunately, it isn't,' Stephen drawled mildly. 'And if you try to claim it,' he added in a voice that stopped DuVille cold, 'I will have to tell her that my sister-in-law put you up to playing the gallant suitor.' Without a backward glance, Stephen shoved away from the pillar and presented himself to his unwilling partner.

'Nicki has the next dance,' Sherry informed him with stony hauteur, deliberately using the familiar form of address to show the earl what particularly friendly terms she was already on with 'Nicki.'

'He's relinquished the privilege to me.'

Something about his implacable tone made Sherry reverse her earlier decision and decide it was wiser to get the dance over with instead of delaying it or attempting to refuse, or causing any sort of scene. 'Oh, very well.'

'Are you having a pleasant evening?' Stephen inquired

as the music began and she moved woodenly in his arms, dancing with none of the grace he'd seen in her in the last set.

'I *was* having a pleasant evening, thank you very much.'

Stephen looked down at her shining head and caught a glimpse of her resentful profile. The letter in his pocket went a long way to dilute his annoyance over her attitude. 'Sherry,' he said with quiet determination.

Sherry heard the strange softness in his voice and refused to look up. 'Yes?'

'I apologize for anything I've said or done that has hurt you.'

The reminder that he knew he had hurt her, and undoubtedly believed he still could, was more than her lacerated pride could withstand. Her temper ignited and burst into flames. 'You needn't give a thought to any of that,' she said, managing to sound bored with the topic and disdainful of him. 'I feel certain I'll have several more suitable offers of marriage by the end of the week, and I'm excessively happy that you gave me this opportunity to be introduced to other gentlemen. Until tonight,' she continued, her voice beginning to vibrate with the raging hostility she really felt, 'I naturally assumed all Englishmen were arbitrary, moody, vain, and unkind, but now I know that *they* are not. *You* are!'

'Unfortunately for you and for them,' Stephen stated, stunned by the apparent depth of her anger at his tardiness, 'you happen to be already betrothed to me.'

Sherry was riding her wave of triumphant defiance, and that remark didn't slow her down in the least. 'The gentlemen I've met tonight are not only the soul of amiability, but they are also *much* more desirable than you!'

'Really?' he said with a lazy grin. 'In what way?'

'For one thing, they are younger!' Sherry fired back, longing to slap that arrogant, insufferable smile off his face. 'You are much too old for me. I realized that tonight.'

'Did you, indeed?' His gaze dropped meaningfully to her lips. 'Then perhaps you need a reminder of times you found me *very* desirable.'

Sherry jerked her gaze from his. 'Stop looking at me that way! It isn't seemly, and people will talk! They are staring at us!' she hissed, trying to pull back, only to have his arm tighten, imprisoning her with infuriating ease.

In a conversational tone more appropriate to a casual discussion of the latest *on-dits*, he said, 'Do you have any idea of what will happen if I follow my inclinations and either toss you over my shoulder and haul you out of here, or else kiss you right in the middle of this dance? For a start, you would be off-limits to every respectable male in the room. I, of course, wouldn't care, being the "arbitrary, vain, unkind" man that I am—'

'You wouldn't dare!' she exploded.

Her eyes shot daggers at him as she boldly called his bluff, while all around them dancers were missing their steps in their eagerness to witness the altercation that seemed to be taking place between the mysterious American girl and the Earl of Langford. Stephen looked at her flushed, entrancing, rebellious face, and a reluctant smile tugged at his lips. 'You're right, sweetheart,' he said softly. 'I wouldn't.'

'How *dare* you call me by an endearment after the things you have done to me!'

Momentarily forgetting that she would be thrown off balance by the sort of sophisticated sexual banter that was commonplace among his own set, Stephen let his gaze drop suggestively to the rounded breasts displayed enticingly above the square bodice of her gown. 'You have no idea what I would dare to do to you,' he warned with a lazy, suggestive smile. 'Have I complimented you on your gown, by the by?'

'You can take your compliments, and yourself, right to hell,' she whispered furiously, yanking out of his arms and leaving him in the middle of the dance floor.

'Egad!' said Makepeace to his current partner, 'did you see that? Miss Lancaster just left Langford standing on the dance floor.'

'She must be insane,' said his partner in a stricken voice.

'I do not at all agree,' the young baronet proudly declared. 'Miss Lancaster did *not* treat me shabbily at all. She was the soul of civility and sweetness.' When the dance was over, he hurried off to make certain his own friends had noticed that the stunning redheaded American preferred his attentions to those of the lofty Earl of Langford.

That astounding fact had already been noted by a great many of the gentlemen in the ballroom, many of whom had been sorely rankled by Langford's appearance in their own arena and who were greatly mollified to note that at least one female in the room had the superior taste and foresight to prefer Makepeace to Westmoreland.

Within minutes, Makepeace's stature escalated to un-paralleled heights among his peers. The lovely American girl, who clearly preferred him, ergo all of them, to the vastly more popular Earl of Langford, became an instantaneous heroine.

Furious with her for her outrageous display of temper, Stephen stood off to the side, watching an entire wall of bachelors make their way straight toward his fiancée. They clustered about her, asking for dances and flattering her so outrageously that she sent a glance of helpless appeal in his direction. But not to him, Stephen noticed, growing even angrier – to DuVille.

Nicki put down his glass of lemonade and started for her, but the men were closing around her so tightly that she began backing away, then she turned and beat a hasty retreat in the direction of the retiring rooms. Left with no choice, Nicki leaned back against the same pillar that he had shared with Stephen earlier and folded his arms over his chest as Stephen had just done. Unaware of how identical they looked, they stood side by side, two darkly handsome, urbane men in flawlessly tailored black evening clothes, wearing matched expressions of bored civility. 'By spurning you, she has just become a heroine to every male in this ballroom,' Nicki observed.

Stephen, who had reached the same conclusion, was somewhat mollified to note that DuVille sounded almost as frustrated as he himself felt. 'By tomorrow,' DuVille continued, 'my fiancée will be unanimously declared an Original, an Incomparable, and Joan of Arc by every mincing fop and young Corinthian in London. You have set my courtship back by weeks.'

'I've turned down your suit,' Stephen retorted with flat satisfaction. Tipping his head toward the debutantes and their mothers who were lined up on the opposite side of the room, he said, 'Feel free to lavish your attentions on any one of those eager hopefuls, however. I feel certain you could propose tonight to any one of them and be wed with their family's blessing and a special license by tomorrow.'

Nicki automatically followed his gaze and for the moment the two men set aside their hostilities in favor of shared observations on the drawback of being deemed a brilliant catch. 'Do you ever have the feeling they see you as a platter of tempting trout?' Nicki inquired, nodding politely and distantly toward a young lady who was fluttering her fan invitingly at him.

'I think they see me more as a blank bank draft with legs,' Stephen replied, staring unencouragingly at Lady Ripley, who was whispering frantically to her daughter and casting beckoning looks at him. He inclined his head imperceptibly at Lady Ripley's very pretty daughter, who seemed to be one of the few females in the room who seemed not to be either coyly pretending the two men weren't there or else gazing longingly at them. 'At least the Ripley girl has enough sense and enough pride to ignore us.'

'Allow me to introduce you to her, so your evening

will not be an entire waste of time,' Nicki volunteered. 'I am already committed to an exquisite redhead who seems to be developing a tendre for me in a gratifyingly short time.'

'DuVille?' Stephen drawled in a steely voice that was in vivid contrast to the expression of bland courtesy he was wearing for the sake of their fascinated audience.

'Langford?'

'Back *off* !'

Nicki returned Westmoreland's sideways glance with an identical one of his own, hiding his amusement behind a mask of genteel imperturbability. 'Am I to assume you've had a change of heart, and no longer desire to be free of your obligation to Miss Lancaster?' he taunted.

'Are you *itching* to meet me at dawn in some pleasant, secluded glen?' Stephen bit out.

'Not particularly, although the idea is beginning to have a certain appeal,' DuVille said as he shoved away from the pillar and walked into the card room.

Sherry became aware of her change of status among her own sex – as well as the reason for it – as soon as she entered the crowded retiring room. Conversations instantly broke off and curious smiles were aimed at her, but no-one spoke to her until a large-boned girl with a friendly smile spoke up. 'It was very diverting to see you give the earl such an unprecedented setdown, Miss Lancaster. I am sure he has never received such a rebuff.'

'I feel perfectly certain he has had dozens of them coming, however,' Sherry said, trying to seem completely unemotional when she was angry and embarrassed.

'Hundreds,' the girl declared gaily. 'Oh, but he is so very handsome and manly, do you not agree?'

'No,' Sherry lied. 'I prefer fair men.'

'Are fair men de rigueur in America?'

Since Sherry had no recollection of that, she said, 'They are to *this* American.'

'I heard you had suffered a loss of memory recently from an accident?' one of them asked with a mixture of sympathy and curiosity.

Sherry responded with the dismissive smile that Miss Charity had assured her would make her seem more mysterious than bacon-brained, and the remark Whitney had suggested, 'It's very temporary.' Since something else seemed to be expected, she improvised flippantly. 'In the meantime, it's very nice to feel as if I have not a worry in the world.'

By the time Sherry walked back into the ball-room, she'd learned many new things about Stephen Westmoreland, and she detested every piece of new-found knowledge, along with the conclusions she'd drawn from them. Despite what Whitney thought, Stephen Westmoreland was apparently a libertine, a rake, a hedonist, and a notorious flirt. His amorous affairs were numerous, and his lechery was obviously sanctioned by the *ton*, who seemed to dote on him, and everyone – absolutely everyone – apparently felt that an offer of marriage from him was second only to the crown of England! Worse, much worse, even though he was temporarily betrothed to her, he kept a mistress – and not an ordinary mistress, either, but a member of the fashionable impure who was reportedly breathtakingly beautiful.

Feeling insignificant, appalled, and outraged, Sherry returned to the ballroom and took furious glee in using her heretofore untapped ability at flirtation. She smiled gaily at the gentlemen who were still clustered around a flustered Miss Charity, waiting for her return, and during the next two hours, she promised to save at least two dozen dances for those gentlemen who were invited to the Rutherfords' ball later that evening. Her fiancé, however, did not appear to notice or mind her flirtatious triumphs, but merely stood watching her from the side-lines, his expression casual and pleasantly detached.

In fact, he seemed so utterly uninvolved that she felt

no qualm whatsoever when he finally approached her and stated that it was time to leave for the Rutherfords', and he didn't seem displeased with her as they waited with Nicholas DuVille and Miss Charity for their carriages to be brought round. He even smiled blandly when Charity Thornton remarked ecstatically, 'Sherry was such a success, Langford! I cannot wait to tell your mama tonight, and your sister-in-law, how excellently everything went!'

Nicholas DuVille had called for them in a fashionably sleek landau with its top folded back, but the Earl of Langford's luxurious town coach made Sherry's eyes widen as it glided to a stop in front of them. Drawn by six identical, flashy gray horses in silver harnesses, its body was lacquered a gleaming black, with the earl's coat of arms emblazoned on the door panel. Sherry had encountered the coachmen and grooms in the kitchens at the house on Upper Brook, but tonight they were turned out in formal livery of white leather breeches with bottle-green-striped waistcoats and bottle-green top-coats adorned with gold buttons and braid. With their shiny black top boots, white shirts, snowy cravats, and white gloves, Sherry thought they looked as fine as any of the fashionable gentlemen inside Almack's, and she told them so.

Her artless compliment drew fond smiles from the servants and an appalled look from Miss Charity, but when the earl's expression didn't change in the least, Sherry felt a prickle of uneasy foreboding – enough so that when she realized he intended her to ride alone with him to the Rutherfords' ball, she balked. 'I prefer to ride with Miss Charity and Monsieur DuVille,' she said firmly, already turning toward their carriage.

To her startled horror, his hand clamped on her elbow like a vise and forced her toward the open door of his coach. 'Get in!' he said in an *awful* voice, 'before you make a greater spectacle of yourself than you already have tonight.'

Belatedly realizing that beneath his smooth veneer of bland sophistication, Stephen Westmoreland was burningly furious, Sherry cast an anxious glance toward Miss Charity and Nicholas DuVille, who were already pulling away. Several other groups from Almack's were waiting for their own carriages to be brought round, and rather than make a useless scene, she got into the coach.

He climbed in behind her and snapped an order at the groom as he put up the steps. 'Take us the long way, through the park.'

Seated across from him, Sherry unconsciously pressed back into the luxurious silver velvet squabs and waited in tense silence for what she was certain was going to be an explosion of fury. He was staring out the window, his jaw clenched, and she wished he would get on with it, but when he finally turned his icy gaze on her and spoke to her in a low, savage voice, she instantly wished for the return of the suspenseful silence. 'If you ever,' he bit out, 'embarrass me again, I will turn you over my knee in front of everyone and give you the thrashing you deserve. Is that clear?' he snapped.

She swallowed audibly, and her voice wavered. 'It's clear.'

She thought that would finish it, but he seemed to have only begun. 'What did you hope to accomplish by behaving like an ill-bred flirt to every ass who approached you for a dance?' he demanded in a low, thunderous voice. 'By leaving me in the middle of the dance floor? By clinging to DuVille's arm and hanging on to his every word?'

The reprimand for her behavior on the dance floor was deserved, but the rest of his tirade about *her* behavior with the opposite sex was so unjust, so hypocritical, and so infuriating, that Sherry's temper ignited. 'What would you expect except foolish behavior from any woman who was *stupid* enough to betroth herself to the likes of you!' she fired back and had the satisfaction of seeing shock momentarily crack his mask of fury. 'Tonight I heard all the disgusting gossip about you, about your conquests and your *chère amie*, and your flirtations with married women! How dare you lecture *me* on decorum when *you're* the biggest libertine in all England!'

She was so carried away with her own furious humiliation over the gossip she'd heard tonight, that she didn't heed the muscle that was beginning to tick in his tightly clenched jaw. 'No wonder you had to go to America to find a bride,' she scoffed furiously. 'I'm surprised your reputation for profligacy didn't reach there, you – you unspeakable rake! You had the gall to engage yourself to me when everyone in Almack's has been expecting you to offer for – Monica Fitzwaring and a half dozen others. No doubt you've deceived every unfortunate female you've cast your eye at into believing you plan to offer for them. I wouldn't be surprised to find out you did exactly what you did to me – engage yourself to them "in secret" and then tell them to find someone else! Well,' she finished on a note of breathless, infuriated triumph, 'I no longer consider myself betrothed to you. Do you hear me, my lord? I am breaking our engagement as of this moment. Henceforth I shall flirt with whomever I please, whenever I please, and it is no reflection on your name, so you have nothing to say about it. Is *that* clear?' she finished, mocking his own phrase, then she waited in angry triumph for the satisfaction of his reaction, but he said not a word.

To her utter disbelief, he lifted his brows and gazed at her with enigmatic blue eyes and an impassive expression for several endless, uneasy moments, then he leaned forward and stretched his hand to her.

Unnerved completely, Sherry jerked back thinking he intended to strike her, then she realized he was casually offering his hand to her – a handshake to seal the end of their betrothal, she realized. Humiliatingly aware that he hadn't protested in the least to the breaking of it, her pride still forced her to look him right in the eye and place her hand in his.

His long fingers curved politely around hers, then abruptly tightened like a painful vise, yanking her off her seat. Sherry gave a muffled scream as she landed in a sprawling, uncomfortable heap on the seat beside him, her shoulders against the door, his glittering eyes only inches from hers as he leaned over her. 'I am sorely tempted to toss up your skirts and beat some sense into you,' he said in a terrifyingly soft voice. 'So heed me well, and spare us both the painful necessity: My *fiancée*,' he emphasized, 'will conduct herself with proper decorum, and my *wife*,' he continued with icy arrogance, 'will never discredit my name or her own.'

'Whoever she is,' Sherry panted, hiding her terror behind scorn as she squirmed ineffectually beneath his weight, 'she has my deepest sympathy! I—'

'You outrageous hellion!' he said savagely, and his mouth swooped down, seizing hers in a ruthless kiss that was meant to punish and subdue while his hand gripped the back of her head, forcing her to hold the contact. Sherry struggled in furious earnest, and finally managed to twist her head aside. 'Don't!' she cried, hating the terror and plea in her voice. 'Please don't . . . please!'

Stephen heard it too, and he lifted his head without relaxing his grip, but as he studied her pale, stricken face and realized that his hand was on her breast, he was amazed by his unprecedented loss of temper and control. Her eyes were huge with fear, and her heart was racing beneath his palm. He had merely intended to tame her, to bend her to his will and force her to yield to reason, but he had never meant to humble or terrify her. He did not want to do anything, ever, to break that amazing spirit of hers. Even now, when she was pinned beneath him and completely at his mercy, there were still traces of stormy rebellion in those long-lashed gray eyes and stubborn chin, a courageous defiance that was gaining strength in the few moments he'd been still.

She was magnificent even in her defiance, he decided

as he noticed the flaming curls covering her cheek. Impertinent, proud, sweet, courageous, clever . . . she was all of that.

And she was going to be his. This delectable stormy titian-haired girl in his arms was going to bear his children, preside at his table, and undoubtedly pit her will against his, but she would never bore him – in bed or out of it. He knew it with the experience gained from two decades of intimate dalliance with the opposite sex. The fact that she didn't know who she was, or who he was, and that she was not going to like him very well when she finally recovered her memory did not concern him overmuch.

From the moment she'd put her hand in his and fallen asleep, some bond had sprung up between them, and nothing she'd said or done tonight had convinced him she wanted to break it, or that she didn't want him as badly as he wanted her. She was merely overreacting to a storm of gossip she'd heard about him because she didn't understand that there was rarely more than a grain of truth – if that – in any of it.

All this raced through his mind in the space of seconds, but it was long enough for his fiancée to sense that his anger was under control and to adjust her tone to exactly the right combination of appeal and firmness. 'Let me up,' she said quietly. Stephen added 'keenly perceptive' to her many other desirable wifely traits, but he shook his head. Holding her gaze pinned to his, he spoke in a tone of quiet implacability. 'I'm afraid we need to reach an understanding before you leave this coach.'

'What is there to understand?' she burst out.

'This,' Stephen said as he twined one hand through her hair and caught her chin with the other, turning her face up to his, and slowly lowered his mouth to hers again.

Sherry saw the purposeful gleam in those heavy-lidded eyes, and she drew in a swift breath, trying to twist her head away. When she couldn't escape his grip, she braced herself for another punishing onslaught, but it never came. He touched her mouth with an exquisite gentleness that stunned her into stillness and began to assault her carefully erected defenses. His mouth brushed back and forth over her lips, lazily coaxing, shaping, and fitting them to his own while his hand loosened its grip in her hair and slid downward, curving around her nape, stroking it sensually. He kissed her endlessly, as if he had all the time in the world to explore and savor every contour of her mouth, and Sherry felt her pulse begin to hammer in fright as her resistance to him began to crumble. The man who was kissing her had suddenly become the concerned fiancé who'd slept in a chair beside her bed when she was ill; the fiancé who'd teased her to laughter and kissed her to insensibility; only now there was a subtle difference in him that made him even more lethally effective: his seeking mouth was breathtakingly insistent and there was a possessiveness in the way he was holding and kissing her. Whatever the difference was, her treacherous heart found him utterly irresistible. Wrapped snugly in his strong arms, with his mouth caressing hers, and his thumb slowly stroking her nape, even the gentle swaying of the coach became seductive. His tongue traced the trembling line between her lips, coaxing them to open for him, and with her last ounce of will, Sherry managed to resist his urging. Instead of forcing her, he lifted his mouth from hers and switched tactics, brushing a hot kiss along the curve of her cheek to her temple and the corner of her eye. His hand tightened on her nape – imprisoning or supporting her – as his tongue touched the edge of her ear and then began to slowly explore each curve, sending shivers of desire darting through her. As if he sensed that victory was within his grasp, he dragged his mouth roughly across her cheek, and when his lips lightly touched the corner of hers, seeking and inviting, Sherry went down to defeat. With a shudder of surrender, she turned her head to fully receive his kiss. Her lips parted beneath the pressure of his, and his tongue made a brief, sensuous foray into her mouth, probing lightly at hers.

Stephen felt her hand slide up his chest, felt her press closer to him, and he claimed his victory, plundering her mouth with his, teasing and tormenting her, and she responded instinctively. The fires within her that had fueled her tempestuous rebellion earlier, now burned hot and bright with passion, and Stephen found himself in the midst of a kiss that was wildly erotic – and rapidly getting out of control. His hand was sliding over her breast, cupping it, and she was straining toward him in sweet abandon, offering her mouth to him. He told himself to stop and kissed her deeper instead, making her moan softly, and when she kissed him back, tentatively touching her tongue to his lips, it was the gasp of his own breath that he heard. He shoved his fingers into her thick hair, and the rope of pearls that had bound it broke loose, sending a shower of pearls and a gleaming waterfall of red tresses spilling over his hands and arms. He kissed her until they were both senseless and his hand was caressing her breast. He forced his hand to still, reminded himself that they were in a coach on a public street on their way to a ball . . . but her full breast was filling his palm, and he tugged the bodice of her gown down enough to expose it. She panicked when she realized what he had done, her fingers grasping his wrist, and with a laughing groan, he ignored her and bent his head to her breast . . .

33

Weak from the turbulence of her own emotions, Sherry let her hand slide from his shoulder to his chest and felt his heart beating hard and fast, which meant he, too, must have been affected by their kisses. That knowledge, combined with the gentle stroking of his hand down her back, went a long way toward banishing her feeling of having been vanquished. There was something different about him tonight, something indefinably more tender. And more authoritative. She didn't understand the reason for that, but she was certain she'd discovered the reason for something else. Leaning her forehead against his chest, she said it aloud:

'What we just did – it's the real reason I considered marrying you, isn't it?'

She sounded so abject, so defeated by the amazing passion they shared, that Stephen smiled against her hair. 'It's the reason you are *going* to marry me,' he corrected with finality.

'We aren't at all suited.'

'Aren't we?' he whispered, curving his hand around her narrow waist and moving her closer against him.

'No, we are not. There are a great many things about you that I do not approve of.'

Stephen stifled his laughter. 'You can take your time enumerating all my shortcomings on Saturday.'

'Why on Saturday?'

'If you mean to become a shrewish wife, you should wait until after the wedding.'

He felt her body tense even before she slowly raised her head and stared at him. Her eyes were still languorous, but her refusal had a trace of strength in it. 'I cannot marry you on Saturday.'

'Sunday, then,' he magnanimously agreed, erroneously believing her objection to the day was based on a feminine concern over a suitable trousseau.

'Not then either,' she warned, but the desperation in her voice told him that she lacked conviction. 'I want to have my memory back before I take such an irrevocable step.'

Stephen's goal was precisely the opposite. 'I'm afraid we can't wait that long.'

'Why on earth not?'

'Allow me to demonstrate,' he said and took her lips in a swift, hard, demanding kiss. Finished, he looked into her face and quirked a brow, suggesting she state an opinion of his demonstration.

'Well, there is that,' she admitted, and Stephen stifled a shout of laughter at her tone and expression, 'but it is not reason enough to rush into a ceremony.'

'Sunday,' he repeated flatly.

She shook her head, showing him a glimpse of an amazing strength of will, even though he could see she was beginning to falter.

'I am not yet subject to your wishes, my lord, so I suggest you not use that particular tone on me. It is most arbitrary, and for some reason it seems to raise my hackles. I insist on having a choice – What are you doing?' she burst out as he slid his hand inside her bodice, cupping her breast and fondling her nipple, forcing it into a tight bud.

'Giving you a choice,' Stephen said. 'You can admit you want me, and agree to let me make an honorable woman of you on Sunday, or you can deny it . . .'

He let the sentence hang in a way that was intended to alarm her. 'And if I do deny it . . .' she argued softly.

'Then we will go home instead of to the Rutherfords' ball, and I will continue there what we left off a few minutes ago, until I either prove it to you or you admit it. Either way, the result will be a wedding on Sunday.'

Beneath his velvet baritone, there was a steely

determination, an arrogant confidence that he could and would succeed in anything he decided to do, that made her feel even more helpless and bewildered. Sherry knew he could and would make her admit it. He could kiss her into insensibility in a matter of minutes. 'Yesterday, you were not at all eager to wed, or even honor our betrothal,' she pointed out. 'What has brought about your change of heart?'

Your father is dead, and you have no-one left in the world but me, Stephen thought, but he knew there was another reason that was far more compelling, though not entirely true: 'Yesterday, I didn't fully recognize how badly we want each other.'

'Yes, but earlier tonight, I was perfectly certain I did *not* want you at all. Wait, I have a suggestion—' she said, and Stephen grinned at the way her face lit up, even though he knew he was neither going to like, nor to agree to, any alteration in his plans. Five hundred years of undiluted nobility flowed in his veins, and with the true arrogance of his illustrious forebears, Stephen David Elliott Westmoreland had already decided that his will was going to prevail in the matter. All that was important was that she wanted him, and he wanted her. Beyond that, his only reason for haste was that he wanted her to be able to enjoy some time as his wife before she had to confront her father's death.

'We could go on as we are, and if you don't become disagreeable, and *if* we continue to like kissing one another, *then* we could be married.'

'A tempting suggestion,' Stephen lied politely, 'but as it happens, I have a great deal more in mind than merely kissing you, and I am . . . uncomfortably eager . . . to satisfy us both on that score.'

Her reply to that remark proved that she'd forgotten more than merely her own name, and her fiancé's name. Either that, or like many of her gently bred English counterparts, she'd never been told what was actually going to happen on her wedding night. With her delicate russet brows drawn together over quizzical gray eyes, she confirmed it. 'I don't know what you mean or what precisely you have in mind, but if I am making you uncomfortable, it's little wonder. I am practically sitting on your lap.'

'We'll discuss all my meanings and motives later,' he promised in a voice roughened by the pleasure she gave him as she wriggled her way off his lap.

'When will we discuss it?' she persisted stubbornly when she was seated across from him again.

'Sunday night.'

Unable to summon the fortitude to argue with him further or even meet the challenge of his gaze, Sherry parted the curtain at the side window of the coach and looked out. Two things hit her at once: First, they were stopped in front of a house with footmen standing at attention on every step, holding torches to welcome the droves of splendidly garbed guests who were moving inside in a steady stream while casting curious looks over their shoulders at the door of the coach. And worse, if her reflection in the coach window was even close to accurate, Sherry's elaborate coiffure had been hopelessly damaged by her fiancé's marauding fingers. 'My hair!' she whispered, aghast, reaching up and confirming that the intricate curls had come loose and were hanging about her shoulders in what Stephen privately thought was delightful, artless disarray. But then the moment she'd called attention to her hair, his thoughts had immediately gone to his regular fantasy of seeing those locks spilled over his bare chest. 'I can't go in there, looking like this. People will think—' When she trailed off in embarrassed silence, Stephen's lips twitched.

'What will they think?' he prompted, studying her flushed cheeks and rosy lips knowing damned well what some of them were going to rightfully assume.

'It does not bear contemplating,' she said with a shudder, pulling the pins out of the gleaming mass and letting it tumble over her shoulders.

Sherry pulled the comb through her hair, growing increasingly aware of the way his warm gaze lingered on her movements, and it only added to her confusion. 'Please stop looking at me in that way,' she said helplessly.

'Looking at you has been my favorite pastime from the moment you asked me to describe your face,' he said solemnly, looking straight into her eyes.

The velvet roughness of his voice and the amazing words he'd spoken were more seductive than any kiss could have been. Sherry felt all her resistance to marrying him begin to collapse, but pride and her heart demanded she mean more to him than she apparently had. 'Before you think any further about a marriage on Sunday,' she said hesitantly, 'I think you should know I have a freakish aversion to something that English ladies seem not to mind in the least. I myself did not recognize, until earlier tonight, how strongly I feel.'

Baffled, Stephen said, 'To what do you have this aversion?'

'The color lavender.'

'I see.' Stephen was stunned by her temerity and unwillingly impressed by her courage.

'Please consider it very carefully before you decide if we should even remain betrothed another day.'

'I'll do that,' he replied.

He hadn't conceded as she'd hoped, but at least he wasn't angry, and he had taken her seriously. Sherry told herself to be satisfied with that and lifted her hands to try to restore more order to her tumbled hair. Self-conscious as the focus of his lazy, admiring glance, she said with a helpless smile, 'I can't do this if you're going to watch me.'

34

Reluctantly Stephen withdrew his gaze, but no-one else who saw her walking along the balcony beside him and down the steps into the Rutherfords' crowded ballroom a few minutes later looked away from her. Her head was high, her lips were rosy from his kisses, and her smooth skin seemed to glow. In contrast to the image of quiet serenity she presented in the cool ivory gown, her hair was loose, flowing over her shoulders and down her back in a molten mantle of graceful waves and curls.

To Sherry, it seemed to take forever to work their way through the guests who stopped the earl on the balcony, the steps, and the floor of the ballroom to speak to him – which wouldn't have mattered to her in the least if so much of their conversation hadn't been littered with joking references that made her feel excruciatingly uncomfortable. 'I say, Langford,' a gentleman on the balcony said with a laugh the instant the butler finished announcing their names, 'I heard you've developed a recent fondness for the assembly rooms at Almack's!'

The earl sent him a look of comic horror, but the joking had only just begun. An instant later, another man stopped a servant who was in the act of offering the last two glasses of champagne on his tray to Stephen and Sherry. 'No, no, no!' he said to the startled servant as he whisked the glasses off the tray and out of their reach. 'His lordship prefers *lemonade* these days. Oh, and be sure it is nice and warm,' he instructed the servant, 'just the way they serve it at Almack's.'

The earl leaned forward and said something that made the other man guffaw, and the good-natured joking went on and on and on as they wended their way slowly down the stairs . . .

'Langford, is it true?' a middle-aged man joked, when they finally reached the ballroom floor. 'Did some red-haired chit at Almack's actually give you the cut-direct in the middle of the dance floor?' Stephen tipped his head meaningfully to Sherry, acknowledging it was true and that she was the 'red-haired chit' who had done it. With a large group of people looking on, the other man demanded an introduction, then he grinned widely at her. 'My dear young lady, it is a privilege to meet you,' he declared as he raised her hand for a gallant kiss. 'Until tonight, I didn't think there was a female alive who was immune to this devil's charm.'

Moments later an elderly man leaned heavily on his cane and said with a wheezing cackle, 'Heard your dancing isn't up to snuff these days, Langford. If you'll come round tomorrow, I could give you a lesson or two.' Overcome by his own humor, he banged his cane on the floor for emphasis and cackled with glee.

The earl bore it all with amused indulgence, declining to reply to most of their quips, but Sherry had to struggle to maintain even a surface appearance of being blasé. She was horrified at how closely he was watched and how swiftly gossip about him spread. Everyone, but everyone, seemed fully aware of every move he'd made in the last few hours, and she had a horrifying vision of people peeking into the windows of his coach, their hands curved round their temples, spying on them.

Just thinking of what they would have seen made her cheeks hot. Miss Charity noticed it as soon as they located her in the crush, standing with Whitney and Clayton and a group of the Westmorelands' friends. 'My goodness,' she exclaimed happily, 'you're in fine color, my dear. Strawberries and cream, that's just what you remind me of at this moment. The ride in the coach with the earl must have done you a world of good! You looked quite pale when we left Almack's.'

Sherry began vigorously fanning her face, and that was before she noted that several members of the

Westmoreland enclave had turned, waiting for introductions, and they heard it all. So did her fiancé, who
looked down at her with a knowing smile and leaned
close. 'Did it do you a world of good, sweet?' he asked.

In the midst of her mortifying predicament, his smile
made her laugh. 'You wretch!' she whispered, shaking her head in admonishment.

Unfortunately, that movement drew Charity Thornton's attention to a matter she had heretofore overlooked.
'Your hair was up when we left Almack's!' she exclaimed
worriedly. 'Did the pins come out, dear? I shall have
a word to say to my maid for her shoddy work
upon our return this very night!'

Sherry felt as if the entire group had stopped talking
in favor of listening to this amazingly revealing commentary from a woman whose job it was to protect the
very reputation she was demolishing. Several of them
had, including the Duke of Claymore, who gave Sherry
a secretive, knowing smile so much like Stephen's that
she quite forgot to be intimidated by him and instead
rolled her eyes at him. He burst out laughing at her
impertinence and introduced her to the two couples
closest to him – the Duke and Duchess of Hawthorne
and the Marquess and Marchioness of Wakefield. Both
couples greeted her with a warmth and cordiality that
made her like them instantly. 'I gather you were the
attraction that lured Stephen to Almack's?' said the
Duke of Hawthorne, and his wife smiled at Sherry and
added, 'We were all longing to have a look at you. Now
that we have,' she added, glancing at the Wakefields and
including them in her flattering assessment, 'it is little
wonder that he went tearing out of The Strathmore
when he realized Almack's doors were soon to close.'

Oblivious to all of that conversation, Miss Charity
was concentrating on a half dozen young men from
Almack's making their determined way across the
crowded ballroom. So was Stephen. 'Langford, do go
away!' she said, turning to him. 'Those young men are

heading straight for Sherry, and you'll run them off if you intend to stand here as you are doing with that – that very *unwelcoming* expression upon your face.'

'Yes, Stephen,' Whitney teased, linking her arm happily through his, her smile telling him that Clayton had already told her a wedding was imminent, 'could you not contrive to look more congenial when several of London's most desirable bachelors are about to surround Sherry?'

'No,' he said bluntly and temporarily eliminated the problem by touching Sherry's arm and turning her to meet their host.

Marcus Rutherford was a tall, imposing man with a warm smile and the relaxed congeniality and unshakable confidence that came from a privileged life and an illustrious bloodline that few could match. Sherry liked him instantly and rather regretted the necessity to turn away and acknowledge the gentlemen from Almack's who were lined up to speak with her and ask for dances.

'You seem to have a great deal of competition, Stephen, and it's little wonder,' Rutherford remarked as Makepeace drew Sherry onto the dance floor with Miss Charity waving daintily and beaming approvingly at the pair.

'And for once,' Clayton chuckled, watching Charity Thornton's satisfied expression as she kept a close watch on the dance floor, 'the object of your attentions has a chaperone who does *not* seem to be overcome with joy to have you nearby.'

Stephen heard that, but an idea was taking shape that suited him perfectly, an idea that would also immediately undo whatever damage to Sherry's reputation her own chaperone had just done.

'I heard Nicki DuVille finds her very out-of-the-ordinary,' Rutherford commented, lifting his glass of champagne to his lips. 'Enough so that he actually went to Almack's too. Gossip has it that the two of you stood off to the side, holding up the same pillar, when you couldn't get close enough to the young lady because of her other beaux. That must have been a sight,' Rutherford continued, his shoulders shaking with mirth. 'You and DuVille both at Almack's and on the same night. Two wolves in a roomful of cubs. Where is Nicki, by the by?' Rutherford added, idly searching across a sea of six hundred faces.

'Nursing his broken heart, I hope,' Stephen replied, putting his idea into action.

'DuVille?' Rutherford said, laughing again. 'That is almost as difficult to imagine as the two of you at Almack's. Why would he have a broken heart?'

With a mocking lift of his brows and an amused smile, Stephen replied, 'Because the object of his affections has just agreed to marry another.'

'Really?' he said, fascinated and looking at Makepeace with new respect as he danced with Sherry. 'You can't mean Makepeace. Tell me all that beauty won't be wasted on that young pup.'

'She's not marrying Makepeace.'

'Then who is she marrying?'

'Me.'

His face went from shock, to delight, to comic anticipation. Gesturing with his glass to the entire ballroom, he added, 'Would you consider letting me announce it tonight? I would love to see their faces when they hear the news.'

'I'd consider it.'

'Excellent!' he said, sending a censorious look at Whitney Westmoreland as he added, 'If you recall, your grace, I once tried to announce your betrothal, but you had some maggot in your head that night about wanting to keep it secret.'

That seemingly innocent remark caused her husband and brother-in-law to cast her matched looks of amused admonishment for having rebelled against marrying her husband in ways that had wreaked havoc all over London. 'Stop it, both of you,' Whitney said with an embarrassed laugh. 'Do you ever intend to let me forget it?'

'No,' said her husband with a tender grin.

Sherry was standing by Stephen's side for the first time in an hour, enjoying the friendly conversation of his friends, when Lord Rutherford abruptly detached himself from the group. She saw him wend his way through the crowd toward the orchestra, but she paid it no heed until the music rose to an imperative crescendo, then died completely in the classic musical call for attention. Conversations broke off and surprised guests slowly turned, looking about for the cause of the odd occurrence.

'Ladies and gentlemen,' Stephen's friend said in a surprisingly carrying voice, 'I have the very great honor of announcing an important betrothal tonight, before it is formally announced in the paper—' Sherry looked around, as did many of the guests, wondering who the newly engaged couple might be, and in her curiosity, she overlooked the tender amusement in Lord Westmoreland's smile as he watched her study the crowd alertly, trying to guess. 'I know this particular betrothal will come as a vast relief to many of the bachelors in this ballroom, who will be thankful to have this gentleman finally out of their way. Ah, I see I have aroused your curiosity,' he said, obviously enjoying his role as he looked around at hundreds of faces alive with amused curiosity.

'In view of that, I think I'll prolong your suspense a moment longer and instead of telling you the names of the parties, I will ask them to do me the honor of performing their first formal duty as future husband and wife, by officially opening our ball.' He left the vacant dance floor, accompanied by murmurs and laughter, but no-one was looking at him. As the orchestra leader signalled a waltz and the music began to fill the room, everyone was scanning the crowd and even looking suspiciously at one another. 'What a wonderful way to announce an engagement,' Sherry confided to her amused future in-laws.

'I am very glad you approve,' Stephen said, covering her hand with his and slowly leading her to the edge of the dance floor – so that she could have a better view, Sherry presumed. But when they were there, and the music continued to flow and soar in its rich tempo, he stepped slightly in front of her, blocking her view. 'Miss Lancaster,' he said quietly, pulling her attention to him when she was trying to see around him.

'Yes?' Sherry said, smiling at the inexplicable amusement in his eyes.

'May I have the honor of the next dance?'

There was no time for stage fright, no time to react at all, because his arm was already sliding around her waist, drawing her forward, then whirling her off the sidelines and onto the dance floor. The moment the crowd realized who was leading off the dance, laughter and cheers exploded in the room, building to a deafening roar.

Overhead, crystal chandeliers glittered and gleamed with fifty thousand candles while the mirrored walls reflected a couple dancing alone beneath them – a tall, dark-haired man who waltzed with easy grace, his arm possessively encircling a young woman in an ivory gown. Sherry saw their reflection in the mirrors, sensed the heady, romantic magic of the moment, and she lifted her gaze to his. Somewhere in the depths of those knowing blue eyes smiling down at her, she saw another sort of romantic magic sparking to life . . . something deep and profound and silent. It held her captive, promising her something . . . asking . . . inviting.

I love you, she thought.

His arm tightened around her waist, as if he'd heard her and had liked the sound of it. And then she realized she'd said it aloud.

On the balcony above the ballroom, the Dowager Duchess of Claymore looked down upon the couple and smiled with pleasure, already thinking of the splendid grandchildren they would have. She wished her husband could have been with her, watching his son with the woman who was going to share his life. Robert would have approved of Sherry, she thought. Unconsciously rubbing her thumb over the marriage ring Robert had slid on her finger nearly four decades before, Alicia tenderly watched their son waltzing with his affianced bride, and she could almost feel Robert standing at her side. *'Look at them, my love,'* she whispered to him in her heart. *'He's so like you, Robert, and she reminds me so much of me in little ways.'* Alicia could almost feel Robert's hand slide around her waist as he leaned down, and his smiling voice whispered in her ear, *'In that case, my sweet, Stephen is going to have his hands full.'*

A proud smile trembled on her lips as she thought of her own contributions toward bringing this moment about. Her eyes sparkled as she thought of the names she'd placed on the list of suitors Stephen had asked her to prepare, and his thunderstruck reaction to her candidates. They'd all been so *old* that Stephen hadn't even realized they were also infirm. *'I did it!'* she thought.

Beside her, Hugh Whitticomb was observing the same sight and thought of the long-ago nights that Alicia and his own Maggie had kept Robert and himself on the dance floor until dawn. As he watched Sherry and Stephen moving together, he chuckled with delight at how successfully he had manipulated the situation. True, there were going to be some rough seas when she recovered her memory, but she loved Stephen Westmoreland and he loved her. Hugh knew it. *'I did it, Maggie girl,'* he told her in his heart. Her answer floated through his mind. *'Yes you did, darling. Now, ask Alicia to dance. This is a special moment.'*

'Alicia,' he said dubiously, 'would you like to dance?'

She turned a dazzling smile to him, as she placed her hand on his arm. 'Thank you, Hugh! What a wonderful idea! It's been years since we danced together!'

Standing off to one side of the dance floor, Miss Charity Thornton tapped her toe in rhythm to the magic of the waltz, her faded blue eyes bright with pleasure as she watched the Earl of Langford perform his first official function as Sherry's future husband. As the other dancers finally moved onto the floor, Nicholas DuVille spoke at her ear, and she turned in surprise. 'Miss Thornton,' he said with a lazy, white grin, 'would you honor me with this dance?'

Stunned with pleasure that he had sought her out at this momentous occasion, she beamed at him and placed her small hand upon his sleeve, feeling like a girl again, as one of the handsomest men in the room led her onto the floor. 'Poor Makepeace,' she confided without a hint of sympathy, 'he looks quite devastated over there.'

'I hope *you* are not devastated,' Nicki said with concern, and when she seemed confused, he added kindly, 'I had the impression you were very much in favor of *my* suit.'

She looked charmingly flustered as he whirled her around and around, adjusting his steps for her diminutive size. 'Nicholas,' she said, 'may I confide something to you?'

'Certainly, if you like.'

'I am old, and I nod off when I don't at all wish to sleep, and I am dreadfully forgetful at times . . .'

'I hadn't noticed,' Nicki gallantly replied.

'*But*, dear boy,' she continued severely, ignoring his disclaimer, 'I am not enough of a *ninnyhammer* to have believed for more than the first hour that you were besotted with our dear Sherry!'

Nicki nearly missed a step. 'You . . . did not think I was?' he said cautiously.

'Certainly not. Things have worked out exactly as I planned they should.'

'As *you* planned they should?' Nicki repeated a little dazedly, completely reassessing her and coming up with answers that made him feel like shouting with laughter

264

and flushing with embarrassment over his own naiveté.

'Certainly,' she said with a proud little wag of her head. 'I do not like to boast,' she tipped her head toward Sherry and Langford, 'but I did that.'

Uncertain if the unbelievable notion forming in his head was correct, Nicki studied her closely from the corner of his eyes. 'How did you do whatever it was you think you did?'

'A little nudge here, a little push there, dear boy. Although I did wonder tonight if we should have let Sherry leave with Langford. He was jealous as fire over Makepeace.' Her little shoulders shook with merry laughter. 'It was the most *diverting* thing I've seen in thirty years! At least, I *think* it was . . . I shall miss all this excitement. I have felt so very useful from the moment Hugh Whitticomb asked me to be chaperone. I knew, of course, that I wasn't supposed to do a good job of it, or else he'd have got someone else to do it.' She looked up inquiringly after Nicholas's long silence and found him staring at her as if he'd not seen her before. 'Did you wish to say something, dear boy?'

'I think so.'

'Yes?'

'Please accept my humblest apologies.'

'For underestimating me?'

Nicki nodded, grinning, and she smiled back at him. 'Everyone does, you know.'

35

I feel like a guest in my own house,' Stephen remarked ironically to his amused brother as they waited for the women to join them in his drawing room so they could leave for the opera. He had not been alone with Sherry since he'd announced their engagement last night at the Rutherfords' ball, and he found it absurd that his change in public status to being her fiancé supposedly had to mark the end of all possibilities for the slightest intimacy.

At his mother's suggestion, he'd moved into Clayton's house, and she had moved into his, where she planned to remain with Sherry during the three days before the wedding – 'to absolutely eliminate any possible reasons for gossip, since Sherry is under the very nose of the *ton* here in London.'

Stephen had graciously agreed to her suggestion only because he had every reason to expect Whitticomb to maintain his earlier position that Sherry would require the security of his reassuring presence, and that Charity Thornton was an adequate chaperone.

Instead, the unreliable physician had agreed with Stephen's mother that Sherry's reputation might suffer now that Society knew Stephen was personally interested in her.

Tonight, his brother and sister-in-law were playing chaperone, accompanying Sherry and him to the opera, while his mother attended her own functions, but she would be there when they returned, she'd promised.

'You could always move Sherry in with us,' Clayton pointed out, enjoying Stephen's discomfiture and his healthy eagerness to be alone with his fiancée, 'and then you could stay here.'

'That's as absurd as this arrangement. The point is that I'm not going to preempt the damned wedding and take her to bed when there are only three more days to wait—'

He broke off at the sound of feminine voices on the staircase, and they both stood up. Stephen picked up his black coat and shrugged into it as he strolled forward, then nearly walked into his brother, who had stopped to watch the two women rushing into the hall together laughing. 'Look at that,' he said softly, but Stephen was already looking, and he knew what Clayton meant even before he added, 'What a portrait they would make.'

Their musical laughter made both men grin as they watched the Duchess of Claymore and the future Countess of Langford trying on each other's capes and bonnets in front of the mirror while Colfax and Hodgkin stood with hands clasped behind their backs, staring straight ahead, as if oblivious to the girlish antics. Hodgkin wasn't as good as Colfax at hiding his thoughts, and his gaze kept sliding to Sherry and a smile kept tugging at his cheek.

Whitney had been wearing a bright blue gown when they arrived. Sherry had said she intended to wear a bright green gown even though, she'd softly added, as she looked at the huge sapphire Stephen had given her that afternoon for a betrothal ring, 'sapphire blue is my favorite color of all.'

They had evidently changed their minds *and* their gowns upstairs because Whitney was now wearing Sherry's green gown and Sherry was wearing her deep blue one.

As both men started forward, they heard Whitney gaily predict, 'Clayton will never notice the change, mark my word.'

'And I doubt Lord Westmoreland paid the slightest heed to my comment about which gown would look best with my ring,' Sherry said, laughing. 'He was preoccupied with—' She choked back the word 'kissing,' and Stephen stifled a laugh.

'Shall we?' he said to his brother.

'By all means,' Clayton agreed, and without further communication, Stephen walked up behind Whitney while Clayton offered his arm to Sherry, startling a peal of laughter from her as he joked in a low voice, 'Did I tell you earlier how lovely you look in green, my love?'

Whitney was pulling on her gloves when masculine hands touched her shoulders and Stephen's voice whispered tenderly in her ear beside her bonnet. 'Sherry,' he

267

whispered, and beneath his hands her shoulders shook with laughter as she carefully kept her face hidden, 'I've arranged with my brother to leave us alone for a while when we return from the opera, so we can be private. He'll distract Whitney—' She whirled around and had already begun her indignant reprimand before she saw his knowing grin. 'Stephen Westmoreland, if you *dare* to even—'

Outside Number 14 Upper Brook Street carriages paraded in dignified pomp, their lamps glowing and flickering like a procession of golden fireflies. As the conveyance belonging to the Duke and Duchess of Dranby passed by the house, her grace looked admiringly at its splendid Palladian facade and sighed. 'Dranby, who shall we find to wed Juliette, now that Langford is taken? Where will we find his equal in taste and elegance, in refinement and—' She broke off as the front door of the house opened and four laughing people erupted from it – the earl running down the front steps in pursuit of his new fiancée. 'Sherry,' he called, 'I knew she wasn't you!'

The American girl called a laughing reply back as she headed straight for the Duke of Claymore's coach, which was pulled up behind the earl's. The duke and duchess pressed closer to their coach window staring with disbelief as the Earl of Langford caught his new fiancée by the waist as she climbed into the duke's coach, swung her into his arms, and firmly deposited her into his own coach.

'Dranby,' said the duchess, 'we have just witnessed the most delicious *on-dit* of the year! Wait until I tell everyone what we saw!'

'If you'll take my advice, you won't bother,' said the duke, leaning back in his seat.

'Whyever not?'

'No-one will believe you.'

36

A steady stream of luxurious conveyances were packed into Bow Street, waiting to pull up before Covent Garden's brightly lit facade to unload their passengers. 'It looks like a Grecian temple!' Sherry exclaimed in delight as she peered out the window of their coach. 'Like the painting hanging in your library.'

Her enthusiasm was so infectious that Stephen actually leaned over and looked at the Royal Opera House's facade with her. 'It was modelled after the Temple of Minerva at Athens.'

Careful to lift her beautiful skirts, Sherry took Stephen's hand as she alighted from the coach and paused to look about her before they went inside. 'It's wonderful,' she said, ignoring the amused glances being cast her way as they made their way across the expansive vestibule and proceeded up a grand staircase past imposing Ionic columns and glittering Grecian lamps. It was the fashion in London to appear quite bored and blasé at all times, but Sherry didn't care. Her face glowing with pleasure, she stopped in the lobby that led to the lower tier of boxes and looked about at the graceful pillars and arched recesses that contained paintings of scenes from Shakespeare.

Loath to rush her, yet conscious they were blocking the other patrons, Stephen touched her elbow and said softly, 'We'll stay late so that you may look around at your leisure.'

'Oh, I'm sorry. Only, it is hard to imagine that people can walk by all this without pausing to notice it.'

Stephen's box was located for maximum view, and when they entered it, he actually peered around to get a look at Sherry's face, but she was gazing in admiration at the identical tier of elegant boxes opposite them, each with its own chandelier and with gold flowers and stars painted on the box's front.

'I hope you like the opera,' he said, sitting down beside her and nodding casually to friends in the box on their right. 'I try to come every Thursday.'

Sherry looked up at him, so happy that she was almost afraid to trust it. 'I think I do. That is, I feel excited, which must be a very good sign.' His eyes had been smiling into hers, but as she spoke she saw their expression change and his lids lowered, his gaze dropping to her lips, lingering long on them, then lifting.

It was a kiss! she realized. It was a kiss, and he'd meant for her to feel it, to understand that was what he was doing. Without conscious volition, her hand moved imperceptibly, seeking his as it had the first day she'd returned to consciousness.

It was a tiny movement, one he might have missed, even if he had been looking instead of turning to greet friends who'd stopped into the box. And yet, as Sherry turned her head to do the same, his hand slid into her open palm, covering it, strong fingers lacing with hers. A jolt streaked up Sherry's spine as his thumb slowly rubbed her palm, brushing left and right, then back again. It was another kiss, she realized, her breath catching. This one slower, longer, deeper.

Her heart swelling, she looked down at the beautiful male hand partially covered by the open fan in her lap, watching his finger stroking while her body seemed to melt from the touch.

Below, in the gallery and pits, the crowd was noisy and curious, openly studying the occupants of the boxes, and Sherry tried to look perfectly casual, while the simple touch of a finger on her palm made her pulse continue to escalate.

When the movement finally stopped and her pulse slowed to normal, she felt very foolish to be so susceptible to what was very probably an idle touch on his part. Partly out of curiosity and partly for mischief, Sherry experimented. While he chatted with his brother, she stroked her thumb over Stephen's knuckles, concentrating far more on that than the conversation. It had no noticeable effect on him. In fact, he opened his hand, and for a second Sherry thought he was going to pull it away. Since he left it there instead, palm up, she dipped her gaze and thoughtfully traced each long finger from its tip to the vee where it met his wide palm, while he continued his absorbed conversation with his brother. Since he seemed not to notice or object, Sherry touched his palm, her fingertip following each intersecting line. *I love you,* she thought helplessly, telling him so with her fingertip. *Please love me too.* Sometimes when he kissed her or smiled at her, she was almost certain he did, but she wanted to hear the words, needed to hear them. *I love you,* she told him through her fingertip as it stroked his open palm.

Stephen gave up all pretense of trying to carry on an intelligent conversation and slid a glance at her bent head. He was sitting in a noisy public place, with a bulging arousal that felt as if he'd been indulging in an hour of intense sexual foreplay instead of merely holding hands with an inexperienced virgin. His heart was beating in the heavy, insistent tempo that came with denying himself a climax while he maximized his pleasure, and still he did not stop her. Instead he opened his hand more, fingers splaying in willing submission to his own torture.

He could not believe what she was doing to him, and he was deriving almost as much pleasure from knowing she *wanted* to touch him as from her sweet stroking.

In the glittering, sophisticated world he inhabited, the roles were clearly defined: wives were for the breeding of an heir; husbands were a social and financial necessity; mistresses gave and received passion. Couples who had nothing in common with their own spouses had affairs with other people's spouses. Stephen could think of perhaps twenty couples, among the thousands he knew, who shared anything stronger than mild affection. He could think of hundreds who shared nothing at all. Wives did not yearn for a husband's touch, they did not deliberately incite a husband's yearning for theirs. And yet that was *exactly* what Sherry was doing.

Beneath lowered lids, he gazed at her profile as she delicately traced something onto his sensitized palm, then traced the same thing again. The third time she did it, he tried to distract himself from the desire that was flowing from the nerve endings in his open palm throughout his entire nerve stream, and to concentrate on what she was doing. With her fingertip she drew an open circle on his palm and then two perpendicular lines joined at the bottom:

C L

Her initials.

Stephen drew a ragged breath and lifted his gaze to her profile while in his mind he dragged her into a darkened corner and covered that soft mouth with his . . .

He was mentally kissing her breasts when a commotion below heralded the beginning of the opera and he wasn't certain whether he was relieved or sorry to have her distracted, but distracted she was.

Sherry leaned forward expectantly, watching as the crimson draperies swept open beneath a graceful arch with painted figures of women holding trumpets and wreaths of laurel. And then the orchestra began to play, and she forgot the world.

Stephen held her hand on the way home, feeling a little foolish for his boyish pleasure in the simple touch. 'I gather you liked the performance,' he said idly as he walked beside her to the front door of his house, their path illuminated by a bright full moon.

'I loved it!' she said, her eyes filled with excited wonder. 'I think I *recognized* it. Not the words, but the melody.'

That piece of good news was followed by another: as Colfax helped Sherry off with her light cape, he volunteered the gratifying information that Stephen's mother had retired for the night. 'Thank you, Colfax, I suggest you do the same,' Stephen hinted flatly, his mind instantly replaying his fantasy at the opera. The butler took himself off down the hall, snuffing out all but the candles in the entry, and Stephen looked down at Sherry as she started to bid him good night.

'Thank you for a wonderful evening, my lor—'

'My name is Stephen,' he told her, wondering how in God's name he could have forgotten to ask her to use it.

Sherry tried it out, loving the strange intimacy of it. 'Thank you, Stephen.' There was little time to relish it, however, because he took her elbow and guided her firmly down the dark hall into a moonlit salon, closed the door, and turned to her instead of walking further into the room.

With the door behind her and his body in front of her, Sherry looked at his moonlit face, trying to imagine what he intended to do in the dark. 'What—?'

'This—' he answered. Bracing his flattened palms on the door on either side of her head, he leaned his body into hers and lowered his head.

Before Sherry could react, his mouth seized hers, stealing her breath while his hard body pressed into hers, his hips moving slightly, and the effect on her senses was stunning. With a silent moan, she slid her hands around his neck and kissed him back, welcoming the invasion of his tongue, glorying in the rasp of his breath as he kissed her harder, helplessly yielding her body to the insistent movements of his hips.

37

Carrying the morning *Post* in his hand, Thomas Morrison strolled into his cozy dining room and looked cautiously at his new wife, who was toying with her breakfast, staring out the window at the noisy London street. 'Charise, what has been bothering you these last few days?'

Charise looked up at the face she'd thought so handsome on the ship, and then at the tiny little dining room in his tiny little house, and she was so furious with him and herself that she didn't deign to reply. On the ship he'd seemed so dashing and romantic in his uniform, and he'd spoken to her so gallantly, but all that had changed as soon as she'd said her vows. After that, he'd wanted her to do that disgusting thing in bed with him, and when she told him she hated it, he'd been cross with her for the first time. Once she made him understand that she was not going to put up with him or that, their brief honeymoon in Devon had been pleasant enough for her. But when he brought her back to London and she saw his house, she'd been dumbstruck. He'd lied to her, misled her into believing he had a fine house and an excellent income, but by her standards, this was near-poverty, and she despised it, and him.

If she'd married Burleton, she would have been a baroness; she could have shopped in the fabulous shops she'd seen in Bond Street and Piccadilly. Right now, right this very minute, she'd be wearing a beautiful ruffled morning gown and paying a morning call on one of her fashionable new friends who lived in those splendid mansions along Brook Street and Pall Mall. As it was, she'd spent all her money on a single gown, and then gone for a stroll in Green Park, where the Quality walked in the afternoon, and they'd ignored her as if she didn't exist! She hadn't realized what a necessity a noble title was until she'd strolled in the park yesterday afternoon and witnessed the sort of tightly knit, closed society that existed here.

Not only that, when her loathsome husband asked the cost of the gown and she told him, the man had looked as if he was going to cry! Instead of being admired and praised for her excellent taste and lovely figure, all he'd thought about was the money.

She was the one who had a right to cry, she thought furiously, glancing contemptuously at him as he read the newspaper. At home in Richmond, she'd been the one whom people envied and imitated. Now she was nothing – less than nothing – and she was consumed by envy every day when she went to the park and watched the *ton* promenading about, and ignoring her.

The problem with Thomas Morrison was that he didn't realize she was special. Everyone in Richmond had known it, even her papa, but the tall, handsome clod she'd married didn't grasp it. She'd tried to explain that to him, but he'd insulted her by saying she hadn't been behaving as if she were special! Furious, she'd informed him that 'people behave as they are treated!' That remark had been so clever that it sounded as if it came straight from Miss Bromleigh herself, and still he didn't respond as he should have.

But then, what could she expect from a man so lacking in refinement and taste that he didn't know the difference in desirability between a paid companion and an heiress?

At first, he'd paid more attention to that Bromleigh woman than Charise herself, and no wonder – Sheridan Bromleigh didn't know her place at all. She read romance novels about governesses who married the lord of the house, and when Charise had mocked that ludicrous idea, she'd boldly said she didn't think titles or wealth would or should matter between two individuals who *truly* loved each other.

In fact, Charise thought bitterly as she stabbed a slice of ham with her knife, if it hadn't been for Sheridan Bromleigh, she wouldn't be in this heartbreaking mess! She would never have felt compelled to draw Morrison's attention away from her lowly paid companion when the two of them seemed to like each other, would never have eloped with him to show everyone on the ship, especially Miss Bromleigh, that Charise Lancaster could have any gentleman she wanted. Her awful life was the fault of that redheaded witch who'd put all that romantic nonsense in her head about love and fairy-tale marriages where money and titles didn't matter!

'Charise?'

She hadn't spoken to him in two days, but something about the odd note in his voice made her respond by looking up, and when she saw his incredulous expression, she almost asked him what he was reading that made him look so foolish.

'Was there anyone else aboard our ship whose name happened to be Charise Lancaster? I mean it is not an extraordinarily common name, is it?'

She glared at him contemptuously. Stupid question. Stupid man. There was nothing common about her, including her unique name.

'According to this newspaper,' he said in a dazed voice, looking at her, 'Charise Lancaster, who arrived in London three weeks ago aboard the *Morning Star*, has just become betrothed to the Earl of Langford.'

'I don't believe you!' Charise said with blazing scorn, snatching the newspaper out of his hand so she could read the announcement herself. 'There was no other Charise Lancaster on the ship.'

'Read it for yourself,' he said needlessly, because she'd already snatched the newspaper from him.

A moment later, she flung the paper down on the table,

her face mottled with fury. 'Someone is impersonating me to the earl. Some scheming, vile, evil . . .'

'Where the deuce are you going?'

'To call upon my "new fiancé."'

38

Humming softly to herself, Sherry took out the gown she was going to wear for her wedding in an hour and laid it across the bed. It was still too early to change from her day dress into the dressier blue gown she was going to wear later, and the hands on the clock above the mantel seemed to be moving at half speed.

Since it had been impossible to invite some of their friends and omit others, the decision had been made to limit the wedding guests to immediate family only, which avoided offending the sensibilities of friends who were not invited and also kept it a quiet intimate affair, which Sheridan preferred. It also enabled the family to wait a few weeks before announcing the marriage so that it didn't look too sudden.

According to the dowager duchess, who had gently asked Sherry to call her 'Mother,' last night, hasty weddings inevitably brought on a storm of gossip and conjecture about the reasons for the haste. Miss Charity had been invited because no-one had the heart to exclude her, and she was due here any moment. Dr Whitticomb was the only other non-family member asked to attend, but he'd sent word this morning that a patient of his was in urgent need of him, and that he'd come round later for a glass of champagne.

According to the plan, the Duke of Claymore was to escort his mother and Whitney here in an hour, and Stephen would arrive a half hour later, precisely at eleven A.M., when the wedding was to take place. English weddings, she had learned, traditionally took place between eight o'clock in the morning and noon, so that the bridal couple had the benefit of bright daylight and a full night's sleep to contemplate for the last time the import of the step they were about to take. The vicar was obviously aware of the import of his own role in the marriage of the Earl of Langford, because he'd arrived an hour ago to make certain he was on time – a precaution that Colfax clearly found a little amusing when he imparted the information to Sherry. Clad in formal livery for the occasion, as were all the servants she'd seen downstairs earlier, Colfax had also imparted the information that the household staff wished to sing for her, on this momentous occasion, an old and traditional song they had been rehearsing in the kitchen. Touched by their thoughtfulness, Sherry had instantly and delightedly agreed.

Based on what Sherry had witnessed so far, it appeared that only the butler and the bride were taking things in stride. Her maid was so nervous that she'd fussed half the morning over Sherry's bath and hair, dropping pins and mislaying towels everywhere, until Sherry finally sent her off in order to savor her anticipation in solitude.

Wandering over to the dressing table, Sherry gazed down at the diamond and sapphire necklace lying in a large, white-velvet-lined jeweler's case that Stephen had sent over to her this morning. Smiling, she touched the necklace, and the triple band of diamonds and sapphires seemed to sparkle happily back at her, matching her mood. The lavish piece was more formal than her gown required, but Sherry intended to wear it anyway because it was from Stephen.

Stephen . . . He was going to be her husband, and her thoughts drifted inevitably to the minutes she had spent in the dark salon with him after the opera. He had kissed her into mindless insensibility, his hard body pressed into hers, and shock waves of sensation had rushed over her with every grinding shift of his hips, every deep demand of his tongue, every possessive, intimate stroke of his hands over her breasts. By the time he moved away a little, his breathing sounded strangely ragged, and Sherry was clinging to him in helpless abandon. 'Do you have any idea,' he'd whispered in a rough voice, 'how passionate you are, and how unique?'

Not certain how to answer that, she searched her empty memory for some specific cause for the uneasy guilt she felt for allowing him to kiss and touch her. Finding nothing in particular, she'd slid her hand around his nape and pressed her cheek against his hard chest. With a half-laugh, half-groan, he'd gently pulled her hand down and stepped back. 'Enough. Unless you want the honeymoon to precede the wedding, young lady, you're going to have to content yourself with a few chaste pecks. . .' She must have looked disappointed, because, laughing softly, he'd leaned into her and kissed her again.

Sherry's thoughts were disrupted by a knock on her door and she called for whoever it was to enter. 'Your pardon, milady,' Hodgkin said, his narrow face pinched and pale, as if he were in pain. 'There is a young – I hesitate to use the word "lady" in view of the sort of language she used – woman downstairs who insists she must see you.'

Sherry looked at him in the mirror above the dressing table. 'Who is she?'

The elderly under-butler spread his hands and they trembled with the force of his reaction. 'She says she is you, miss.'

'I beg your pardon?'

'She says *she* is Miss Charise Lancaster.'

'How very. . .' Sherry's heart began to thunder for no apparent reason, and her voice strangled on the word 'odd.'

Sounding as if he were begging her to claim the other

woman was a mystic or a fraud, he added, 'She is . . .
is in possession of a great many facts that might seem
to prove her claim. I – I know this to be true, my lady,
because I was once employed by Baron Burleton.'

Burleton . . . Burleton . . . Burleton . . . Burleton. The
name began to howl like a banshee in her brain.

'She – she was demanding to see the earl, but you
have been very good to me . . . to all of us, and I
would hope that were our positions reversed, not that
they ever could be, you would at least come to me with
any possible falsehood, instead of carrying the tale to the
earl . . . to someone else. I will, naturally, have to tell
him of the woman's wish to see him when he arrives for
the nuptials, but if you perhaps had a chance to see her
first and she were to be more calm . . .'

Sherry leaned her hands on the dressing table for support, nodding to him to show the woman who claimed
to be her upstairs, and she closed her eyes tight, concentrating.

Burleton . . . BURLETON . . . BURLETON.

Images and voices began to flash through her mind,
speeding up faster and faster, spinning so quickly that
the next one appeared before the other had spun away.

. . . A ship, a cabin, a frightened maid. *'What if
Miss Charise's fiancé thinks we killed her, or sold her,
or something evil like that? It would be the baron's word
against yours, and you aren't nobody, so the law will be on
his side. This is England, not America . . .'*

. . . Torchlight, stevedores, a tall, grim man standing at
the end of a gangplank. *'Miss Lancaster, I'm afraid there's
been an accident. Lord Burleton was killed yesterday.'*

. . . Cotton fields, meadows, a wagon filled with goods,
a little girl with red hair . . . *'My papa calls me "carrot"
because of my hair, but my name is Sheridan. There is a rose
– a flower – called Sheridan, and my mama named me for
it.'*

. . . A restless horse, a stern-faced Indian, the smell of
summer. *'White men are not as good as Indians for giving*

names. Not flower, you. Fire, you. Flames. Burn bright.'

. . . Campfires, moonlight, a handsome Spaniard with smiling eyes and a guitar in his hands, music pulsing in the night. *'Sing with me, cara.'*

. . . A tiny, neat house, indignant little girl, angry woman.

'Patrick Bromleigh, you ought to be horsewhipped for the way you've reared that child. She can't read, and she can't write, her manners are deplorable, and her hair is wanton. She announced to me, as bold as brass, that she "fancies" someone named Rafael Benavente and she'll probably ask him to marry her someday. She actually intends to propose matrimony herself and to some Spanish vagabond who cheats at cards. And I haven't even mentioned her other favorite companion – an Indian male who sleeps with dogs! If you have any conscience, any love for her, you will leave her here with me.'

. . . Two solemn men standing in the yard, a third one in the doorway, his face tense. *'You mind your aunt Cornelia, darlin'. I'll be back for you before you know it – a year or two at most.'*

. . . A distraught child clinging to him. *'No, Papa, don't! Don't leave me here! Please! Please, I'll wear dresses and fix my wanton hair, just don't leave me here. I want to go with you and Rafe and Dog Lies Sleeping! That's where I belong, no matter what she says! Papa, Papa, wait—'*

. . . A stern-faced woman with gray hair, a child who was supposed to call her 'Aunt Cornelia.' *'Do not try to stare me out of countenance with that expression, child. I perfected that very look long ago in England, and I'm quite immune to it. In England, it would have served you well, were you Squire Faraday's acknowledged granddaughter, but this is America. Here, I teach deportment to the children of people whom I would have once regarded as my inferiors, and I am lucky to have the work.'*

. . . Another woman, stout, pleasant, firm. *'We may have a position for you at our school. I've heard some very good things about you from your aunt, Miss Bromleigh.'*

. . . Little girls' voices. 'Good morning, Miss Bromleigh.' Miniature young ladies in white stockings and ribbons practicing their curtsies while Sheridan demonstrated.

Her palms were perspiring on the dressing table's top, her knees were turning to liquid. Behind her, the door opened and a blonde girl stalked in, her voice raised in fury. 'You unspeakable fraud!'

Reeling from the fleeing visions, Sherry forced her eyes open, lifted her head, and stared into the mirror above her dressing table. Framed beside her own face was another face, a FAMILIAR FACE. 'Oh, my God!' she moaned as her arms began to shake and give way, forcing her to either straighten from her hunched position or fall to the floor. Slowly, she lifted her palms off the dressing table, and very slowly, she turned, while terror began to hammer through her, banishing weakness and lethargy. Her entire body vibrating with panic, she faced Charise Lancaster, and felt each of her enraged words as if it was a blow to her head:

'You *evil*, despicable, scheming *slut!* Look at this place. Look at you!' Her eyes were wild as she looked around at the luxurious green and gold suite. 'You've actually taken my place.'

'No!' Sheridan burst out, but her voice was unrecognizable, brittle and frantic. 'No, not on purpose. Dear God, don't—'

'It will take more than prayer to save you from prison,' her former student snapped, her face contorted with fury. 'You've taken my PLACE . . . You tricked me into marrying Morrison with all your talk of romance, and then *YOU TOOK MY PLACE*. You actually intended to MARRY AN EARL!'

'No, please, listen to me. It was an accident. I lost my memory.'

That only made her more infuriated. 'Lost your memory!' she screamed contemptuously. 'Well, you know who *I* am!' Without another word, she swung on her heel. 'I'll be back with the authorities within minutes, and we'll see how they feel about your memory loss, you vile—!'

Sherry ran without realizing she was moving, clutching the other girl's shoulders, trying to make her listen before she did the unthinkable, her words tumbling over themselves. 'Charise, please, listen. I was hit in the head – accident – and I didn't know who I was. Please wait – just listen to me – You don't know, don't understand what it would do to them to have a scandal.'

'I'll have you in a dungeon before nightfall!' she raged, flinging off Sheridan's hands. 'I'll have your precious earl exposed for the fool he is—'

Blackness rose up before Sheridan's eyes. Black on white. Headlines screaming. Scandal. Dungeons. *This is England, and you aren't nobody, so the law will be on his side.*

'I'll leave!' she cried, her voice plaintive and demented and confused as she began backing toward the door. 'I won't come back. I won't cause trouble. Don't bring authorities. Scandal will kill them. Look at me – I'm leaving.' Sherry whirled and ran. She fled down the staircase, nearly knocking over a footman. A lump rose in her throat at the realization that Stephen was going to walk into this hall in an hour, thinking he was about to be wed, only his bride would have deserted him. Her heart hammering, she raced into the library, scribbled a note, and thrust it at the stricken elderly butler, then she tore open the door, and raced down the steps, down the street, around the corner.

She ran and ran until she couldn't run anymore, and then she leaned against the side of a building, listening to a voice of her more recent past – a beloved voice – a beloved voice explaining things that had never happened to a woman he'd never met: *'The last time we were together in America, we quarrelled. I didn't think about our quarrel while you were ill, but when you began to recover the other night, I found it was still on my mind.'*

283

'What did we quarrel about?'

'I thought you paid too much notice to another man. I was jealous.'

Staggered by yet another shock, Sherry stared blindly at a passing carriage as she wandered slowly down the street. But he hadn't been jealous. His attitude had hardened from the moment she'd asked him if they were 'very much in love.'

Because they'd never been in love.

Her mind went numb with confusion and shock.

39

Stephen grinned at Colfax as he strode into the main hall, dressed formally for his wedding. 'Is the vicar here?'

'Yes, my lord, in the blue salon;' the butler said, his expression oddly withdrawn for such a festive occasion.

'Is my brother with him?'

'No, he's in the drawing room.'

Cognizant of the fact that he was not supposed to see his bride before the ceremony, Stephen said, 'Is it safe to go in there?'

'Perfectly.'

Stephen walked swiftly down the main hall into the drawing room. Clayton was standing with his back to the room, looking into the empty fireplace. 'I'm early,' Stephen began. 'Mother and Whitney are a few minutes behind me. Have you seen Sherry? Does she need any—'

Clayton slowly turned around, his expression so foreboding that Stephen stopped in mid-sentence. 'What's wrong?' he demanded.

'She's gone, Stephen.'

Unable to react, Stephen stared at him in blank disbelief.

'She left this behind,' Clayton said, holding a folded sheet of notepaper out to him. 'Also, there is a young woman here, waiting to see you. She claims to be the real Charise Lancaster,' Clayton added, but he made that last announcement in a tone of acceptance, not ridicule.

Stephen opened the short, disjointed letter that had obviously been written in haste, and each unbelievable word seemed to sear his mind, branding his soul.

As you will soon discover from the real Charise Lancaster, I am not who you thought I was. Not who I thought I was. Please believe that. Until the moment Charise Lancaster walked into my bedchamber this morning, I did not remember anything about myself except what I was told after the accident. Now that I do know who I am and what I am, I realize that a marriage between us would probably be impossible. I also realize that when Charise is finished telling you her opinion of what I intended to accomplish, it may sound far more believable than my truths in this note.

That would hurt me more than you can imagine. I wonder how I would go on, knowing that somewhere in this world you would be living your life, forever believing that I was a fraud and a schemer. You won't believe that, I know you won't.

She'd crossed out the last word and simply signed the letter:

Sheridan Bromleigh

Sheridan Bromleigh.

Sheridan. In the most painful moment of his life, with her letter in his hand and the unbelievable words scored into his brain, Stephen stared at her real name – a strong, beautiful name. Unique.

And he thought Sheridan fit her far better than Charise.

'The woman who is waiting for you says that you've been duped. Deliberately.'

Stephen's hand closed on the letter, wadding it into a ball, and he tossed it in the direction of the table. 'Where is she?' he snapped.

'Waiting for you in your study.'

His expression as murderous as his feelings, Stephen stalked out of the room, determined to prove that this new Charise Lancaster was a liar, or a fraud, or that she was mistaken about Sherry's having deliberately duped him.

But the one painfully irrefutable fact that he could not ignore, or disprove, was that Sheridan had run from him, rather than facing him and explaining. And that hinted unbearably of guilt . . .

40

As he walked swiftly toward his study, Stephen told himself Sherry would return in an hour or two. She'd run away because she was upset – hysterical. Whitticomb had said memory loss was a form of hysteria. Perhaps hysteria came with its return as well.

With visions of her wandering through London streets, alone and confused, he strode into his study. With only a curt, icy nod to the blonde who was waiting for him, he flung himself into the chair behind his desk, determined to disprove her contention that Sherry had deliberately deceived him. 'Sit down,' he ordered curtly, 'let's hear what you have to say.'

'Oh, I have a great deal to say!' she burst out, and Stephen was momentarily disconcerted by the fleeting irony that this Charise Lancaster looked exactly like the curly-haired blonde he'd expected to meet at the ship.

Charise sensed his desire to disbelieve anything she said, and as it sank in that this handsome, rich man might somehow have belonged to her, her fury and determination grew to new proportions. Daunted by his glacial manner, she was trying to decide how to best begin, when he said in a savage voice, 'You've made a damning accusation against someone who isn't here to defend herself. Now, start talking!'

'Oh, I see you don't want to believe me,' she burst out in alarm and rage. 'Well, I didn't want to believe it either when I read the announcement in the newspaper. She's duped you, just the way she dupes everyone.'

'She had amnesia – memory loss!'

'Well, she certainly found it when I appeared – how do you explain that?'

He couldn't, and he didn't want to let her see his reaction to that point or to the rest of what she was saying.

'She's a liar and an ambitious schemer, and she always was! On the ship, she told me she intended to marry someone like you, and she almost pulled it off, didn't she? First she tried to lure my husband away, and then she set her sights on you!'

'Until she returns and can answer you face to face, I'll ignore that as the anger of a jealous little minx.'

'Jealous!' Charise exploded, leaping to her feet. 'How dare you imply I'd be jealous of that red-haired witch! And for your information, my lord, she ran away because she was *exposed*. She is never coming back, do you hear me? She admitted to me she'd lied to you.' Stephen felt as if his chest had a rope around it that was being tightened with every word the blonde said. She was telling the truth – it was all over her contemptuous face – the hatred she felt for Sheridan Bromleigh and the scorn she had for him.

'On the way over from America, she talked me out of marrying Burleton and convinced me I ought to elope with Mr Morrison instead! Now that I think about it, I'm surprised she didn't betroth herself to my own *fiancé!*'

In the midst of his own rampaging emotions, Stephen realized the girl seated in front of him with tears in her eyes and her fists clenched in furious frustration had two pieces of very bad news coming. In his current mood, he was not inclined to postpone or dissemble. Fed up with all the convoluted lies and his own disastrous efforts to spare Sherry news that didn't even pertain to her, he tempered his voice and said flatly, 'Burleton is dead.'

'Dead?' Charise wailed in genuine despair as her secret hope that Burleton might still take her as his wife if she could get rid of Morrison was crushed to splinters. 'How?' she whispered chokily, reaching into her reticule for a lacy handkerchief and dabbing at her eyes.

Stephen told her and watched her face crumple. She wasn't lying now either, he realized. She was completely distraught.

'My poor father. I didn't know how I was ever going to face him after that Bromleigh woman talked me into eloping with Mr Morrison. I've been so afraid I haven't even written him yet. I'm going home!' Charise decided, already inventing a plausible lie that would persuade her father to take her back, to buy a divorce or an annulment or whatever was necessary. 'I'm going straight home.'

'Miss Lancaster,' Stephen said, and it seemed so odd, so ugly, to be calling this woman by a name he thought belonged to Sherry, 'I have a letter for you from your father's solicitor. It was sent to me by Burleton's landlord.' Setting aside his own monumental concerns for the moment, Stephen unlocked his desk drawer, extracted the letter and bank draft, and reluctantly held them out to her. 'I'm afraid it isn't good news.'

Her hand trembled violently as she read the contents of the letter and looked at the bank draft, then she slowly raised glazed eyes to his. 'Is this all the money I have in the world?'

Her financial situation wasn't Stephen's problem or

his concern, since she had evidently jilted Burleton and wed someone else en route to England, but keeping her silent was very much his concern. 'Without implying that I believe Sheridan Bromleigh deliberately impersonated you,' he said flatly, 'I would be willing to give you a substantial sum to . . . shall we say, ease your plight . . . in return for your silence on this entire matter.'

'How substantial?'

Stephen loathed her at that moment. He loathed the idea of paying her off to keep her from spreading what would become a scandal that would explode all over England if it came out. He loathed himself for the twinge of doubt growing inside him about Sherry's intention to return in a few hours. Her letter hadn't been a final farewell, it had been a plea – a hysterical plea from a lovely, overwrought girl who feared he wouldn't listen, wouldn't believe. She had run from the house to give his temper time to cool, in case he did believe Charise.

She would come back, confused and distraught and indignant; she would come back and face him. She was entitled to answers and explanations from him about why he'd impersonated Burleton. She would come back for those. She had enough spirit to confront him. She had so damned much spirit.

He repeated that to himself over and over again as he watched the Lancaster woman leave with the enormous sum he'd paid her, then he got up and wandered over to the windows, staring down at the street watching for his bride to return . . . to explain. He saw Charise Lancaster climb into a hired hack as his brother walked in behind him and quietly said, 'What do you intend to do?'

'Wait.'

For one of the few times in his life, Clayton Westmoreland felt and sounded helpless and hesitant. 'Do you want me to send the vicar home?'

'No,' Stephen clipped. 'We'll wait.'

41

Holding up a coat of wine-colored superfine, Nicholas DuVille's superior valet cast an approving eye over his master's gleaming white shirt and neckcloth. 'As I've oft said, sir,' he remarked as Nicki finished buttoning his wine velvet waistcoat, 'no Englishman has quite your excellent knack with a neckcloth.'

Nicki cast him an amused glance. 'And as I've oft replied, Vermonde, that is because I am more French than English, and you are biased against the British—' He broke off as the valet went to answer an imperative knock at the door of his bedchamber.

'Yes, what is it?' Nicki asked, surprised that his haughty valet had admitted a lowly footman into his private domain.

'I am to tell you that there is a young lady here to see you, my lord. She's in the blue salon and very distraught. She says you know her as Miss Lancaster. The butler tried to send her off, seeing that she arrived in a rented hack and is not known to him, but she was very persistent. And unwell, we think, because . . .'

His voice trailed off at the sight of the dire look on his employer's face as he stalked swiftly toward the doorway, almost knocking the surprised footman out of his way in his haste.

'Sherry?' Nicki said, his alarm escalating as she looked up at him with a haunted, wild expression. Tears were streaking down a face that was so white her silvery eyes looked dark in contrast, and she was sitting on the very edge of the sofa as if she were thinking of either bolting or falling over. 'What has happened?'

'I – have my – memory back,' Sherry said, gulping for

air as if she were strangling. 'I – I'm a fraud. Everyone is a – a fraud! Charise was betrothed to *Burleton*. Why did Stephen pre-pretend? No, *I'm* the pretender—'

'Don't try to talk,' Nicki ordered sharply and went over to a tray of glasses and decanters. Pouring a liberal draught of brandy into a glass, he brought it over to her. 'Drink this. All of it,' he added when she took a sip, shuddered, and tried to thrust it back. 'It will help calm you very quickly,' Nicki added, thinking she was hysterical because she now knew she'd never been betrothed to Stephen Westmoreland.

She looked at him as if his concern for her was madness, then she obeyed like an automaton, drinking the sharp liquor in gulps and coughing.

'Don't try to talk for a few minutes,' he said when she opened her mouth to begin again. Sherry obeyed helplessly, feeling the liquor burning a path all the way down to her stomach as she stared at her folded hands. The original shock of getting her memory back, of realizing who she was and had been, of seeing Charise, of listening to the ghastly accusations she was making, had sent her fleeing from the house like a heartbroken madwoman. She'd wandered for nearly an hour, wildly trying to think of some way to convince Stephen that she loved him, that she would never have lied to him, no matter what Charise convinced him was true, when another revelation finally hit her and sent her reeling: Stephen Westmoreland had never been betrothed to Charise Lancaster. Her fiancé's name had been Burleton! Everyone had been playing some sort of charade.

After that, came one stunning revelation and rec-ollection after another, and she'd sat in a park, her mind stumbling over itself, her head spinning. Now she wanted answers from someone with the least reason to lie to her, and the brandy made her feel that she could cope with whatever explanations she heard.

'I'll send for Langford,' Nicki said, watching a little

of her color return, but her answer was so frantic that he realized she was still hovering close to hysteria.

'No! No! Do not!'

He sat back down in the chair opposite her and said soothingly, 'Very well. I won't move from this room until you say I may.'

'I have to explain,' Sherry said, forcing herself to sound calm and lucid. Then she changed her mind and decided her best chance of getting honest answers to what seemed to be a world of deception was to ask questions before she gave out information. 'No, *you* have to explain,' she corrected carefully.

Nicki noticed that she was measuring her words, and he began to realize that she had not come to him on a whim, no matter how hysterical she was about being duped. Her opening sentence confirmed that and also neatly entrapped him.

'I came here because you are the only one I could think of with nothing to gain by . . . by continuing to play out this . . . this unbelievable deceit that's been practiced by the entire Westmoreland family.'

'Would it not be better to discuss all this with your fiancé?'

'My fiancé!' She laughed a little wildly, shaking her head. 'Arthur Burleton was betrothed to Charise Lancaster, Stephen Westmoreland wasn't! If I hear another falsehood, I'll—'

'Have some more brandy,' Nicki interrupted, leaning forward.

'I don't need brandy!' Sheridan cried. 'I need answers, can't you understand that?' Realizing that she wasn't likely to get them if she didn't sound more rational, Sheridan took a firm grip on her rampaging emotions and very carefully steadied her voice. Looking imploringly into his eyes, she explained, 'I came here, to you, because as I looked back, I couldn't recall that you ever actively participated in this – this monstrous farce. You never even referred to the earl as my

292

fiancé as everyone else did. Please help me now. Tell me the truth. All of it. If you don't, I very much fear I will go quite mad.'

Nicki had been appalled when Westmoreland had announced their betrothal two days ago, but when Whitney explained about Sherry's father's death, he'd at least found the notion of rushing her into marriage before she regained her memory less noxious. Whitticomb had repeatedly warned everyone not to tell her anything that would distress her, but Nicki was now certain that she did need and want the truth, all of it.

Glad that the physician wasn't here to complicate his decision with opposing advice, Nicki braced himself for the unpalatable task of answering for other people's actions because Charise Lancaster trusted him and, evidently, him alone.

'Please help me,' she said with quiet desperation. 'I have things to explain to you too when you're finished . . . difficult, shameful, embarrassing things, but I won't hide the truth from you. I *hate* dissembling.'

Sherry saw him lean back, as if resigned to a difficult discussion, but his gaze didn't waver from hers as he said, 'I will be very frank, if you are certain you are well enough to hear it.'

'I am well enough,' she said emphatically.

'Where do you want me to begin?'

'Begin,' she said with a grim laugh, 'at the beginning. Begin with why he let me believe until yesterday that he *was* Lord Burleton. The last thing I remember, before I woke up in the earl's house with my head in bandages, was that he'd met me at the ship and told me Lord Burleton was dead.'

Nicki noted that she had sounded solemn at the mention of Burleton's death, but not devastated. Westmoreland had obviously been correct in his assumption that she'd not known Burleton well enough to form any deep attachment to him. 'Burleton died in a carriage accident the night before your ship arrived,' he began in a gentle, but straightforward voice.

'I was sorry to learn of his death,' she said, matching his tone and somehow reinforcing Nicki's conclusion that she deserved to hear the whole truth and would be able to handle it better than she could handle confusion and deception. 'But I do *not* understand how the earl became involved in all this.'

'Langford was driving the carriage,' Nicki said flatly. He saw her wince, but she remained amazingly and gratifyingly calm, so he added, 'It was foggy and close to dawn. Burleton was foxed, and he walked right in front of the horses, but Langford blamed himself for the young man's death, and in his position, I suspect I might have felt exactly the same. He was driving an untried team, unused to the city, and perhaps if that hadn't been the case, Burleton would still be alive. I do not know.

'In any event, when Langford made inquiries a few hours after the accident, he discovered that Burleton's fiancée was arriving the next day from America, and that Burleton had no family and no friends whom Langford could trust to meet you and give you the news. In fact, if Burleton's butler hadn't known about you and your impending arrival in England, no-one would have been there to meet your ship at all. You probably remember the rest – Langford went to the ship to give you the news and offer you whatever assistance you desired. Evidently, he was so absorbed in that, he failed to notice a cargo net loaded with crates was heading straight for you, and it struck you in the head.'

Watching her closely, Nicki leaned forward, letting all that sink in while he poured himself a brandy. She seemed very calm, he thought admiringly, and he continued, 'Langford brought you to his house and summoned their family physician. For several days, you were unconscious, and Whitticomb had little faith in your chances of ever waking up. When you finally did come round, and he realized the trauma to your head had caused you to lose your memory, he was adamant that no-one ought to say anything to cause you any form of distress. You seemed to think Langford was your fiancé, and so they – we – let you go on believing it. That is about all I know, except,' Nicki added, in fairness to Stephen Westmoreland, 'I do know that Langford blamed himself for not protecting you from harm, and for giving you dire news in such a clumsy way that you were too overcome to protect yourself. I also know he has carried a great burden of guilt and remorse over depriving you of your fiancé.'

Drowning in humiliation, Sherry reached the obvious, the agonizing, conclusion: 'And so he felt *obliged* to provide me with another fiancé by volunteering himself. That's it, isn't it?'

Nicki hesitated, then he nodded. 'That's it.'

Sherry turned her head aside, fighting desperately not to weep for her stupidity, for her gullibility, and for falling in love with a man who felt nothing for her but responsibility. No wonder he'd never said he loved her! No wonder he'd wanted her to find someone else to wed! 'He was actually going to marry me out of guilt and responsibility.'

'I wouldn't say those are his only reasons as of this time,' Nicki said cautiously. 'I suspect he feels something for you.'

'Of course he does,' Sherry replied scornfully, reeling with humiliation. 'It is called *pity*!'

'I'll escort you back to Langford's.'

'I can't go back!' she cried.

'Miss Lancaster,' Nicki began in a sharp, authoritative voice that normally quelled anyone who heard it. It made the stricken young woman across from him double over with hysterical laughter, her arms wrapped around her stomach. 'I am *not* Charise Lancaster!'

Nicki quickly went round to her, cursing himself for letting her trick him into believing she was well enough to handle whatever he told her.

'I am *not* Charise Lancaster,' she repeated, and her

laughter abruptly gave way to sobs. 'I was her paid companion on the trip.' Her arms still wrapped around her stomach, she rocked back and forth, weeping. 'I am a glorified governess, and he was going to marry me. What a laugh his friends would have had over that. He was drowning in pity for a glorified governess who'd never laid eyes on Lord Burleton.'

Nicki stared at her in blank shock, but he believed her. 'Good God,' he whispered.

'I thought I was Charise Lancaster,' she whimpered, her shoulders beginning to shake with sobs. 'I thought I was, I swear it.'

Belatedly it occurred to Nicki to pull her into his arms and offer her some form of comfort, and he did it, but he was at a complete loss for words to match the gesture. 'I thought I was,' she wept against his chest. 'I thought I was her until she came to the house today. I thought I was, I swear it!'

'I believe you,' Nicki said, and was a little amazed that he did.

'She wouldn't go away. She had to tell him herself. He – he was getting ready for the wedding. A s-secret wedding. I don't have anywhere to go – no clothes – no money.'

Trying to offer her one small bright spot out of all this, he said, 'At least it was not your father who died.'

Very slowly, she lifted her head, her eyes dazed, unfocused. 'What?'

'Langford received a letter one night last week that was forwarded to him from Burleton's landlord. It had been intended for Charise Lancaster, written by her father's solicitor, and informing her that her father had died two weeks after she sailed for England.'

She drew a shaky breath, coming to grips with that, and said bleakly, 'He was a harsh man but not an unkind one. He spoiled Charise quite terribly—' Another wrenching probability struck her, and she thought she was going to retch. 'Last week – was it the same night I went to Almack's and the Rutherfords' ball?'

'So I was told.'

Her head bowed with further humiliation and fresh tears spilled down her cheek. 'No *wonder* he changed so abruptly from wanting me to find another fiancé, to deciding we should wed at once.' She remembered the way she'd touched his hand at the opera and thought of how repelled he must have been at having to sit through that – and pretend to want to kiss her and—

'I wish I were dead!' she whispered brokenly.

'Stop that sort of talk at once,' Nicki said mindlessly. 'You can stay here tonight. Tomorrow, I'll go with you to Langford's and we'll explain.'

'I did explain in a letter! I can't go back. I won't, I tell you, and if you send for him, I'll go mad. I know I will. I can never go back now.'

She sounded as if she meant it, and Nicki couldn't blame her.

Sherry wasn't certain how long she cried in his arms or when she stopped, but as the silence lengthened, a blessed numbness finally took over. 'I can't stay here,' she whispered, her voice hoarse from the storm of emotions.

'As you said, you have nowhere else to go.'

She pushed free of his soothing embrace and sat up, then she stood, swaying a little. 'I shouldn't have come here. I would not be surprised if there are charges filed against me.'

The thought that Langford might do that filled Nicki with an anger that was almost uncontainable, but he couldn't deny the possibility or the unthinkable results. 'You're safe here, at least for tonight. In the morning, we'll discuss how I can be of help.'

The feeling of unworthiness and relief that surged through her at the realization that he was actually offering to help her nearly broke Sherry's fragile grip on her control. 'I – I will have to find some sort of position. I have no references. I can't stay in London. I don't—'

'We'll discuss it in the morning, *chérie*. I want you to lie down now. I will have your dinner sent up.'

'No-one who knows him or his family will consider employing me, and he – everyone in London seems to know him.'

'In the morning,' he said firmly.

Too weary to protest, Sherry nodded. She had started up the stairs with a servant when something hit her and she turned around.

'Monsieur DuVille?'

'I gave you leave to call me Nicki, mademoiselle,' he tried to tease.

'Paid companions do not address their "betters" by their given names.'

She looked as if she were at the end of her tether, and so Nicki did not argue with her decision and let her ask her question.

'You won't tell any of them where I am – promise me you won't!'

Nicki hesitated, reviewed the alternatives and their consequences, and finally said, 'I give you my word.' He watched her walk up the stairs, beaten and humbled. She had never resembled a meek servant, but she did then, and it made him want to do violence to Westmoreland. And yet, he had acted honorably until today. More than honorably, Nicki reluctantly decided.

42

'Will there be anything else, my lord, before I retire?'

Stephen lifted his gaze from the glass of liquor in his hand and stared at the elderly under-butler standing in the doorway of his bedchamber. 'No,' he said shortly.

He'd kept his family and the cleric waiting until three hours ago, in the asinine belief that Sheridan Bromleigh would come back and face him. If she were innocent, if she'd really lost her memory, not only would she have wanted to explain and exonerate herself, she'd have demanded explanations from him about why he'd pretended they were engaged. Since she didn't seem to need those explanations, the only answer was that she'd *always* known the truth.

Now, however, there was no way to avoid the truth and not enough liquor in the world to douse the rage that was beginning to burn like an inferno inside him. Sheridan Bromleigh had obviously never lost her memory. When she regained consciousness, she'd simply seized on a brilliant ploy to lead a better life for a while, and he'd sweetened the deal a thousand times by offering to marry her. She must have been laughing herself into a seizure while he pretended to be Burleton and she pretended to be her own employer.

After all his experience, his alleged sophistication, Stephen thought, as his wrath continued to build, he'd fallen like a rock for the oldest female ploy in the world – the helpless damsel in distress! TWICE! First with Emily and now with Sheridan Bromleigh.

With Sheridan's talent, she should have been on the stage. That's where she belonged, along with the rest of the ambitious semiharlots who danced and cavorted and recited their lines. He took another swallow of his drink, remembering some of her best performances: Her first one had been truly impressive. The morning he'd slept by her bed, he'd awakened to the sound of her weeping. *'I don't know what I look like,'* she'd wept, wringing his heart with her tears. *'It's a trifling thing, really, but since you're already awake, could you just describe me a little?'* Then there had been the morning she'd decided to point out her hair to him – in case he hadn't already noticed its siren appeal, Stephen thought viciously: *'My hair is not brown. Look at it. It's red—'*

Like the ass he was, he'd stood there transfixed by the sight of that glossy mantle, mentally likening her to a red-haired Madonna. *'It's so . . . so brazen!'* she'd pointed out to him, managing to look unhappy about a head of hair that obviously suited her perfectly.

Then there was her charming confusion over how she ought to behave. 'I understand from Constance – the maid – that you're an earl, and that I ought properly to address you as "my lord." Among the things I do seem to know is that in the presence of a king, one does not sit unless invited to do so.'

But his absolute favorite, Stephen decided with blazing cynicism, was the first night she'd been out of her bed, when she'd begged him prettily, *'And my family – what are they like?'* After he'd explained her father was a widower and she was his only child, she'd looked at him with those big, beseeching eyes of hers and said, *'Are we very much in love?'*

In all their conversations, she'd only slipped once that he could remember. He'd been in the process of telling her she had to have a chaperone if she stayed in his house, and she'd laughed. *'I don't need a companion, I am a—'* Her only slip, but in retrospect damning proof.

She'd been comfortable with the servants because she was one, or close to it.

'Jesus, what a scheming, brilliant little opportunist she was,' Stephen thought aloud, grinding his teeth. She'd probably been hoping she could persuade him to offer her his protection and set her up in a house of her own, and instead he'd offered her his name!

He tossed the rest of his drink down as if he could wash away his self-loathing, then he got up and headed into his dressing room.

Despite her strong protests in the coach when they left Almack's, that redheaded sorceress had agreed to marry him in less than one hour and made it seem as if *he'd* convinced *her*.

He jerked off his shirt and flung it on the floor. It dawned on him that he'd intended to wear the clothes he had on at his wedding, and as he removed each piece of clothing, he dropped it carefully onto the growing heap. Damson came in just as he was pulling on a robe, and the appalled valet bent down to pick them up.

'Burn them!' Stephen bit out. 'Get them out of here and go to bed. In the morning, have someone get rid of everything she left behind.'

He was standing at the fireplace, the last of the bottle of liquor in his glass, when he heard another knock at his door. 'What the hell is it now?' he demanded when Burleton's butler was standing just inside the room, looking as tormented as if he was being stretched on a rack.

'I – I do not wish to intrude into a situation that is none of my affair, my lord, but neither – neither would I – would I feel right were I to conceal information that – you might wish to know.'

Stephen had all he could do to contain his loathing for the old servant who now reminded him of Sheridan Bromleigh. 'Do you intend to tell me or to stand there all night?' he snapped scathingly.

The old man seemed to wilt from the cutting tone. 'Dr Whitticomb privately told me that I was to keep an eye on Miss Lan – on the young lady.'

'And?' he gritted furiously.

'And so, when she left today in such a state, I felt obligated to send a footman to watch after her. She – she went to the home of Monsieur DuVille, my lord. That is where she is . . .' He trailed off at the sight of the murderous look on the earl's face as he heard that news and hastily backed out of the doorway, bowing.

DuVille! She'd gone to DuVille. 'Little *bitch*!' he said aloud.

He did not consider going after her. She was dead to him now, and he didn't give a damn where she went or whose bed she occupied. She had a highly refined sense of survival, and she'd land on her feet wherever she went. With a malicious smile, he wondered what Banbury tale she'd fed DuVille today to persuade him to let her stay under his roof. Whatever it was, DuVille had an equally good sense of survival, and he had never been besotted by her, as Stephen had been.

No doubt DuVille would set her up in a nice little house somewhere if she asked him prettily and pleased him in bed.

The redheaded sorceress was a born courtesan, if ever there'd been one.

Standing at the window of a guest suite in Nicholas DuVille's house, Sherry stared into the night, her forehead resting on the cold glass, her eyes aching with tears she couldn't let herself shed. In the six hours since she'd come up here at Nicholas's insistence, her mind had cleared, and with that clarity came the full realization of what she had almost had – and lost – and she didn't know how she was going to bear it.

Turning away, she walked listlessly over to the bed and lay down, too exhausted to fight down the memories. She closed her eyes, willing sleep to come, but all she saw was his lazy smile and the tender way he'd looked at her at the Rutherfords' ball. 'Miss Lancaster . . . may I have the honor of this dance?' Swallowing convulsively, she squeezed her eyes tighter closed, but in her mind, she felt him kissing her the way he had in the coach. *'This is why we are going to be married,'* he'd said in that husky voice he used when they'd been kissing. Surely, she thought achingly, he hadn't been pretending he liked to kiss her. Surely that had not been pretending. She needed to believe, had to believe, that much had been real. If she couldn't believe in that, she didn't know how she would go on after today.

The memory of that and the other times he'd kissed her were hers alone to cherish. They did not belong to 'Charise Lancaster.' They belonged to her. She rolled onto her stomach, holding the memories close, and she fell asleep to dream of strong arms crushing her tightly and demanding kisses that stole her breath . . . of caressing hands that gentled and tantalized her and made her forget it was wrong to let him touch her in that intimate way. She slept, dreaming of things she would never know again in reality.

Wrapped in a dressing gown, Whitney stood in the nursery, gazing down at her sleeping son's cherubic face. She looked up as the door opened, admitting a wedge of light, and her husband walked in, his face more grim than she'd seen it in years. 'I couldn't sleep,' she whispered, leaning down and smoothing the light blanket over Noel's shoulders. He already had his father's square chin and dark hair.

Behind her, Clayton slid his arms around her waist, silently offering her comfort. 'Have I thanked you recently for my son?' he whispered near her ear, smiling down at the three-year-old.

'Not since this time last night,' she said, tipping her face up to his and trying to smile.

He wasn't fooled by her smile any more than she was fooled by his careful avoidance of the discussion of to-day's aborted wedding. 'I feel so terrible,' she confided.

'I know you do,' he said quietly.

'I will never forget the look on Stephen's face as it became later and later and he realized she wasn't coming back.'

'Nor I,' he said tersely.

'He kept the vicar there until after ten o'clock. How could she do a thing like that to him? How *could* she?'

'None of us really knew her.'

'Stephen was insane about her. I could see it every time he looked at her and when he was trying not to look at her.'

'I noticed,' he said curtly.

Swallowing over the lump of sorrow in her throat, she said, 'If it hadn't been for Stephen's intervention, you would be married to Vanessa and I'd be wed to someone else, and Noel wouldn't exist.'

Clayton reached up and smoothed her tousled hair off her shoulder and pressed a reassuring kiss against her temple, as she continued in an aching voice, 'I always wanted to repay him for that, but all I could do was wish and *wish* that he would find someone who would make him as happy as we are.'

'Come to bed, darling,' Clayton said, leaning down and lightly tousling his son's hair. 'Stephen is a grown man,' he said as he drew her firmly toward their own bedchamber. 'He'll get over her because he wants to get over her.'

'Did you get over me as easily as that when we were—' she hesitated, carefully refraining from any mention of the hideous night that had nearly destroyed all chances of a marriage between them, 'when we were estranged?'

'No.'

When they were both in bed and she had curled into his arms, he added, 'However, I had known you longer than Stephen knew Ch – Sheridan Bromleigh.'

She nodded, her soft cheek sliding against his arm, and he tightened his hold, drawing her tighter against him because he, too, remembered the event that had nearly torn them apart.

'Time has little to say to the matter. Do you remember how long after we met again in England it was before you loved me?' she said into the darkness.

Clayton smiled at the memory. 'It was the night you confessed you used to pepper your music teacher's snuff-box.'

'If memory serves me well, I told you that story only a week or two after I came home from France.'

'Something like that.'

'Clayton?'

'What?' he whispered.

'I do not think Stephen is going to get over this as easily as you think. He could have any woman he wants, and yet in all this time, she was the only woman he ever wanted – except for Emily, and look how *cynical* he became after that!'

'All Stephen has to do is crook his finger, and dozens of desirable women will line up to soothe him. This time, he'll let them because his pride and his heart both took a more serious beating than the last,' Clayton predicted grimly. 'In the meantime, he'll get completely foxed and stay that way for a while.'

She tipped her face up to his. 'Is that what you did?'

'That's what I did,' he confirmed.

'How very typically male,' she said primly.

Clayton smothered a laugh at her tone and tipped her soft mouth up to his. 'Are you feeling superior, madam?' he asked, a brow quirked in amused inquiry.

'Very,' she replied smugly.

'In that case,' he said, rolling onto his back and taking her with him, 'I suppose I'd better let you be on top.'

Some time later, sleepy and sated, Clayton settled her more comfortably against his side and closed his eyes.

'Clayton?'

Something in her voice made him warily force his eyes open.

'I don't know if you noticed, but Charity Thornton was in tears today when Sheridan Bromleigh didn't return.' When he didn't reply, but continued to watch her, she said, 'Did you notice?'

'Yes,' he said cautiously. 'Why do you ask?'

'Well, she told me in the most – most heartbreaking way – that she'd felt truly useful for the first time in decades because she was needed to act as chaperone. And she said she felt a useless old failure because she hadn't found another husband for Miss Bromleigh, besides Stephen.'

'I heard her and so did Stephen,' Clayton said, his unease and suspicion vibrating in his voice. 'However,

I believe her exact words were that she was sorry she hadn't been able to find some other unfortunate, gullible male for Miss Bromleigh to deceive and abandon, instead of her dear Langford.'

'Well, that's almost the same thing . . .'

'Only if you consider idiocy almost the same thing as sense. Why,' he said with gravest reservations about hearing the answer, 'are we having this discussion right now?'

'Because I – I invited her to stay with us for a while.'

To Whitney it seemed as if he had stopped breathing. 'I thought she could help look after Noel.'

'It would make more sense to ask Noel to look after her.'

Uncertain whether his mocking tone disguised annoyance or amusement, she said, 'Naturally, Noel's governess would be secretly in charge.'

'In charge of who – Noel or Charity Thornton?'

Whitney bit back a nervous smile. 'Are you angry?'

'No. I am . . . awed.'

'By what?'

'By your sense of timing. An hour ago, before I wore us both out making love, I might have reacted more violently to having her in my house than I am able to now – when I'm too weak to hold my eyes open.'

'I rather thought that would be the case,' she admitted guiltily after he deliberately let the silence lengthen.

'I rather thought you did.'

He sounded almost disapproving of that, and she bit her lip, carefully lifting her gaze to his face, searching his inscrutable features, one by one. 'Finding what you're looking for, my love?' he asked mildly.

'I was looking for . . . forgiveness?' she hinted, and her glowing eyes were almost Clayton's undoing as he struggled to keep his face straight. 'A manly attitude of benevolence toward his overwrought wife? A certain nobility of spirit that manifests itself in the quality of tolerance for others? Perhaps a sense of humor?'

'All of that?' Clayton said, a helpless grin tugging at his lips. 'All of those qualities in one beleaguered male with a wife who has just invited the world's oldest living henwit into his home?'

She bit her lip to keep from laughing, and nodded.

'In that case,' he announced, closing his eyes, a smile on his lips, 'you may count yourself fortunate to have married just such a paragon.'

43

'I've come to ask you a favor,' Stephen announced without preamble two weeks later as he walked into the morning room of his brother's house, where Whitney was supervising the installation of sunny yellow draperies.

Startled by his abrupt arrival and curt tone, Whitney left the seamstresses alone, and walked with Stephen into the drawing room. In the past three weeks since the aborted wedding, she'd seen him at different functions, but only at night and always with a different woman on his arm. Rumor had it that he had also been seen at the theatre with Helene Devernay. In the revealing daylight, it was obvious to Whitney that time wasn't soothing him. His face looked as hard and cold as granite, his attitude even to her was distant and curt, and there were deep lines of fatigue etched at his eyes and mouth. He looked as if he hadn't been to sleep in a week and hadn't stopped drinking while he was awake. 'I'd do anything you asked of me, you know that,' Whitney said gently, her heart aching for him.

'Can you make a place for an old man – an under-butler? I want him out of my sight.'

'Of course,' she said, and then cautiously she added, 'Could you tell me why you want him out of your sight?'

'He was Burleton's butler, and I don't ever want to see anyone or anything that reminds me of her.'

Clayton looked up from the papers he was studying as Whitney walked into his study, her face stricken. Alarm brought him quickly to his feet and around his desk. 'What's wrong?'

'Stephen was just here,' she said in a choked voice. 'He *looks* awful, he *sounds* awful. He doesn't even want Burleton's servant around because the man reminds him of her. His pride wasn't all that suffered when she left. He loved her,' she said vehemently, her green eyes shimmering with frustrated tears. 'I knew he did!'

'It's over,' Clayton said with soft finality. 'She's gone and it's over. Stephen will come around.'

'Not at this rate!'

'He has a different woman on his arm every night,' he told her. 'I can assure you he's a long way from becoming a recluse.'

'He has shut himself away, even from me,' she argued. 'I can *feel* it, and I'll tell you something else. The more I think about it, the more convinced I am that Sheridan Bromleigh wasn't playacting about anything, including her feelings for Stephen.'

'She was an ambitious schemer, and a gifted one. It would take a miracle to convince me otherwise,' he stated flatly, walking back around his desk.

Hodgkin stared at his employer in stricken silence. 'I – I am to be dismissed, milord? Was it something I did, or did not do, or—'

'I've arranged for you to work in my brother's home. That's all.'

'But was I derelict in any of *my* duties, or—'

'NO!' Stephen snapped, turning away. 'It has nothing to do with anything you've done.' Normally he never interfered with the hiring or dismissal or discipline of the household staff, and he should have left this unpleasant task to his secretary, he realized.

The old man's shoulders sagged. Stephen watched him shuffle off, moving like a man who was ten years older than he'd been when he walked in.

44

It was a mistake to seek Stephen out, even from this safe distance, and Sherry knew it, but she couldn't seem to help herself. He'd told her he went to the opera on most Thursdays, and she wanted – needed – to see him just one more time before she left England. She'd written to her aunt three weeks ago, the day after her aborted wedding, explaining everything that had happened and asking Cornelia to send her enough money for passage home. In the meantime, Sherry had secured a position as governess to a large family without the means to hire a more desirable, older woman or the sense to verify the recommendation letter Nicholas DuVille had given her with Charity Thornton's name listed as a secondary reference – a reference that Sherry suspected the elderly lady knew nothing about.

The crowded pit at Covent Garden was occupied by boisterous, restless people who stepped on Sherry's feet and bumped her shoulder constantly, but she scarcely noticed. Her eyes were on the empty box, the seventh from the front, and she stared at it until the gilt flowers and stars on the front of it began to blur and merge. Time ticked past and the ruckus within the opera house rose to a deafening roar. The curtains behind the seventh box suddenly parted and Sherry froze, panicked because she was finally going to see him . . . and then she was devastated because she did not see him in the group at all.

She must have miscounted, she thought wildly, and began to count each box, searching the aristocratic faces of its occupants. Each box was separated from its neighbor by a slender gold pillar, and from each pillar a cut-glass chandelier was suspended. Sherry counted and recounted them, then she looked at her hands in her lap, clasping them tightly to stop their trembling. He wasn't coming tonight. He'd given his box to others. It would be another week before she could come again, providing she saved enough money to buy another ticket.

The orchestra gave out a blast of sound, the crimson curtains swept open, and Sherry mentally counted the minutes, ignoring the music she had once loved, glancing up compulsively at the two empty seats in the box, willing to see him there, and when she didn't, praying that he would be there when she looked again.

He arrived between the first and second acts, without her seeing him enter the box or take his seat – a dark spectre from the mists of her memory who materialized into the realm of her reality and made her heart thunder. Her eyes clung to his hard, handsome face, memorizing it, worshipping it, as she blinked away the sheen of tears that blurred her vision.

He hadn't loved her, she reminded herself, torturing herself with the sight of him, she'd merely been a responsibility he'd mistakenly assumed. She knew all that, but it didn't stop her from looking at his chiseled lips and remembering how softly they had touched hers, or from gazing at his rugged profile and remembering how his slow dazzling smile could transform his entire face.

Sheridan was not the only woman whose attention wasn't on the performance. On the opposite side of the theatre, in the Duke of Claymore's box, Victoria Fielding, Marchioness of Wakefield, was staring hard at the occupants of the pit, searching for the young woman she'd glimpsed earlier making her way into the opera house. 'I *know* the woman I saw was Charise Lanc— I mean Sheridan Bromleigh,' Victoria whispered to Whitney. 'She was in the lines going into the pit. Wait – there she is!' she exclaimed in a low voice. 'She's wearing a dark blue bonnet.'

Oblivious to the curious looks of their husbands, who were seated behind them, the two friends peered hard at the woman in question, their shoulders so close together that Victoria's auburn hair nearly touched the glossy dark strands of Whitney's.

'If only she didn't have that bonnet on, we'd know her in a minute by the color of her hair!'

Whitney didn't need to see the color of her hair. For the next half hour, the woman in question never looked anywhere but at Stephen's box, and it was confirmation enough. 'She hasn't stopped looking at him,' Victoria said, her voice filled with some of the same confusion and sorrow that Whitney felt about the sudden disappearance and behavior of Stephen's fiancée. 'Do you suppose she knew he would be here tonight?'

Whitney nodded, willing the young woman to look in her direction for just a moment, instead of the opposite one. 'She knows Stephen comes here on Thursday nights and that he has that box. She was here with him a few days before she . . . vanished.' Vanished was the least damning thing Whitney could say at the moment, which was why she chose the word. Victoria and Jason Fielding, who were also friends of Stephen's, were two of the very few people amongst the *ton* who were privy to most of the full story because they'd been invited to attend the small celebration that had been planned for after the private affair.

'Do you think she intends to meet him "accidentally" for some reason?'

'I don't know,' Whitney whispered back.

Behind them, their husbands observed the pretty pair who were ignoring a rather excellent performance. 'What is that all about?' Clayton murmured to Jason Fielding, tipping his head toward their two wives.

'Someone must have the gown of the century on.'

'Not if she's down there in the pits,' Clayton pointed out. 'The last time Whitney and Victoria indulged in a similar huddle, it was because Stephen's mistress was in his box with him and Monica Fitzwaring was in the next box with Bakersfield, trying to look as if she didn't know who was one narrow pillar away from her shoulder.'

'I remember,' Jason said with a grin. 'As I recall, they were on the side of Helene Devernay that night.'

'Whitney laughed all the way home,' Clayton said.

'Victoria declared it the most diverting three hours of the entire Season,' Jason added, and leaning forward he whispered jokingly, 'Victoria, you are in imminent danger of toppling out of this box.'

She sent him an abashed smile but did not cease her scrutiny of whatever they were watching.

'She's leaving!' Whitney said, feeling both relieved and crestfallen. 'She didn't wait for the performance to end, and she didn't leave her seat between acts, which means she doesn't intend to meet him here accidentally.'

As puzzled as he was amused by their girlish whispering, Clayton leaned sideways, scanning the rows in the pit, but he waited until they were on their way to their next engagement – a lavish midnight supper – before he brought the subject up to his pre-occupied wife. 'What were you and Victoria doing all that whispering about tonight?'

Whitney hesitated, knowing he would not be pleased that Sheridan Bromleigh had reentered their sphere or be interested in the reasons. 'Victoria thought she saw Sheridan Bromleigh tonight. I couldn't get a good enough look at her face to say for certain that Victoria was correct.' Clayton's brows drew together into a dark hostile frown at the mention of the woman's name, and Whitney decided to let the subject drop.

★   ★   ★

The following Thursday, after seeing that their husbands were occupied elsewhere, Victoria and Whitney arrived early at Covent Garden, and from the vantage point of their box, scanned the faces of every new arrival who entered the pit and the gallery, searching for one particular face. 'Do you see her?' Victoria asked.

'No, but it's a miracle you noticed her in the crowd at all last week. It's impossible to see everyone's features clearly from up here.'

'I don't know whether to be relieved or disappointed,' Victoria said, sitting back in her chair when the curtain went up, and they still hadn't had a glimpse of the woman they'd thought was Sheridan Bromleigh last week.

Whitney sat back too, silently sorting out her own reaction.

'Your brother-in-law just arrived,' Victoria said a few minutes later. 'Is that Georgette Porter with him?'

Whitney looked across the theatre at Stephen's box and nodded absently.

'She's exceedingly lovely,' Victoria added in the tone of one who is trying very hard to find and give encouragement about a situation that is not particularly encouraging at all. She liked Stephen Westmoreland very well, and he was one of a very few people whom her husband considered among his close friends. She had also felt an instantaneous liking for Sheridan Bromleigh, who, like herself, was also an American.

Whitney contemplated Stephen's attitude toward the woman at his side, who was smiling at him and talking animatedly. He was listening with a look of fixed courtesy, and Whitney had the impression he didn't know Georgette Porter was talking, or that she had a face, or that she was even in his box. Her gaze shifted inexorably to the seats below in the pits, scanning the rows of heads again. 'She's here, I *know* she is. I mean, I have a feeling she is,' she amended as Victoria glanced sharply at her.

'If I hadn't seen her arriving last week and been watching for her to come into the pit, I'd never have been able to point her out to you. We could never find her now, among all these rows of people.'

'I know a way!' Whitney said on an inspired stroke. 'Look for a head that is turned toward Stephen's box instead of the stage.' A few minutes later, Victoria grabbed her arm in her excitement. 'Right there!' she said. 'The same bonnet too! She's practically beneath us, which is why we didn't see her.'

Now that she'd spotted the other woman, Whitney observed her steadily, but not until she stood up to leave did she get a clear look at the other woman's wistful face. 'It *is* her!' Whitney said fiercely, feeling a swift stab of helpless sympathy for the naked sorrow and longing she'd seen on Sheridan's face as she stood up to leave just before the opera's end.

Sympathy was not an emotion her husband was likely to share – at least not unless he too saw the way Sheridan Bromleigh had sat in silence, her gaze on Stephen. But if he were to see it, and if his attitude toward Sheridan were to soften, then Whitney thought he might be persuaded to talk to Stephen, to urge him to seek her out. Clayton was the only one, she knew, who had enough influence on Stephen to possibly sway him.

45

'We mustn't be late.' Whitney cast an anxious look at the clock as her husband lingered over a glass of sherry. 'I think we ought to leave now.'

'How is it I never realized you were so inordinately fond of opera?' Clayton said, studying her curiously.

'Lately the . . . the performance has been quite riveting,' she said. Bending down, she wrapped their son in a tight hug before he padded off sleepily between his governess and Charity Thornton.

'Riveting, really?' Clayton repeated, eyeing her with puzzled amusement over the top of his glass.

'Yes. Oh, and I exchanged our box for the Rutherfords' just for tonight.'

'May I ask why?'

'The view from Stephen's side is much better.'

'The view of what?'

'The audience.'

When he tried to question her further about that baffling answer, Whitney said, 'Please, just trust me and don't ask more questions until I can show you what I mean.'

'Look,' Whitney whispered, clutching Clayton's wrist in her agitation, 'there she is. No – don't let her see you looking. Just turn your eyes, not your head.'

He did not turn his head, but instead of looking in the direction she indicated, her husband slanted his gaze at her and said, 'It would help immensely were I to have some slight idea whom I'm supposed to be looking for.'

Nervous because so much could hinge on his reaction and his help, Whitney admitted, 'It's Sheridan Bromleigh. I didn't want to tell you in advance for fear she wouldn't be here, or you wouldn't come.'

His expression hardened instantly at the mention of the other woman's name, and she lifted beseeching green eyes to his cool gray ones. 'Please, Clayton, do not condemn her out of hand. We have never heard her side in the matter.'

'Because she ran off like the guilty little bitch she is. The fact that she likes opera, which we already knew, doesn't change that.'

'Your loyalty to Stephen is clouding your judgment.' When that didn't have any noticeable effect, Whitney persevered with gentle but firm determination. 'She doesn't come here for the performances. She never even looks at the stage, she only looks at Stephen, and she always sits in rows behind his box so that he wouldn't see her if his attention wandered from the stage. Please, darling, just look for yourself.'

He hesitated for an endless moment, then conceded with a curt, wordless nod, and slid a glance in the direction she'd indicated, off to their right. 'Plain dark blue bonnet with a blue ribbon,' Whitney added to help, 'and a dark blue dress with a white collar.'

She knew the moment Clayton found Sheridan in the crowd, because his jaw hardened, his gaze snapped back to the stage, and it remained there until the curtain went up. Disappointed, but not defeated, she watched him from the corner of her eye, waiting for the merest change in his posture that might indicate he was taking a second look. The moment she felt it, she stole a swift glance at him. He'd moved his head only a fraction of an inch to the right, away from the stage, but his gaze was far off to the right. Praying that this was not the only time in weeks that Sheridan Bromleigh had decided to watch the performance, Whitney leaned slightly forward to peer around Clayton's shoulders and smiled with relief.

For the next two hours, Whitney kept her husband and Sheridan Bromleigh under cautious surveillance, careful not to move her body in any way that would alert him. By the end of the evening, her eye sockets hurt, but she was feeling absolutely triumphant. Clayton's gaze had returned to Sheridan throughout the entire evening, but Whitney did not bring the topic up again until two days later, when she felt he'd had time to perhaps readjust his attitude toward Stephen's former fiancée.

46

'Do you recall the other night at the opera?' she began cautiously as the footmen cleared away their breakfast dishes.

'I thought it was a "riveting" performance, just as you'd said,' Clayton said straight-faced. 'The tenor who—'

'You were not watching the performance,' she interrupted firmly.

'You're right.' He grinned. 'I was watching you watch me.'

'Clayton, please be serious. This is important.'

His brows lifted inquiringly, and he gave her his fullest attention, but he looked amused, wary, and prepared.

'I want to do something to bring Stephen and Sheridan Bromleigh face to face. I discussed it yesterday with Victoria, and she agreed they ought to at least be forced to talk to each other.'

She braced herself for an argument and ended up gaping at him as he said casually, 'Actually, a similar thought occurred to me, so I discussed it with Stephen last night when I saw him at The Strathmore.'

'Why didn't you tell me! What did you say? What did he say?'

'I said,' Clayton recited, 'that I wanted to discuss Sheridan Bromleigh with him. I told him that I believe she goes to the opera specifically to see him.'

'And then what happened?'

'Nothing happened. He got up and walked out.'

'That's all? He didn't say anything?'

'As a matter of fact he did. He said that, out of respect for our mother, he would ignore the temptation to resort to physical violence against my person, but that if I ever brought up Sheridan Bromleigh's name to him again, I should not depend on his ability to exercise similar restraint.'

'He actually *said* that?'

'Not in exactly those words,' Clayton said with grim irony. 'Stephen's were shorter and more – colorful.'

'Well, he can't threaten me. There must be something I could do.'

'Have you considered prayer? A pilgrimage? Sorcery?' Despite his light tone, he wanted her to let matters rest, and she could see that he did. When she didn't smile, he put his cup onto the saucer and leaned back in his chair, frowning a little. 'You're absolutely determined to get involved in this, no matter what Stephen says or I say, is that it?'

She hesitated, and then nodded. 'I have to try. I keep remembering the expression on Sheridan's face when she looks at him in the opera, and the way she was looking at him at the Rutherfords' ball. And Stephen looks more haggard and grim each time I see him, so being apart isn't doing either of them any good.'

'I see,' he said, studying her face with a reluctant smile lurking at the corners of his mouth. 'Is there anything I can say to persuade you it's a mistake?'

'I'm afraid not.'

'I see.'

'I may as well confess – I've contacted Matthew Bennett to ask him to have his firm make inquiries about where she is. I can't do anything to bring them together until I can find her.'

'I'm surprised you didn't decide to hire a lackey during the intermission to follow her home from the opera, and *then* have Bennett's firm make inquiries.'

'I didn't think of it!'

'I did.'

His voice had been so unemotional, his expression so marvelously bland, that it took a moment for the true import of those two words to register. When they did, she felt the familiar fierce surge of love that had grown stronger over the four years of their marriage. 'Clayton,' she said. 'I love you.'

'She's working as a governess for a baronet and his family,' he informed her. 'Surname is Skeffington. Three children. I've never heard of them. Bennett has their direction.'

Whitney put her teacup down and stood up, intending to send a note to the solicitor's firm at once, asking for all the information they had.

'Whitney?'

She turned in the doorway of the morning room. 'My lord?'

'I love you too.' She smiled at him in answer, and he waited a moment before issuing a serious warning: 'If you persist in your determination to bring them face to face, be very cautious how you handle this, and be prepared for Stephen to leave the moment he sees her. You should also be prepared for the possibility that he will not forgive you for this, not for a very long time. Think carefully before you take steps you may sorely regret.'

'I will,' she promised.

Clayton watched her leave and slowly shook his head, knowing damned well she wasn't going to waste time in contemplation and inaction. It simply was not in her nature to watch life happen and not wade in. It was, he decided wryly, one of the things he most loved about her.

He did not, however, expect her to act as swiftly as she did.

'What's that?' he asked late that same afternoon as he strolled past the salon and saw her sitting at a rosewood secretary, thoughtfully brushing the feathered end of a quill against her cheek while she studied a sheet of paper in her hand.

She looked up as if she'd been far away, and then smiled swiftly. 'A guest list.'

The frenetic activities of the Season were finally

winding to a close, and they'd both been looking forward to returning to the peace and serenity of the country for the summer, so Clayton was naturally surprised she was evidently planning to entertain. 'I thought we were going back to Claymore the day after tomorrow.'

'We are. This party is three weeks off – it's a birthday party for Noel. Nothing too large, of course.'

Over her shoulder, Clayton glanced at her list and muffled a laugh as he read the first item aloud, 'One small elephant, safe for children to touch—'

'I was thinking of a circus theme, with clowns and jugglers and such, with all the festivities and meals taking place on the lawn. That's so much more relaxed, and the children will be able to enjoy everything right alongside with the adults.'

'Isn't Noel a little young for all this?'

'He needs the society of other children.'

'I thought that was the reason he spends every day with the Fieldings' and the Thorntons' children when we come to London.'

'Oh, it is,' she said, giving him a breezy smile. 'Stephen volunteered to give Noel's party at Montclair when I told him about it today.'

'Having been to enough parties in the last six weeks to last a lifetime, I rather wish you'd have let him,' he joked. 'As Noel's uncle *and* godfather, it's Stephen's prerogative to have *his* country house overrun with parents who'll stay for a week and expect to be entertained, children's party or no.'

'I suggested Stephen give your mother's sixtieth birthday ball at Montclair instead, and let us have Noel's birthday party at Claymore. Since her birthday is only three days after Noel's, that seemed the best plan.'

'Clever girl,' Clayton replied, instantly reversing his opinion of who ought to have the party. 'Mother's ball will be a huge crush.'

'Our party will be small – a few carefully chosen guests with their children and governesses.'

As she spoke, Clayton glanced idly at the sheet of paper near her wrist and his eyes riveted on the name Skeffington. He straightened, and when he spoke, his voice was filled with amused irony. 'Interesting guest list.'

'*Isn't* it?' she replied with an incorrigible smile. 'Five couples whose absolute discretion we can depend upon, no matter what they see or hear, and who already know most of the situation. And the Skeffingtons.'

'And their governess, of course.'

Whitney nodded. 'Of course. And the beauty of the plan is that Sheridan won't be able to leave, no matter how badly she wishes, because she works for the Skeffingtons.'

'How do you intend to prevent *Stephen* from leaving when he sets eyes on her?'

'Leave?' she repeated, looking even more pleased. 'And abandon his nephew who adores him? The nephew he positively dotes on? How would that look to Noel? And how would it look to everyone else if he's so overset by the presence of a mere governess in a house with over a hundred rooms that he can't bear being there and has to leave? I wish there were a less public way to bring them together, but since Stephen clearly won't countenance a private meeting, I had to find a method of getting him where we want him to be and then preventing him from leaving. Even if he could rationalize that Noel wouldn't notice his absence, he'd still lose face in front of the Fieldings and Townsendes and everyone else. He has a great deal of pride, and Sheridan already trampled it. I doubt he'll be willing to sacrifice one iota more by leaving when he sees her. And by keeping the party outdoors, the governesses will be in constant view of the guests, so Stephen won't be able to avoid Sherry, even in the evenings.'

She paused, glancing thoughtfully at the guest list. 'I daren't invite Nicki. For one thing, he'll try to dissuade me, and even if he didn't, he'd refuse to come under these circumstances. He disapproved of everything Stephen did where Sheridan was concerned, including the fact that Stephen didn't try to find her and explain. Nicki is very hostile on the entire subject. He admitted to me the day after I saw her at the opera for the first time that he knew where she was, but he refused to tell me where when I asked. Nicki's never refused me anything. He said very firmly that she's suffered enough from Stephen and she doesn't wish to be found.'

'She left. Stephen didn't,' Clayton pointed out curtly.

'I'm inclined to agree, but Nicki is adamant.'

'Then you're wise not to maneuver them into the same shire, let alone the same house.'

Whitney heard that with a troubled frown. 'Why not?'

'Because Stephen has developed a pronounced, highly refined loathing for DuVille since Sheridan vanished.'

She looked so distressed that Clayton shifted his thoughts back to the plan to bring Sheridan into Stephen's presence. Her scheme was fraught with possibilities for failure, but he could not think of another that was better. 'What if the Skeffingtons decline?' he said idly.

His wife dismissed that possibility by tapping her fingers on a folded missive on her desk. 'According to the information in this letter from Matthew Bennett's firm, Lady Skeffington persuaded her husband, Sir John, to bring the family to London for the Season, specifically so they could mingle with the "right sort of people." Lady Skeffington has very little money, but very big social aspirations, it seems.'

'She sounds delightful,' Clayton said ironically. 'I can hardly wait to have them occupy my home for seventy-two consecutive hours, twelve meals, three teas . . .'

Preoccupied with making her point, Whitney continued, 'They came to London in high hopes of gaining an entrée into the sort of elevated circles where their seventeen-year-old daughter might have an opportunity to make a brilliant match. As of yesterday, they'd succeeded in neither goal. Now, given all that, can you honestly believe the Skeffingtons will decline a personal invitation from the Duke of Claymore to attend a party at his country seat?'

'No,' Clayton said, 'but there is always hope.'

'No, there isn't,' his incorrigible wife said as she turned back to her note making with a laugh, 'not when your brother happens to be considered the most splendid match in England.'

'Maybe it will snow that weekend,' he said, looking appalled by the forthcoming house party. 'Surely at some time in the history of the world, it must have snowed on this continent in June.'

47

With her aching feet propped up on a footstool, Lady Skeffington sat in blissful silence in the salon of their small rented London house. On the opposite side of the room, her husband read *The Times*, his gouty foot propped up on another footstool. 'Listen to how quiet it is,' she said, tipping her head to the side, her expression blissful. 'Miss Bromleigh has taken the children for ice cream. They will return at any moment, and all I can think about is how nice it is to have them gone.'

'Yes, my dove,' her husband replied without missing a word of text.

She was about to continue that topic when their footman, who doubled as coachman and also butler, intruded on the solitude, a missive in his outstretched hand. 'If this is another notice about our rent—' she began, then her fingers registered the extraordinary thickness of the heavy cream paper in her hand, and she turned it over, staring at the seal embedded in the wax. 'Skeffington,' she breathed, 'I think – I am almost certain – we have just received our first important invitation—'

'Yes, my dove.'

She broke the seal, unfolded the note, and her mouth dropped open as she beheld the gold crest at the top of the parchment. Her hands began to shake as she read each word, and she stood up as excitement flowed through her shaking limbs. '*Claymore!*' she uttered in awe, her free hand clutching her chest, where her heart was beginning to thunder. 'We have been invited . . . to *Claymore!*'

'Yes, my dove.'

'The Duke and Duchess of Claymore request the honor of our company at a small party to celebrate the birthday of their son. And—' Lady Skeffington paused to reach out for her hartshorn on the table, before she could continue, 'the Duchess of Claymore has written me a note in her own hand. She says she is sorry that she did not have the pleasure of making our acquaintance during the Season, but is hoping to remedy that at . . . *Claymore* . . .' She stopped for a dose of hartshorn before she continued. '. . . in three weeks. And we are to bring the children. How does that sound to you?'

'Devilish queer.'

She pressed the invitation to her ample bosom, her voice a reverent whisper. 'Skeffington, do you know what this means?' she breathed.

'Yes, my dove. It means we have received an invitation intended for someone else.'

Lady Skeffington whitened at the possibility, snatched the paper from her chest, reread it, and shook her head. 'No, it is directed to us, right there – look.'

His attention finally drawn away from *The Times*, Sir John took the note from her outstretched hand and read it, his expression going from disbelief to smug satisfaction. 'I told you there was no need to hare all over London hither, thither, and yon, hoping for invitations.

This letter would have found us had we stayed right at home in Blintonfield, where we belong.'

'Oh, this is not merely an invitation!' she said, her voice gaining girlish strength. 'This means a great deal more than that!'

He picked his paper back up. 'How so?'

'This has to do with Julianna.'

The paper lowered a scant inch, and his eyes, red-rimmed from a pronounced fondness for Madeira, appeared over the top. 'Julianna? How so?'

'Think, Skeffington, think! Julianna has been in London all Season, and though we could never get her vouchers to Almack's or anywhere else where she'd be seen by the best people, I did insist she stroll in Green Park each day. I was very regular about it, and we saw *him* there one day. He looked straight at Julianna, and I thought then . . . I thought, Yes, he sees her. And *that* is why we have received an invitation to Claymore. He noticed how lovely she is and has spent all this time searching for her and thinking of a way to bring her into his company.'

'Rotten way for him to go about it – having his own wife send the invitation for him. I can't say I approve. Smacks of bad taste.'

She rounded on him in dismayed disbelief. 'What? Whatever are you talking about?'

'Our daughter and Claymore.'

'The duke?' she cried in frustration. 'I want her to have Langford!'

'I don't see how you'll pull that off. If Claymore has set his heart on her, and Langford were to want her too, there's bound to be trouble. You'll have to make up your mind before we go, dearest'.

She opened her mouth to launch an angry tirade at him for his obtuseness, but was diverted by the outburst of animated voices in the hall. 'Children!' she exclaimed, rushing down the hall and hugging the one she encountered first. 'Miss Bromleigh!' she cried, so excited she inadvertently hugged the governess too. 'We shall be working night and day to prepare for a trip. I can't think what we will need for a house party of this magnitude.

'Julianna, where are you, dear?' she said belatedly, momentarily nonplussed when all she saw were two ruddy-faced dark-haired boys between the ages of four and nine.

'Julianna went up to her room, Lady Skeffington,' Sheridan said, hiding a weary smile at her employer's excitement and a wary fear of what sort of extra work was likely to be required of her to get the children ready for 'a house party of this magnitude.' As it was, she only had one evening off each week, and in order to have it, she worked from dawn to eleven every evening, doing an endless variety of additional chores that were normally relegated to seamstresses and maids, not governesses. Sherry took advantage of the uproar about the house party to escape to her own room in the attic for a while. Standing over the pitcher and bowl on her bureau, she washed her face, reassured herself that her hair was neatly bound in its coil, then she sat down by the little attic window and picked up her sewing. There was bound to be more mending, more ironing, more work for her involved in the house party being discussed, but Sheridan didn't actually object to the extra work. Being governess to three children kept her too busy during the day to think about Stephen Westmoreland and those magical days she'd been an integral part of his life. At night, when the house was quiet and she was sewing by candlelight, then she could give free rein to her memories and her daydreams, even though there were times she feared her hopeless obsession with him would someday make her quite insane. With her head bent over her sewing, she invented entire scenes with him and improved on others that had been real.

Time after time, she rewrote in her mind the awful ending to their betrothal. She started most of those imaginary scenes the same way – with Charise Lancaster storming into her bedchamber – and in the midst of Charise's damning tirade about Sherry's motives and trickery, Stephen always walked in. From there Sheridan had several favorite variations on possible endings:

. . . Stephen listened to Charise's incriminating lies, threw Charise out of his house, then he turned to Sheridan, listened sympathetically to her side of the story, and they were married that day as planned.

. . . Stephen refused to listen to a word Charise said before throwing her out of his house, then he listened sympathetically to Sheridan's side of the story, and they were married that day as planned.

. . . They were already married when Charise appeared, and so he had to listen to Sherry's side of the story and believe her.

None of that solved Nicholas DuVille's painful revelation that Stephen had felt bound to wed her out of guilt and responsibility, but Sherry circumvented that mortifying fact with a simple solution – Stephen also loved her. She had variations aplenty for that ending too:

. . . He had always loved her but didn't realize it until after she had gone away, then he searched for her until he found her. And they were married.

. . . They were already married, and he learned to love her despite everything.

She vastly preferred the first ending, because that was the only possible reality, and she kept the dream so close to her that sometimes she found herself looking out the window, half expecting to see him striding to the door. In addition to her fantasies, she had the real-life pleasure – as well as torture – of seeing him at the opera.

She had to stop going there, had to stop tormenting herself by waiting for the moment when he would finally turn to whatever woman was with him and focus his lazy, intimate smile on her. That, Sherry knew, would mark her last trip to the pits of Covent Garden. That she could never endure.

Sometimes, she even imagined that her disappearance was the reason he looked stern and distant when he sat beside the women he escorted to his private opera box. He looked weary and cold because he missed Sherry . . . because he regretted losing her . . .

It was still full daylight and too early for sweet dreams, and Sherry gave her head a shake to banish the thoughts, then she looked up with a determined smile as Julianna Skeffington slipped into the room.

'Miss Bromleigh, may I hide in here?' the seventeen-year-old said, her lovely face a mirror of dismay as she closed the door with a silent click and walked over to the bed. Careful not to mess the coverlet, she sat down, looking like a drooping angel. In her more uncharitable moments, Sherry wondered how two dreadful people like Sir John and Lady Skeffington could have produced this sweet, sensible, intelligent golden girl. 'The worst thing imaginable has happened!' Julianna said with disgust.

'The *very* worst thing?' Sheridan teased. 'Not merely a horrid thing or a disastrous thing, but the worst thing imaginable?'

A hint of an answering smile touched her lips then vanished as Julianna sighed. 'Mama is up in the boughs, believing some nobleman has developed a partiality for me, when the truth is that he scarcely glanced in my direction, and he never spoke a word to me.'

'I see,' Sheridan said gravely, and she did see. She empathized as well. She was thinking of something to say when Lady Skeffington threw open the door, looking wild-eyed.

'I can't think what we have that is suitable to wear in such illustrious company. Miss Bromleigh, you came recommended by a duke's sister, could you possibly advise us? We shall have to go to Bond Street straightaway. Julianna, straighten your shoulders. Gentlemen do not like a female who slouches. What shall we do, Miss Bromleigh? There are coaches to hire, and we shall have to go with a full retinue of servants, including you, of course.'

Sherry let that summation of her status pass without flinching. It was the truth, especially in this household. That was what she was, and she was fortunate to have the position.

'I am not an expert on how the Quality dresses,' she said carefully, 'but I shall be happy to lend you an opinion, ma'am. Where is the party taking place?'

Lady Skeffington straightened her shoulders and puffed out her ample chest, reminding Sheridan of a herald announcing the arrival of the king and queen: 'At the country seat of the Duke and Duchess of Claymore!'

Sherry felt the room tip, then right itself. Her ears were deceiving her, of course.

'The Duke and Duchess of Claymore have invited all of us to an intimate gathering at their home!'

Sherry groped behind her for the bedpost, gripping it and staring at the other woman. Based on what she'd seen firsthand of the *ton*'s social ladder, the Westmorelands occupied the very pinnacle of it, while the Skeffingtons were on the bottom rung, completely beneath the Westmoreland family's notice. Even if it weren't for the ludicrous differences in wealth and prestige between the two families, there was the matter of good breeding. The Westmorelands had it and so did everyone they knew. Sir John and Lady Glenda Skeffington had none. This was impossible, Sherry thought. She was dreaming one of her daydreams, and it had turned into a nightmare.

'Miss Bromleigh, you are losing your color, and I must caution you that there simply isn't time for you to have vapors over this. If I haven't time for a nice swoon,' she added with a robust smile, 'then neither do you, my good girl.'

Sherry swallowed and swallowed again, trying to find her voice. 'Are you—' she rasped, 'are you acquainted with them, with the duke and duchess, I mean?'

Lady Skeffington issued a warning before she confided the truth: 'I trust you would not betray a confidence, and risk losing your position with us?'

Sherry swallowed again and shook her head, which Lady Skeffington correctly interpreted was Sherry's promise of confidentiality. 'Sir John and I have never met them in our lives.'

'Then how, that is, why—?'

'I have very good reason to believe,' Lady Skeffington confided, proudly, 'that Julianna has caught the eye of the most eligible bachelor in all England! This party is merely a ploy, in my opinion – a clever method devised by the Earl of Langford – to bring Julianna into his own circle so that he may look her over at his leisure.'

Sheridan was beginning to see bright flashes of vivid color at the edges of her eyes.

'Miss Bromleigh?'

Sheridan blinked, warily surveying the woman who had obviously devised this entire Banbury tale as some form of diabolical torture designed to break down Sheridan's carefully constructed foundation for sanity.

'Miss Bromleigh, THIS WILL NOT DO!'

'Mama, give me your smelling salts quickly,' Julianna said, her voice coming from farther and farther away, as if Sheridan were hurtling down a tunnel.

'I'm quite all right,' Sheridan managed, turning her head away from the odious salts that Lady Skeffington was determined to wave under her nose. 'I was just a little . . . dizzy.'

'Thank heavens! We are all depending upon you to provide us with any information on how the inner circles of the *ton* go about.'

Sheridan gave a laugh that was part hilarity and part hysteria. 'How would I know?'

'Because Miss Charity Thornton wrote your reference letter and said very specifically that you were a woman of rare gentility who would set an example of the highest social standards for any child entrusted to your care. She did write that letter, did she not? The one you showed to us?'

Sherry had her own suspicion that Nicholas DuVille had dictated it and somehow gotten Miss Charity to sign it without reading it, since the recommendation of a bachelor, who also happened to be a notorious rake, was hardly the thing to gain a young woman respectable employment. Either that or he'd not only written it but signed both their names to it. 'Have I given you any reason to doubt the truth of those words, ma'am?' Sherry evaded.

'Certainly not. You're a good sort of girl, despite the wild color of your hair, Miss Bromleigh, and I hope you will not let us down.'

'I will try not to,' Sheridan said, amazed that she was able to speak at all.

'Then I give you leave to lie down and rest for a few minutes. It is rather stuffy up here.'

Sherry plopped down on the bed like a limp, obedient child, her heart beginning to thud in fast, furious beats. An instant after she'd closed the door, Lady Skeffington poked her head back into the room. 'I shall want the boys to show up to their very best advantage too while we are there. Even when my daughter becomes Julianna, Countess of Langford, we will still have their futures to consider, you know. Do practice them with their singing. It is very appealing the way you have taught the children to accompany you on that tired old instrument you suggested we purchase, that—'

'Guitar,' Sherry provided lamely.

When she left, Sherry looked at her lap. Not for one minute did she believe that nonsensical notion of Lady Skeffington's that Stephen Westmoreland had glimpsed Julianna in the park and gone to all this trouble to bring her to him. Julianna was undeniably appealing to look at, but her special qualities only became apparent in conversation, which Stephen had not had with her yet. Furthermore, according to the gossip she'd heard the one time she'd visited Almack's, he had women at his beck and call wherever he turned, ready to make complete cakes of themselves over him. He did not need to bother with an elaborate ploy like a house party.

No, that wasn't why the Skeffington family – and their *governess* – was being summoned to Claymore for a command appearance. The invitation had nothing to do with them at all, Sheridan thought as a hysterical laugh that was part dread and part helplessness welled up in her. The truth was that the Westmorelands – and probably a large group of their friends who'd also be at Claymore – had devised the most exquisite vengeance in the world to punish Sheridan Bromleigh for what they thought was her deceitful misuse of them: they were going to force her to return to their society, only not as an equal this time, but as the glorified servant she *really* was.

And the most painful part of it . . . the humiliating, agonizing part . . . was that she didn't have a choice in the world except to go there.

Sherry felt her chin tremble and angrily stood up. Her conscience was clear. Furthermore, there was no shame in her position. She had never aspired to be a countess.

Her conscience reminded her that wasn't entirely true. The truth was that she *had* wanted to be Stephen Westmoreland's countess. And so this was to be her punishment for daring to dream, daring to reach above herself, Sherry realized, feeling furious at fate for doing this to her.

'I want to go home!' she said fiercely to the empty room. 'There has to be some way to go home!' Only five weeks had passed since she'd written to Aunt Cornelia, explaining everything that had transpired since she boarded the *Morning Star*, and asking her aunt to send her money for passage home. The money would be coming, of that Sheridan was certain, but at best it would take a total of eight to ten weeks for her letter to cross the Atlantic and reach her aunt, and then for her aunt's response to reach her.

Even if the Atlantic seas stayed calm and the ships didn't tarry in any port between Portsmouth and Richmond, there was still three weeks left before she could hope to hear from her aunt. Three more weeks before the money for her passage home could possibly arrive. Three more weeks before the party at Claymore. If Fortune would smile down on her just one time since she set foot on English soil, then she might still be able to deprive the Westmorelands of their petty vengeance after all.

48

With so much time to prepare mentally for whatever unpleasantness the Westmorelands had planned for her at Claymore, Sheridan had almost convinced herself she was well-fortified against her fate. For weeks, she had reminded herself that she was completely innocent, and that goodness and righteousness were therefore on her side. To further insulate herself against heartbreak, she had firmly put an end to her ritual daydreams about Stephen.

As a result, she was able to endure the trip to Claymore with what she thought was stoic nonchalance. Instead of wondering how long it would be before she saw Stephen – or if she was going to see him – she concentrated on the cheerful chatter of the Skeffington boys, who were travelling with her in the third of the rented coaches that comprised the entourage. Rather than wondering what Stephen would do or say when he saw her, she insisted the children sing merry songs with her during the two-hour trip. In lieu of peering out the coach window for her first glimpse of the house, Sheridan steadfastly devoted all her thoughts, all her attention, to the boys' appearance while the Skeffington cavalcade proceeded along a winding, treelined drive and across a stone bridge that led up to the Duke of Claymore's country seat. She did not allow herself more than a passing, disinterested glance at the facade of the immense house with its double wings sweeping forward around a vast terraced entrance, nor allow herself to notice the balconies and mullioned windows that adorned its front.

Except for her treacherous heartbeat, which insisted on accelerating as she alighted from the coach, she was so well-fortified against feeling anything at all that she managed a polite, fixed smile at the servants who rushed from the house in maroon and gold Westmoreland livery to assist the new arrivals. Garbed in a plain dark blue bombazine gown, with her hair twisted into a severe coil at the nape, and her narrow white collar demurely buttoned at the throat, Sheridan looked exactly like the governess she was as she alighted from the coach. With her hands resting on the shoulders of the two boys, she proceeded up the flight of shallow steps, behind Sir John and Lady Skeffington and Julianna.

Her chin was high, but not aggressively so, and her shoulders were straight, but then she had nothing whatsoever to be ashamed of or to defend, not even her respectable, if menial, position as a governess. For the thousandth time in three weeks, she reminded herself very firmly that she had never knowingly deceived the Westmorelands or anyone else. The Earl of Langford had willfully and wrongfully deceived *her* about being her fiancé and about actually wanting to marry her. His family had gone along with it, therefore the responsibility and the guilt and the shame were theirs, not hers.

334

Unfortunately, Sheridan's hard-won poise took its first severe blow as soon as she shepherded her charges into the three-story skylit foyer, where more liveried servants were standing at attention, waiting to show the new arrivals to their rooms as soon as the under-butler had formally greeted them and indicated to which rooms each guest was to be shown.

'Her grace thought you would enjoy the particularly fine view from the blue suite,' he told Sir John and Lady Skeffington. 'When you have had all the time you desire to refresh yourselves from your journey, she will be pleased to have you join her and the other guests in the drawing room.' As he finished, a footman stepped forward from the front of the line to escort them to the blue suite.

'Miss Skeffington, the suite next to that has been readied for you.' He turned to the boys as Julianna began her trip up the broad winding staircase accompanied by another footman.

'Young sirs,' Hodgkin continued, 'your rooms are on the third floor, where the playrooms are located. And your governess will, of course—' He turned to Sheridan, and even though she'd had time to brace herself for the moment when he saw and recognized her, she still wasn't prepared for the horror that flashed across Hodgkin's face as his pale eyes riveted on her features, slipped to her cheap gown, then snapped back to her face. '—will, of course—' he stammered, 'be close at hand – in a room directly – across the hall.'

Sheridan had a wild impulse to reach out and pat his parchment cheek, to tell him that it was all right that she was here as a governess, and that he shouldn't look as if he were going to cry. Instead, she managed a semblance of a smile. 'Thank you very much—' she said and softly added, 'Hodgkin.'

Her room was small in comparison to the boys' and simply furnished with a bed, a chair, and a small bureau with a washbowl and pitcher, but it was palatial compared to the attic room she occupied at the Skeffingtons'. Better yet, the house was so vast that if she stayed on the third floor, she could easily avoid all sight of the owner and his family. In an effort to keep busy, she washed her hands and face, unpacked her night garments, and went to check on the boys.

Two other governesses were installed at the end of the hall, and as Sherry ushered the boys into the playroom, they appeared there with their own charges, two little boys of perhaps four. After friendly introductions, those governesses insisted on involving the Skeffington children in a game with the little boys, and Sheridan found herself with the last thing she wanted: time on her hands.

Left out of the playful ruckus created by four boys, she wandered around the huge, sunny room, past a large table covered with an entire army of wooden soldiers, then she bent down to pick up two books that had fallen out of the shelves. She put them back, idly picked up an old sketchbook lying atop the bookcase, opened the cover. . . and felt her heart stop. Beneath a childish drawing of what appeared to be a horse grazing in a field – or drinking water from a lake – was a name, awkwardly and painstakingly inscribed: STEPHEN WESTMORELAND.

Sherry slapped the cover closed and swung around, but her carefully erected defenses took another hit – this time a broadside: a few feet away, framed upon a table beside a wooden rocking horse, was a painting of a little boy with his arm slung round the horse's neck and a grin on his face. The painting had obviously been done by a talented amateur, and the smile on the dark-haired child's face was impish, rather than boldly caressing, but it was just as irresistible, and just as unmistakably Stephen's.

'I think I'll join the game,' Sherry burst out, turning her back on the painting. 'What are we playing?' she asked Thomas Skeffington, the seven-year-old, who was already on his way to being seriously overweight.

'We have too many players right now, Miss Brom-leigh,' Thomas said. 'And the prize is a special sweet, so it wouldn't be right for you to win it because I want it.'

'No, *I* do!' the six-year-old whined.

Appalled by their manners, which had actually shown a slight sign of improvement under Sheridan's care, she sent an apologetic glance at the other two governesses, who answered with smiles of understanding sympathy. 'You must be weary,' one of the governesses said to her. 'We both arrived yesterday and have the benefit of a night's sleep. Why don't you rest for a few minutes before the festivities begin, and we'll look after these gentlemen?'

Since it was already taking all her self-control to stop herself from opening the sketchbook again or study-ing the picture of the sturdy dark-haired boy with the heartbreakingly familiar smile, Sheridan took advantage of their offer and practically fled across the hall. Leaving the door open, she walked over to the chair near the bed and sat down while she fiercely concentrated on *not* thinking about the fact that this was the house where Stephen had grown up. However, three weeks of unabated anxiety and hard work, compounded by the events of the last half hour, had all combined to take their toll, and for the first time in weeks, Sheridan let herself daydream: closing her eyes, she fantasized that the invitation to the Skeffingtons had nothing to do with her, that she would be able to remain on the third floor, undiscovered for three days, and that Stephen Westmoreland was not going to be here.

Julianna's appearance a short time later not only removed all hope of any such possibilities but also made it obvious that Sheridan was due for more than just periodic humiliation. 'Are you resting, or may I come in?' Julianna asked hesitantly, and Sheridan pulled herself from her prayerful fantasy.

'I'd enjoy the company,' Sheridan said truthfully, and then because she couldn't choke back the words, she added, 'Is the Earl of Langford here?'

'No, but he's expected momentarily, and Mama is up in the boughs with ridiculous notions about making a match between us. I don't know how I'll endure this weekend.' Anger flared in her eyes. 'Why does she *do* this to me, Miss Bromleigh? Tell me why her greatest desire in life is to foist me off on the richest man with the biggest title, no matter how old or how ugly or how unpalatable I might find him! Tell me why she behaves like such a – a *toadeater* when she's among anyone she regards as her social superior!' Sheridan's heart went out to her as she watched the seventeen-year-old struggle to keep her shame and anger under control. 'You should have *seen* her in the drawing room a while ago with the Duchess of Claymore and her friends. Mama was so – so *pushing* – and so *eager* to win their favor that it was horrid to watch.'

Sheridan couldn't answer any of those questions without betraying her secret revulsion at the same attitudes Julianna found so abhorrent in her ambitious, cloying mama. 'Sometimes,' she said cautiously, 'mothers simply desire a better life for their daughters than they themselves have had—'

Scornfully, Julianna retorted, 'Mama doesn't care about my life. My life would be happy if she would leave me to my writing! My life would be happy if she would stop trying to marry me off like I was a—'

'A beautiful princess?' Sheridan provided, and it was partially true. In Lady Skeffington's mind, Julianna's face and figure made her a precious asset to be bartered in return for a more elevated place in Society for the rest of the family, and her daughter was sensible enough to know it.

'I wish I were ugly!' Julianna exploded, and she obviously meant it. 'I wish I were so ugly no man would look at me. Do you know what my life was like before you came to us? I have spent it all reading books. That's all the living I've ever done. I have never been allowed to go *anywhere*, because Mama has lived in daily fear that some scandal would attach itself to me and spoil my value on the marriage market! I wish it had happened,' she said wrathfully. 'I wish I were ruined, so I could take the little portion Grandmama left to me. I would live in a tiny place in London and have friends. I would go to the opera and the theatre and write my novel. Freedom,' she said softly, wistfully. 'Friends. You are my first friend, Miss Bromleigh. You are the first female anywhere close to my age that Mama has ever let me be near. She does not approve, you see, of the modern behavior of females my own age. She thinks they are fast, and if I were to socialize with them—'

Sheridan felt absolutely called upon to at least show she understood. 'Then your reputation might suffer,' she provided, 'and you would be—'

'Ruined!' exclaimed Julianna, but she sounded positively jubilant about the prospect. Her eyes lit with the irrepressible humor and spirit Lady Skeffington was trying so hard to suffocate as she leaned forward and confided in a comic whisper, *'Ruined.* Rendered unmarriageable . . . Doesn't it sound divine?'

In Julianna's specific circumstances, it did sound like a permanent reprieve, but as Sheridan knew, Julianna had no real idea of the ramifications of such a thing. 'No, it doesn't,' she said firmly, but she smiled.

'Miss Bromleigh, do you believe in love? I mean, love between a man and a woman, of the sort one reads about in novels? I don't.'

'I—' Sheridan hesitated, remembering the exhilaration she'd felt when Stephen walked into a room, the delight that came from talking with him or laughing with him. And she remembered most of all the odd sense of rightness she'd experienced when she believed he derived intense pleasure from kissing her. For a while, she had felt as if she were playing her part in the natural order of things. She had felt . . . complete . . . because she pleased him. Or because she stupidly thought she pleased him. Realizing that Julianna was suddenly watching her too closely, she said, 'I used to believe in love.'

'And?'

'And it can be very painful when it is one-sided,' she confessed and then was astonished her guard had dropped so far, merely by allowing herself to think of a kiss.

'I see,' Julianna said, her violet eyes too wise for her age, too knowing. She was, in Sheridan's opinion, a talented writer and extraordinarily observant.

'I don't think you do,' Sheridan lied with a bright smile.

Julianna proved otherwise with blunt simplicity. 'When you first came to stay with us, I sensed . . . a deep hurt in you. And courage, and determination. I won't ask you if it was unrequited love, though I feel certain it was, but may I ask you something else?'

It was on the tip of Sheridan's tongue to sternly point out the wrongness of prying into another person's life, but Julianna was so lonely, and so appealing, and so sympathetic, that she didn't have the heart to do it. 'Only if what you ask is something that will not make me feel uncomfortable,' Sheridan said instead.

'How do you manage to seem so serene?'

Sheridan felt anything but serene at the moment, and she attempted a joke, but her laugh was strained. 'I'm a paragon, obviously. Courageous – determined. Now, talk to me about more important things. What are the plans for the weekend, do you know?'

Julianna reacted with an admiring smile when Sheridan adroitly switched the topic away from herself, but she complied by answering the question. 'It's to be a weekend spent outdoors, including meals, which seems quite odd, I thought. In any case, the children and their governesses will be seated at tables next to us – I know that part because I went out onto the lawn for a stroll before I came up here and saw how everything is being set up.' She had leaned down to remove a pebble from her slipper and so missed the look of dawning horror and hostility on Sheridan's face. 'Oh, and you are to play the guitar and sing with the boys—'

Instead of being stricken, Sheridan was slowly standing up, propelled to her feet by a boiling wrath beyond anything she'd ever known. Based on what Julianna had said, it was obvious that the entire party had been deliberately organized in a way that would keep Sheridan constantly in view. The guests were limited to those couples whom Sheridan had known the best. They were also close friends of the Westmorelands, which meant they could be relied upon to relish humiliating Stephen's former-fiancée-turned-governess, but not to repeat anything they saw to the London gossips because that would embarrass the earl. She was not even going to be allowed to dine in peace. Far more infuriating, she was supposed to perform like a court jester for their amusement. 'Those monsters!' she exploded, her voice hissing.

Julianna looked up as she put her slipper on. 'The boys? They are across the hall.'

'Not *those* monsters,' Sheridan said unthinkingly. 'The adult monsters! Did you say they were in the drawing room earlier?'

Oblivious to Julianna's open-mouthed stare, the woman she'd just praised for her serenity marched forward with a militant look in her eye that would have given Napoleon Bonaparte second thoughts. Sheridan knew she was going to lose her position over what she was about to do, but then the Skeffingtons would dismiss her anyway after this weekend. Lady Skeffington was ambitious and sly, and it wouldn't take her more than an hour to realize that her children's governess was an object of scorn, in addition to being the focal point of the occasion. Lady Skeffington was perfectly willing to sacrifice her only daughter in hopes of being included in the Westmorelands' social circle. She wouldn't hesitate one minute to send Sheridan packing if she sensed the Westmorelands had a low opinion of her.

None of that mattered to Sheridan as she marched down the long staircase. She would sooner starve than let these haughty British aristocrats torture her out of some sick, distorted need for vengeance.

49

Blind to everything but her intention, Sheridan located the drawing room with the help of a footman, and there she confronted yet another servant who was stationed in front of the drawing room's closed door.

'I wish to see the Duchess of Claymore at once,' she informed him, fully expecting to be informed that was impossible – and fully prepared to force her way inside if necessary. 'My name is Sheridan Bromleigh.'

To her shock, the footman bowed at once and said, as he opened the door, 'Her grace has been expecting you.'

That announcement removed for Sheridan any question that this party might have been organized for some purpose other than to punish her. 'I'll wager she has been!' Sheridan said scornfully. Feminine laughter stopped and conversations broke off the instant she swept into the immense room. Ignoring Victoria Seaton and Alexandra Townsende, Sherry walked past the dowager duchess and Miss Charity without a nod and confronted the Duchess of Claymore.

Her eyes blazing, she looked down her nose at the composed brunette she had once thought of as a sister, and her voice shook with the violence of her outrage. 'Are you so poor of entertainment that torturing a servant titillates you?' she demanded scathingly, her hands clenched into fists at her sides. 'How much amusement did you honestly expect me to provide for you, besides playing and singing? Did you hope I would dance for you as well? Why isn't Stephen here yet? He must be as eager as you to see it all begin.' Her voice shook with wrath as she finished, 'You have all wasted your time, because I am leaving! Do you understand? You have put the Skeffingtons to an expense they can ill afford and dragged them here with their hopes all built up, when all you wanted was vengeance on me! What sort of – of *monsters* are you, anyway? And don't you *dare* to pretend you haven't planned this entire weekend for the simple purpose of dragging me here!'

Whitney had expected this visit from Sheridan, but she hadn't expected it to begin with the angry aggression of a duel. Instead of gently explaining what she hoped to accomplish, as Whitney had intended to do, she entered the verbal swordplay with a thrust aimed straight at Sheridan Bromleigh's heart: 'For some reason,' she announced coolly, with a challenging lift of her brows, 'I rather thought you might appreciate our efforts to bring you into Stephen's sphere.'

'I have no desire to be in any such place,' Sheridan fired back.

'Is that why you go to the opera every Thursday?'

'Anyone can go to the opera.'

'You don't watch the performance. You watch Stephen.'

Sheridan paled. 'Does he know? Oh, please, do not say you've told him. Why would you be that cruel?'

'Why,' Whitney said very, very carefully, sensing that she was a hair's breadth from finally hearing the truth about Sheridan's disappearance and that if she made one mistake, she wouldn't, 'would it be a cruelty if he knew you went there to see him?'

'*Does* he know?' Sheridan countered stubbornly, and Whitney bit her lip to hide an admiring smile at the

343

other woman's spirit. Sheridan Bromleigh might be a servant in a roomful of nobility, but she bowed to no one. On the other hand, her caution and spirit were creating a standoff. Whitney drew a breath, hating to resort to blackmail, but she did it anyway and without compunction. 'He does not know, but he will know if you cannot make me understand why you go to the opera to look at him, after jilting him at the altar.'

'You have no right to ask me that.'

'I have every right.'

'Who do you think *you* are?' Sheridan exploded. 'The Queen of England?'

'I think I am the woman who appeared for your wedding. I think you are the woman who did not appear for it.'

'For that, I would have expected you to thank me!'

'Thank you?' Whitney uttered, looking as stunned as she felt. 'For what?'

'Why are you asking me all this! Why are we caviling over trifles?'

Whitney studied her manicure. 'I do not consider my brother-in-law's heart and life a trifle. Perhaps that is where we differ?'

'I liked you much better when I didn't know who I was,' Sheridan said in a voice so bewildered that it would have been comic in another context. She looked around the room as if she needed confirmation that the furnishings were firmly anchored to the floor and that the draperies hadn't become bed linens. 'You didn't seem quite so . . . difficult and unreasonable. After Monsieur DuVille explained to me the day of the wedding why Stephen had suddenly decided to marry me, I did the only thing I possibly could. Poor Mr Lancaster . . . dying without Charise there.'

Mentally, Whitney consigned Nicki DuVille to perdition for his inadvertent part in this debacle, but she kept her mind focused on their plan.

'May I leave now?' Sheridan said stonily.

'Certainly,' Whitney said as Victoria and Miss Charity looked at her in shock. 'Miss Bromleigh,' Whitney added as Sheridan reached for the door, but her voice was gentle now, 'I believe my brother-in-law was in love with you.'

'Don't tell me that!' Sherry exploded, her hand clenching the door handle, her back to them. 'Don't do this to me. He never pretended to love me, never even bothered to lie about it when we discussed marriage.'

'Perhaps he didn't acknowledge the feeling by name, even to himself, perhaps he still does not, but he has not been the same man since you left.'

Sherry felt unbalanced by the explosion of hope and fear, of denial and joy, inside her brain. 'Do not lie to me, for the love of God.'

'Sherry?'

Sherry turned at the soft sound in her voice.

'On your wedding day, Stephen wouldn't believe you weren't coming back. Even after Miss Lancaster poured all her venom, he didn't believe her. He waited for you to come back and explain.'

Sherry thought her heart would break and that was before the duchess added, 'He kept the cleric there until late that night. He wouldn't let him leave. Does that sound like a man who didn't want you? Does that sound like a man who was only marrying you out of guilt and responsibility? Since he knew by then you weren't Charise Lancaster, why would he have felt any guilt or responsibility to you? Your head injury was healed and your memory was returned.'

Sherry felt shattered at the thought of what she might have had . . . and what she had lost.

'He wouldn't believe you'd run away. He wouldn't let the cleric leave,' Whitney emphasized. 'The vicar was adamant that the wedding had to be performed in daylight, before noon, as is custom, but Stephen overrode him.'

Sherry turned her head away because her eyes were glazing with tears. 'I never thought . . . never imagined

. . . He could not possibly have been thinking clearly,' she said with more strength, turning to look at Whitney. 'He would never have considered marrying a common governess.'

'Oh, yes he would,' Whitney said with a teary laugh. 'I can tell you from personal experience – and from all I've read about the family's history – that Westmoreland men do *exactly* as they please, and they always have. May I remind you that when Stephen kept the vicar at his house, he was already aware of your former position as Charise Lancaster's paid companion. It didn't matter to him. He'd made up his mind to marry you, and nothing could have stopped him. Except you.'

She paused, watching Sheridan's expressive face mirror joy and anguish . . . and then hope. Tentative, fragile, but there, and though that pleased Whitney immensely, she also felt obliged to issue a sobering warning. 'Unfortunately,' she said, 'Westmoreland men are extremely difficult to manage when they have been provoked beyond what they deem reasonable, and I'm afraid Stephen is already far, far beyond that unlucky state.'

'Provoked beyond reason?' Sheridan said cautiously.

Whitney nodded. 'I'm afraid so.' She waited, hoping for a sign of the courage Sheridan was going to need if things were to be set to rights. 'If matters are to be set to rights between you, I very much fear the burden for it will fall completely to you. In fact, the best thing you can hope to receive from Stephen is opposition. Cold, unresponsive opposition. At worst, he'll unleash some of the rage he feels toward you.'

'I see.'

'He wants nothing to do with you, will not even allow the mention of your name by any of us.'

'He . . . hates me?' Her voice faltered at the agonizing certainty he did – and the realization that she could have prevented all this.

'Thoroughly.'

346

'But he – I mean you do think that he didn't hate me before?'

'I think he loved you. I told you once before I've never seen Stephen treat a woman quite the way he treated you. Among other things, he was possessive, which is not at all in his normal style.'

Sheridan looked down at her hands, afraid to hope she could rekindle any of those feelings in him. Unable to stop herself from hoping. Raising her eyes to Whitney's, she said, 'What can I do?'

'You can fight for him.'

'But how?'

'That's the delicate part of the problem,' Whitney said, biting her lip to hide a smile at Sheridan's alarmed expression.

'He will avoid you, of course. In fact, he would have left here the moment he realized you were here if it hadn't been Noel's birthday, and if leaving wouldn't cause him to lose all face.'

'Then I suppose I should be grateful matters happened this way.'

'Actually, they didn't "happen this way." You were quite right when you assumed all this was planned very carefully, but it was never intended to embarrass you, only to force Stephen to be in your company the maximum amount of time over the weekend. Also, the other two governesses will step in to look after the Skeffington boys while you're here. To that end, I've suggested to Lady Skeffington that you might better serve if you were to be where you could chaperone Julianna – from a distance, of course. That will allow you to wander about the grounds, ride if you wish, and generally be visible.'

'I – I don't know how to thank you.'

'You may not want to thank me,' Whitney said with a nervous smile. And then because she desperately wanted to give the other woman enough reassurance to make her able to face up to whatever Stephen did to her, she confided something that only the family knew. 'Several years ago, I was betrothed to my husband by my father without my knowledge. I – I had some foolish girlhood notion of marrying a local boy I thought I'd love forever, and I – I did several things to try to avoid this marriage that caused my husband to break the betrothal and withdraw his offer. Unfortunately, it wasn't until then that I realized I was long over my infatuation with the other man. By then, Clayton wouldn't even acknowledge that he knew me.'

'Eventually, however, he obviously changed his mind.'

'Not quite,' Whitney admitted with a rosy blush. '*I* changed his mind. He was on the verge of marrying another, and I – I came here to see him, to try to dissuade him. Stephen stepped in and forced me to stay. Actually, I only conceived this party because a similar ploy worked with my husband and me.'

'But everything came about as soon as he saw you?'

That evoked a musical laugh from the duchess and a firm shake of her head. 'He seemed to hate the sight of me. It was the most mortifying night of my life. But when it was over, when I won – when we both won – I had no pride left. I had him.'

'And you are warning me that my pride is going to suffer?'

'Terribly, unless I miss my guess.'

'Thank you for confiding in me. In a way it helps to know another woman made an enormous mistake and had to rectify it herself.'

'I didn't,' Whitney said gently, 'confide in you to share misery. I had a much more important reason, else I wouldn't have done it.'

'I know.'

Sheridan hesitated, then stood up, her smile wobbly but her voice strong. 'What should I do?'

'First, you must be very visible, so that he cannot avoid noticing you. And very available, somehow.'

'Available . . . to him, you mean?'

'Precisely. Having been jilted and deceived, Stephen won't want anything to do with you. It will take an invitation from you – unmistakable, and hopefully irresistible – to lure him to you again.'

Sheridan nodded, her heart thundering with dread and hope and uncertainty, then she slowly turned to the other women, all of whom she'd insulted earlier, and all of whom were watching her with fond, gentle understanding. She looked at the dowager and Miss Charity first. 'I was inexcusably rude,' she began, but Stephen's mother shook her head to stop her and held out her hand.

'Under the circumstances, my dear, I'm sure I would have acted much as you did.'

Taking the dowager's hand in both of hers, Sherry clasped it tightly. 'I'm terribly, terribly sorry—'

Victoria Seaton stopped further outpourings of guilt by standing up and giving Sheridan a fierce hug, then she drew back and laughingly said, 'We are all here to support you, and you may well need it when Stephen arrives.'

'Don't frighten her,' said Alexandra Townsende, laughing as she stood up and clasped Sheridan's hands. With an exaggerated shiver, she said, 'Leave that to Stephen.'

Sheridan's smile wavered a little. 'Do your husbands know what all this is about?'

All three women nodded, and Sheridan found it very touching to know the husbands were also wishing her well.

The task that lay in front of her was daunting. The realization that Stephen had evidently cared enough for her to wait with the cleric for hours after she ran away was heartbreaking. Sherry had never been happier in her life.

50

After Sheridan, Alexandra, and Victoria left the drawing room, the three women who remained within it, despite their valiant efforts to seem normal and confident, were jumpy and tense by the time they heard the sound of a coach arriving an hour later. 'That *must* be Stephen,' the dowager duchess said, putting her teacup down with enough nervous energy to cause the priceless Sèvres cup to clatter and tilt upon its delicate saucer. All morning, guests had been arriving for the birthday celebration, including the Skeffington party, but Stephen had not put in an appearance, and it was becoming obvious something either had detained him or was going to cause him to miss the day completely. 'If he has not been injured or held up by highwaymen on the road,' she continued peevishly, 'I shall be sorely tempted to do him bodily harm myself! My nerves are drawn to the limit. I am entirely too old to be subjected to this sort of suspense.'

Too anxious to wait for the butler to announce the new arrival, Whitney was already on her way to the windows to have a look.

'Is it he, dear?'

'Yes . . . Oh, no!' her daughter-in-law answered, and turning around she pressed against the draperies, looking positively frantic.

'Yes, it is he, or "oh, no," it is *not* he?' inquired Miss Charity.

'Yes, it is Stephen.'

'That's good.'

'With Monica Fitzwaring.'

'That's bad,' said the dowager, handing her three-year-old grandson to Charity, who opened her arms to him, and who'd been included in the plot out of necessity. Since she and Noel had become inordinately fond of each other, Whitney didn't have the heart to send the elderly lady away from him on his birthday, nor could she have allowed Charity to remain if she weren't forewarned of Sheridan's arrival and apprised of the reasons and the plan.

'He has also brought Georgette Porter.'

'That is *very* bad,' the dowager said, sounding more dire.

'I think it is very nice!' exclaimed Miss Charity, drawing their incredulous looks as she grinned at Lord Noel Westmoreland. Picking up the youngster's wrists, she clapped his chubby hands together, making him laugh, before she glanced up at the two duchesses and noticed they were looking at her as if she were demented. 'One woman would occupy his time,' she predicted happily. 'Two women can occupy each other and leave him quite free for our Sheridan.'

'Unfortunately, Monica and Georgette cannot abide each other.'

Miss Charity didn't see that as an obstacle. 'In order to secure Langford's good opinion, they will spend all their time trying to surpass each other for amiability. Or else,' she added, her brow furrowed in thought, 'they will unite and turn all their malice on our poor Sherry, should Langford pay her attention.'

Less than pleased with the second possibility, Whitney looked at her mother-in-law. 'What shall we do?'

Unwilling to be left out of the excitement for more than a moment, Charity said brightly, 'We ought to invite dear Monsieur DuVille to even out the numbers!'

The dowager duchess's nerves were strained enough to cause that lady to turn clear round in her chair and glower at Miss Charity. 'What a perfectly absurd idea! As you well know, Stephen developed an aversion to the mere mention of the man's name from the day Sheridan disappeared!'

Wary of the dowager's unprecedented mood, Whitney hastily interceded. 'Why don't you take Noel outdoors, ma'am,' she suggested to Charity. 'I instructed the governesses to take the children down by the pond at this hour to see the swans and have a sweet. You could keep an eye on our particular governess if she appears there.'

Charity nodded at once, stood up, and took Noel's hand. 'Well, my young lord, shall we endeavor to spy out our prey?' she invited.

Noel pulled back and shook his dark, curly head. 'First, kiss 'bye,' he explained, and ran across the room on sturdy little legs to kiss his grandmother and his mother as he knew they liked for him to do. Satisfied, he grinned at Miss Charity, offered her his hand, and allowed her to lead him outdoors through the French doors that opened onto the lawns.

The Dowager Duchess of Claymore managed to keep her smile in place until Noel vanished, but the moment he was out of sight, she focused her irate gaze on the door that led into the room from the main hall. Stress had finally pushed her past the limit of her endurance. She was irrationally angry with Stephen for foiling their carefully made plans to effect a reconciliation with Sherry by bringing not one, but two women, and she was vastly, if unjustly, annoyed with both women for coming along. Unaware of his mother's strained temper, Stephen escorted his guests into the drawing room and went straight to her chair. 'You look a little weary,' he said, bending to kiss his mother's cheek.

'I wouldn't *look* weary if you wouldn't persist in being late and worrying me when you are.'

Stephen was too startled by her tone to react strongly to the unjust criticism. 'I wasn't aware time was of the essence. I'm sorry you were worried.'

'It is excessively rude to keep your hostess waiting,' she added crossly.

Stephen straightened and eyed her with surprised annoyance. 'My sincerest apologies for my tardiness, your grace.' With a formal bow, he added, 'For the *second* time.'

Dismissing her unnaturally querulous behavior with an imperceptible shrug, he turned so that she could acknowledge his guests. 'Mother,' he said, 'I believe you're acquainted with Miss Fitzwaring—'

'How is your papa, Monica?' the dowager demanded as the young woman made her a pretty curtsy.

'Very well, thank you, your grace. He sends you his warmest regards.'

'Please convey mine to him. And now, since you are clearly exhausted from your trip, I suggest you go straight upstairs and stay there until supper so that you may rest and recover your color.'

'I am not in the least tired, your grace,' Miss Fitzwaring said, stiffening in affront at the bald hint she didn't look her best.

The dowager ignored her, extended her regal hand to the other woman, and announced as Georgette curtsied, 'I heard you have been ill recently, Miss Porter. You must spend the weekend lying down.'

'Oh, but – that was last year, your grace. I'm fully recovered.'

'Prevention is the key to good health,' she persevered doggedly. 'That is what my physician always says, and that is how I have lived all these years with such *robust* health and *cheerful* disposition.'

Whitney stepped in and greeted her unexpected guests before they could pause to mentally challenge her claim to cheerful disposition. 'You both look perfectly fit, but I'm certain you'd like a few minutes to refresh yourselves,' she said with a smile as she escorted the mortified Miss Porter and the offended Miss Fitzwaring to the door so that a footman could show them to their rooms.

'Where is my nephew?' Stephen asked as he pressed a brief kiss to Whitney's cheek. 'And where,' he added in a sardonic whisper, 'is my mother's "cheerful" disposition?'

'Noel is with Miss Charity. . .' Whitney began as it suddenly hit her the time was at hand. It was now. There was no turning back. 'In a half hour, everyone is to go down to the pond, where the children are to have a little party. Noel will be there then, along with some of the cottagers' children.'

51

Swans floated gracefully on water as still as a mirror, as Sheridan and the two other governesses stood near a graceful white gazebo, watching several children who lived on the estate playing happily with small, fledgling dukes on the bank of a small lake on the front lawn. Their happy voices rang out as they tried to coax the lofty swans closer to the bank, mingling with the deeper, more reserved voices of the Fieldings, Townsendes, Skeffingtons, and Westmorelands.

Sheridan kept a close eye on the children, but none of the day's sounds were as loud as the thunder of her heart as she watched Stephen finally emerge from the house with two women. Whitney had already whispered a warning about the women before she joined her guests, but Sheridan scarcely paid it any attention. In her mind, all she could hear was Whitney's earlier words: *Stephen kept the cleric there until late that night. He could not – would not – believe you weren't coming back.*

Tenderness and regret shook through her every time she thought of it, reinforcing her courage, her determination to face him and give him whatever 'invitation' was necessary to bring him back to her.

He was listening to whatever Monica was telling him,

354

but his smile was absent, and his gaze was on the children.

The closer he came, the harder Sheridan's heart beat until it seemed to roar in her ears. Noel came running up to her with Charity close beside him, and he stopped shyly in front of her. 'Flower, for you,' he said, holding out a tiny wildflower that Charity had told him to pick.

Charity's reason was obvious as she said, 'Langford will be looking for Noel, and if he is with you, then we will all be relieved of our tension sooner than if we have to wait until he notices the governesses.'

Sherry didn't care for that idea, but she crouched down to accept the flower, smiling softly at the sturdy three-year-old, who reminded her of his father and Stephen both. 'Thank you, kind sir,' she said, watching Stephen from the corner of her eye as he neared the gazebo. Behind her, beneath a large oak tree, the adults were surreptitiously watching the same scene begin to unfold, and their conversations became halting, while their laughter came to an abrupt end.

Noel looked at the sunlight glinting on the flaming strands of her hair, reached out to touch it, then paused to look inquiringly at Charity. 'Hot?'

'No,' Sheridan answered, loving every feature on his face. 'It's not hot.'

He grinned and reached out to touch it, but Stephen's call drew his instant attention.

'Noel!'

Noel broke into a grin, and before Charity could stop him, he turned and raced to his uncle, who swept him up into his arms. 'You've grown a foot!' Stephen told him, shifting him to his left arm, his gaze on the group of adults beneath the tree. 'Have you missed me?'

'Yes!' Noel said emphatically with a shake of his head, but as they passed within a few feet of Sheridan, Noel saw Sherry watching him with a hesitant smile. He made a sudden decision and wriggled to get down.

'What, leaving me so soon?' Stephen asked, looking surprised and a little hurt. 'Obviously,' he joked to the Townsendes and Fieldings, as well as Georgette and Monica, as he lowered the wriggling little boy to his feet, 'I need to start bringing him more lavish gifts. Where are you going, young man?'

Noel gave him an adoring look, but pointed a chubby finger to a woman who was standing a few paces away, wearing a drab dark blue gown, and explained, 'First, kiss 'bye!'

Unaware that he was the cynosure of a half-dozen pairs of eyes, Stephen straightened, glanced in the direction the child had pointed . . . and froze, his gaze levelling on Sheridan, who was bending to receive her kiss but looking directly at Stephen.

Whitney saw his reaction, saw his jaw clench so tightly that a muscle began to throb in his cheek. She had secretly harbored the hope that he might somehow believe the Skeffingtons were actually acquaintances of hers and that Sherry's appearance here was coincidence, but that hope was in vain. Slowly, Stephen turned his head and looked straight at her, his eyes boring into Whitney's. In frigid silence he accused his sister-in-law of complicity and treachery, and then he turned and stalked purposefully toward the house.

Afraid that he intended to leave, Whitney put down her wineglass, excused herself to her guests, and went after him. His legs were longer, and he didn't care about appearances, so he had gained the house several minutes before she entered it. The butler provided the information that he had called for his carriage to be brought round and gone up to his room.

Whitney ran up the steps. When there was no answer to her knock on his door, she knocked again. 'Stephen? Stephen, I know you're in there—'

She tried the door, and when it wasn't locked, she opened it and went inside. He stalked out of the dressing room wearing a fresh shirt, saw her, and his expression became more forbidding than it had been outside. 'Stephen, listen to me—'

'Get out,' he warned, quickly fastening the shirt up the front and reaching for his jacket.

'You aren't leaving, are you?'

'Leave?' he jeered. 'I *can't* leave! You worked that out too. My compliments to you, *your grace*' – he emphasized contemptuously – 'on your duplicity, your dishonesty, and your disloyalty.'

'Stephen, please,' she implored, taking a few hesitant steps into the room. 'Just listen to me. Sherry thought you were marrying her out of pity. I thought if you had a chance to see her again—'

He started toward her, his expression threatening. 'If I'd wanted to see her, I'd have asked your friend DuVille,' he said scathingly. 'She went to him when she left me.'

Whitney began talking faster as she automatically backed away. 'If you will just try to see it from her perspective.'

'If you are wise,' he interrupted in a soft, blood-chilling voice as he loomed over her, 'you will avoid me very carefully this weekend, Whitney. And when this weekend is over, you will communicate with me through your husband. Now, get out of my way.'

'I know you loved her, and I told—'

He clamped his hands on her shoulders, forcibly moved her aside, and walked around her.

In stunned silence, Whitney watched him stalk swiftly down the hall and bound down the stairs. 'My God,' she whispered weakly. She had known Stephen Westmoreland for over four years, and she had never guessed, never imagined, that he was capable of the kind of virulent hatred she saw in his face when he looked at her.

Slowly, she went back downstairs to rejoin her guests for a party that had already had a very inauspicious beginning. When she reached them, it was to discover that

Stephen had taken Monica and Georgette for a jaunt to
the local village, which meant he would probably be gone
for several hours. Lady Skeffington looked as dismayed
as everyone else over his departure, only for different
reasons, of course. In fact, the only two members of
the party who didn't seem depressed about it were Sir
John, who was having yet another glass of Madeira,
which – thankfully – seemed to make him quiet instead
of effusive, and Julianna Skeffington, who was talking
to Sheridan and helping with the children. With a smile,
she lifted Noel into her arms and hugged him tightly,
then she turned and said something to Sheridan with an
expression on her face that was clearly sympathetic.

From the sidelines, the dowager duchess watched the
blonde girl and, in a halfhearted attempt to distract
their thoughts from Stephen's very violent reaction to
Sheridan's presence, she idly remarked to Whitney,
'Julianna Skeffington knows something is in the wind.
She saw the murderous look Stephen gave Sheridan
when he saw her, and she was at Sherry's side within seconds. She seemed like a thoroughly delightful girl when
I spoke with her earlier – charming and intelligent.'

Whitney dragged her thoughts from the alarming
things Stephen had said to her to Julianna's lovely
features. 'Beautiful, as well.'

'It makes one marvel at the capriciousness of nature
that allowed that man—' she nodded distastefully toward Sir John, 'and that woman—' she grimaced at
Lady Skeffington, 'to produce that heavenly creature.'

52

Normally a full staff of footmen were always on hand
to assist arriving guests from their carriages and see
that the vehicles and horses were taken around back

to the stables, but when Stephen returned from his jaunt to the village, no-one came out of the house. The only servant in evidence was a lone footman who was standing in the drive, staring fixedly in the general direction of the hills that rolled gently away from the stables at the back of the estate. He was concentrating so hard on whatever it was he was trying to see, that he seemed not to hear the carriage wheels until Stephen pulled up behind him, then he turned with a guilty start and trotted over to take the reins.

'Where is everyone?' Stephen asked, noticing that the butler still had not dispatched more servants from the house, nor opened the front door, as was customary.

'They're down at the stables, milord. It's quite a show, if I may say so, and not one to miss. Or so I've heard from them that's watching from the back of the house.'

Stephen took the reins back from the footman, having decided to drive around to the stables and see for himself what the footman meant by 'quite a show.'

A long stretch of fence enclosed the stables and the large grassy area between the buildings where the horses were walked and cooled before being put away. To one side of the fence, pasture stretched all the way to the base of wooded hills, dotted with hedges and stone fences that were used to train Claymore's horses for the hunt. When Stephen pulled the carriage to a stop at the stables, the entire length of fencing was lined with grooms, footmen, coachmen, and stable hands. Stephen helped Monica and Georgette down from the carriage, noting as he did so that the entire house party, minus his treacherous sister-in-law, were standing on the far side of the fence, as absorbed with whatever unknown spectacle was taking place on the hillside as the servants were.

Stephen studied his brother's inscrutable profile as he and his two companions joined the group, wondering if Clay had actually collaborated in Whitney's scheme, and unable to believe he would have. Since Stephen wasn't completely certain, he deliberately addressed his question to Jason and Victoria Fielding. 'What are you watching?'

'Wait and see for yourself,' Jason advised him with an odd grin. 'It wouldn't be right to spoil it with an explanation in advance.'

Victoria Fielding seemed to have a difficult time looking him in the eye, and her smile was overbright. 'It's really quite amazing!'

It occurred to Stephen that the Fieldings and the Townsendes were both behaving oddly. There was a nervousness in the women and an uneasiness about the men. Either they were uncomfortable because they were surprised and unhappy about Sheridan Bromleigh's presence – or else they'd known all along that she was going to be here, and they felt guilty. Stephen studied the four people he regarded as particularly close friends, deciding whether or not that friendship was about to end permanently. The women had definitely known, he decided, watching color stain Alexandra Townsende's cheeks as she felt his gaze on her. Not once in the three hours since he'd looked up and found himself only a few paces away from his former fiancée had Stephen allowed himself to think about her. Shutting out the reality of her presence was the only way he could stomach staying here.

She had pretended to be someone she was not, and when she was about to be exposed, she had fled to DuVille, leaving Stephen to wait for her like a besotted idiot with a cleric and his family standing by.

In the weeks since her disappearance, he had gone over everything she'd said and done while she supposedly had amnesia, and he could remember only that one slip – when she'd objected to having a paid companion. 'I don't need a ladies' companion,' she'd blurted. 'I *am* a—'

She was an amazing actress to have pulled off the whole sham so well, Stephen thought with a fresh surge of disgust for his own gullibility.

A stellar actress, he decided wrathfully, remembering the softness in her eyes during the few moments their gazes had locked this morning. She'd looked straight at him with her heart in her eyes, unflinching. Except she had no heart. And no conscience either, obviously.

She was going to make another try for him. Stephen had realized it within seconds of seeing that wistful expression on her lovely, deceptive face this morning.

He'd assumed DuVille had been keeping her neatly tucked away for his own pleasure all these weeks, but evidently he'd tired of her in a surprisingly short time and sent her packing.

Now she was working as a governess and obviously longing for a better life. Based on that sweet pleading look she'd given him, she was apparently hoping he'd be as stupidly susceptible to her nonexistent appeal as he'd been before.

He shifted his speculative gaze to the men, but Victoria Fielding's exclamation drew his attention.

'There they come!' she said.

Stephen tore his mind from furious thoughts of Sheridan Bromleigh and lifted his gaze to the edge of a wooded hillside where she pointed.

Two mounted riders were galloping at full speed, crouched low over the horses' necks, leaping hedges in graceful unison, side by side. Stephen recognized Whitney at a glance; she was one of the most skilled riders he'd ever seen mounted – man or woman. The lad who was challenging her was slight in stature, clad in a shirt, breeches, and boots, and he was even more skilled than Whitney. Riding at breakneck pace, he took each jump with an effortless, breezy unconcern for style that Stephen had never seen before. With his face pressed close to the horse's mane, there was a jubilation, a simplicity in the way he soared over each jump, as if he were one with his mount – confident, trusting, elated.

'I never knew that animal could jump like that!'

Clayton exclaimed with an admiring laugh. Oblivious to Stephen's private doubts about his fraternal integrity, he added, 'Stephen, you've ridden Commander in the hunt. He's fast on the flat, but did he ever soar like that over the jumps?'

Stephen squinted into the late afternoon sun, watching the riders jumping in perfect tandem, then galloping flat-out, soaring over the next hedge together. Since he couldn't demand answers about Sheridan from his brother at the moment, he reported what he could see of the lad who was riding in a flat, unemotional voice. 'It appears that he's holding Commander back, to keep him from gaining on Khan—'

'Who is normally more willing to take the jumps than Commander,' Clayton added to his friends.

The riders took the last fence, then turned their mounts in unison at full speed toward the open gate of the enclosure, where the spectators were gathered. Since Clayton had been trying out new trainers for the past year, Stephen naturally assumed his brother had probably decided to give the slightly built lad a chance at the position. As the horses thundered closer, he was about to suggest his brother make the position permanent, but two things happened at once that made him break off in mid-sentence: a stable hand rushed forward into the field and dropped a grain sack on the ground – and as Commander's rider began to lean to the right, her hair came unbound.

Piles of fiery tresses unfurled like a flag behind her, swirling about, and she leaned farther and farther down to the right, and began to fall. Monica screamed in fear, Stephen took an involuntary step, starting to run toward her . . . and Sheridan swept the grain sack off the ground while the servants and houseguests erupted in wild cheers.

In the space of one second, rage replaced Stephen's fear – rage that she had terrified him with her stupid stunt, and fury that she had been able to evoke any emotion in him at all. And while he was still struggling to get that under control, she headed the lightly galloping horse straight at Stephen. Monica and Georgette jumped back with cries of alarm, but Stephen folded his arms and stood his ground, knowing damn well she was in full control. Not until she was almost on top of him did she haul Commander to a smart stop, and at the same time, she swung her leg over the horse's back and slid gracefully to the ground. While the servants erupted in cheers, and the houseguests applauded, Sheridan landed on both feet in front of him, a smile on her soft mouth, her color gloriously high. But what Stephen noticed, as he gazed impassively at her, was the look in those liquid-silver eyes. They were imploring him to soften, to smile at her.

Instead, he raked her with an insulting glance from the top of her gloriously tousled flame-colored hair to the tips of her booted feet. 'Didn't anyone ever teach you how to dress?' he asked contemptuously.

He saw her flinch at the same moment Georgette laughed, but Sheridan's gaze never faltered. With everyone looking on, she smiled at him, and said with a catch in her soft voice, 'In days of old, it was customary for the winner of a tournament to bestow his favor on someone at the tournament as a gesture of his – his very *high* regard and – and *deepest* respect.'

Stephen didn't know what the hell she was talking about until she held out the empty grain sack to him and softly said, 'My favor, Lord Westmoreland—'

He took it before he realized what he was doing.

'Of all the brazen, the outrageous—' Monica exploded, and Lady Skeffington looked as if she were going to burst into tears of mortification.

'Miss Bromleigh!' she cried angrily. 'You forget yourself! Apologize to these good people and then go at once and tend to your pack—'

'Tend to me!' Julianna interrupted sharply, linking her hand through Sheridan's arm and drawing her toward the house. 'You must tell me when you learned to ride like that and how you did it . . .'

Victoria stepped away from the group and glanced at the Skeffingtons. 'Miss Bromleigh and I are both Americans,' she explained. 'I am longing to talk to someone from my own country. Will you excuse me until supper?' she added, looking at her husband.

Jason Fielding – who had once been the subject of ugly gossip and an outcast from polite society – grinned at the young wife who had changed all that. With a tender smile, he bowed slightly and said, 'I will be desolate without your company, madam.'

'I, too, would love to know more about America,' Alexandra Townsende announced as she broke away from the group. Turning to her own husband, she said with a smile, 'And you, my lord? May I count upon you to be equally desolate without *my* company?'

Jordan Townsende – who had once regarded his marriage to a besotted young Alexandra as an 'obligatory marriage of *in*convenience' – looked at her with unhidden warmth. 'I am always desolate without you, as you perfectly well know.'

Whitney waited until her coconspirators were well on their way to the house before she fixed a bright smile on her face and prepared to invent an excuse to leave, but Lady Skeffington forestalled her.

'I cannot imagine what has got into Sheridan Bromleigh,' she said, her face red with ire. 'I am always saying to Sir John that it is so very hard to find good help. Isn't that what I always say?' she asked him.

Sir John nodded and hiccupped. 'Yes, my dove.'

Satisfied, she turned to Whitney. 'I must implore you to tell me how it is done, your grace.'

Whitney pulled her thoughts from Stephen, who was conversing with Monica and Georgette as if nothing had happened – the grain sack Sheridan had sweetly

364

offered him on the ground beneath the heel of his boot. 'I'm sorry, Lady Skeffington, my thoughts wandered. You wished to know something?'

'How do you find adequate servants? Were it not so difficult, we certainly wouldn't be employing that brassy American woman. I have the gravest misgivings about keeping her in our employ for another hour.'

'I do not regard a governess as a servant—' Whitney began. She had thought Stephen wasn't listening, but at that remark, he looked over at her and replied to Lady Skeffington in an acid voice, 'My sister-in-law regards them as *family*. One might even say she holds them in higher esteem than mere family.' His dagger gaze shifted to Whitney. 'Don't you?' he snapped sarcastically.

It was the first remark he had addressed to Lady Skeffington since their introduction, and that lady seized on it as a source of great encouragement; at the same time she missed the sarcasm in his voice. Dropping the subject of a governess altogether, she hastened to his side and said, 'My dear Julianna is the same way, as you will have noticed. She leapt right to Sheridan Bromleigh's defense. Julianna is such a wonderful girl,' she continued, and somehow managed to squeeze herself between Stephen and Monica, 'so very loyal, so sweet . . .'

When Stephen walked off to the house, she stayed at his side with Sir John trotting along in their wake.

'I could almost feel sorry for him,' Clayton remarked idly, watching Lady Skeffington continue her one-sided monologue.

'I cannot,' Whitney said, still stinging from his cutting remark about her misplaced loyalty. With a quick apologetic look at the men, she said, 'I want to talk to Victoria and Alexandra.'

They watched her leave, all three of them silent and thoughtful. 'Despite what our wives think, this was a mistake,' Jason Fielding said, echoing all their thoughts. 'It's not going to work.' He looked at Clayton and added, 'You know Stephen far better than Jordan or I. What do you think?'

'I think you're right,' Clayton said grimly, remembering the expression on Stephen's face when Sherry sweetly offered him the 'favor.' 'I think it was an *enormous* mistake, and Sheridan Bromleigh is the one who's going to be hurt by it. Stephen has marked her down permanently as a scheming opportunist who fled out of fear of prosecution, but who has now gained enough confidence because he *didn't* file charges against her to try to insinuate herself again. Nothing she says or does is going to matter, because she is going to have to prove he's wrong. And she can't.'

Their wives, who had gathered in the blue salon to discuss the situation, were of a like opinion.

Whitney slumped back in her chair, staring dully at her hands, then she glanced around at her coconspirators, including the dowager duchess. 'It was a mistake,' she told her mother-in-law, who'd watched the 'show' from the window of her bedchamber.

'I felt like crying when he ignored her gesture,' Alexandra said with an ache in her voice. 'Sheridan was so brave about it, so open, and so terribly vulnerable.' She looked over her shoulder to politely include Miss Charity in the conversation, but the elderly lady had nothing to say. She sat on the window seat, her brow furrowed in concentration, looking straight ahead, giving the impression that she was either listening intently or not listening at all.

'We still have another full day and evening,' Stephen's mother said. 'He might soften by then.'

Whitney shook her head. 'He won't. I was counting on proximity to make him listen, but even if he listened, he wouldn't change his mind. I realize that now. For one thing, I discovered earlier that he knows she went to Nicki the day she left his house, and you know how he feels about Nicki.'

Miss Charity turned her head sharply at that, her frown deepening with intense concentration.

'The thing is that Stephen wouldn't believe anything Sherry says without proof. Her actions spoke so loudly that nothing else matters. Someone would have to present him with some other viable reason for her to have run away—' She broke off as Miss Charity stood up and walked silently out of the room. 'I don't think Miss Charity is holding up very well under the added stress of all this.'

'She told me she finds it all very exciting,' the dowager announced with an irritated sigh.

From Sheridan's perspective as she stood at the window of her room and watched Stephen laugh at something Monica said to him, the situation looked even more bleak. She couldn't get him off alone to try to talk to him because he clearly wouldn't cooperate with anything she wanted, and she couldn't talk to him in front of the others because she'd tried to communicate with him when she gave him her 'favor,' and that had been a disaster.

53

Stephen's decision to ignore her existence became harder and harder to adhere to as evening drifted into night, and he saw her hovering on the edge of the torchlit area where the tables had been set up for supper. The shock of seeing her had fortified him for the first few hours, but now he no longer had the advantage of that barrier. Standing off to one side, behind the other guests, his shoulders propped against an oak tree, he could watch her without being observed, while the memories he couldn't seem to stifle paraded across his mind.

He saw her standing outside his study doors, talking to the under-butler. *'Good morning, Hodgkin. You're looking especially fine today. Is that a new suit?'*

'Yes, miss. Thank you, miss.'

'I have a new gown,' she'd confided, doing a pirouette for the under-butler's inspection. *'Isn't it lovely?'*

A few minutes later, when Stephen had stalled for time before he told her he wanted her to look for another husband, he'd asked why she hadn't read the magazines he'd ordered for her.

'Did you actually look at any of them?' she'd asked, making him grin even before she embarked on her description. *'There was one called* The Ladies Monthly Museum, or Polite Repository of Amusement and Instruction: being an Assemblage of what can Tend to please the Fancy, Instruct the Mind or Exalt the Character of the British Fair,' she'd explained. *'The article in it was about how to rouge one's cheeks! It was absolutely riveting,'* she'd lied with an irrepressible smile. *'Do you suppose such an article falls under the heading of "Instructing the Mind" or of "Exalting the Character"?'*

But most of all, he remembered how she felt when she melted in his arms, the sweet generosity of that romantic mouth of hers. She was a natural temptress, Stephen decided. What she lacked in expertise she more than made up for with willing passion.

A few minutes ago, she'd gone into the house to get the Skeffington boys, who were evidently going to sing for the amusement of the guests, and when she emerged, he could see she was carrying some sort of an instrument. He had to drag his gaze from her and force himself to stare at the brandy glass he held, so that he wouldn't meet her gaze and wouldn't start wanting her.

Wouldn't *start* wanting her? he thought with bitter disgust. He had started wanting her the moment she opened her eyes in his bed in London, and he wanted her no less badly now, within hours of seeing her again. Clad in that plain gown with her hair scraped back off her forehead and twisted into a stern coil at her nape, she made his body harden with lust.

He glanced at Monica and Georgette who were talking to his mother. They were both beautiful women – beautifully gowned, one in yellow and the other in rose, beautifully coiffed, *and* beautifully behaved. Neither one of them would have considered dressing like a groom and galloping about on that damned horse.

But then, neither one of them would have looked so glorious had they tried.

Neither one of them would have offered him a grain sack with a beguiling smile and pretended she was bestowing a 'favor' upon him.

But then, neither one of them would have been brazen enough to gaze into his eyes, *inviting* him to pull her into his arms, *daring* him to do it.

In the past, he'd thought of Sheridan Bromleigh as a sorceress, and as the first strains of music began to throb from the instrument she was playing, the thought hit him again. She mesmerized everyone, especially him. Conversations among the guests had broken off completely, and even the servants were pausing to look at her, to listen in awe. Stephen glowered at the brandy in his glass, trying not to look at her, but he could actually feel her gaze on him. She'd looked at him often enough tonight to make that likely. The glances were always soft, always inviting, sometimes pleading. They infuriated Monica and Georgette, who were confused and disdainful of how forward she was, but then Stephen hadn't had his hands all over either of their bodies. Sheridan alone knew exactly what she could make him want . . . and make him remember.

Furious with his weakening resolve, Stephen shoved away from the tree and put his glass down on the nearest table, then he bade the guests good night and headed for his room, intending to drink himself into a private stupor if that's what it would take to keep him from going to her.

54

Her head reeling from the tension of the day, Sheridan opened the door to the small bedchamber across from the playroom. Moving cautiously in the dark, unfamiliar room, she found the bureau and felt for the tinder to light the candles in the holder on her bureau. She was in the process of lighting the fourth candle when a deep masculine voice made her choke back a startled scream as it said, 'I don't think we're going to need much light.'

She spun around, her hand falling away from her mouth, her heart beginning to beat in deep, fierce thuds of pure joy. Stephen Westmoreland was sitting in the room's only chair, the image of relaxed elegance with his white shirt open at the throat and one booted foot propped casually atop the opposite knee. Even his expression was casual. Too casual. Somewhere in her whirling thoughts she registered that he was treating this momentous meeting with a cool nonchalance that didn't seem at all appropriate, but she was so happy to see him, so achingly thrilled to have him this close, and so much in love with him that nothing mattered. Nothing.

'As I recall,' he said in the lazy, sensual drawl that always made her heart melt, 'the last time I waited for you we were planning a wedding.'

'I know and I can explain,' she said. 'I—'

'I didn't come up here for conversation,' he interrupted. 'Downstairs, I had the distinct impression you were offering me a great deal more than talk. Or did I mistake the matter?'

'No,' she whispered.

Stephen looked at her in impassive silence, noting

with the eye of a connoisseur, not the besotted fool that he'd been, that she was every bit as enticing and exotic as he'd recalled . . . except for the severe style of her hair. He didn't like that look, especially not when he was letting lust and revenge drive him to consort with this scheming, ambitious slut who looked more like a prim virgin at the moment. 'Take the pins out of your hair,' he instructed with curt impatience.

Startled by the request and his tone of command, Sheridan obeyed, reaching up and pulling out the dozen or so pins it took to hold the heavy mass securely in its coil. She turned to drop them on the bureau, and when she turned back, he was standing, slowly unbuttoning his shirt.

'What are you doing?' she gasped.

What was he doing? Stephen wondered savagely. What the hell was he doing up here, invited or otherwise, dallying with the same woman who'd left him without a word on their wedding day? In answer to her question, he reached for his neckcloth. 'What I am doing is leaving,' he clipped, already stalking the three steps to the door.

'No!' The word burst out of her. 'Don't leave!'

Stephen turned, intending to give her the scathing reply she deserved, but she flung herself against his chest, all soft, entreating woman, drugging his senses with the sudden familiar scent and feel of her. 'Please don't go.' She was crying, her nails biting into his shoulders, and still he kept his hands at his sides, but he was losing the battle, and he knew it. 'Just let me explain . . . I love you . . .'

He grabbed her face between his hands to silence her, his eyes already on her parted lips. 'Understand this. There is nothing you could say that I would believe. Nothing!'

'Then I'll show you,' Sheridan said fiercely, clutching his neck as she crushed herself against him and kissed him with that strange combination of naive inexpertise and instinctive sensuality that used to drive him wild.

And still did. Shoving his hands hard into the soft hair at her nape, Stephen kissed her back, forcing her to show him the sensual desire she was making him feel. With the last thread of rationality he possessed, he lifted his mouth an inch from hers, and gave her one last chance to call a halt. 'Are you sure?'

'I know what I'm doing.'

He took what she was offering, took what he had wanted from the first moment he'd touched her. He took it mindlessly, driven by a violent compulsion to have her; he took with a determination and urgency and hunger that stunned and aroused him. A wild, primitive mating for him and yet one he wanted – needed – to know was as exciting for her. Pride drove him to make certain she wanted him with a desperation that matched his, and he used all his sexual experience to battle down the defenses of an inexperienced girl who hadn't any idea how to withstand it. He shoved his finger deep into her wet warmth, drawing hard on her taut nipple until she was arching and crying and clutching him tightly. Then and only then did he take her, parting her thighs with both hands and driving into her with just enough restraint to keep from shoving her into the headboard, and he felt her body jerk with pain and her nails bite into his back, heard her muffled cry of shock and pain, and he froze. *'I know what I'm doing.'*

With dread and confusion he forced his eyes open. Hers were damp with tears, devoid of either accusation or triumph for having got him to do this for whatever reason she could have had. Her choked, whispered words reinforced the drugged expression in her eyes as she curved her hands over his taut shoulders. 'Hold me,' she whispered magically. A gentle benediction. 'Please . . .'

Stephen complied, letting the mindless pleasure overtake him again. Wrapping his arms around her, he took her mouth in a stormy demanding kiss and felt her hands shifting softly over his shoulders, gentling him at the same time her melting body was welcoming him, sheathing him, offering them both release . . . offering and offering and offering . . .

Every nerve in his body was screaming for release and still he held himself back, driving deeply into her, while the muscles in his arms strained with the rest of his body, refusing to deprive her of the same pleasure she was going to give him any second now. She was whimpering, eyes closed tightly, desperate for something she didn't understand, afraid to have it. Afraid not to. Sobbing with desire, needing reassurance. He gave it to her in a hoarse whisper. '. . . Any second now . . .'

She went up in flames before he finished the sentence, her body clenching his, and Stephen heard himself groan with the extravagant splendor she was somehow making him feel. And then he gave himself over to it, driving toward it . . . and then past it, climaxing, his body jerking as he poured himself into her.

Whatever thoughts of revenge and wounded pride had driven him to bed her, they were forgotten as he wrapped his arms around her back and hips and pulled her with him onto his side. She was too magnificent to be used for vengeance, too exquisitely soft in his arms to be anywhere else. From the first moment his mouth touched hers, he'd known they were an oddly combustible combination, but what had just passed had been the most wildly erotic, satisfying sexual encounter of his life. Lying there while she slept in his arms, he marvelled at the heady, primitive sensuality of her. Whatever she'd felt during their coupling had been real – that was one of the few things about her he did not doubt. That at least was real and uncontrived. No woman on earth could have feigned those responses, not without a great deal of practice, and as he now knew, she'd had no practice at all.

Sheridan awoke alone in her bed, which seemed normal enough and yet . . . not. Her eyes snapped open, she saw him sitting in the chair beside the bed, and sweet relief flooded through her. He was dressed already, his shirt open at the front, his handsome face unreadable. Self-consciously, she drew the sheets up to her breasts and sat up against the pillows, wondering a little desperately how he could look so utterly casual after the things they had just done. Somewhere at the edges of her mind, she was beginning to realize they were shameful things, but she shut the thought out. His eyes dipped to the sheet she was clutching to her breasts, then slowly lifted to her face, telling her as clearly as if he had spoken that he was amused by her modesty. Sheridan couldn't blame him for that, but she wished he didn't look quite so nonchalant or quite so amused or quite so distant . . . not when she was struggling to look even a little normal in the aftermath of the things they had done with each other. On the other hand, she realized, he no longer looked cold or cynical or angry, and that struck her as a wondrous change. Tucking the sheet tightly under her arms, she drew up her knees and linked her fingers around them. 'Can we talk now?' she began.

'Why don't you let me begin?' Stephen suggested blandly.

Not that eager to bring up the matter of Charise Lancaster when things seemed almost cozy, Sheridan nodded.

'I have an offer to make to you.' He saw her eyes kindle with happiness at the word 'offer' and could not believe she thought him stupid enough to actually suggest marriage. 'A *business proposition,*' he emphasized. 'Once you've had time to consider it, I think you'll find it sensible for both of us. Certainly, you'll find it preferable to working for the Skeffingtons.'

Uneasiness doused Sheridan's momentary happiness at his mention of an offer. 'What sort of proposition?'

'It's obvious that despite our many differences, we are extremely compatible, sexually.'

She couldn't believe he could sit there and describe the stormy intimacies they had just shared with such

374

clinical calm. 'What is your proposition?' she asked shakily.

'You share my bed when I'm wishful of your body. In return for that, you will have a home of your own, servants, gowns, a coach, and the freedom to do as you please so long as no other man is given the use of what I'm already paying for.'

'You're suggesting I become your mistress,' she said dully.

'Why not? You're ambitious and clever, and it's a hell of a lot better than what you're doing now.' When she didn't respond, Stephen said in a bored drawl, 'Please tell me you didn't expect me to offer to *marry* you because of what just happened. Tell me you aren't that naive or that stupid.'

Flinching from the sting of his tone, Sherry looked at his hard, handsome face, at the cynicism she hadn't recognized in his eyes before. Swallowing convulsively, she shook her head and answered him honestly. 'I did not know what to expect, of anything we did, but I did not expect it would make you ask me to marry you.'

'Good. There's been enough deceit and misunderstanding between us before. I wouldn't like to think you misled yourself.'

He thought he saw the sheen of disappointed tears in her wide gray eyes and stood up, pressing a perfunctory kiss on her forehead. 'At least you are wise enough not to indulge in a fit of ire over my offer. Think about it,' he said.

Sherry stared at him in mute misery as he added with a chilling bite in his voice, 'Before you decide, there's a warning I feel obliged to give you. If you ever lie to me about anything, ever – just one time – I will throw you out on the street.' He reached for the door as he added over his shoulder, 'There's one more thing – Don't ever say "I love you" to me. I never want to hear those words from you again.'

Without another word or a backward glance, he walked out. Sherry laid her forehead on her knees and let the tears slide, but she was crying for her own lack of character and restraint when he took her in his arms, and for actually being tempted, for just a few moments, to accept his indecent, coldhearted proposal.

55

The full realization of what she had done last night had set in long before Sheridan dragged herself out of bed and got dressed the next morning. In the bright light of full day, there was no way to deny the awful truth: she had sacrificed her virtue, her principles, and her morals, and now she would have to live with the shame of that until the end of her life.

She had done it all in one desperate gamble to regain his love – if he had ever really loved her – and how had he reacted to the enormity of her deed? The agonizing answer to that question was below her bedchamber window – on the side lawn, where everyone was having luncheon – and it was there for her to see in every humiliating detail: the man she had lain with last night was dining with Monica, who was turning herself inside out to entertain him, and he looked perfectly willing to be entertained this morning. As Sheridan watched from her window, he leaned back in his chair, his gaze intent on Monica's face, then he threw back his head, laughing at whatever she was telling him.

Sheridan was a mass of shame and anxiety, while *he* looked more contented and more relaxed than she had ever seen him. Last night, he had taken everything she had to give and thrown it in her face with an offer to prolong her humiliation by making her his mistress. Today, he was socializing with a woman who'd never have been stupid enough to do what Sheridan had . . . a woman worthy of his own inflated opinion of himself, she thought bitterly. A woman to whom he would offer marriage, not some tainted liaison in exchange for her virtue.

All those thoughts and more marched through Sheridan's tormented mind as she stood at the window, staring down at him, refusing to cry. She *wanted* to remember this scene, she wanted to remember it every single moment of her life, so that she would never, ever soften in her thoughts of him. She stood still, welcoming the icy numbness that was sweeping away her anguish and demolishing all her tender feelings for him. '*Bastard,*' she whispered aloud.

'May I come in?'

Sheridan started and whirled around at the sound of Julianna's voice. 'Yes, of course,' she said, trying for a bright smile that felt as strained as her voice sounded.

'I saw you standing up here when I was having breakfast. Would you like me to bring something up here for you?'

'No, I'm not hungry, but thank you for thinking of me.' Sheridan hesitated, knowing some explanation was in order for her behavior yesterday when she had offered Stephen her favor, but she hadn't been able to think of a single reasonable excuse.

'I was wondering if you would like to leave here?'

'Leave?' Sheridan said, trying not to sound as desperate as she felt to do exactly that. 'We aren't to leave until tomorrow.'

Julianna walked over to the window and stood beside her, quietly looking down at the same tableau that Sheridan had been torturing herself with. 'Julianna, I feel I ought to explain about what happened yesterday, when I said what I did to the Earl of Langford about holding him in deepest respect.'

'You don't need to explain,' Julianna answered with a reassuring smile that made Sheridan feel like the seventeen-year-old ingenue instead of her paid chaperone.

'Yes, I do,' Sheridan persevered doggedly. 'I know how much your mother was hoping for a match between you and Lord Westmoreland, and I know you must wonder why I – why I behaved to him in such a *forward*, and *familiar* way.'

In what seemed like a change of subject, Julianna said, 'Several weeks ago, Mama was quite despondent. In fact, I remember that it was less than a week before you came to stay with us.'

Seizing her conversational reprieve like the coward she was at the moment, Sheridan said brightly, 'Why was your mama upset?'

'Langford's betrothal was announced in the paper.'

'Oh.'

'Yes. His fiancée was American.'

Uneasy under the unwavering gaze of those violet eyes, Sherry said nothing.

'There was some gossip about her, and you know how Mama adores being privy to any gossip about the ton. His fiancée reportedly had red hair – very, very red hair. And he called her "Sherry." They said she'd lost her memory due to a blow to the head, but that she was expected to recover quickly.'

Sheridan made one more bid for anonymity. 'Why are you telling me this?'

'So you'll know you can ask me for help if you need it. And because you are the real reason we were invited here. I realized that something was very strange when I saw the way Lord Westmoreland reacted to seeing you at the pond yesterday. I'm surprised Mama hasn't figured out what's in the wind.'

'There is nothing in the wind,' Sheridan said fiercely. 'The whole awful matter is closed, over.'

Julianna tipped her head toward Monica and Georgette. 'Do they know who you are?'

'No. I'd never met them when I was—' Sheridan

broke off as she started to say, *When I was Charise Lancaster.*

'When you were betrothed to him?'

Sheridan drew in a long breath and then reluctantly nodded.

'Would you like to go home?'

A hysterical laugh bubbled up in Sheridan. 'If I had anything to trade for the opportunity, I'd do it in a trice.'

Julianna turned on her heel and started from the room. 'Start packing,' she said with a conspiratorial smile over her shoulder.

'Wait – what are you going to do?'

'I am about to draw Papa aside and tell him I'm feeling unwell and you must accompany me home. We'll not be able to pry Mama out of here early, but she will not want me to stay and give Langford a disgust of me by becoming quite terribly ill in front of him. Would you believe,' she said with an incorrigible laugh, 'she *still* cherishes hope that he'll look up at any moment and fall madly in love with me, despite everything that should be very obvious to her.'

She was closing the door when Sherry called to her, and she poked her head back into the room. 'Would you tell the duchess I'd like to see her before we leave?'

'All the ladies left for the village a bit ago, with the exception of Langford's ladies, that is, and Miss Charity.'

The last time Sheridan had left them, she'd made herself look guilty and ungrateful. This time, she did not intend to flee in secret. She intended only to flee. 'Would you ask Miss Charity to come up then?' When Julianna nodded, Sheridan added, 'And don't say a word about our departure to anyone except your father. I intend to tell the earl myself, face to face.'

56

Miss Charity's face fell as Sheridan explained that she was leaving.

'But you haven't had a chance yet to speak to Langford alone and make him understand exactly why you disappeared,' she argued.

'I had that chance last night,' Sherry said bitterly. She glanced at her bedroom window as she packed the few things she'd brought into a valise. 'The result is out there.'

Charity walked over to the window and looked down at the two women who were entertaining the earl. 'How very vexing men are. He does not care in the least about either of those two women, you know.'

'He does not care about me either.'

Charity sat down on the chair, and Sheridan thought poignantly of the first time she'd seen her and been reminded of a china doll. She looked like one now – a very perplexed, unhappy one.

'Did you explain to him why you ran away and never came back?'

'No.'

'Why *did* you do it?'

The question came so quickly that it took Sheridan aback. 'I told you most of it yesterday. One minute I thought I was Charise Lancaster, and the next minute, Charise was standing there, accusing me of deliberately impersonating her, and threatening to tell Stephen that. I panicked and ran, but before I could recover from the shock of realizing who I really am, I began to realize that everyone else had been lying to me about who *they* were. Among the things I remembered was that Charise had been betrothed to a baron, not an earl, whose name was Burleton, not Westmoreland. I wanted answers, I needed them, and so I went to see Nicholas DuVille. He at least was honest enough to tell me the truth.'

'What truth did he tell you, dear?'

Still embarrassed by what she had learned, Sheridan looked away and pretended to check the neatness of her hair in the mirror as she said, 'All of it. Every mortifying bit of it, beginning with Lord Burleton's death and why Stephen felt obliged to find another fiancé for me – for Charise Lancaster, I mean. He told me everything,' Sheridan finished, pausing to swallow over the lump of humiliated tears in her throat as she thought of her gullible belief that Stephen had wanted to marry her. That same deadly streak of naiveté had led her to sacrifice her virginity and her pride to him last night. 'He even explained the greatest mystery of all, though I let myself believe otherwise when I talked to all of you yesterday.'

'What mystery was that?'

Sheridan's laugh was choked and bitter. 'Stephen's sudden proposal of marriage, the night we went to Almack's, coincided exactly with the news he'd received earlier that day of Charise's father's death. He proposed to me out of pity and responsibility, not because he cared for me or even wanted to marry me.'

'It was very bad of Nicholas to put it exactly that way.'

'He didn't have to. I am only a fool when it comes to that man out there.'

'And you discussed all this with Langford last night?'

'I tried, but he said he wasn't interested in conversation,' Sheridan said bitterly as she picked up her valise.

'What *was* he interested in?' Charity tipped her head inquiringly to the side.

Something about the sudden way she asked made Sheridan look swiftly at her. There were times when she wasn't certain whether the Duke of Stanhope's sister was quite so vague as she seemed, times like right now, when she was studying the hot flush staining Sheridan's cheeks with a distinctly knowing look. 'I suppose he would be interested in proof of my innocence, if he were interested in me at all, which he is not,' she evaded hastily. 'When you look at it from his side, which I tried to do yesterday and last night, I ran away and hid because I was guilty. What other excuse could I have had?'

Charity stood up and Sheridan looked at her, knowing that she was never going to see her again, and tears burned the back of her eyes as she enfolded the tiny lady in a swift hug. 'Tell everyone good-bye for me, and tell them I know they truly tried to help.'

'There must be something else I can do,' Charity said, her face looking as if it were going to crumple.

'There is,' Sheridan said with a fixed, confident smile. 'Please tell his lordship that I would like to see him privately for a moment. Ask him to meet me in that little salon immediately off the front hall.'

When Charity left to do that, Sheridan drew a steadying breath and walked over to the window, watching a few minutes later as Charity went over to him and delivered the message. He got up so quickly, striding swiftly toward the house, that Sheridan felt a sharp stab of hope that perhaps – just perhaps – he wasn't going to let her leave. Perhaps he would beg her forgiveness for his callousness last night and ask her to stay.

As she walked down the steps she couldn't stop herself from indulging in that last, tormentingly sweet fantasy. The frail hope made her heart accelerate as she walked into the salon and closed the door, but the hope began to die the instant he turned and looked at her. Clad in a shirt and riding breeches, with his hands shoved into his pockets, he looked not only casual, but supremely unconcerned. 'You wanted to see me?' he suggested mildly.

He was standing in the middle of the small room, and a few steps brought her almost to within arm's reach of him. Displaying a calm she didn't at all feel, Sheridan nodded and said, 'I came to tell you I'm leaving. I didn't want to simply disappear this time, as I did the last.'

She waited, searching that hard, sardonic face for some sign that he felt something, anything, for her, for the fact that she was leaving, for the gift of her body. Instead, he lifted his brows as if silently asking her what she expected him to do about it.

'I'm not accepting your offer,' Sheridan clarified, unable to believe he could be so completely uninterested in a decision that affected her entire life – a decision made after a night spent in his arms, after she had surrendered her virginity and her honor to him.

He lifted his broad shoulders in a slight shrug and said in an indifferent voice, 'Fine.'

That did it – that single bored word sent her from the depths of humiliated despair to a fury that was almost uncontainable. Turning on her heel, she started to walk out on him, then she stopped and turned back.

'Was there something else?' he prodded, looking impatient and unconcerned.

Sheridan was so infuriated, and so *pleased* with her intention, that she actually gave him a bright, disarming smile as she stepped up to him. 'Yes,' she said lightly, 'there is something else.'

One brow lifted in arrogant inquiry. 'What is it?'

'This!' She slapped him so hard his head jerked sideways, then she took an automatic step back from the rage in his face and held her ground, her chest heaving with fury. 'You are a heartless, evil monster, and I cannot believe I let you touch me last night! I feel filthy and defiled—' A muscle began to tick in the side of his jaw, but Sheridan wasn't finished and she was too infuriated to care that he looked murderous. 'I committed a sin when I let you do what you did to me last night, but I can pray for forgiveness for that. But, I will never be able to forgive my stupidity for trusting you and loving you!'

Stephen watched the door crash into its frame behind

her, and he stood perfectly still, unable to shake off the image of a tempestuous beauty with blazing silver eyes and a face alive with fury and disdain. The picture branded itself on his mind along with a voice that shook with emotion. *'I will never be able to forgive my stupidity for trusting you and loving you!'* She'd actually looked and sounded as if she meant every single thing she'd said to him, including that last. Christ, she was a superb actress! Better by far than Emily Lathrop. Of course, Emily hadn't had the advantage of Sheridan's aura of virtuous innocence or her tempestuous temper. Emily had been sophisticated and carefully restrained, so she couldn't have pulled off this scene.

On the other hand, Emily probably wouldn't have flung his proposition in his face . . .

Somehow, he hadn't expected Sheridan to do that either. She'd been clever enough and ambitious enough to turn a brief loss of memory after her accident into what appeared to be a full-fledged case of amnesia that seemed to last for weeks, and to very nearly raise her status from a governess to a countess as well. The proposition he'd offered last night wouldn't have made her a countess, but it would have given her a hell of a lot more in the way of a luxurious life than she could possibly expect otherwise.

Either she wasn't as clever as Stephen had credited her with being . . .

Or she wasn't as ambitious . . .

Or she wasn't interested in luxury . . .

Or she'd been innocent of deviousness all along – as innocent of it as she'd been sexually innocent before last night.

Stephen hesitated uneasily and then rejected the last possibility. Innocent people did not run away and hide – not when they had Sheridan's kind of courage and daring.

57

Out of consideration for Noel's birthday, and in a futile effort to maintain a semblance of a festive atmosphere, Whitney declared the subject of Sheridan Bromleigh and her departure off limits for the rest of the weekend, but the failed attempt at a reconciliation hung like a pall over most of the guests at Claymore. Within hours after Sheridan left, storm clouds rolled in and rain began to fall, driving everyone indoors and further dampening feminine spirits. Only Charity Thornton was immune to the atmosphere and so energized that she declined to follow suit when all the other ladies and most of the men repaired to their chambers for a nap before supper. In fact, their absence suited her perfectly.

Seated upon a tufted leather sofa in the billiard room, with her legs crossed at the ankles and her hands folded in her lap, she watched the Duke of Claymore playing billiards with Jason Fielding and Stephen Westmoreland. 'I have always found billiards so very intriguing,' she lied, just as Clayton Westmoreland poked a long cue stick at the balls on the table and missed his shot entirely. 'Was that your strategy – to miss all the balls on the table so that Langford will now have to deal with them?' she inquired brightly.

'That's an interesting way of looking at it,' Clayton replied dryly, stifling his annoyance with her outburst that had caused him to miss his shot.

'Now what happens?'

Jason Fielding answered with a chuckle. 'Now Stephen will take over and neither of us will have another opportunity at this game.'

'Oh, I see.' Charity smiled innocently at her intended victim as he rubbed something on the end of his cue stick and bent over the table. 'Does that mean you are the most skilled player here, Langford?'

He glanced up at the sound of his name, but Charity had the feeling he wasn't listening to her or concentrating on the game either. Ever since Sheridan had left, he'd looked as grim as death. Despite that, when he took his shot, balls clattered against one another, collided against the sides of the table, and three of them rolled into the pockets.

'Nice shot, Stephen,' Jason said, and Charity saw the opportunity she'd been waiting for.

'I so enjoy the society of gentlemen,' she announced suddenly, watching as Clayton Westmoreland poured Madeira into his guests' glasses.

'Why is that?' he asked politely.

'My own sex can be quite petty and even vindictive for no cause at all,' she remarked as Stephen aimed and made his next shot. 'But gentlemen are so very stalwart in their loyalty to one another and their own sex. Take Wakefield, for example,' she said, smiling approvingly at Jason Fielding, Marquess of Wakefield. 'Had you been a female, Wakefield, you might have felt jealous of Langford's superior shot a moment ago, but were you?'

'Yes,' Jason joked, but when her face fell he quickly said, 'No, of course not, ma'am.'

'Exactly my point!' Charity applauded as Stephen walked around the table for his next shot. 'But whenever I think of loyalty and friendship among gentlemen, do you know who immediately comes to mind?'

'No, who?' Clayton said, while he watched Stephen line up his next shot and aim.

'Nicholas DuVille and Langford!'

The cue ball slid sideways off of Stephen's cue stick and rolled to the side of the table, where it gently nudged the ball he'd intended to aim at. That ball slowly headed for the pocket, hovered at the edge, and finally dropped in. 'That wasn't skill, that was blind luck,' Jason told him. Trying to change the subject, he added, 'Did you ever stop to calculate how many times you win a game with luck instead of skill? I've meant to do that.'

Ignoring Wakefield's attempt to divert the topic, Charity forged ahead, carefully directing her animated conversation to Jason Fielding and Clayton Westmoreland and avoiding a glance at the earl as he walked around the table for his next shot. 'Why, if Nicholas hadn't been such a *loyal* friend of Langford's, he would have sent Sheridan Bromleigh straight back home the day she ran away and landed on his doorstep, crying her heart out, but did he do that? No indeed, he did *not*!'

She glanced at the mirror on the opposite wall and saw Stephen Westmoreland arrested in the act of shooting, his eyes narrowed to slits, his gaze levelled on the back of her head. 'Sheridan begged for the truth about why Langford wanted to marry her, and even though it wasn't poor Nicholas's responsibility to tell her everything and break her heart, he did it! It would have been so much easier to lie to her, or send her home to ask Langford, but he took it upon himself to help his dear friend and fellow man.'

'Exactly what,' Stephen asked in a low, savage voice as he slowly straightened without having taken his shot, 'did my *friend* DuVille tell Sheridan?'

Charity looked around at him, her face a miracle of startled, vapid innocence. 'Why, the truth, of course. She realized she wasn't Charise Lancaster anymore, so Nicholas told her about Burleton's death and how responsible you felt for it. That is why you pretended to be Sheridan's fiancé, after all.'

Three silent men were staring at her in various states of shock and anger, and Charity looked brightly at each of them. 'And of course, being a romantic girl, Sheridan still wanted to think – to believe – that you might have had some other reason for asking *her* to marry you, but dear Nicholas had to tell her, very *firmly*, that you'd only proposed after you got word of Mr Lancaster's unfortunate death – out of pity, as it were. Which was dreadfully distressing to the poor girl, but Nicholas did what needed to be done, out of unselfishness and loyalty to his own sex.'

Stephen slammed the cue stick into the rack on the wall. 'That *son of a bitch!*' he said softly as he strode swiftly out of the room.

Startled by the use of profanity in front of her but not by his departure, Charity looked at Jason Fielding. 'Where do you suppose Langford is going?' she asked, hiding her smile behind a blank frown.

Jason Fielding slowly withdrew his gaze from the doorway through which the earl had departed, then he glanced at Clayton Westmoreland and said, 'Where would you say he's going?'

'I would say,' the duke replied dryly, 'that he is going to have a "talk" with an old "friend."'

'How nice!' Charity said brightly. 'Would either of you consider letting me play billiards with you, now that Langford is gone? I'm certain I could learn the rules.'

The Duke of Claymore studied her in amused silence for a very long moment, so long in fact that Charity felt a little uneasy. 'Why don't we play chess instead? I have a feeling that strategy is your particular forte.'

Charity considered that for a moment and wagged her head. 'I think you're quite right.'

58

Although the Season had wound to a close, the exclusive gaming rooms at White's were not lacking for wealthy occupants willing to wager enormous sums of money on the turn of a card or spin of the wheel. The oldest and most elegant of the clubs on St James's Street, White's was far noisier than The Strathmore, and brightly lit, but not without its own hallowed traditions.

At the front, looking out upon the street, was a wide bow window in which Beau Brummell had once held court with his friends the Duke of Argyll, Lords Sefton, Alvanley, and Worcester, and, on occasion, the then Prince Regent.

More famous than its bow window, however, was White's Betting Book, into which distinguished members had, for many years, entered wagers on events ranging from the solemn to the sordid to the silly. Included among the entries were wagers on the outcome of a war, the likely date of the death of a relative with a fortune to bequeath, the predicted winners in contests for ladies' hands, and even the outcome of a forthcoming race between two prime pigs owned by two of the club's members.

At a table near the back of one of the card rooms, William Baskerville was playing whist with the Duke of Stanhope and Nicholas DuVille. In the spirit of good-fellowship, those three gentlemen had permitted two very young gentlemen from excellent families to join them. Both young men were Corinthians of the first stare, obsessed with sporting and eager to make a name for themselves in town by excelling at the manly vices of gaming and drinking. Talk at the table was slow and desultory; betting was fast and heavy. 'Speaking of crackwhips,' said one of the young gentlemen, who'd been speaking of little else, 'I haven't seen Langford at Hyde Park all week.'

William Baskerville provided the answer to that as he counted out his chips. 'His nephew's birthday, I believe. Duchess of Claymore is giving a small party to celebrate the occasion. Lovely woman, the duchess,' he added. 'I tell Claymore that every time I see him.' Glancing at Nicholas DuVille who was seated on his left, he said, 'You were friendly with her grace in France, before she came home to England, I believe?'

Nicki nodded without looking up from his cards, then he automatically added a proviso to forestall any gossip.

'I count myself fortunate to be on friendly terms with *all* the Westmoreland family.'

One of the youths who'd been drinking heavily heard that with some surprise and then demonstrated his lack of polish – as well as his inability to hold his drink – by verbalizing it: 'You don't say! Gossip had it that you and Langford nearly came to fisticuffs at Almack's over some red-haired girl you both fancied.'

Baskerville snorted at such a thought. 'My dear young fellow, when you've more experience in town, you'll learn to separate rubbish from truth, and to do that, you need to be better acquainted with the individuals involved. Now, I heard the same story, but I also know DuVille and Langford, so *I* knew the whole story was pure faradiddle. Knew it the moment I heard it.'

'As did I!' the more sober of the young men announced.

'A lamentable bit of nonsense,' Nicki confirmed, when everyone seemed to wait for his response, 'that will soon be forgotten.'

'Knew it was,' said Miss Charity's brother, the distinguished Duke of Stanhope, as he shoved chips into the growing heap at the center of the table. 'Doesn't surprise me in the least to discover you and Langford are the best of friends. Both of you are the most amiable of men.'

'No doubt about it,' the sober young man said to Nicki with a mischievous grin, 'but if you and Langford *were* ever to come to blows, I'd want to be there!'

'Why is that?' the Duke of Stanhope inquired.

'Because I've seen Langford and DuVille box at Gentleman Jackson's. Not with each other, of course, but they're the best I've ever seen with their fists. A fight between them would have lured even *me* to Almack's.'

'And me!' exclaimed his companion with a hiccup.

Baskerville was appalled by their youthful misconception of civilized manhood, and he felt obliged to point out their gross lack of understanding. 'Langford and

DuVille would never stoop to settling matters with their fists, my good fellow! That's the difference between you hotheaded young pups and gentlemen like DuVille and Langford and the rest of us. You ought to study the excellent manners of your elders, acquire some of their town polish, don't you know. Rather than admiring DuVille's skill with his fists, you'd be wise to imitate his excellent address and his way with a neckcloth.'

'Thank you, Baskerville,' idly murmured Nicki because Baskerville seemed to be waiting for some sort of affirmative response.

'Welcome, DuVille. I speak only the truth. As to Langford,' Baskerville continued, waiting for his turn to bet, 'you couldn't have a finer example of refinement and gentlemanly arts. Fisticuffs to settle a disagreement, indeed!' he scoffed. 'Why, the very thought of it is offensive to any civilized man.'

'Ludicrous to even discuss it,' the Duke of Stanhope agreed, studying the faces of the other players before he decided whether to wager on his rather poor hand of cards.

'My apologies, sirs, if—' the sober one of the young pair began, but he broke off abruptly. 'Thought you said Langford was rusticating,' he said in a bewildered tone that implied there was evidence at hand that proved otherwise.

All five men glanced up and saw Stephen Westmoreland heading straight toward them wearing an expression that, as he came nearer, looked far more ominous than amiable. Without so much as a nod to acknowledge acquaintances calling out greetings to him, the Earl of Langford stalked purposefully around tables and chairs and gamblers, bearing down on the five men at Baskerville's table and then circling around their chairs.

Four of those men stiffened, eyeing him with the wary disbelief of innocent men who are suddenly and unaccountably confronted with a threat they neither understand nor deserve from a predator they had mistaken for tame.

Only Nicholas DuVille seemed unconcerned with the tangible danger emanating from Langford. In fact, to the population of White's, who were all turning to watch in incredulous fascination, Nicholas DuVille seemed to be positively *inviting* a confrontation by his deliberate and exaggerated nonchalance. As the earl stopped beside his chair, DuVille leaned back, shoved his hands deeply into his pockets, and with a thin cheroot clamped between his white teeth, he acknowledged the earl with a sardonic questioning look. 'Care to join us, Langford?'

'Get up!' the Earl of Langford bit out.

The challenge was unmistakable and imminent.

It caused a minor commotion as several young bucks sprinted for White's Betting Book to enter their wagers on the outcome. It caused a lazy, white smile to work its way across DuVille's face as he slouched deeper into his chair, thoughtfully chewed the end of his cheroot, and appeared to contemplate the invitation with considerable relish. As if he wanted to be certain his hopes weren't unfounded, he quirked a brow in amused inquiry. 'Here?' he asked, his smile widening.

'Get out of that chair,' the earl snarled in a dangerously soft voice, 'you son of a—'

'Definitely, here,' DuVille interrupted, his smile hardening as he shoved up from his lounging position and jerked his head in the direction of one of the back rooms.

News of the impending fight reached White's manager within moments, and he rushed out from the kitchen. 'Now, now, gentlemen! Gentlemen!' the manager entreated as he shoved through the crowd exiting in polite haste from the back room. 'Never in the history of White's has there ever—'

The door slammed in his face.

'Think of your attire, gentlemen! Think of the furniture!' he shouted, opening the door just in time to hear the savage sound of a fist connecting with bone and to see DuVille's head snap back.

Yanking the door closed, the manager spun around, his faced drained of color, hands still clutching the door handle behind his back. A hundred male faces eyed him expectantly, all of them interested in the same information. 'Well?' said one of them.

The manager's face contorted with pain as he contemplated the possible damage to the back room's expensive green baize faro tables, but he managed to gasp out a quavering reply. 'At this time . . . I would suggest . . . three-to-two odds.'

'In whose favor, my good man?' demanded an impatient, elegantly dressed gentleman who was standing in the long line, waiting to write his wager in the Betting Book.

The manager hesitated, cast his eyes heavenward as if praying for courage, then he twisted about and opened the door a crack, peeking inside at the same moment a body collided with a wall with a thunderous crash. 'In favor of Langford!' he called over his shoulder, but as he started to pull the door closed, another explosion like the last one rattled the rafters, and he took another look. 'No – DuVille! No, Langford. No—!' He jerked the door closed barely in time to avoid having it snap off his head as a pair of heavy shoulders slammed into it.

Long after the sounds of human combat finally ended, the manager remained with his spine riveted against the door, until it suddenly gave way behind him, sending him careening backward into the empty room as the Earl of Langford and Nicholas DuVille walked out. Alone in the room and dazed with relief, the manager slowly turned and surveyed a room that, at first glance, looked miraculously undisturbed. He was uttering a fervent prayer of gratitude when his eyes beheld a polished end table resting upon three sound legs and a fourth that was badly splintered, and he clutched at his heart as if it, too, were splintering. On shaking limbs he walked over to the faro table and removed a tankard that oughtn't to have been on it, only to discover that the tankard concealed a dreadful gouge in the faro table's green baize top. Narrowing his eyes, he inspected the room more closely . . . In the corner of the room, four chairs were neatly arranged around a circular card table, but now he noticed that each chair possessed only three legs.

An ornate gilt clock which normally graced the center of an inlaid serving board was now on the right end of it. With shaking hands, the manager reached out to slide the clock back to its rightful place, then he cried out in horror as the clock's face fell forward, its hands swinging limply from side to side.

Shaking with outrage and anguish, the manager reached out to brace himself and grabbed the back of the nearest chair.

It came off in his hand.

On the other side of the wall, in the main room of White's, an outburst of unnaturally boisterous conversation erupted when DuVille and Langford strolled out – conversation of the sort used by adult males as a diversionary tactic intended to convey the impression that one's attention was everywhere except where it actually was.

Either indifferent to, or unaware of, the unnatural atmosphere and watchful eyes that followed them, the two former combatants parted company at the center of the room, Langford to search for a servant with a tray of drinks, and DuVille to return to his empty place at the card table. 'Was it my turn to deal?' he asked, settling into his chair and reaching for the deck.

The two young men answered in unison that it was, the Duke of Stanhope courteously replied that he wasn't entirely certain, but Baskerville was in high dudgeon over having been made to look a fool before the young gentlemen, and he brought up the subject on everyone's mind. 'You may as well tell these two what happened in there, since they won't be able to concentrate or even sleep without knowing the outcome,' he said testily. 'Disgraceful behavior, I don't scruple to tell you, DuVille. On both your parts!'

'There is nothing to tell,' Nicki said blandly, picking up the abandoned deck of cards from the center of the table and shuffling it expertly. 'We discussed a wedding.'

Baskerville looked hopeful but unconvinced. The two younger men looked serenely amused, but only the drunken one of them had the temerity and bad manners to scoff at the offered explanation.

'A wedding?' he hooted, casting a meaningful eye upon Nicki's torn collar. 'What could two men discuss about a wedding?'

'Who the groom is going to be,' Nicki replied with casual nonchalance.

'And did you decide, sir?' the courteous one asked, sending his companion a warning glance and trying desperately to pretend he believed the whole tale.

'Yes,' Nicki drawled, leaning forward to toss his chips into the center of the table. 'I am going to be the best man.'

His careless friend took another long draught of wine, and gave a laugh. 'A wedding!' he snorted.

Nicholas DuVille slowly lifted his head and gave him a long, speculative look. 'Would you prefer to make it a funeral?'

Fearing that the worst might yet be to come, Baskerville leapt into the breach. 'What else did you and Langford discuss? You were gone a good while.'

'We discussed little old ladies with faulty memories,' Nicki replied ironically. 'And we marvelled at the wisdom of a God who, for some incomprehensible reason, occasionally allows their tongues to go on working long after their brains have ceased to function at all.'

The Duke of Stanhope looked up sharply. 'I hope you are not referring to anyone I know.'

'Do you know anyone called by the unlikely name of "Charity," instead of "Birdwit"?'

The Duke choked back a horrified laugh at that deliberate, and unmistakable, description of his oldest sister. 'I may.' He was spared further discussion of that embarrassing topic by the arrival of another gambler, who nodded a casual but friendly greeting at Baskerville and himself as he pulled out the chair beside DuVille and settled into it.

Stretching his long legs out beneath the table, the new arrival gazed pointedly at the two young gentlemen, who were not known to him, clearly awaiting the formality of an introduction before acknowledging them. DuVille was the only one who seemed either cognizant of the need for introductions or able to respond to it. 'These two fellows with the slack jaws and deep pockets are Lords Banbraten and Isley,' he said to the newcomer. To the youths, he said, 'I believe the Earl of Langford is already familiar to you?' When they nodded in unison, Nicki finished dealing out the cards and said, 'Good. Since that's over, the earl and I will now endeavor to divest you of the rest of your fathers' money.'

He picked up the cards he'd dealt for himself and winced at the pain in his rib.

'Bad hand, eh?' chuckled the Duke of Stanhope, mistaking the reason for Nicki's grimace.

In the erroneous belief the question had been directed to him, Stephen glanced at his swollen knuckles and flexed his hand. 'Not too bad.' He turned as a servant approached the table with two glasses of excellent brandy, and he took them both, keeping one for himself and passing the other to DuVille. 'With my compliments,' he said blandly, pausing for an inquiring glance at one of the youths, who'd overturned his wine as he reached for it.

'Can't hold his drink,' Nicki explained, following the direction of Stephen's gaze.

Stephen crossed his feet at the ankles and glanced in

disapproval at the red-faced, glassy-eyed youth. 'You would think,' he said, 'that someone would have taught them how to conduct themselves before turning them loose on the rest of society.'

'My thoughts exactly,' Nicki agreed.

59

The Skeffingtons had given up their rented house in town and repaired to the village of Blintonfield. As a result, it took Nicki three more hours than he'd anticipated to reach Sheridan and put into effect the romantic plan that Langford felt was the best – and only – way to bring her to him as well as convince her his intentions were honorable.

The fact that Nicki was now Stephen Westmoreland's emissary instead of his adversary did not strike Nicki as odd in the least. For one thing, he was merely doing his best to repair a relationship he had inadvertently helped to damage. For another, he was thoroughly enjoying his role, which was to persuade Sheridan to resign her position with the Skeffingtons and accompany him at once to an interview for a 'new position' at an estate several hours away.

To that end, he had brought with him two impeccably qualified governesses to take her place.

Since Lady Skeffington had taken her daughter to Devon, where she had heard the future Duke of Norringham spent his bachelor days during July, Nicki had only to convince Sir John to accept two governesses in place of one – an easy feat since Stephen Westmoreland would be secretly paying more than half their wages for the first year.

Having accomplished all that, Nicki was now attempting to persuade Sheridan of the logic – and the need – to pack her clothes at once and accompany him to meet an unknown nobleman who had a 'better position' to offer her. In keeping with that end, he was providing her with as much of the truth as he could tell her and improvising when the occasion – or his sense of humor – required it.

'Viscount Hargrove is a bit temperamental, even disagreeable, at times,' he told her, 'but he dotes on his nephew, who is also his heir at the moment, and wants only the best for him.'

'I see,' Sheridan said, wondering just how temperamental and disagreeable the viscount was.

'The wages are excellent – to compensate for the viscount's personal shortcomings.'

'How excellent?'

The figure he named made Sherry's lips part in a silent O of stunned delight.

'There are also other benefits that go with the position.'

'What sort of benefits?'

'A large suite of your own, a maid to attend you, a horse of your own . . .'

Her eyes were widening with each word. 'Is there more?' she asked when he let the sentence hang. 'How could there be?'

'As a matter of fact, there is more. One of the most appealing benefits of this position is what I would call . . . tenure.'

'What do you mean by that?'

'I mean that if you accept the position, it will be yours – along with all its benefits – for as long as you live.'

'I wasn't planning to stay in England above a few months.'

'A small complication, but perhaps you can persuade the viscount to give it to you anyway.'

Sheridan hesitated, trying to get a clearer picture of the man. 'Is he an elderly gentleman?'

'Comparatively speaking,' Nicki confirmed, thinking

with amusement that Langford was a year older than himself.

'Has he had other governesses in the past?'

Nicki choked back several highly amusing, but inappropriate, answers as to the likelihood of that and gave her the answer she'd expect, 'Yes.'

'Why did they leave him?'

Another set of diverting speculations occurred to him, and he uttered one of them. 'Perhaps because they expected tenure and he didn't offer it?' he suggested smoothly, then to prevent more questions, he said, 'As I said a moment ago, this is a matter of some urgency to the viscount. If you are interested in the position, then pack your things, and we will be on our way. I promised to bring you to him at two o'clock today, and we are already going to be three hours late.'

Unable to trust in the first good fortune that had befallen her since coming to England, Sheridan hesitated and then stood up. 'I don't understand why he's interested in employing someone like me when he could surely have his choice of better-qualified English governesses.'

'He's set on having an American,' Nicki said with amused certainty.

'Very well, I'll meet with him, and if we are at all compatible, I'll remain with him.'

'That is what he is hoping for,' Nicki said. As she turned to go upstairs and pack, he added, 'I have brought you a better gown to wear, one that does not look so—' He looked for some fault with her perfectly neat but drab dark gown. '—so somber,' he finished. 'Viscount Hargrove dislikes somber things around him.'

60

'Is something wrong, *chérie?*' he asked as the sun began its lazy descent.

Pulling her gaze from the verdant countryside passing by the coach's window, Sherry shook her head. 'I am only – anticipating the change – a new position, wonderful wages, a large room of my own, and horses to ride. It seems almost too good to be true.'

'Then why do you look so inexpressibly solemn?'

'I don't feel right about leaving the Skeffingtons so suddenly,' Sherry admitted.

'They have two governesses now, instead of one. Skeffington was so excited, he'd have helped you pack your valise.'

'If you'd met their daughter, you'd understand why. I left her a note, but I hated not to say good-bye to her. In fact, I hated to leave her to them at all. In any case,' Sherry added, shaking off her unease and smiling, 'I am exceedingly grateful to you for everything you've done.'

'I hope you will still feel as you do in a little while,' Nicki replied with a touch of irony. He took out his watch and frowned at the time. 'We are very late. He may have decided we aren't coming, after all.'

'Why would he think that?'

He took a moment longer to answer than should have been necessary, but Sherry dismissed that as soon as he said, 'I could not guarantee the viscount that I could lure you away from your present position.'

She burst out laughing. 'Who in their right mind would pass up such an offer as his?' Another possibility occurred to her, and she sobered abruptly. 'You aren't trying to tell me that he might have given the position to someone else by the time we arrive?'

For some reason, that question seemed to amuse him as he shifted position, turning so that his back was propped against the side window and one long leg was draped over the seat beside him. He caught her worried look and said with complete assurance, 'I feel certain the position will still be yours. If you want it.'

'It's such a beautiful day—' Sherry began half an hour later. She broke off and grabbed for leverage as the horses slowed suddenly and the coach began to sway hard on its frame. Then, with a loud bump, it turned sharply to the left, off the main road. 'We must be getting near his home,' she said, straightening the wide, tight cuffs and full sleeves of the lovely pale blue embroidered gown Nicki had brought her, then she reached up to make certain her hair was securely anchored in its neat coil.

Nicki leaned forward and looked out at the ancient stone buildings at the side of the overgrown, narrow lane, then he smiled with satisfaction. 'The viscount's country seat is still some distance from here; however, he was going to be here at this hour, and he felt this was the most suitable place for you both to discuss the position he wishes to offer.'

Curious, Sheridan leaned sideways and looked out the window, her delicate brows drawing together in confused surprise. 'Is this a *church*?'

'As I understand, this is a chapel that was once part of a Scottish priory during the sixteenth century. It was later dismantled with permission and brought here. It has great significance in the viscount's ancestral history.'

'What sort of significance could a chapel have in a family's history?' Sherry inquired, baffled.

'I believe the viscount's earliest known ancestor forced a friar to marry him to his unwilling bride within the chapel's walls.' When she shivered, Nicki added dryly, 'Now that I think about it, it seems to be something of a family custom.'

'It sounds Gothic and – and not amusing or appealing in the least! I see two other coaches around the other side, but no-one is in them. What sort of service could he be attending at this hour and in such an out-of-the-way place as this?'

'A private one. Very private,' Nicki said, then he changed the subject. 'Let me see how you look.'

She faced him, and he frowned. 'Your hair seems to be sliding free of your tidy coil.' Puzzled because her hair had felt secure, Sherry reached up, but he was too quick.

'Here, let me. You have no looking glass.'

Before she could protest or warn him, he'd pulled on the long pins instead of pushing them in and twisting, and the whole mass came tumbling down around her shoulders in hopeless disarray. 'Oh, no!' she cried.

'Do you have a brush?'

'Yes, of course, but, oh, I wish you hadn't—'

'Do not fret. You will feel better able to voice your objections if you know you look more – festive,' he lied lamely.

'What possible objections could I have to his offer?'

Nicki waited for the coachman to let down the steps, then he climbed out and offered her his hand, before he replied vaguely, 'Oh, I think you may have an objection or two. At first.'

'Is there something you haven't told me?' Sherry said, pulling back a little, then stepping aside in surprise as the coachman abruptly moved the horses forward. The breeze caught her skirt, blowing it gently and teasing her hair as they walked side by side. From the corner of her eye, Sherry searched the side yard of the picturesque little chapel for some sign of the sort of man who would have to pay a fortune to keep a governess.

She thought she saw something move off to the left, and her hand went to her heart at the same time Nicki looked sharply at her. 'What's wrong?'

'Nothing. I thought I saw someone.'

'It was probably him. He said he would be waiting for you over there.'

'Over there? What is he doing out here?'

'Meditating, I imagine,' Nicky said succinctly, 'on his sins. Now, run along and listen to what he has to say. And, *chérie*?'

She turned to step across the rutted lane and stopped. 'Yes?' she said over her shoulder.

'If you truly do not wish to accept the position he offers, you will leave here with me. Do not feel obliged to remain if you wish to leave. You will receive other offers, though not perhaps as – diverting in some ways – as this one would turn out to be. Remember that,' he said firmly. 'If you truly wish to decline, you may leave here with me under my protection.'

Sherry nodded and turned back, picking her way across the road, avoiding getting her slippers dusty, then she walked up to the little white fence and pushed it open, blinking to adjust to the dimmer light of the grove. Ahead of her, a man was in the shadow of a tree, his arms crossed over his chest, feet braced slightly apart, gloves clutched in one hand, idly tapping his hip. Only dimly aware there was something familiar about that stance, she continued forward, her heart beginning to hammer in nervous anticipation and a little dread of the coming interview.

She took three steps forward. So did he. Sherry stopped cold at the sound of his solemn voice. 'I was afraid you weren't coming.'

For a split second, her feet felt rooted in the ground – then she whirled and ran, rage and shock propelling her with unusual speed, but she still couldn't outdistance him. Stephen caught her just as she neared the gate and pulled her back around, his hands clamped on her arms. 'Let go of me!' Sherry warned, her chest heaving with each tortured breath.

Quietly, he asked, 'Will you stand here and listen to what I have to say?'

She nodded, he released her, and she swung at him, but this time he had expected it and recaptured both her arms. With a pained look in his eyes, he said, 'Don't make me restrain you.'

'I'm not making you do anything, you loathsome – despicable – lech!' she raged, trying ineffectually to twist free. 'And to think Nicki DuVille was a part of this! He brought me here – he convinced me to resign my position, he made me believe you had a position to offer me—'

'I do have a position to offer you.'

'I'm not interested in any more of your offers!' she raged, giving up her futile physical struggle and facing him in a fury of helplessness. 'I'm still hurting from the last one!'

He winced at the mention of his last offer, but he went on talking almost as if he hadn't heard her. 'The new position comes with a house – several of them.'

'I've heard all this before!'

'No you haven't!' he said. 'It comes with servants to do your every bidding, all the money you can spend, jewels, furs. And it comes with me.'

'*I don't want you!*' she cried. 'You've already used me like a – a common doxy, now stay away from me! God,' she said, her voice breaking, 'I'm so ashamed – it was so trite – the governess who falls in love with the lord of the manor, only in the novels he doesn't do the things to her you did to me in bed. It was so ugly—'

'Don't say that!' he cut in, his voice raw. 'Please don't say that. It wasn't ugly. It was—'

'Sordid!' she cried.

'The new position comes with me,' he continued, his face white with strain. 'It comes with my name and my hand and all I possess.'

'I don't want—'

'Yes you do,' he said, giving her a shake, just as his full meaning sunk in. Sheridan felt a brief spurt of joy before she realized he was merely having another attack of conscience and duty, this time over seducing her, evidently.

'Damn you!' she choked. 'I am not some foundling you're obliged to propose to every time you have an attack of guilt. The first time you did it, I wasn't even the right woman to feel guilty about.'

'Guilty,' he repeated with a harsh, embittered laugh. 'The only guilt I ever felt where you were concerned was for wanting you for myself from the moment you regained consciousness. For God's sake, look at me and you'll see I'm telling the truth.' He put his hand under her chin, and she neither resisted nor cooperated, but focused her gaze over his shoulder instead. 'I stole the life of a young man, and then I saw his fiancée and I wanted to steal her too. Can you understand just a little of how that made me feel about myself? I killed him and then I *lusted* after the fiancée he couldn't have because he was dead. I wanted to marry you, Sheridan, right from the beginning.'

'No you didn't! Not until *after* you were informed Mr Lancaster had died, leaving his poor, helpless daughter alone in the world except for *you*!'

'If I hadn't wanted an excuse to marry his "poor, helpless daughter" I'd have done anything I could for her, but marriage was not one of them. God forgive me, but an hour after I got that letter, I was drinking champagne with my brother to toast our wedding. If I hadn't wanted to marry you, I'd have been drinking hemlock.'

Sheridan bit back a teary smile at his quip, afraid to believe him, afraid to trust him, and unable to stop herself because she loved him. 'Look at me,' Stephen said, tipping her chin up again, and this time her glorious eyes looked into his. 'I have several reasons for asking you to walk into that chapel, where there is a vicar waiting for us, but guilt is not among them. I also have several things to ask of you before you agree to go in there with me.'

'What sort of things?'

'I would like you to give me daughters with your hair and your spirit,' he said, beginning to enumerate his reasons and requests. 'I would like my sons to have your eyes and your courage. Now, if that's not what you want, then give me any combination you like, and I will humbly thank you for giving me any child we make.'

Happiness began to spread through Sheridan until it was so intense she ached from it. 'I want to change your name,' he said with a tender smile, 'so there's no doubt who you are ever again, or who you belong to.' He slid his hands up and down her arms, looking directly into her eyes. 'I want the right to share your bed tonight and every night from this day onward. I want to make you moan in my arms again, and I want to wake up wrapped in yours.' He shifted his hands and cradled her cheeks, his thumbs brushing away two tears at the edges of her shimmering eyes. 'Last of all, I want to hear you say "I love you" every day of my life. If you aren't ready to agree to that last request right now, I would be willing to wait until tonight, when I believe you will. In return for all those concessions, I will grant you every wish that is within my power to grant you.

'As to what happened between us in bed at Claymore, there was nothing sordid about it—'

'We were *lovers*!' she countered, flushing with guilt.

'Sheridan,' he said quietly, 'we have been lovers since the first moment your mouth touched mine.'

He wanted her to find pride, not shame, in that, and to accept it as a special gift from fate, and then he realized he was expecting the impossible of a young, inexperienced girl. He was about to absolve her completely by assuming all of the blame for the desire they'd shared, but after a moment the woman he loved turned her face into his hand to brush a soft kiss against his palm. 'I know,' she whispered simply.

The two words filled him with so much pride that he thought he would burst with it. *I know*. No more recriminations, no pretense, no denials. In place of that, she lifted her eyes to his, and in their fathomless depths he saw only sweet acceptance and quiet joy.

'Will you come inside with me now?'

'Yes.'

61

His bride of two hours stirred reluctantly as the coach came to a smart stop, and with equal reluctance Stephen lifted his mouth from hers. 'Where are we?' she asked, her voice a languorous, thready whisper.

'Home,' Stephen said, a little surprised at the husky timbre of his own voice.

'Yours?'

'Ours,' he corrected, and Sherry felt a shiver of delight at the sound of that.

A servant was opening the coach's door and reaching inside to let down the steps. Sherry made a halfhearted effort to straighten her hair by raking her fingers through it and shoving it back off her forehead. As she did, she noticed the way his gaze strayed to her hair, following it almost caressingly down to her shoulders while the tiny lines at the corners of his eyes creased into a thoughtful smile. 'What are you thinking about?' she asked.

His smile deepened. 'Something I've been thinking about ever since you marched out of the dressing room in London, pulled a towel off your head, and announced to me in the direst tones that your hair was "brazen".'

'What did that make you think of?' she persisted as he alighted and offered her his hand.

'I'll tell you later. Better yet, I'll *show* you,' Stephen promised.

'It sounds mysterious,' Sherry teased.

For four years, women had flung themselves at Stephen in the hope of someday becoming mistress of the palatial house he had designed and built and called Montclair. Now he waited for a reaction from the woman he had finally chosen to be its mistress.

Sherry tucked her hand in the crook of his arm, smiled cordially at the footmen who'd come out to help them, took one step forward, and looked up at the majestic, sprawling stone mansion in front of her. She stopped dead, staring in disbelief at the brightly lit windows that were spread across its entire facade, then she looked over her shoulder at the long winding drive that was lined with luxurious coaches on both sides as far as she could see. She looked at it, and then at him, and said in a tone of blank shock, 'Are you giving a *party*?'

Stephen threw back his head and shouted with laughter, then he wrapped his arms around her and buried his laughing face in her hair. 'I am insane about you, Lady Westmoreland.'

She wasn't impressed by a palace, but she was pleased and impressed with the sound of her newly acquired name. 'Sheridan Westmoreland,' she said aloud. 'I like that very much.' Behind them, Nicholas DuVille's coach pulled to a stop and Sherry remembered her original concern. '*Are* you giving a party?'

Stephen nodded, looking over at DuVille and waiting as he walked toward them. 'This is my mother's sixtieth birthday. I'm giving a ball in honor of the occasion, which is why my brother and sister-in-law weren't at the chapel. They've been playing host in my absence.' She looked a little dismayed, and he explained, 'The invitations had gone out weeks ago, but I didn't want to wait until after the ball for our wedding. More correctly,' he amended wryly, 'I couldn't endure the suspense of waiting another day to find out if there was going to *be* a wedding.'

'It's not that,' she said a little desperately as they walked up a flight of terraced steps, 'it's that I'm not dressed—'

Nicki heard that and gave her a wounded look. 'I chose that gown myself in London.'

'Yes, but it isn't a ball gown,' Sheridan explained as the butler opened the door and an explosion of laughter and music came at her from all sides. Ahead of her a Palladian staircase swept upward in a graceful U on both sides of an immense foyer. Beside her, a butler with a familiar face and a beaming smile stood at attention, waiting for her notice, and Sherry forgot about the problem of a gown. 'Colfax!' she exclaimed joyously.

He bowed formally. 'Welcome home, Lady Westmoreland.'

'Is everyone here?' Stephen asked, pulling his thoughts from the large bed that awaited them upstairs to the more immediate issue of a change of attire.

'They are.'

With a nod, Stephen looked at his best man. 'Why don't you go ahead to the ballroom, and Sherry and I will change clothes.'

'Not a chance. I want to see their faces.'

'Very well, we'll change and join you in—' Stephen actually considered the possibility of a tryst with his bride before he attended a ball that would last well into the small hours of early morning.

'In twenty minutes,' DuVille emphasized with a knowing look.

Sherry listened to that with only half her attention while she wondered what she was expected to change into. She asked Stephen that as he led her upstairs, but his reply was interrupted by Nicki DuVille who called after them from the foot of the stairs, 'Twenty minutes, or I come in after you.'

That innocent reminder caused her new husband to say something under his breath. 'What did you just call Nicki?'

'I called him the "Soul of Punctuality,"' Stephen lied with a helpless grin at the dubious look on her face.

'It didn't sound quite like that.'

'It was close enough,' he said, stopping outside a suite of rooms at the end of the hall. 'There wasn't time to have an appropriate gown made for you, so Whitney brought one she thought was well-suited to the occasion – providing you came back with me.' As he spoke, he reached out and swung open the door. Sheridan looked around him and saw three maids standing in readiness, but her attention was drawn to a breathtaking ivory satin gown that was lovingly spread out across the huge bed, its long train swirling over the side of the coverlet and down all the way to the floor. Mesmerized, she took a step forward, then stopped and looked from the lavish gown to her husband's tender smile. 'What is that?'

In answer, he curved his hand around her nape, pressed her cheek tightly to his chest, and whispered, 'Whitney's wedding gown. She wanted you to wear it if you came back with me.'

Sheridan decided it was absurd to cry merely because she was happy.

'How long will it take you to get ready?'

'An hour,' Sheridan said regretfully, 'if we have to try anything elaborate with my hair.'

For the second time, he bent his head and whispered something the maids couldn't hear: 'Brush it if you must, and then leave it alone.'

'Oh, but—'

'I have a distinct partiality for that long, shining, brazen red hair of yours.'

'In that case,' she said a little shakily as he let her go, 'I think I'll wear it down tonight.'

'Good, because we only have fifteen minutes left.'

The dowager duchess looked at Hugh Whitticomb

when the under-butler, who was stationed on the balcony, called out the name of the Duke and Duchess of Hawthorne as they passed by him and made their way into the crowded ballroom. 'Hugh, do you have the time?' she asked.

Clayton, who had just looked at his own watch, answered for the physician. 'It's after ten o'clock.'

The answer caused the small group of people to look despondently at one another. Whitney expressed all their thoughts in a voice filled with sad resignation. 'Sherry refused him or they would have been here three hours ago.'

'I felt so very certain—' Miss Charity began, then broke off, her narrow shoulders drooping with despair.

'Perhaps DuVille couldn't get her to agree to go to the chapel,' Jason Fielding suggested, but his wife shook her head and said flatly, 'If Nicki DuVille wanted her to accompany him, he'd have found a way to persuade her to do it.'

Unaware that she'd made it sound as if no woman could refuse Nicki anything, she glanced up and saw her husband frowning at Clayton Westmoreland. 'Is there something about DuVille that I haven't noticed?' he demanded of the duke. 'Something that makes him irresistible?'

'I have no trouble resisting him,' Clayton said dryly, then he stopped while one of his great-aunts came over to congratulate his mother on her birthday.

'This is such a lovely ball, Alicia. You must be very happy tonight.'

'I could be happier,' the dowager duchess said with a sigh as she turned to begin mingling with the guests in the ballroom.

On the balcony above, the under-butler called out more new arrivals. '*Sir Roderick Carstairs. Mr Nicholas DuVille . . .*'

The dowager whirled around and looked up, along with the rest of the small group that had been waiting for word of the day's outcome. Nicki looked down at them, his handsome face solemn as he walked slowly along the balcony toward the stairs leading down to the ballroom. 'It didn't happen!' Whitney whispered achingly, studying his expression. 'We failed.'

Her husband slid his hand around her waist and pulled her close. 'You tried, darling. You did everything that could be done.'

'We all did,' Charity Thornton agreed, her chin trembling as she looked sadly at Hugh Whitticomb and then up at Nicholas DuVille.

'The Earl and Countess of Langford!'

That announcement caused an immediate reaction among the inhabitants of the ballroom, who began looking at one another in surprise and then turned to the balcony, but it was nothing compared to the reaction among the small group of seven people who'd been keeping a vigil of hope. A jolt went through the entire group; hands reached out blindly and were clasped tightly by other hands; faces lifted to the balcony, while joyous smiles dawned brightly and eyes misted with tears.

Attired in formal black evening clothes with a white waistcoat and frilled white shirt, Stephen Westmoreland, Earl of Langford, was walking across the balcony. On his arm was a medieval princess clad in a pearl-encrusted ivory satin gown with a low, square bodice that tapered to a deep V at the waist. A gold chain with clusters of diamonds and pearls in each link rode low on her hips, swaying with each step, and her hair tumbled in flaming waves and heavy curls over her shoulders and back.

'Oh, my—' Charity breathed in awe, but her exclamation was drowned by the thunder of applause that had begun all over the ballroom and was gaining in volume, until it seemed to shake the very rafters.

62

It was his wedding night.

With his shirt open at the collar and his cuffs rolled back on his forearms, Stephen sat in a wing-backed chair in his bedchamber, his feet propped upon a low table, while he lingered over a glass of brandy, giving his bride ample time to disrobe and dismiss her maids.

His wedding night . . .

His bride . . .

He looked round in surprise as his valet let himself into the suite. 'May I be of assistance this evening?' Damson suggested when his master seemed baffled by what was actually a routine appearance each night.

Assistance? Stephen stifled a smile as his wayward thoughts refused to switch from the pleasurable task that lay ahead of him to Damson's offer to assist him tonight. His mind conjured a comic image of his conscientious valet hovering at Sheridan's bedside, his clothing brush in hand, waiting for Stephen to hand him his trousers so he could hang them properly, then bustling back to the bedside for each additional piece of clothing as Stephen removed it.

'My lord?' Damson prompted and Stephen gave his head a slight shake as he realized he was staring past the servant with what surely must look like an idiot's smile.

'No,' he said with polite firmness. 'Thank you.'

Damson eyed Stephen's open shirt and rolled-back cuffs with disapproval. 'Your dressing robe perhaps, my lord, the black brocade?'

Stephen tried, very seriously, to imagine what possible use he was going to have for a dressing robe, and felt the smile tug at his cheek again. 'No, I think not.'

'The wine silk, then?' Damson persevered doggedly. 'Or the dark green, perhaps?' It hit Stephen that his middle-aged valet, who had never been married, was gravely concerned that Stephen was not likely to make a good impression on his new bride were he to walk into her bedchamber casually attired in trousers and shirtsleeves.

'Neither one.'

'Perhaps the—'

'Go to bed, Damson,' Stephen said, cutting off any discussion of silk neckcloths and appropriate shirt studs, which he felt certain would be the valet's next point of concern. 'And, thank you,' he added with a brief smile to take any sting out of the dismissal.

Damson obeyed with a bow, but not before he cast a tortured look at Stephen's open shirtfront and the glimpse of bare throat and chest it allowed.

Half-convinced the man would make one more attempt to save him from the unspeakable indignity of appearing for his wedding night inappropriately attired, Stephen put the brandy glass on the table. Then he got up, walked over to the door, and threw the bolt.

Damson did not know, of course, that Stephen had already precipitated his wedding night with Sherry, and as Stephen opened the connecting door between the suites, he felt a sharp stab of guilty regret for the way he had begun and ended that night, but not for what they had done in the middle of it. Resolved to atone for everything their last encounter lacked, he walked into the connecting bedchamber. He stopped in surprise when she wasn't waiting for him in bed, since he'd given her more than enough time to disrobe. Then he walked slowly toward the adjoining bathing room. He was partway there when the hall door of her bedchamber opened, and a maid rushed in carrying a pile of fluffy towels.

His wife was in her bath, Stephen realized.

His wife . . . Revelling in the thought and all it

implied, he reached for the towels and took them from the scandalized maid. Then he dismissed her for the night.

'But – but my lady will require me to help her dress for bed!'

Stephen was beginning to wonder if every husband and wife, with the single exception of Sherry and himself, went to bed in a full suit of clothes and a ball gown as some sort of modest ploy to prevent servants from realizing they might actually see each other's bodies. He was smiling about that as he walked into the bathing room and saw his wife in the sunken marble bath. Her back was partially turned to him, her hair was piled in a loose knot atop her head with charming tendrils down her nape, and there were bubbles up to the tops of her breasts.

The sight was more than charming, it was downright enticing. His wife! The scent of lavender rising from her bath suddenly made him remember her bold ultimatum about Helene – an ultimatum with which he'd already complied. That memory called to mind her angry tirade about all the other women she'd heard mentioned by the gossips in connection with him. With an inner smile, Stephen decided that although she didn't approve of his sexual dalliances before their marriage, she was certainly going to benefit from them tonight. In fact, he intended to make certain that she did so by using every bit of skill and knowledge he possessed to give her the wedding night she deserved, one she would never, ever forget.

Feeling relatively confident of his ability to do that, he sat down on the edge of her tub, intending to play lady's maid. Reaching into the warm, scented water, he wet his hands, then put them on her shoulders, his thumbs working lightly over her slick, wet skin.

'I'd like to get out now,' she said without turning around.

Smiling a little at the joke he was playing on her, Stephen stood up and opened the towel, holding it out for her. Sherry stepped out of the water, and he wrapped the towel around her from behind, folding his arms around her as he did so. She stiffened in shock when she saw his bare forearms encircling her, instead of a maid's hands holding the towel. And then, very lightly she leaned back against him, bringing her back and hips and legs into contact with his full length, and she wrapped her arms over his, turned her cheek, and rubbed it against his shirt. It was a silent gesture of wanting, of tenderness, of love, and yet when he turned her around, she trembled slightly, looking at him with nervous uncertainty. 'May I put on my dressing robe?'

It was a request for permission, which struck him as odd in an indefinable way, but since he'd already resolved to linger over her, he answered unhesitatingly and with a smile. 'You may do anything you like, Lady Westmoreland.' When she hesitated, holding the towel around her, Stephen politely turned his back and went into the bedchamber, a little surprised by her sudden modesty. A little off-balance.

When she strolled into the room a minute later, the sight of her did much more violent things to his balance. Dripping wet, wrapped in a towel, she was delectable. Clad in a low-cut dressing gown made entirely of white lace as fragile as a spider's web, with shadowy glimpses of skin offered up to his view from the tops of her breasts all the way to her ankles, she was the haunting temptress of a male's dreams . . . ethereal, inviting, not quite naked, but not quite covered. A siren. An angel.

Sherry saw the banked fires kindle in his eyes as they drifted over her, and with only the one night at Claymore to rely on for clues as to what was going to happen, she waited for him to instruct her to take her hair down. She stood there, feeling awkward and helplessly aware of her lack of knowledge – a situation that might not have occurred had the maid not poured handfuls of lavender scent into her bathwater. The reminder of Helene Devernay wouldn't have been quite so bad if Sherry hadn't also gotten a good look at Stephen's mistress two weeks ago, riding through Bond Street in a silver-lacquered carriage with lavender velvet squabs. Julianna Skeffington had pointed her out and provided her identity, but Sheridan had already guessed who she was. Stephen's mistress – his *former* mistress if Sheridan had her way about it – was the sort of female to make any other woman feel ordinary and gauche. And Sheridan did.

It was not a feeling she liked in the least. She wished Stephen had told her he loved her. She wished he had said he didn't see Helene anymore. Now that her memory was functioning, she had a vivid childhood recollection of Helene Devernay's American equivalent – a lady in a startlingly low-cut red gown with feathers in her hair whom Sheridan saw sitting in Rafe's lap one night when she peeked in the windows of a gambling house. The female had been running her fingers through his hair, and Sheridan had felt a burst of jealousy that was as nothing compared to the way she felt about the thought of Helene Devernay sitting in Stephen's lap.

She wished she had the courage right now to demand that he break off his relationship with the beautiful blonde if he hadn't already done so. On the other hand, common sense dictated that such an ultimatum might be far more successful if Sheridan were to first make Stephen want his wife more than he wanted his stunning *chère amie*. The only thing standing in her way at the moment was that she didn't have the slightest idea how to make him want her without some guidance from him. Thinking of the way he'd ordered her to take her hair down at Claymore, Sheridan lifted her hands. 'Should I?'

Stephen watched her breasts threaten to spill over the low, square-cut bodice of the lace gown. 'Should you what?' he asked softly, as he started toward her.

'Should I take my hair down now?'

Permission again. She was thinking about his callous

demand to loosen her hair that night at Claymore, he realized with a fresh stab of regret. He put his hands on her shoulders, trying not to look at the rosy swell of breasts. 'I'll do it,' he said gently.

She backed up a half step. 'No, really, if you'd prefer that I do it, I will.'

'Sheridan, what's wrong? What's bothering you?'

Helene Devernay is bothering me, she thought. 'I don't understand what I'm supposed to do. I don't know the rules.'

'What rules?'

'I would like to know how to please you,' she finally forced out. He looked as if he were struggling to keep his face straight and she said in an imploring voice, 'Oh, please, don't laugh! Don't . . .'

Stephen stared down at the temptress in his arms and, very reverently, he whispered, 'Good God . . .' She was serious. She was glorious, and sensual, and sweet, and courageous. And she was very, very *serious*. So much so that he had the distinct feeling that a wrong answer, a wrong reaction now, could hurt her beyond belief. 'I was not laughing, darling,' he said somberly.

Satisfied that he understood and did not object, she began with the subject of clothing, her eyes searching his. 'What is allowed?'

He laid his hand against her cheek and ran it back, smoothing her hair. 'Anything is allowed.'

'Is there a . . . a goal?'

Stephen's earlier confidence that his prior experience with women had equipped him for this particular evening slipped a notch. 'Yes,' he said, 'there is.'

'What is it?'

He slipped his arms around her and put his hands lightly on her back. 'The goal is for us to be as close as we can possibly be, and to enjoy that closeness in every way we can.'

'How will I know what you enjoy?'

He was beginning to get an erection just from enjoying

the conversation. 'In general, if you enjoy something, I will.'

'I don't know what I enjoy.'

'I see. Then I think it's only right that you have time to find out.'

'When?' Sheridan said, afraid he meant 'someday.'

He tipped her chin up, and she watched his sensual lips form one word. 'Now.'

She waited with a mixture of embarrassment and anticipation for him to do something, to give her some sort of direction, but Stephen could only gaze down into her eyes, thinking that he had gone to heaven. He bent his head to kiss her, very slowly rubbing his lips on hers, letting his hand drift down her throat to her bare bodice, and he felt her lean closer to kiss him back. She liked that, Stephen knew. She liked something else, too, he realized as she tentatively put her fingers against the narrow vee of his open shirt. 'Would you like me to take my shirt off?' he heard himself ask.

Sheridan had a feeling that question was a prelude to having her own gown removed, but she was also certain that was going to happen anyway. She nodded, and Stephen complied. She stepped back, watching him unfasten the front of his shirt. When the last stud came free, Stephen put them down on the table. Then he slowly opened his shirt and removed it, surprised to find that the act of deliberately undressing while a woman looked on, watching, was strangely erotic.

Sheridan gazed in admiration at the heavily muscled broad shoulders and a wide chest with dark, springy hairs. She lifted her hand, then stopped when it neared his chest and gave him a swift look of inquiry. He nodded slightly, smiling at the sheer joy of her; she put her hand on his rib cage, slowly spreading her fingers, sliding them upward toward his nipple, and then she put her other hand beside it. He was beautiful, she thought, like a statue of a Greek god, all hard planes and bunched muscle. As her hands slid upward and her fingers brushed his small nipples, the muscles beneath her questing fingers leapt reflexively and she stopped instantly. 'You don't like it?' she asked, looking into those heavy-lidded smoldering blue eyes.

'I like it,' he said almost gruffly.

'So do I,' she admitted without thinking, smiling at him.

'Good,' he said as he took her hand and led her to the bed. He sat down and when she started to sit next to him, he caught her waist and drew her down on his lap with a muffled laugh. 'Go on,' he invited, and Sheridan resumed the exploration of his chest and arms, mildly puzzled about his comment that it was good that she liked touching him there. A moment later, she understood what he meant. *If you like it, I will*, he'd said. Obviously, that was supposed to work both ways, because his large hand came to rest on the bodice of her gown, cupping her full breast, and Sheridan felt her pulse leap. She looked down, watching his long fingers sliding over her nipple as she'd touched his, and she wondered if her leaping pulse was the equivalent of the reflexive bunching of his muscles. She drew a shaky breath, and waited, but his hand stopped moving, his fingers at the frog-closing of her bodice.

Stephen waited for her to decide whether she wanted to open it or wanted him to open it or if she wanted it left alone. Half expecting her to decide the latter, he waited, and to his infinite delight, she solved the problem by sliding both her hands around his neck and pressing her breasts to his bare chest. She wanted him to open it, he realized, but she didn't want to ask. He had the complicated closing open in seconds, and he slid his hand into the open bodice, holding her breast, teasing the nipple, feeling it harden into a taut bud while the soft globe seemed to swell to fill his hand. . . And his erection swelled and hardened with it.

Stephen felt in charge again, in territory where his experience was of value to them both, and he bent his head, touching his tongue to the tight nipple, then drawing it into his mouth, feeling her swift indrawn breath. Sheridan looked down at the dark head at her breast, while sparks of feeling began shooting rhythmically from her breast to her knees and she slid her fingers into his thick beautiful hair. He switched to the other breast, lavishing it with the same attention. Then his lips closed tightly on it and she gasped and clutched his head to her breast, suddenly desperate to make him feel the melting sensations he was giving her.

As if he sensed it, he shifted her down onto the bed, so that her head was on the pillows, and he stretched out beside her. Sheridan turned into his arms, touching her tongue to his nipple, tightening her lips around it, and she felt his fingers sinking slowly into her hair as he gave her free use of his body.

Stephen knew he was going to die before this was over.

He had moved her to the bed because it was more comfortable and gave him freer access to the rest of her. He had not expected her to do what she was doing to him. Desire was exploding through his body and he swallowed, clutching her more tightly as she brushed her fingers up and down his chest and kissed it. Unable to endure any more, he rolled her onto her back, unfastened the rest of her bodice, pushed the lace aside with his fingers, and then closed his eyes and drew a steadying breath. The gown had no fasteners beneath the bodice; the whole thing was open. He didn't know how he'd failed to notice that. He didn't know why he hadn't expected it, except that it had been a gift from Whitney. At Claymore, the room had been virtually dark. Somehow, he hadn't noticed that his wife had long, exquisite legs and graceful hips and a tiny waist and gorgeous breasts. His plan for a leisurely night of lovemaking took another battering as his body surged with alarming urgency.

Sheridan swallowed, watching him leaning up on his

elbow, looking at her, then closing his eyes, and her heart sank. Feeling it was better to know about her flaws so that she could either disguise them or hide them, she said in a shaky voice, 'What's wrong with me?'

'What's wrong with you?' he repeated in disbelief. He tore his gaze from the bounty before him and leaned over her to kiss her. 'What's wrong with you,' he whispered achingly, sliding his hand around her waist and pulling her closer, 'is that you are exquisite, and I want you so damned much . . .'

The words were as seductive as the kiss that followed it. He opened her mouth with his, moving his lips back and forth almost roughly, and then his tongue drove between her parted lips in a fiercely erotic kiss, retreating and plunging again and again, until desire was streaking through Sheridan like lightning bolts. Leaning over her, he kissed her until she heard herself moaning softly, and then his lips were at her aching breasts again and his hand was sliding downward over her stomach, reaching lower, covering the soft mound between her legs. His fingers teased and tormented her, until Sheridan was clinging to him, parting her legs and giving him access.

She was damp and more than ready for him, and the bed shifted as he got out of it, leaving her feeling cold and alone. She opened her eyes and saw him standing beside the bed, his hands at his waistband, and then he came back to her, and the magic began again, only hotter this time, and Sheridan gave herself up to it. She turned to him in trembling need, her fingers flexing against his shoulders, her body arching against his hand.

Stephen was half demented with need. Cupping her bottom in both hands, he pulled her tightly against him. Then he wedged his knee between hers, probing with his body and then finding. He shifted his hips and slid into her, feeling her opening for him and then sheathing him while her nails dug into his shoulders. She was helping him, her knee lifted to give him deeper access, and he tried, one last time, to slow them both down. Keeping one arm around her hips, he cradled her face against his chest and rocked gently inside her, increasing the depth and tempo of each stroke imperceptibly, but when she crushed her soft mouth to his and began to move her hips with his, Stephen was lost.

Sheridan felt the thunder of his heart beneath her ear and the driving force of his powerful strokes deep within her, and she felt her body begin to soar and reach and clasp him tighter. 'I love you,' she cried on a sob as the universe began to come apart, and he rolled her swiftly onto her back, driving deeper, kissing her with fiery urgency. His hand found hers on the pillow near her head as his hips rammed deeper, and his fingers threaded through hers, holding tightly.

He was holding her hand like that when the universe exploded in a burst of pleasure that tore a sobbing moan from her, and she felt his life pumping into her, his body shuddering again and again with the force of the explosion, his hand tightening.

Stephen fought his way back from oblivion with an effort, leaning up on his forearms to take his weight off her, and he forced his eyes open. Her satin curls were spread all over the pillow in wild disarray, exactly as he'd imagined they would be someday, and his hand was holding hers.

His hand was holding hers . . .

Filled with a feeling that was part joy, part awe, and part reverence, he gazed down at the woman who had just sent him to unparalleled heights of desire and unequalled depths of satisfaction. Her eyes fluttered open, and he tried to smile, to tell her that he loved her, but his chest was constricted with emotion, and there was an unfamiliar lump in his throat as he looked at their clasped hands on the pillow.

He had never held a woman's hand at a time like this in his life.

He had never thought of it.

He had never wanted to.

Until now.

Sheridan felt his hand tighten on hers and sensed instinctively what he was looking at with that strange expression of tenderness on his handsome face. Weak from the passion they'd shared, it took an effort to move her right hand from his nape and to put it on the pillow beside her face, where he could reach it. His long fingers slid over her palm and then twined with hers, closing tightly.

Stephen bent his head and kissed her lips, their bodies joined, their hands clasped. He closed his eyes, swallowed, and tried to tell her again what he felt, to explain that he'd never known there were feelings like this, but the emotions were still too raw, and he was still out of breath. All he could manage to say was, 'Until you . . .'

She understood. He knew she did, because her hands tightened convulsively on his and she turned her face and kissed his fingers.

EPILOGUE

Seated in the drawing room at Montclair amidst exquisite furnishings that had once occupied European palaces, surrounded by all the trappings of his wealth and position, Stephen Westmoreland looked up at the gilt-framed portraits of his ancestors that lined the silk-panelled walls, and he wondered if *they'd* had as much trouble as he was having trying to be alone with his bride of two days.

Above the fireplace mantel, the first Earl of Langford looked down at him from atop a mighty black warhorse, a visored helmet under his arm, his cloak swirling behind him. He looked like the sort of man who would have tossed his knights into the moat to get rid of them if they didn't have sense enough to leave him alone in his castle with his new bride.

On the wall across from Stephen, the second Earl of Langford reclined in front of his fire with two of his knights. His wife was seated nearby, surrounded by women working on a tapestry. The second earl had a more civilized look than his father, Stephen decided. That ancestor would have been more likely to send his knights on a trumped-up errand and then order his drawbridge pulled up.

Bored with studying his ancestors, Stephen turned his head slightly and indulged in the more pleasurable occupation of studying his wife who was seated across from him, surrounded by his mother, his brother, Whitney, and Nicholas DuVille. Mentally, he tipped her chin up and kissed her while, with his free hand, he teased the shoulder of her lemon gown off, slipping it down her arm, then cupped her full breast and deepened the kiss. He was trailing a kiss down the side of her neck, working slowly to the nipple he wanted to kiss, when he realized Nicholas DuVille was watching him with a look that was both amused and knowing. Stephen was spared the embarrassment of blushing like an errant schoolboy by the arrival of Hodgkin, whom he'd retrieved from exile yesterday, and who walked to his side. 'Excuse me, my lord,' Hodgkin said, 'but you have guests.'

'Who are they?' Stephen said irritably, swallowing the impulse to tell the old man to pitch the new arrivals into the lake – since he had no nice, deep moat with which to dispose of them – and then to bar the gates at the entrance to the estate.

Hodgkin lowered his voice and whispered. As he explained the situation, Stephen's annoyance gave way to resignation that he would have to see Matthew Bennett, who'd evidently just returned from America – and then to puzzlement that Bennett had evidently brought people with him. 'Excuse me,' he said to his guests, who were too absorbed in a discussion of Sherry's housekeeping decisions to notice he was leaving. His wife noticed, however. She stopped listening to advice on the running of a large household and looked up at him with a smile that said she, too, wished they were alone.

Matthew Bennett launched into his explanation before Stephen was clear into his study. 'I apologize for my untimely arrival, my lord,' the solicitor said. 'Your butler explained that you were newly wed and not receiving visitors, but your instructions when I left for America were that I was to locate Miss Lancaster's relatives and escort them back to England at once. Unfortunately, Miss Lancaster's only living relative – her father – died before I reached the Colonies.'

'I know,' Stephen said. 'I received a letter that was intended for Burleton and it contained that information. Since she had no other relatives, who did you bring back with you?'

The solicitor looked defensive and a little harassed. 'You see, Miss Lancaster was travelling with a paid companion, a young woman by the name of Sheridan Bromleigh, who was expected to return at once to America. No word has been heard from Miss Bromleigh, and her aunt – a Miss Cornelia Faraday – was most insistent that a search be instituted all over England to discover her whereabouts. Unfortunately, Miss Faraday did not feel she could rely upon either you or myself to handle that search. She was *most* insistent about accompanying me back to England in order to supervise it herself.'

During one of their two nights alone together, Sheridan had told him about the aunt who had partially raised her and about the father who had disappeared without a word several years ago. Now, it looked as if he would be able to give Sherry an unexpected 'wedding gift.' The fact that he was obviously acquiring another houseguest rankled, but it was compensation enough to know how happy she was going to be. 'Excellent!' Stephen said with a smile.

'I hope you feel that way when you meet the lady,' Bennett said wearily. 'She is quite – determined – to locate her niece.'

'I think I can handle that with surprising speed,' Stephen said with a smile of anticipation over the scene which was sure to unfold in the drawing room in a few minutes. 'I know exactly where Miss Bromleigh is.'

'Thank God!' Bennett said wearily. 'Because Miss Bromleigh's father, who'd been missing for four years, returned while I was in America. He and his friends were every bit as worried about her – and every bit as determined to see that you did what needed to be done to ensure she was safely returned to them.'

'Miss Bromleigh is very safe,' Stephen assured him with a grin. 'She is not, however, going to be "returned" to them.'

'Why not?'

Ten minutes ago, Stephen wanted nothing more than to be alone with Sherry. Now he wanted nothing more than to see her face when she realized who was waiting to see her, and he rather relished seeing Matthew Bennett's face when events unfolded as well. In high spirits, he invited the solicitor into the drawing room, sent Hodgkin after the visitors, and then walked over to the fireplace where he could have the best view while Matthew Bennett found a chair that suited him. 'Sherry,' he said mildly, interrupting DuVille's laughing recitation of the antics he had had to go through in order to get her to agree to go to the chapel where Stephen was waiting. 'You have visitors.'

'Who?' she said, sending him a look that said she wished she didn't. While she was looking from Stephen to Hodgkin, a handsome, middle-aged man who was bridling with impatience walked into the drawing room. Behind him, hovering in the doorway, Stephen saw a gray-haired woman in a simple high-collared gown pause just inside the doorway. 'We regret intruding on your privacy,' the man said bluntly to Stephen, 'but my daughter is missing.'

Stephen shifted his gaze to Sherry, who had whirled around on her chair at the sound of his voice and was slowly standing up. 'Papa?' she whispered, and her father's head jerked toward her. She stood frozen in place, her eyes roving lovingly over the man as if he were an apparition she was afraid would vanish if she moved. *'Papa . . . ?'*

In answer he opened his arms and she ran flying into them.

Stephen looked away from the outpouring of emotion, giving them time, and as he did so, he noticed the rest of his family and DuVille had done likewise. 'Where have you been?' she said, weeping and cradling his face in her hands. 'Why didn't you write to us? We thought you were dead!'

'I was in prison,' he said with more disgust than embarrassment as he glanced apologetically at the silent occupants of the room. 'Your friend Rafe and I had the bad judgment to believe a horse we won in a card game was the legitimate property of the thief we won him from. We were lucky not to be hanged when they caught us with him. Your aunt Cornelia always warned me that gambling at cards was going to get me into trouble.'

'And I was right,' the woman said from the doorway.

'Fortunately, she doesn't object to marrying a reformed gambler, who still knows how to farm, and who's even willin' to make peace with Squire Faraday, for her sake,' he added, but no-one heard him. Sherry had already turned toward the voice in the doorway and she was laughing and hugging the woman who'd spoken.

Remembering her manners, Sherry took her aunt and her father over to Stephen to introduce them, but before she could begin, her father said, 'There's someone else who would like to see you, Sherry. Although I doubt he's going to recognize you,' he added with a proud smile as his gaze moved slowly over her.

Rafe's smiling voice spoke from the doorway as he sauntered into the room, looking more handsome than she remembered, and as at ease in an English drawing room as he'd been beside a campfire with a guitar in his hands. 'Hello, *querida*,' he said in that deep, caressing voice of his. At the fireplace, Stephen stiffened, and that was *before* his new wife hurtled herself into the arms of another man, who lifted her off the ground and whirled her around and around, holding her outrageously close to his lean body. 'I have come to make good on my promise to marry you,' Rafe teased.

'Goodness!' said Miss Charity, stealing an alarmed look at Stephen's forbidding expression.

'Dear God,' said the dowager duchess, glancing at her son's ominously narrowed eyes.

'What does he mean by that?' Whitney said in a choked whisper.

'I'm afraid to think about it,' her husband replied.

Nicholas DuVille leaned back in his chair, looking amused and wary, and said nothing at all.

'How soon can we be wed, *querida*?' Rafe joked, putting her down and inspecting her from head to toe. 'I spent the long days in prison, thinking of my little carrot—'

To everyone's amazement, the object of his frankly admiring regard ignored what sounded like a serious discussion of honorable intentions, put her hands on her hips, and took issue with his use of a nickname. 'I will thank you not to address me by such an undignified name in the presence of my husband. Furthermore,' she confided with a soft smile at Stephen as she took the other man's arm and led him forward, 'my husband thinks my hair is quite special.'

That remark caused her father, her aunt, and Rafe to turn abruptly to the man at the fireplace while Sheridan quickly handled the introductions.

When she was finished, Stephen found himself the object of a thorough inspection being conducted by three people who seemed not to care in the least that he owned the mansion in which they stood, or that he was the Earl of Langford, or even that he was tentatively deciding whether it was necessary, or advisable, to do physical harm to Rafael Benavente, who struck him as too free with his attentions to Sherry, too virile to be left in the same room with any female under the age of seventy, and too damned handsome to be trusted by anyone.

Postponing that decision, he slid his hand around Sherry's waist, drawing her possessively close, and let them look him over. 'Are you happy, darlin'?' her father asked after a moment. 'I promised Dog Lies Sleeping I'd find you and bring you back. He'll want to know you're happy.'

'I'm *very* happy,' she said softly.

'You're quite certain?' her aunt asked.

'Very certain,' Sherry assured her.

Rafael Benavente withheld judgment for another moment, and then held out his hand to Stephen. 'You must be a fine man, and an exceptional one, for Sherry to love you as much as she obviously does.'

Stephen decided to offer the man a glass of his best brandy, instead of his choice of weapons. Rafael Benavente was very clearly a man of exceptional judgment and refinement. It was actually quite a pleasure to have him as a guest beneath his roof, for one night.

He mentioned that to Sheridan much later that night, as he held her in his arms, his body sated, his spirit quietly joyous.

His wife tipped her face up to his and splayed her fingers over his bare chest in a sleepy exploration that was beginning to have a dramatic effect on the rest of his body. 'I love you,' she whispered. 'I love your strength and your gentleness. I love you for being so kind to my family and so nice to Rafe.'

Stephen decided they could stay as long as they liked. He told her that with a laughing groan as her hand drifted lower.

THE END

A SELECTED LIST OF FINE NOVELS
AVAILABLE FROM CORGI BOOKS

THE PRICES SHOWN BELOW WERE CORRECT AT THE TIME OF
GOING TO PRESS. HOWEVER TRANSWORLD PUBLISHERS
RESERVE THE RIGHT TO SHOW NEW RETAIL PRICES ON
COVERS WHICH MAY DIFFER FROM THOSE PREVIOUSLY
ADVERTISED IN THE TEXT OR ELSEWHERE.

13255 1	**GARDEN OF LIES**	*Eileen Goudge*	£5.99
13872 X	**LEGACY OF LOVE**	*Caroline Harvey*	£4.99
13917 3	**A SECOND LEGACY**	*Caroline Harvey*	£4.99
14299 9	**PARSON HARDING'S DAUGHTER**	*Caroline Harvey*	£4.99
14220 4	**CAPEL BELLS**	*Joan Hessayon*	£4.99
14262 X	**MARIANA**	*Susanna Kearsley*	£4.99
14045 7	**THE SUGAR PAVILION**	*Rosalind Laker*	£5.99
14331 6	**THE SECRET YEARS**	*Judith Lennox*	£4.99
14025 2	**PRISONER OF MY DESIRE**	*Johanna Lindsey*	£4.99
14113 5	**ANGEL**	*Johanna Lindsey*	£4.99
14222 0	**THE MAGIC OF YOU**	*Johanna Lindsey*	£4.99
14292 1	**LOVE ONLY ONCE**	*Johanna Lindsey*	£4.99
13210 1	**HEARTS AFLAME**	*Johanna Lindsey*	£4.99
13075 3	**FIRES OF WINTER**	*Johanna Lindsey*	£4.99
14289 1	**SURRENDER MY LOVE**	*Johanna Lindsey*	£4.99
13737 5	**EMERALD**	*Elisabeth Luard*	£5.99
13910 6	**BLUEBIRDS**	*Margaret Mayhew*	£4.99
13569 0	**A KINGDOM OF DREAMS**	*Judith McNaught*	£4.99
13252 7	**ONCE AND ALWAYS**	*Judith McNaught*	£4.99
13478 3	**SOMETHING WONDERFUL**	*Judith McNaught*	£4.99
12728 0	**WHITNEY, MY LOVE**	*Judith McNaught*	£4.99
13826 6	**ALMOST HEAVEN**	*Judith McNaught*	£4.99
13972 6	**LARA'S CHILD**	*Alexander Mollin*	£5.99
10249 0	**BRIDE OF TANCRED**	*Diane Pearson*	£2.99
10271 7	**THE MARIGOLD FIELD**	*Diane Pearson*	£2.99
13987 4	**ZADRUGA**	*Margaret Pemberton*	£4.99
14123 2	**THE LONDONERS**	*Margaret Pemberton*	£4.99
14298 0	**THE LADY OF KYNACHAN**	*James Irvine Robertson*	£5.99
14296 4	**THE LAND OF NIGHTINGALES**	*Sally Stewart*	£4.99
14118 6	**THE HUNGRY TIDE**	*Valerie Wood*	£4.99